ORACLES ALWAYS WIN

Willow Lake Supernaturals

Book 3

LORI AMES

—

Oracles Always Win by Lori Ames

Published by November Snow
Copyright © 2024 by S.L. Paton. All rights reserved.
Digital edition / 2024 - ISBN 978-1-989764-72-5
Print edition / 2024 - ISBN 978-1-989764-73-2
Large Print edition / 2025 / ISBN 978-1-989764-87-9

Cover by: S.L. Paton
Beta Reading by: Kirk Waite at Rare Bird Beta Reading

Thank you for respecting the hard work of this author.
loriames.com

Content Warning

Generally, this book and series are lighter reads, but there may be moments or situations that some readers may find distressing.

Note: This list may contain spoilers.

Content warnings include: swearing, violence, sexual content, bombing of one character's home, injuries, vomiting, patricide prior to start of book, threats of murder, mention of trafficking of supernatural people (not of main characters), concerns about mental health.

Chapter One

JAKE

I had always suspected there might be something… well, *off* about the town of Willow Lake. But I'd nearly convinced myself Van Clark, the Chief of Police, didn't have fire in his eyes. It was just a trick of the light. And Hayden Walker, the mechanic down at the garage, didn't growl. He just had something wrong with his throat, maybe damage from smoking. True, I'd never seen the man light up, but it didn't matter. He must have quit before I moved to town.

And that figure I'd just seen running through the shadow-cloaked garden outside my inn? That was definitely a regular old horse. It did *not* have the torso of a human.

It just didn't.

And if sometimes other people looked at me the same way I looked at Chief Clark, Mr. Walker, or that horse? It just confirmed how fanciful my imagination was, because I was absolutely, completely ordinary.

The fact I was currently hunched over the sink in my room, gagging into the old and severely chipped porcelain sink basin, with a paintbrush in my hand, not knowing how I got there *again*...

Well, no one needed to know about that.

Sometimes strange things happened.

It was all perfectly understandable. Really. My psyche was just finding ways to cope with the year I'd endured. Painting was relaxing. It helped. It was a form of art therapy. Of course, mine was the sub-conscious kind. The middle-of-the-night, paint-while-you-sleep kind. The kind that made me puke every single time it happened.

Okay.

So maybe what I was going through wasn't one hundred percent normal, but it could be worse. Maybe. So what if I had some strange kind of sleep-walking condition that ended with me painting creepy pictures and not remembering anything about doing it. Everyone had problems, right? This was just my own personal slice of crazy with extra olives.

I wiped the back of my hand over my mouth and stared at the paintbrush in my other hand. The bristles were covered in black and white paint. No surprise there. My painterly alter-ego abhorred color. Every time I woke up like this, it was the same thing. I'd find a strange picture done in black, white, and varying shades of gray. It was all depressing shit. Weird shit.

Even this latest one—the one on my easel with its still

wet and glistening gobs of paint I'd barely glimpsed before sprinting to the sink—wouldn't be normal. I knew it wouldn't. It'd be another study in twisted horrors.

Certainly nothing marketable in this tiny little town. Or anywhere. Really. And, no, I wasn't being melodramatic. This one, just like all the others, would be another waste of my limited resources.

Maybe if all my other paintings sold or the inn I'd inherited from my grandfather wasn't constantly dancing with bankruptcy, I wouldn't care about these strange midnight painting sessions. Maybe then I'd just laugh and happily jump online to buy more Mars Black, Titanium White, and canvases. Maybe then I could pretend these painting sessions weren't desperate pleas from my deteriorating mind.

Except... My paintings weren't selling, the inn flirted with debt like Sally at closing time, and a little part of me died every time I had to order more black and white paint.

So where did that leave me?

With a shaky hand, I brought a plastic bottle of mouthwash to my lips. If only my anxiety could be washed away with a swish and a spit too. I stared at the green froth at the bottom of the sink for several long minutes, as I hunted for enough oomph to deal with what I'd done.

How long had I been standing here?

I was never sure how long these things lasted, but I'd crash hard soon—yet another lovely side effect of my nightly endeavors. But first, I had to look. I had to see what I'd painted this time. I just needed to muster enough energy to go across the room and look. And then I'd have to figure out what to do with it. I was running out of space to store all these horridly awful pictures in my room.

"Deep breath in. Deep breath out," I muttered. I braced against the vanity with my paintbrush still clenched in one hand. "This one will be nice and chocolate boxy, something I can sell."

Honestly, I'd just be happy if it wasn't *too* odd. The worst thing would be if it was another one of the imaginary man—the one with the horns, of all things—that my subconscious seemed fixated on.

I mean, how was a devilish-looking man with horns sexy? Based on all those messed up medieval paintings of the devil eating people I had to study in art school, I'd have thought it'd be impossible, but here we were anyway. Apparently I had a Lucifer kink no one else needed to know about.

Not that I showed *any* of my black-and-white paintings to *anyone*. Ever. That was just a big ol' nope.

But the ones with that strange man? Those I hid under my bed like dirty little secrets.

He—the imaginary man—called to me on a primal level. And how crazy did that sound? The paintings were a figment of my imagination. The guy in the pictures wasn't real. He couldn't be. I would have remembered meeting someone like that, even without the horns. And no one was that… that… *Perfect* was the word that came to mind first, but could a horned man be perfect? Anyway, maybe my brain mashed together all my wet dreams and coalesced them into an unrealistic perfection, just to remind me I'd never find an actual real person who'd do it for me.

But if the guy was real?

Heat raced over me as I thought about the dark and intense look in his eyes, the dimple in his cheek, the way strands of his thick black hair fell over his forehead…

"Stop. Thinking. About. Him."

How much time had I lost to fantasizing about that imaginary guy since I'd first painted him?

Hours, for sure. Hopefully not days or weeks.

I sucked in a deep, bracing breath, then turned toward the canvas.

It wasn't the man.

"Thank Picasso for small mercies," I murmured as I stepped closer.

The canvas was covered in black with only a couple of small white clumps of paint to break up the monotony. The bright cone-like blobs looked like headlights on a vehicle. The smaller, streaky organic shapes might be puddles reflecting those lights.

Why would I paint something like that? What was my brain trying to tell me? What kind of hidden anxiety was it trying to work through that this was how it manifested?

I should paint over it—cover it in white, bury it under something normal—but I couldn't. Just like I couldn't paint over any of the others. Not right away, anyway. Like everything else about these paintings, my reluctance was a mystery to me. It was like my brain had an unpredictable internal clock with a silent ticking countdown to when one of my black-and-white eyesores could be destroyed. The expiry date on each of the paintings was different. The first one I'd painted, for example, was still hidden under my bed. I couldn't destroy it. Not yet.

I had no idea why.

But maybe this time it would be different.

I scowled at the painting.

"Yes. I can do it." I nodded as I gave myself a pep talk. "This time *will* be different. Absolutely. It'll be so freaking easy."

I had to get rid of it. I wanted to get rid of them all, but I'd be happy to start with one. There was no good reason to hang on to something so... so... ridiculously ugly. I squeezed an enormous glob of white onto my palette.

As soon as I brought the white-laden paintbrush close to the canvas, my fingers clenched, and my muscles seized. I gritted my teeth to fight through the strange need to preserve this artistic monstrosity, but my body just *would not cooperate*. No matter how much I tried, the brush would not get any closer to the canvas.

"You ugly shitting shit," I shouted at the painting as I flung the paintbrush across the room. It hit the far wall, spattering white paint over the faded floral wallpaper before dropping unceremoniously to the hideous royal blue carpet.

I screamed, forcing every bit of my anger and frustration into it.

Unfortunately, my screams didn't help one little bit.

I stared at the splattered paint until I blinked and became aware I'd lost another stretch of time. At least half an hour or more. I glanced around for another hideous work of art but didn't find anything. Thank Monet for that. One possessed painting session a night was more than enough.

Anger at this whole situation built inside me again

until I pierced the quiet with another scream. And then another.

The inn didn't have a single room rented so I could make all the noise I wanted. Being completely vacant wasn't something most inn owners would be happy about, but I'd always been a little different from other people.

I heaved a defeated sigh and let my shoulders drop as my mind circled back to the muffled shout that'd woken me from my sleep painting. The sound of hooves hitting the ground still clopped through my mind. Had I imagined it? That would be good, right? Then I'd only have the sleep-painting problem, not the sleep-painting problem *and* hallucinations about horse/man creatures too.

I glanced out the window.

"There's nothing there, Jake," I whispered, wishing I sounded a little more confident. "Of course there isn't."

The roiling in my stomach didn't calm like it should have.

I squinted into the darkness. Still nothing. So… Was it never there? Or was the creature thing—definitely a horse! —just gone?

No matter how I clung to the idea of it being a horse, my brain refused to mollycoddle me, bringing up a sharp image of exactly what I'd seen after I was jolted awake. I clearly remembered four legs like a horse. That was okay. But then there were two arms like a human—which, okay, those might have belonged to a rider, right? But what about the beast's head? If I didn't know better, I'd swear the human-ish torso had replaced it instead.

Except I did know better. And that wasn't possible.

I rubbed my forehead as I searched my memory for the horse's stupid head. It must have been hidden behind the man's naked torso… and his head, with his long billowing blond hair. That hair was something else. Maybe that's why I couldn't remember the horse's head. The rider's hair had totally distracted me since it was like a video clip from a shampoo commercial.

But what about the rider's legs?

"Fuck."

My stupid brain was an asshole, pointing out all the holes in my logic like that.

"Come on, Jake. You can do it. Just think about it, nice and calm, and you'll remember everything. He had to have legs." I grunted and pulled on my hair when my brain refused to cooperate.

I swallowed hard, desperately wanting to believe I'd seen someone riding a horse, but my memory kept telling me something else.

Because it really, really hadn't looked like a rider on a horse.

It was more like a mythical creature instead. A centaur? Or was it a satyr? I couldn't remember the difference right now. The last time I'd seen something like that was on an old cartoon. I hadn't seen many episodes, only sneaking them in when my mom was running errands. When she'd discovered what I'd been doing, she sold the television and that was the end of that. Which explained why I couldn't remember them very well.

Who knew I'd regret choosing Contemporary Art History over Ancient Greek and Roman Art History? It didn't really matter, though, did it? Because either way, mythical creatures weren't real.

"I'm losing my mind." I moaned, rubbing my hands over my face.

Between the nocturnal painting and the hallucinations, what other conclusion was there?

I laughed bitterly, whether from the absurdity of my life or the real fear for my sanity, I wasn't sure. I ground the heels of my hands into my burning eyes. Panic wasn't helping anything. I needed to get a grip.

"I'm okay," I said as I bounced on my toes and shook out my arms. "It's just stress and lack of sleep. It'll be okay. I'll be okay."

I had to be.

Right now, it felt like the only things holding me together were this weird little town and this inn. They gave me something to think about besides my own problems, anchoring me when I felt afloat.

The townsfolk were always checking up on me, sometimes more than I would have liked. But they knew I was new to town, and they'd really liked my grandfather, so they took me under their wing, so to speak. Apparently, the old guy had been quite the pillar of the community, so they extended the same warmth to me. They were nice. Friendly. The quintessential small town welcome party. Really.

But that horse.

What was I supposed to think about that lousy horse?

If I'd been drinking, this would be so much easier to dismiss. But I'd been drug and alcohol free when I'd climbed into bed—I glanced at the time on my phone—

three hours ago. I really needed to get some sleep. Tomorrow was Saturday, the busiest day of the week at the bar, and coincidentally the only time my bank account didn't hate me.

A yawn erupted from me. I washed my hands over my face. Right. Nothing would be solved tonight anyway. The best plan was to return to bed and try to get a few hours of sleep.

"I'll deal with you in the morning," I said as I flipped the bird at the painting, before retrieving my paintbrush from the floor where I'd thrown it. I wiped the acrylic paint from the wall and the rug with a wet rag—it came up, mostly—then returned to my painting corner to wash out the brush. I'd just dipped the brush into a Mason jar of water when a faint noise from outside made me pause.

Leery of seeing another part horse/part man hallucination, I swallowed and gripped the jar tightly. I needed to look. I really did.

"It'll be fine," I said. "I'll see the animal for what it really is. Yes. Absolutely. Good idea. A good dose of reality will wash away all the weirdness."

The fear snaking through my belly was unfounded. Completely ridiculous, really.

With my heart pounding, I killed the light I'd turned on after I'd been jarred awake by an unfamiliar noise in time to see the... *horse*. Darkness surrounded me as I peered out at the moonlit night. The grooves on the lip of the jar dug into my fingers as I tightened my grip even more and stepped closer to the window. Fresh air, tinged with the peaty damp smells that always erupted after a rain—petrichor, I thought it was called—wafted in through the screen and cooled my sweat-slicked skin.

There.

I clasped the curtain tightly as I caught movement to the left.

"It isn't a horse." I hooted and did a fist pump. Relief exploded through me.

Light flickered through the leaves of the trees lining the driveway. I held my breath. Then the lights grew brighter. Seeing a vehicle on the road outside the inn shouldn't be so mesmerizing. At this time of year, a lot of kids drove out to the lookout at the end of the lake. They raced along the winding road that followed the contours of the lake edge before stopping at the lookout to make out. Or so I'd heard. I'd been too old when I moved here to have any personal experience with the local teenage hangouts.

So a bit of traffic, even at this hour, wasn't a new or unusual thing, but something kept me at the window tonight. The faint moonlight was still trying to break through the clouds, but there was enough light to see a massive older-model motorhome with a utility trailer behind it. The beast of a machine coasted over the road sluggishly, moving much too slowly to be teenagers hoping to get lucky. The low hum of the engine and the crunch of tires over the gravel road filtered through my open window.

"Oh, no…"

I gulped and stared unblinkingly at the scene emerging outside my window. The headlights formed wedge-like cones and caught on the small puddles that'd pooled on the road following the shower earlier in the evening.

I couldn't see my painting in the darkness, but I didn't have to. I remembered well enough what I'd seen there moments earlier, and the view from my window matched it. I stood, transfixed, until the vehicle disappeared and the noise from the engine faded away.

I yanked the drapes closed. The urge to hide was too compelling to ignore. It was only then, after I confirmed no one could see inside my room, that I fumbled with the light switch on my lamp again. Then I set the Mason jar down with a thud on my table. Water sloshed over the lip of the jar and hit my fingers.

My eyes watered with the sudden brightness. I blinked rapidly. And then I saw it again. The painting with its still wet paint. The one I'd finished in my sleep. The one that matched what I'd just seen outside my window.

My earlier desperate need to preserve the painting was gone now, like it'd never existed. I scooped the white paint off my palette with my fingers and smeared it over the tacky paint on the canvas. I grabbed the tube of white and squeezed out more, directly onto the painting, and pushed it around.

A scratching noise and an inquisitive mew came from the other side of my door. After everything else that had happened tonight, I didn't have the energy to deal with the cat too. My grandfather's cat always had a knowing look in his eyes, and I swore some of the regulars tried to have conversations with him. And, on really bad days, I even imagined he talked—as in made words that sounded English and everything.

"Go away," I shouted at the cat. "I'm busy."

I had to cover over this painting. Now that I could, I had to hide it. That took precedence over everything else.

Fatigue wore at me, but I pressed on. I had to do this.

"Just a little bit more, it's almost done..." I murmured.

I didn't stop until the earlier painting was lost under a thick layer of white.

"Ha! There!" I'd done it. My panting breath burst from my lips as I studied the glistening wet paint. My T-shirt, soaked through with sweat now, was plastered to my chest.

My hands shook as I washed the remnants of paint from my fingers a moment later. Even as I stood there at the sink, a newfound clarity hit me. The truth was obvious and indisputable. I *was* going insane. One hundred per cent. It was the only explanation. I mean, I'd been suspecting it for a while, but there came a point when you couldn't deny the truth, right?

This was that point.

How long would it be before anyone else noticed?

I studied my reflection in the small, tarnished mirror above the sink. What did crazy look like? I didn't think I had any obvious signs.

That was good.

Because I really wanted to accomplish some stuff before it was too late.

Losing my virginity was at the top of the list, despite my horrific previous attempts to do just that. That was followed by getting the pub firmly into the black for the next owner, whoever that might be. I owed it to my grand-father to not let his business fail. And, lastly, I wanted to sell one of my nice paintings—none of that black-and-white shit—for more than a hundred bucks.

There.

Done.

Three things to conquer before I was tossed in a locked room that was noticeably devoid of any sharp objects. Out of all my new goals, I expected losing my virginity would be the most difficult, but if you didn't try, you never knew, right?

Chapter Two

GAGE

"Ready?" I asked Isaac and Nelson.

They both nodded.

On the way to the campground just outside of town where we'd set up last night, we'd driven past the Willow Lake Inn, so it was easy enough to open a portal there this morning. Under normal circumstances, I'd have taken my motorhome, which my team had long ago dubbed the Pink Lady when its red panels had faded to a dull pink. I preferred to have both it and my team close to me, but it'd been a challenge getting the beast into the campsite and my team was apprehensive about having me fight with it again so soon. As if something like that would tip me over the edge.

It probably hadn't helped that ever since we'd tracked down the goblin Babette and dismantled her part in a supe trafficking ring, we'd been trapped in the city as we sifted through her belongings and hunted for clues. Being in places like that made everyone anxious. At least our best lead had led us out here now, miles and miles away from the polluted air. How supes lived in those places permanently was a mystery to me. Although, if my magic chose a place like that as its anchor, I'd figure out how to cope. Then again, after all this time, I doubted I'd find a place —*any* place—to call my own.

But I didn't feel like arguing with them about how I was doing just fine. I'd never convince them anyway. So we were using a portal.

If I'd been with anyone other than my team, I wouldn't have been able to move them through the portal without striking a deal with at least one of them first, but these two were mine. I'd bound them to me in one of the most sacred deals a demon could make… at least that's the way it'd felt when the Eternal Magic guided me through the process the first time. These people were special to me.

Davina, my second, liked to call them my minions. The Supernatural Council identified them as my team, which was the name I usually adopted too. Although I really considered them my family. A family I'd asked to destroy me if—or *when*—the time came.

Every family had its problems.

I opened a portal to a spot in the woods by the inn's gate but didn't step through immediately. I let my magic push through first, needing to know it was safe before we walked over there. Isaac, already in his centaur form, charged through before I could stop him. Fucking idiot. As soon as he was through, he pranced and kicked at the ground with his hooves.

"Wow, you need to feel this," Isaac enthused as he

trotted up to the portal and peered through it at Nelson and me. He grinned and waved exuberantly for us to follow.

His words put me on alert. He didn't sound scared, so I waited for him to explain. He didn't. He was too busy frolicking in the trees.

"Feel what?" I narrowed my eyes and scanned the area for threats. The woods seemed normal enough, but magic could hide a lot of things, even from a demon. If Isaac sensed something, I needed to know.

"The energy... It's amazing." A rosy-cheeked Isaac grinned.

Beside me, Nelson drew on his magic. His body faded around the edges into the shadowy smoke of his shifted form, getting ready to either attack or defend.

"What are you waiting for?" Isaac waved us forward. "Get over here. You need to feel it. It's trippy."

"So no threats?" I asked to be clear.

"I don't think so. Why? Do you sense something?" Isaac glanced around the area as if the thought hadn't occurred to him.

I had invited Isaac to join my team. I just needed to remind myself why sometimes, like when he made impulsive decisions and charged into unknown situations without evaluating things first. He had skills I valued, and he brought a youthful perspective to the team, but he had a lot to learn. Nelson snorted, as if he read my thoughts, and let his magic fade.

As soon as I stepped through the portal, the hairs on the back of my neck tingled. Unfamiliar magic rushed over me like a warm tropical breeze.

"What the—?" I grunted.

I scanned for threats again but didn't see anything. A few animals, both mundane and supernatural ones, were close, but nothing powerful enough to pose a serious threat to us. I brought my magic closer to the surface and cautiously stepped forward.

An enchanting array of otherworldly sparks exploded in the air as my magic entwined with that of Willow Lake. Since neither Isaac nor Nelson reacted, the sparkly light show must have just been for me. I'd never thought of my demonic magic as an enthusiastic and joyful entity. Ever. But that was how it felt as it surged forward to greet this foreign essence.

Given the strange mix of supernatural beings I knew lived in Willow Lake, I'd been prepared to feel a chaotic mix of latent magic, but I never anticipated this. When we'd driven through the town last night, I hadn't felt any of this through the ward on the Pink Lady.

It wasn't a welcome surprise. It was too strange. Too unexpected.

My every muscle tensed, ready to fight, but nothing appeared. I sucked in a breath, drawing the strange air into my lungs before exhaling. I savored the taste of the magics, drawing out each distinct thread one by one. The more I dissected the eclectic blend, the more I calmed. The magic wasn't overtly threatening. It was just *potent*, for lack of a better word.

I'd never tasted anything so sweet.

But it wasn't just the typical magic generated by a blend of supernatural beings. No, the strongest magic came from deep in the earth under my feet. There had to be a nexus of ley lines through here for the magic to vibrate so forcefully.

It was intoxicating.

As if it was encouraging me to let myself go, to wallow in it, to bask in its vibrating energy like a dragon shifter on a sun-heated rock.

And that was dangerous.

The last time I'd been close to Willow Lake, I hadn't crossed the town boundary. I met the local Chief of Police, Van Clark, by the town sign, so I didn't realize this was here. Now I wondered if Van decided to meet me outside town for a reason. Had he anticipated how it would affect me? Had he kept me out of here on purpose?

For centuries I'd wandered the earth searching for a place to call my own. How dare he keep Willow Lake hidden from me?

Then, as quickly as my ire rose, it ebbed. During that brief interaction with the hellhound, I'd felt his strong sense of duty. Even if most people didn't know a lot about my kind, he would at least have known having a demon tethered to the place he called home, acting as a guardian, would be advantageous.

Of course, that arrangement was even more advantageous for the demon.

But as this foreign magic danced around me, a fragile hope I hadn't realized still lived inside my heart unfurled. It whispered to me. *Could this be the place I've been searching for?* I swallowed hard and shoved that hope back down. Sure, this was the first time I'd experienced such an intense reaction to a place, but I needed more information before I got too excited.

As if sensing my reluctance, those invisible fingers of magic pulled at me, inviting me to sink into the earth and never leave. They tugged at my psyche, luring me into their embrace with seductive promises: *This is the place. Welcome. You are here. You are home. We've been waiting for you. We're thrilled to have you. So happy you finally found us.*

It was too much. *Too* tempting. A siren's temptation.

Was it a trick? Something meant to trap me here?

I'd certainly made enough enemies over the years to warrant that kind of retribution. Even in our current case, we were sure another demon was involved. The last thing I needed was to blindly fall into a trap they'd set. Sure, I needed to find a place to tether or my demonic magic would eventually break free—which no one wanted to happen—but a false connection to a place would be just as detrimental to me as having none at all. I gritted my teeth and fought for control.

For now, until I knew more, my focus needed to be on the job. Nothing else.

"Boss? You okay?" Isaac asked as he bounded over to me and ducked down to peer right into my face. I wasn't a short man by any means, but, in his centaur form, Isaac stood at least a head taller than me.

Still clenching my teeth, I nodded sharply.

"Okay. Thought I should ask because you're shimmering a bit."

"Fucking hell," Nelson gasped as he stepped through the portal behind me.

The edges of his body flickered from solid to wispy and back to solid again. The shadow jumper was capable of manipulating the solidity of his body until he became nothing more than a curl of smoke in the air. Right now, though, his body seemed to be changing without his permission.

He reached out with one hand to brace himself against an aspen tree.

"What the fuck is up with this place?" Nelson asked. His face appeared even paler than normal.

At least I knew now the magic wasn't impacting just me. Of course, that didn't mean it wasn't still a trap.

Isaac hooted, although in his case it sounded more like a neigh, and slapped Nelson's shoulder. "I told you guys it was a rush last night, didn't I?"

"Just thought you were high from your run," Nelson muttered as he drew his hand over his short dark beard. Then he glanced at me. "Did Adrian say anything about this?"

"No."

And Nelson was right: Adrian should have. The wolf shifter had been staying here with his new mate for a couple of weeks now. He had to know about this, so why didn't he say anything?

"Text Davina and Teague," I said to Nelson, referring to the other members of my team who weren't here yet. "Tell them about the high magic levels and that there should be a lot of ghosts."

He pulled out his phone to do as I asked.

Good. That should be enough of a warning. A place with this much energy would attract supes, but it would also attract a lot of other beings too—like ghosts. Although spirits were capable of lying, they rarely did. Most of them were so starved for attention, they were eager to tell you anything you wanted to know. I couldn't see or speak to ghosts, but from what I'd been told, they tended to be eager gossips, which worked out well for us. Information from the local ghosts could make this case go a hell of a lot more smoothly. They were also a great early warning system if, say, a demon had snapped and started killing people, creating a lot of ghosts all of a sudden. That's why I had Davina on my team.

As a medium, she could interrogate those spirits, or if we needed to summon one back from beyond the veil, Teague could do that, although that was only a small part of what he could do. Most of the time, he just acted as a medic if the situation called for it, but as a death mage, he could bridge the gap between the living and the dead. Even after working with him for so long, I doubted we'd seen the full extent of what he was capable of.

I needed them here. Their current case had already gone on longer than it should have, which seemed to be a theme for us lately.

Nelson shoved his phone away without waiting for an answer.

Isaac bounced lightly on his toes, sending his long, wavy blond hair bouncing too. "Awesome, right?"

"Don't think awesome is the right word," Nelson muttered as he eyed the portal I hadn't closed yet like he was ready to jump back through and get out of here.

Isaac clapped his hand on Nelson's shoulder and laughed. "Who knew a guy who dressed in black like he's channeling the Grim Reaper would be such a wimp."

"Fuck off," Nelson mumbled, shaking off Isaac's hand.

He adjusted the collar of his black leather jacket before smoothing his trembling hands down his black jeans. Nelson's wardrobe was as dark as his supernatural form, not that I was one to talk about fashion since I preferred blacks and grays too.

Long ago, my species had been maligned as evil entities by many human religions to discredit our role in society. It'd worked. People in the past, like now, were always eager to believe the worst. And, since then, many supernatural beings had come to think the same. It might have been different if there were more of my kind around to offset the rumors, but overturning a couple of millennia's worth of bad press was now an impossible task. So I embraced it instead. I used the fear-inspiring lies to my advantage and played to the stereotype. Dressing in black helped with that.

I ignored their bickering and glanced around the area. The inn, a massive century old building, was to our left. It was a familiar design, and I was sure it was originally a pack house for wolves. They tended to all follow the same basic plan. To our immediate right was the road we'd taken last night, and Willow Lake was beyond that. On the far side of the water, people were already setting up on the shore, getting ready for a warm summer's day.

I forced myself to step toward the inn.

We were meeting the police chief later, but I wanted to get a feel for the place first. Since a robbery at the inn is what started our original investigation, this was our first stop. We'd recovered most of the stolen magical artifacts and, in the process, discovered an even worse crime. And now all our leads had brought us back here, where everything started.

The local wolf pack had been using a goblin named Babette to fence the stolen objects, and when we'd gone to retrieve them, we discovered she was involved with trafficking supernatural beings. Her warehouse in the city had been filled with caged supes. We'd released her prisoners, but we still didn't have the answers we needed. There was no way Babette was acting alone, but we hadn't found what we needed to go after the others. Not yet.

But I would find them. They would be punished. It was just a matter of time.

Right now, though, I had a different problem.

My knees shook as the magic under me clung to my feet and impeded my steps. I let out a low curse. That prompted Isaac to put his face in front of mine again. When he reached out to put the back of his hand against my forehead like I was a sickly human child, I smacked it away.

"You okay, boss? You and Nelson look a little weird." Isaac's eyebrows drew together as he studied us, seeming to realize the magic he was so giddy about wasn't doing us any favors. He glanced at Nelson, and they had a not-so-subtle but silent conversation about me, even though the shadow jumper wasn't doing any better than I was. "I can look around on my own if you need to sit this one out."

I gritted my teeth.

They meant well.

I needed to remember that.

And I understood where their concern was coming from. I'd tasked them with killing me if—or *when*—my demonic magic snapped. But that wasn't happening today. And, truthfully, I was getting a little tired of my team constantly trying to cover me in metaphorical bubble wrap.

"I'm fine." I shook my head, then looked at Nelson. "What about you?"

Nelson tilted his chin up. He was as determined to fight off this weakness as I was. "It'll go faster with three of us. I'm getting used to it."

Lucky him.

This strange magic was still clinging to me, but I couldn't tell them that. It would only amplify their unnecessary concern. I sent a pulse of my own magic into the dirt, hoping that would be enough of a greeting and acknowledgement to calm whatever latent energy was there.

I tentatively lifted my foot. It moved easily, so the pulse seemed to have worked. Thank Magic for that.

I still didn't get any sinister impressions from the place. In fact, it all continued to feel rather benign and friendly as we walked toward the inn. I hoped it wasn't an elaborate hoax. And, if anything extraordinarily threatening was happening in Willow Lake, Adrian would have told me, right?

As if my thoughts summoned him, my phone rang with the ring tone Jeremy had set up for Adrian. I hadn't figured out how to change it yet, so I quickly pulled out my phone before the opening chords ended and The Cramps started singing about being a teenage werewolf.

"What?" I said, not bothering with a greeting.

"*Sorry to call, boss. But Nelson just texted and said*

you were heading to Willow Lake Inn and I should join you."

"Can't you people ever say hello like normal people?" Jeremy muttered from Adrian's side of the connection. It was obvious he was further away from the phone.

"Are you coming over now?"

"We were out of town looking at RVs when you called yesterday. We left right away, but the truck we borrowed from Ash broke down on our way back. We're stuck. It took most of the night just to get help."

A new throbbing pain settled in my head at that bit of news.

"Do you need us to come get you?" I didn't want to leave yet, but I would if needed.

"Nah, we're good now."

"Tell him how far we had to walk," Jeremy whined. *"Those are hours I'll never get back. My feet will never forgive me. Ask him if he can share his ability to make portals with us."*

"The tow truck driver is finally coming to pick us up to get the truck," Adrian said, ignoring Jeremy's suggestion. *"Hopefully it'll be something easy to fix and we'll be out of here soon."*

"Understood. Keep me updated."

"Will do."

"We just got into the inn. What do you know about the magic here?"

"It's intense, right? The whole town is like that."

"Why didn't you say anything?"

There was a pause. *"I thought you knew, since you met Van in town that day."*

I frowned. I could see how he'd come to that conclusion. Before I could ask him anything more, a loud screech shot through the phone from Adrian's end of the call.

"*Ah... Emma!*" Jeremy shouted. "*Quit that! Get down from there. Those curtains aren't for climbing... Adrian!*"

"*Gotta go, boss,*" Adrian said quickly.

"Keep me updated," I reminded him, but he'd already ended the call.

And who the hell was Emma?

I wished we'd had more time to talk, but at least he hadn't texted. I hated those ridiculous little emojis and incomplete sentences my team liked to use in texts. Although I hated typing on the little screen on my phone even more, so I'd resorted to messaging that way too. Until the last few decades, I'd thought we'd left hieroglyphs in the ancient past.

When my team called me a technophobe, they weren't wrong. I had no desire to carve out messages on stone tablets or ink feathery scripts on parchment scrolls, but I wasn't convinced my life had been improved with the invention of the cell phone.

As I shoved my phone in my pocket, I frowned at the implications of Adrian's absence. I wanted to debrief him in person before I met with the locals, so I hoped his borrowed vehicle wouldn't take long to repair.

Since Adrian had met his mate, his updates had been so abbreviated they could hardly be called updates. I understood to some extent. Finding your fated mate was a rarity these days and something to celebrate. And his mate Jeremy was even more unusual, since he was a human who'd recently been blessed by the Eternal Magic with magic of his own. It wasn't often a human received such a gift. It was undoubtedly a distracting time for them both, so I was willing to give them time to adjust.

I'd already invited Jeremy to join my team, but the more I thought about it the more I wondered if that was the right move. I'd hate to lose Adrian from our day-to-day operations, but I kept remembering that old saying "obey fate and love your mate".

Adrian's commitment to his mate was more important and took priority over any agreement he had with me. I wouldn't risk hurting him or making my magic unstable by severing the link we shared. I'd been there, done that. It only led to pain and death. Our connection was stronger and deeper than any ordinary deal I made. But there had to be a way for him to still fulfill his duties to me; we just had to find it. It was one more thing we needed to talk about.

"Adrian's been delayed, so it may just be the three of us for now," I informed the others.

Nelson and Isaac merely nodded.

"Okay," I said. "Isaac, you take outside. See if you can find anything suspicious hidden in the woods. Nelson and I will go inside the inn."

"I'll take the top floor and work my way down," Nelson said. "If you take the bottom, we'll meet in the middle."

I opened my mouth to agree with him, but magic poked at me, telling me I needed to take the top of the inn. I hoped this was a message from my magic and not the foreign one. But either way, I needed to do this. If it was a trap, it was better that I face it rather than Nelson.

"Let's do that, but with me on the top floors instead."

Nelson just shrugged and moved toward the inn. "At least we don't have to worry about any locks."

He was right; few locks resisted a demon's magic. In fact, I'd only ever come across one... and that was a worrisome detail of our current case. If we ran into anything that I couldn't get through, it'd at least be a clue.

Still, I hoped I'd adjust to the magic in this place soon so I was steady and able to think clearly by the time we met with Van. Because right now, my every thought centered around one question: *Could Willow Lake be my place?* And that strange magic seemed to be saying *yes, yes, yes.*

Chapter Three

JAKE

I adjusted my leather belt one last time, before dragging my hands over my form-fitting shirt. Then I turned around to look at my butt in the mirror. I wiggled it and grinned.

"Damn, I look good," I punctuated my words with a slap to my ass. While taking my painting classes, I'd lived away from home for a few months until my mother had a conniption and demanded I return home. During that short time, I'd seen my roommate do this time and time again, and he had scores of guys in his bed. If this ritual worked for him, I was willing to give it a try.

I hadn't worn this outfit since those long-ago brief days of freedom. It hadn't worked out the way I'd hoped then, but I really hoped it would work now. Then I'd have started working toward two of my three goals.

Right now, though, I was wishing I'd taken a nap instead of setting up an online shop for my paintings. I hadn't realized how long it'd take, or how hard it'd be to decide on a price, or how much my heart would try to pound its way out of my chest at the mere thought of putting my work out there for strangers to judge.

The whole process had been exhausting, but it was almost done.

All I had to do now was take some pictures of my paintings and post them, which I planned to do after the weekend. By the middle of the week, my art would be out there in the world for anyone to buy.

My mouth stretched around yet another yawn. My eyes watered with the effort. Stupid midnight painting sessions. They were messing everything up.

I turned on the tap to splash my face with cold water. As I patted it dry with a towel, I eyed my clothes again. The jeans cupped my ass nicely and the shirt hugged my narrow chest. I wasn't a big guy, so I wouldn't have anyone drooling over my non-existent muscles or anything, but I remembered these clothes attracting atten-tion, so I was counting on them working again.

Although, truthfully, I didn't have problems getting attention. It was all the stuff that came afterward that made things go sideways. I turned away from the mirror. This time was going to be different. I had a goal. That goal *would* be met.

I straightened my shoulders and marched out of my room, determined to conquer the day.

As soon as I stepped into the hallway and shut the door behind me, a noise drew my attention to the end of the hall. I expected it to be Paws. The cat was the only one other than me who should be in the building right now.

Except it wasn't Paws.

It was a man, but not just any man.

"Oh no," I whispered. My hand flew up to cover my mouth. My life was never easy or simple.

I blinked. Then I blinked again. But no matter how many times I opened and closed my eyes, the stranger's face stayed the same.

"Holy Michelangelo."

My hands grew sweatier. My heart pounded in my chest like a percussion band on fast forward, because his face was the spitting image of the man in the paintings under my bed. Right down to the... I swallowed and stared at the man's head... *Horns*.

He had *horns*.

Just like in the painting.

Two charcoal-colored horns protruded from his short midnight black hair and curled back over his head. I tried not to stare at them as the man paused and waited for my reaction to his presence.

How considerate of my hallucination.

My brain was knocking this one out of the park, what with the man's stunningly handsome face and his broad, deliciously masculine body. It was easy to imagine a six-pack under that black dress shirt. Maybe even an eight-pack.

But I guessed that made sense. He was a fantasy—albeit a very vivid, picture-of-perfection, life-sized fantasy—of the man my psyche liked to paint. I blinked yet again, hoping to shake off the vision.

Nope. No change. He was still there. All of him. Including the *horns*...

Why on earth had my brain given him horns?

"Hello," the man said. Even the imaginary guy's voice was delicious, deep, and melodious.

I, on the other hand, squeaked out a high-pitched "hey." Thankfully, this was all just a figment of my imagination. Otherwise, I'd be horribly embarrassed.

The man's mouth kicked up on one side into a small smile, and my heart pounded even faster. How fast could it beat before I needed to call an ambulance?

But, I mean, who could blame it? Because, wow… I'd never seen a more gorgeous man in my life. Of course, I'd stared at that face a lot over the last twelve months. I knew it very, very well… right down to the shape of that dimple in his cheek.

He was my mystery guy.

He'd even become my wet dream fantasy because of course he had invaded my dreams too—once, twice, a hundred times. Ever since he had shown up on my very first, weird black-and-white painting, his image had always been there with me. I had never been able to paint over a single image of the man, so I had every single one I'd ever created.

Horns apparently weren't much of a deterrent to my libido.

His hair was just as black as I'd painted it. His dark eyes had the same twinkle. His dimple—his freaking *dimple*—teased me when he smiled. All I wanted to do was dip my tongue in the cute little indent on this handsome but dangerous-looking man, which struck me as both horribly unhygienic and tantalizing.

"This is wrong, so very, very wrong," I mumbled, even as I stepped closer to examine what my brain had conjured. I mean, I knew my imagination was good. I was an artist, trained to have an eye for detail, but this... This was above and beyond.

Actually…

If this was a fantasy, maybe I should just enjoy it.

I drew my tongue over my top lip and let my gaze drift down the imaginary man's body. Yes. I just needed to embrace this dream or mirage or whatever it was. If I was going crazy, I might as well enjoy myself, right?

"Sorry," the man said as he approached. "I didn't mean to startle you…"

I eliminated the distance between us and put my finger over his mouth to stop him from talking. This was my delusion: I didn't need words. My fingers collided with warm lips. That was crazy. I could even touch him, which meant… I was ready to try some stuff, stuff I'd never done with someone before. It was the perfect opportunity to practice.

Thanks, brain, for doing this. You're pretty fucked up lately, but this is amazing. I forgive you.

"You have a nice voice," I said. "But let's just skip over the talking part of this and get right to the good stuff."

The man's eyebrows lifted, as if he was surprised.

This daydream was so freaking realistic. It was perfect. As I pulled my hand away from his mouth, I let my finger slip over his smooth, soft lip. Heat from his breath warmed my fingertip.

"Holy Caravaggio, you are so freaking hot," I murmured as I set my hands on his chest. Unlike me, he had a muscular torso. I wished my brain had made his shirt as tight as the one I was wearing so I could drool over his defined pecs. I squinted hard at the shirt and wished it away, but the stubborn thing didn't disappear.

That was disappointing, but whatever. I'd just have to do other things. Sexy things. I loved how my body responded to him. It was such a novelty.

Too bad this wasn't real.

But I shouldn't be surprised by how I was responding to the illusion I'd conjured. This imaginary guy was everything I'd lusted over for months now. Oh, how I wished this was real. I really wouldn't have trouble losing my virginity to a guy like this.

With that in mind, I slid my hands up his hard body, then over his shoulders before bringing them together behind his neck.

"Kiss me," I said.

Normally, I'd never have the guts to do something like this, but in my fantasy, nothing was off limits. His eyes narrowed as he studied me. I narrowed my eyes right back at him.

"Kiss me," I demanded again. "Now."

"You want me to kiss you?"

"I don't think I mumbled."

I'd never be so demanding in real life, but in my fantasy world I could be anything I wanted, have anything I wanted. And today I was channeling a bossy bottom vibe. I may not have ever had sex, but I knew what I wanted: I'd discovered porn in the last year. It'd been very educational.

His smile deepened, making his delightful dimple more visible. Then he ducked his head until his mouth met mine. He tasted of coffee and a little bit like minty toothpaste too. I hadn't expected my imagination to supply little details like that. Fuck, I was good.

His arms came around me, then he was lifting me, so my face was level with his. As I wrapped my legs around his solid body, I was thrilled to discover my cock was fully engaged now. Trapped inside my pants, it felt hard and sensitive.

It'd never done that while I was with someone before.

Of course, I wasn't actually with someone now, either.

If my excitement had been at even half this level when I tried to hook up with guys in the past, my love life would have been a hell of a lot more interesting. I rolled my hips against his bulge, grinding against it, savoring the delicious pressure and friction. Thank Degas my imagination had the decency to give me that... and it'd even made his package nice and generous and hard against mine.

I moaned.

He moaned.

His hands slid down. His fingers tried to grip my ass, but it was like my form-fitting pants were working against me now. With them so tight, my body was squeezed into my pants like a sausage in a casing with nothing soft or grip-able remaining.

It was so weird how my imagination was better in some ways and not in others, because I definitely wanted to feel his fingers digging into my ass cheeks. Kneading me. Separating them a little to give his fingers access to other parts of me.

He felt so good between my legs, pressing against me, kissing me. And although I was sure it'd be easy to come like this, I wanted more.

He spun us around and set me down on the narrow console table I'd always cursed and threatened to throw away whenever I vacuumed the hallway. Thank Rembrandt I hadn't actually done it. Who knew it'd be so useful?

Or, well, it would be if this was real.

I laughed.

My illusion pulled back enough to look at me. His lips were wet and rosy from our kisses. His breath fanned across my mouth, making my lips tingle. "What? What's so funny?"

"Me? You? This? Everything?"

His forehead furrowed. "I don't understand."

"That's okay, Mr. Horny Dude," I said, calling him by the name I'd given him months ago. I gently nudged him back and slid off the table. "I wish I didn't have to work, so I could stay here and play. But now that I know it is possible to do all this—" I waved my hand in the air to encompass the whole imaginary interlude, "—I definitely want to do this again."

Sure. It'd be better if I was kissing a living person, but this was a wonderful substitute. I sighed happily and let my eyes boldly slip down his body again. Unable to resist temptation, just in case I couldn't conjure up another vision like this again, I reached over and patted the thick enticing bulge at his crotch.

He jerked in surprise.

Oh. It was nice and hard. I gave it a little squeeze. Yep. My brain had drawn on some truly outstanding porn to fill in details like this.

"Spectacular," I muttered.

Everything was so unbelievably lifelike. My brain was freaking amazing.

"If this is how things are going to be, losing my mind won't be so bad after all."

Then I sauntered down the hall, feeling better than I had in a long time.

Chapter Four

GAGE

"What in all the Eternal Magic just happened?" I whispered incredulously.

I peered over my shoulder like the answer would be lurking behind me in the hallway. I couldn't ask my team for their opinions because they were elsewhere on the property. When we'd first arrived and my instinct made me take the upper floors for myself, I'd worried, but now I wondered if it had to do with the gorgeous man who'd just kissed me like we were lovers.

Few people or situations surprised me, but this one did.

It wasn't often—if ever—that I just walked down a corridor and boom, a sexy guy was all over me. And now he was skipping down the stairs, leaving me alone and aching to fuck. My gaze clung to his ass until he was out of sight. With the way his tight pants embraced the rounded globes of his ass so perfectly, how could I look away?

His taste still lingered in my mouth. His clean scent, mixed with the distinctive smell of paint, still filled my nose. My fingers tingled with the memory of holding him tight.

I didn't know why he'd just randomly decided to kiss me, but we would do it again. Next time, though, it wouldn't end so fast. Neither of us would leave unsated either.

It didn't look like that'd be happening now, though.

I adjusted my erection, squeezing it until it subsided.

A guy who just randomly went up to a stranger and made out with them wasn't my normal choice for a lover, but his approach had definitely gotten my attention. Even through his ridiculously tight pants, I'd felt his erection pressed against mine. He'd been as turned on as I was. So why weren't we naked and sweaty right now?

But that wasn't my only question.

Was he a guest? If he was, where was the staff? No, I was sure he lived here. He'd talked about going to work. So why hadn't he questioned my presence in the hallway of this supposedly locked building?

If he found Nelson skulking around the ground floor, would he kiss him too? My skin itched as my demonic form surged forward. Everything inside me demanded I not let that happen, even though I had no claim on the guy.

"Fuck. Get a grip," I muttered. "He can kiss whoever he wants."

Except that was a lie. Now that I'd had a taste of him, I wanted more. And what I wanted, I usually got, one way or another. Being a demon had some perks after all. I followed the fascinating man at a distance, curious to see what he'd do next.

Chapter Five

JAKE

I reached to the back of the cooler for the last bottle of a specialty brew called Witch's Milk. As least my tight pants had stretched enough now that I was able to crouch in them without losing feeling in my legs and feet. The chilled air seeped through the thin, tight T-shirt I was wearing. I'd chosen it as part of my gotta-get-laid plan, but I doubted much would come of my plan tonight, not when I had the energy of a slug. It was too bad, because after my imaginary kiss in the hallway earlier, I'd been sure tonight was the night I'd strike the first thing from my list.

Since I was turned away from everyone, I let myself steal a yawn. As my lips stretched, I swore it was like they were still tender from the make out session with my illusion. The details in it still amazed me. It almost made me wish I'd dragged my imaginary lover back to my room and had my way with him.

Except having sex with a vision my mind had created

wouldn't count as losing my virginity, would it? I mean, I'd essentially just be having sex with myself, and over the last year I'd done that a lot already.

I shook my head to shake off my sleepiness. When that didn't work, I pushed my face closer to the cooler, pretending to look for another Witch's Milk in the back. There was nothing there, of course, but the blast of cold air was at least a little invigorating.

Old Thom hadn't been happy to hear our current suppliers didn't carry the specialty brew, making it impossible to order more. I blamed the problem on my grandfather's abysmal record keeping.

None of my regular suppliers had even heard of the drink, which hadn't helped. I'd never tasted the stuff, but it had the same color and aroma as a cream ale, so I'd tried to steer the old guy to one of those. He'd snapped his rotting teeth at me. So, the old grouch had been spacing out his consumption of the drink for months now, only having one bottle a month. This was the last one.

In all that time, no one else had dared ask for one.

My fingers had just curled around the cool bottle when a hush fell over the bar.

Old Thom wasn't grumbling. Sally wasn't cackling. Even the billiard balls weren't clacking against one another from one of Carter Jones' well-executed plays.

Although it was early in the day, it was still a Saturday. Noise should be filling the place and getting progressively louder as the day went on. The strange silence made me freeze, like some sixth sense was warning me to sit tight and not draw any attention to myself. Then Sally let out a soft wheezing sound as footsteps fell heavily on the hard-wood floor.

"Holy mother of dildos," she whispered. She sounded breathless.

And then I *needed* to look...

I needed to make myself move, to turn around, to see what all the fuss was about. But I was still frozen in place like prey in the presence of a powerful predator.

In those few seconds, condensation formed on the bottle I was holding, and it slipped a little. I tightened my grip. If I dropped the bottle and it broke, Old Thom would be livid, and Old Thom's wrath wasn't something I wanted to experience. Certainly not by myself.

Not that Alice, my usual Saturday co-worker, would have been able to stop him if she'd been working tonight either. She bragged about being more street-smart and scarier than me, even if, by her own admission, she'd never lived anywhere but this sleepy little town. But I didn't see it.

She was at least a foot shorter than I was. Since I was on the shorter side of average, Alice was extra short. And her ever-present toothy grin was hardly intimidating. When we worked together, we were good at conquering any problem, but I doubted any of her street smarts or my extra foot of height would deter Old Thom if he decided to show his displeasure.

The guy looked ancient, so you'd think he'd be weak and frail, but that wasn't the case. He was huge and shock-ingly muscular. His skin was rough like it was made of sandstone, his eyes always glinted with anger, and his constant snarl made me uneasy. His huge, rosy-colored bulbous nose was about the only part of the guy that didn't look menacing. I didn't want to find out what he'd do if someone pissed him off. No, if Old Thom or anyone else came after me... Well, hopefully one of my regulars like Carter Jones, who was a big bear of a man, would step in to help.

Most of the time I didn't worry about working the bar by myself, which I did three nights a week. The usual patrons were all well-behaved. But today was Saturday, and I was worried people would get grumpy if they had to wait to be served. There should have been two of us, but Alice had begged for the night off. I'd only known her a year, but she'd become one of my closest friends, which meant I didn't buy the fake cough she started out with. Not one little bit. In the end, she confessed to landing a date with Buddy Jackson and a weird sense of déjà vu swept through me at her confession.

Then I remembered one of my black-and-white paintings was of her... and Buddy... on their wedding day. Well, not *their* wedding. Because they were only just now going on their first date. At the time I'd painted it, I'd been baffled as to why my psyche would ship those two, but now it seemed almost prophetic.

What a ridiculous thought.

"Where's my drink, boy?" Old Thom slammed his hand on the bar.

"I'm getting it," I reassured him, even as the bottle slipped in my fingers again.

Shit. I couldn't drop it.

Cradling the bottle like a fragile newborn against my chest, I slowly stood and shut the cooler door with a thud that resounded through the abnormally quiet bar. It was almost like people were even trying to breathe more quietly than normal. Then a song flipped over on the old jukebox and Imagine Dragons belted out "Demons."

My heart thundered painfully in my chest, just like it had last night when I woke from my latest weird painting episode, as I pivoted toward the bar.

There, with his elbows resting on my bar, was the guy I'd seen upstairs. The one I'd made out with a few hours ago. The one I'd been painting for almost a year. The one who was completely and absolutely imaginary.

"Fuck."

Chapter Six

JAKE

"Hello again," the guy said, a sly smile forming on his lips.

Interacting with my hallucination in private was one thing, but here? In the middle of the bar on a Saturday afternoon? That wasn't good.

I tried to keep my face as blank as possible as I ignored the imaginary man. Nope. I would not look at his broad shoulders. My hands absolutely did not remember the feel of his body. His horns gleaming under the lights? Nope. I didn't see those either. And the knowing smirk on his face? Ha. No way was that drawing me in.

"Jake? You okay, honey?" Sally asked.

"I'm fine." I did not sound fine.

"Because…" She nodded toward the imaginary man who was *not* standing beside her. "Aren't you going to say anything?"

I let my gaze slide past Sally down the bar. The only

thing between her and the wall was my illusion. She pointed right at the man who didn't exist.

"My friends and I," the guy said, drawing my attention back to him. "We heard this was the place to come for a drink." He gestured to two other exceptionally large and good-looking men who were grabbing one of the tables at the far side of the room.

Why the hell would my imagination conjure up friends for my fantasy guy?

My chest tightened as I got a better look at one of the men who'd come in with Mr. Horny Dude. I rubbed my eyes before looking again. No, it couldn't be. Sitting at the table was an athletic-looking guy with sun-bleached blond hair hanging down past his shoulders. And I bet it'd look like it was billowing if the guy was, you know, riding a horse... or something.

The long-haired man caught me looking at him. An affable smile lit his face as he waved at me. The other man at the table seemed entirely too normal, all things considered. He had short dark brown hair and a close-cropped beard, which accentuated his jawline.

Wait... Had the normal-looking guy just gone blurry around the edges?

I snapped my attention back to the man who was *not* real and *not* standing at my bar. I bit the inside of my cheek. Pain should jolt me back to reality, right? Nothing changed.

That didn't mean...

No.

I wasn't seeing this for real, was I?

That was impossible.

People didn't have horns.

Unless he had implants.

I was sure I'd seen some late-night documentary about body modifications during the last year when I'd tried binge watching television. I only did that for a month or so before I lost interest and decided it was impossible to watch everything I'd missed.

I still turned the TV on occasionally, but even then, I avoided anything to do with magic. I doubted I'd ever shake the lingering memories of my mother's anxiety over those types of shows. But documentaries? Those were fascinating, even the ones claiming that every mind-blowing feat of engineering on Earth was thanks to aliens.

But this guy didn't look the type to get horn implants on his head.

I was so confused.

None of this made sense.

He was a figment of my imagination. I'd been painting his face for almost a year. I knew the dips and hollows of it better than I knew my own. I could paint his face in my sleep. I *had*, in fact, painted it in my sleep. Over and over again. He was a fantasy. Imaginary. Made up. Not real.

I couldn't imagine someone into real life.

The world didn't work that way.

Then again, what if it was only the horns I was imagining? Had I seen him before and my brain fixated on him, a real person, without me realizing? But if I had seen him before, why didn't I remember it?

"Ah, Jake, honey? Are you going to serve the man?" Sally coaxed.

Well, that settled that. Sally definitely saw him. Which

begged the question, how on earth was he standing in front of me instead of just existing in the pictures under my bed?

Wait.

Did that mean…?

Holy da Vinci.

Was the reason the kiss had felt so real was because it *was* real?

What did a heart attack feel like? Because I was pretty sure I was having one.

"A drink?" I was squeaking again, just like I had the first time I maybe, possibly, saw him upstairs. I cleared my throat.

"Yes?" the man said.

"Oh, lordy," Sally whispered. "You've broken our little Jake." She leaned forward and leered at the man as she licked her bottom lip. "But I'm not broken."

Sally patted his arm, as if to prove she not only saw my hallucination but was interacting with it too. Okay. That was good. So good. It meant he wasn't just in my head.

Except… My gaze dropped down his body to where his hips would be, but I couldn't see his crotch from here. The counter was in the way, hiding the bulge I'd maybe, possibly, patted and squeezed earlier. Had that been real? If it was, then I'd assaulted him upstairs. That wasn't good. Not at all. Maybe it'd be better if he wasn't real. I'd never assaulted anyone before. I wasn't that kind of person.

I had no idea what to do.

No. This couldn't be real. My mind was messing with me again. This wasn't the same guy as upstairs. No way. They might look similar, but nope. I was just making connections that didn't exist.

I heaved out a relieved breath at that conclusion.

Sally's face contorted into what I guessed was supposed to be a seductive invitation. My grandfather had nicknamed her Sally the Succubus. The internet—yes, I had to look it up—described a succubus as a sexual demon, and I thought the nickname was a little cruel. No one should be slut-shamed, as one of my fellow art students said over and over again during our classes. Most of her art had been sexual in nature and very enlightening. I hadn't even known slut-shaming was a thing before I'd met her. It was the first time I began to see just how sheltered my life had been under my mother's roof. And just because Sally didn't have problems finding companions of any gender or any age to go home with didn't mean she deserved to be called names.

Sally pushed her voluptuous boobs toward the new guy as her fingers dipped into the deep vee of her tight pink shirt. Her breasts were disproportionately generous, considering how small she was. I'd seen her use them to her advantage many times, and she was doing it again. Granddad would be laughing his ass off about now. He always did when Sally turned her attentions on someone. Me? I was usually in awe of the woman, because whoever Sally wanted, Sally usually got.

Tonight, though, I wasn't laughing or in awe. At all. I fought the sudden urge to whack Sally in the face with my bar rag and shoo her away from the picture-perfect man. I didn't want her near him, and I couldn't figure out why. I mean... he wasn't real, right? Not in the true sense of the word. This man may look like the paintings, and he might act like he was the same entity I'd made out with upstairs earlier, but it wasn't true. This was a stranger. I didn't have a claim on him. Hell, I didn't even know his name.

I swore I saw a thin curl of misty vapor waft out of Sally's mouth. Was she spitting on him? Ew. The man sniffed the air—because that wasn't weird at all, although it was pretty much the norm for Willow Lake—and instead of leaning forward to meet her halfway and commence a sloppy French kiss, which was always deeply disturbing no matter how many times I had seen it happen, the mystery man winked at Sally.

"Naughty succubus." It sounded like a reprimand.

Then the air pulsed with energy, the same way the atmosphere got heavy before a thunderstorm. Great. Now there was a new facet to my hallucinations. They were getting really intense now.

I doubted that was a good sign.

"I'm not in the mood to play," the man said.

Paws, my grandfather's cat, jumped onto the bar between Sally and the new guy. The calico cat hissed and smacked Sally with his paw. His fluffy tail twitched back and forth in irritation as he let out a series of un-catlike sounds.

Sally jolted back.

Paws kept talking in his weird cat language. The fact that it sounded a bit like—or *entirely* like—actual words and sentences didn't mean I would give in to this particular hallucination. I'd been ignoring the cat for months; it was something I had down pat.

La la la la la... I screamed in my head so I wouldn't hear what it was saying.

Although, I swore my name was mentioned, but that

was just my mind playing more tricks on me. I was just anxious because what if Paws had seen a few of the paintings I'd done of *the* guy?

Except why would that matter? Paws was a cat; it wasn't like he could spill the beans to anyone about them.

"Oh!" She shrank away from him. "Uh... right... of course."

She glanced at me, in what I swore was an apologetic way, while her fingers fumbled as she buttoned her shirt all the way to the collar. I'd never seen her do that before. This day just kept getting stranger by the minute.

And how did this new guy know Granddad's nickname for Sally? Succubus wasn't a common word.

"Hey, you," Old Thom shouted as he slammed his beefy hand on the bar again, rattling the stacked glasses. "Give me my damn drink."

The grumpy old bastard stood a few feet away at the other end of the bar, but his nasty breath still made it all the way over to where I stood. As always, the stench was strong enough to make me gag and snap me out of my daze. I moved to set the bottle I was holding on the counter, but it slipped from my fingers an inch above the surface and landed with a thud. The bottle teetered, then fell over and rolled across the counter. I shot my hand out to grab it, but I was too slow. Old Thom shrieked as it dropped over the edge.

"Shit, shit, shit..."

Then suddenly the stranger was standing behind the bar beside me with the bottle in his hand. I hadn't even seen him move.

Now that I saw him from head to foot, I realized he

was wearing the same clothes as earlier. That had to mean I'd kissed a real person. Him. This beautiful horned man.

Fuckity fuck.

The stranger's eyes narrowed when he read the label.

"Witch's Milk?"

"Mine," Old Thom shouted as he hobbled closer. He reached across the counter and plucked the bottle from the stranger's hand. Then he twisted off the cap and flicked it at me. I flinched when the metal disc hit me between my eyebrows.

"Hey," the new man shouted at Old Thom.

I swore the horned man grew taller and beefier right in front of my eyes.

Was it possible to feel another person's fury? Because I felt a deep and foreboding sense of impending violence roll through the air with the horned guy at its epicentre. A low, deep rumbling sound poured out of the man's body. His skin turned crimson with his obvious anger.

I gulped, unable to drag my eyes away.

It wasn't normal to get turned on by something so decidedly abnormal, was it?

Nope. I was pretty sure it wasn't. But my unfamiliar stirring of arousal wasn't going away. I'd never been turned on by another person.

Of course, I had to be different. That was the story of my life. The kid who hadn't watched the latest cartoon. The kid who had never dressed up on Halloween. And now, I was the guy who was going through puberty at twenty-three instead of thirteen.

It'd only been during the last year that I'd even discovered all the ways my right hand could be used. It was one of the reasons I put losing my virginity on my list last night. And now, as if given the green light, my body was making up for lost time. I didn't even have a book bag to hold in front of my crotch like teenagers did. And running up to my room to retrieve a jacket to wrap around my hips would just draw more attention.

In other words, I was fucked.

Why did all this have to happen now?

At the shouts, every other movement and sound in the pub halted. Again. I swore people were cowering. Even the guys Mr. Horny Dude had come in with appeared alarmed as they jumped out of their chairs. Paws' furry coat was standing on end, but he didn't screech or hiss or even arch his back. The cat stared at Mr. Horny Dude as if daring him to do something more. That sense of doom increased. The stranger's gaze flitted to Paws before returning to Old Thom.

What the hell was happening? I had to stop this before it got any further out of hand.

"Everyone, calm down. You, Old Thom, go sit down. You…" I pointed at Mr. Horny Dude, then waved my hand through the air. "Knock it off. The whole dark and dangerous attitude might be sexy but wrap it up."

My bossy words flew out of my mouth before I could censor them, but I didn't have the energy or patience to deal with a bar fight. I had enough on my plate, what with losing my mind and all. I couldn't cope with anything more. I held up my hands, like my will alone would stop the men if they really wanted to have a go at one another. The stranger's attention snapped to me. He looked surprised at both himself and me.

"I'm sorry I can't offer you one of those drinks," I said to him. "That was our last bottle and Old Thom asked for it first."

"I didn't want one, but that guy needs an anger management class."

Yeah. I didn't think he was the only one.

Old Thom's snarl sounded like rocks grating against one another.

"Don't worry about him. Witch's Milk is his favorite, and I can't get any more in. He's just cranky."

"Don't tell him that. Don't tell him anything." Old Thom squawked and shuffled toward his regular dark corner, which was on the opposite end of the room from the mystery guy's friends. He dropped into his favorite chair with his back to the wall, hunched his shoulders, and scowled at everyone.

The bar was still quiet. Everyone seemed to be holding their breath. Even Carter Jones seemed fixed in a bent position over the billiard table, with his fingers tight around his pool cue.

"What can I get you?" I asked Mr. Horny Dude, who was still behind the bar with me. I tilted my head back to look at him. Holy Rubens, he was gorgeous. I'd always thought so, right from that first painting I'd done of him. But I couldn't reveal how obsessed I was with him. That'd just be weird and awkward.

Ha! Like molesting him in a hallway wasn't weird and awkward.

Maybe if I pretended everything was normal, it would be. That had become my M.O. in recent months, and I was going to cling to it as long as I could. If it worked for my bizarre midnight painting obsession, it'd work for this too.

The guy, who may or may not have horns, shot one last glare in Old Thom's direction, then nodded. His body lost its redness and seemed to become a little smaller... a little more normal, like it had been when he first walked in. Well, not that it'd *actually* changed, because bodies and skin color and eyes didn't change like that. Not in real life.

The important thing, though, was that everyone seemed to exhale, and the Saturday afternoon din rose up again, not up to its normal decibels, but better than it had been. The guy's companions returned to their seats. It was like the unsettling tension had popped, dissipating like it'd never been.

I wasn't surprised when my regulars started murmuring furtively with one another and exchanging something, money by the look of it. I smiled. That was more like it.

I used to worry about the whispers and seeing hands exchanging money, but Alice and Sally had assured me no one was dealing drugs, so I decided to believe them and just let everyone do what they wanted. The first time it happened, I worried the locals were upset I'd inherited the inn and were badmouthing me and making bets about how long it'd be before I went bankrupt. But they kept coming back to the pub, so now I figured it was just who they were.

After all, it'd been almost a year since I'd taken over the business, and things didn't seem any worse than when my grandfather was running it. Of course, it wasn't any better either, but that was a different problem.

I rubbed my forehead where the bottle cap had hit.

Shit, that stung. As ridiculous as it sounded, it was like the pain ricocheted all the way through me like an out-of-control ping pong ball.

"Come here," the mystery man said, leaning into my space. His voice was deeper now. It had a strange kind of vibration to it, almost like he was compelling me to obey. He wasn't, of course, but I was curious about what he had planned so I did as he asked.

The end of Paws' tail flicked faster, but the cat didn't move, and he didn't meow. Sally whimpered. And me? I moved closer until I was standing directly in front of the man.

I didn't believe in all the woo-woo stuff my mother had feared, but this guy was making me question that. It was almost like he had an aura or an energy around him that reached out to embrace me. It was warm and calming. I leaned toward him, as if drawn in by some unseen force. I'd always thought magnetic attraction was an exaggeration used by romance novelists like Jeremy.

Until this moment.

Now it felt all too real. I moved closer still. I couldn't help myself.

Chapter Seven

JAKE

Had I *actually* kissed this man earlier?

Either way, I wanted to do it again, right now, just to test my theory that the kiss had been real. My lips opened and my breaths quickened as he reached for me. Holy Dali. I couldn't remember the last time someone had brushed their fingers over my skin. I mean, I guess he had possibly touched me earlier, but I hadn't known it was real then. I held my breath and waited.

For the second time in one night, I was frozen in place.

The man's thumb brushed over the place where the bottle cap had struck me. Our gazes locked and I swore the guy's eyes turned red. Not in a bloodshot way. No, this was different. His eyes were just black pupils surrounded by nothing but swirling red. And in his mouth, his tongue did not look like a tongue. At least not a human tongue. It was narrow and long and… *forked*.

It should have been shocking, because that shit wasn't

normal, but then a soothing heat shot out from that feather-light touch and cascaded over me like a gentle waterfall. Oh. That was *nice*. I wanted to fall into that warmth and bathe in it.

Goosebumps pricked along my skin and... my cock was involved again, way more than before. And there was all this... *tingling* happening. My skin tingled. My balls tingled. My cock... Okay, my cock wasn't tingling so much as it felt ready to burst. The last thing I needed was to come in public, in my pants. My head spun at the real-ization I'd not only gotten hard at the mere sight of him, but I was ready to jizz at his fleeting touch to my forehead, of all places.

I jerked back, putting distance between me and this too-tempting stranger.

My body seemed to have forgotten that it didn't do sexual stuff when other people were around. It never had. Sure, I thought about sex. I'd thought about sex a lot in the last year. Before that, I hadn't cared much about it one way or the other. But in the last twelve months, I'd pleasured myself plenty of times, particularly to the images of a certain horned guy I didn't believe existed. But I'd never reacted to another living person before.

As a teenager, I realized not long after puberty that I was different from other kids my age. I did the research and decided I was ace. Then when I started getting horny for the horned dude in my paintings, I figured I was demi instead.

So, what the hell was my body doing reacting to a guy I didn't know? Just because I had dozens of pictures of someone who looked like him hidden under my bed did not mean I knew him. At all. Seriously.

Yes, I'd put losing my virginity on my list, but this whole situation was freaking me out. Maybe I wasn't ready yet, which was a depressing thought because I was running out of time.

"Uh… Yeah…" I stammered. "What did you want to drink?"

"My name is Gage," the man—*Gage*—said. "What's yours?"

And now I knew his name. It was a good name. I wanted to roll it around on my tongue, taste it. I liked the way my lips moved when I repeated it. Particularly at the end, where it was like my lips were puckering to kiss him.

The guy's eyes were almost more mesmerizing now than they had been only a moment earlier. The red had bled away but the intensity in his gaze made my breath hitch. When Gage licked his lips, my gaze zeroed in on the little movement. I stared at his tongue because it looked normal again.

I'd never seen the appeal of tongues—I mean, what was there to like about them? They were covered with someone else's spit and moved in unsettling ways—but suddenly I wanted to lick Gage's tongue. Taste it. Feel how wet and warm it was.

This was insane.

But I couldn't stop my decadent and explicit thoughts now that they'd started. Gage was so much better at seduction than Sally. He wasn't even touching me anymore, but my lips were still parted as if in anticipation of another kiss.

I hadn't paid close enough attention during our first kiss because I hadn't known it was real. It was time to rectify that oversight.

Gage's gaze was fixed on me, like a predator would fixate on its prey. My fight or flight instincts should have kicked in, but they stayed absurdly quiet. I didn't care if he wanted to devour me. Not even a little.

Now that I'd had a moment to catch my breath, I realized I wanted him to touch me again. If he did, I wouldn't run away this time.

No matter how much I thought I should.

The clap of billiard balls hitting one another made me jump and reminded me where I was. Shit. I had a job to do. I couldn't stand around gawking at customers.

"Right, uh, Gage. Okay. What do you want to drink?"

Ignoring my question, Gage leaned closer, causing his midnight black hair to fall over his forehead and shift around his horns. "What's your name, beautiful? I heard someone say the name Jake, is that right?"

Beautiful? No one ever called me beautiful. Cute, occasionally. Adorable, unfortunately. But never beautiful.

"Yep," Sally supplied. "His name is Jake."

Another smile slipped over Gage's mouth. This one looked sinful, despite the cute dimple.

"Drink?" And... I was back to squeaking again.

"What's taking so long?" one of the men Gage had come in with shouted. "Are we waiting for the ale to ferment?"

"Fuck off, Isaac," Gage shouted back. His eyes never left mine. "Sorry about that. I guess my friends are getting thirsty."

I nodded. Not sure what to say.

"I'll have one wheat ale, and two pints of the darkest ale you have on tap," he said.

"Yep. Can do."

I didn't want him to leave, feeling strangely content to have him close, but he was distracting and in the way. Not because he was ginormous or anything like that, but because my body kept gravitating toward him.

"But... uh..." I motioned for him to move. "I need room to work."

He nodded but didn't move away. Instead, he leaned closer until his lips brushed my ear. His breath fanned across my neck like a caress. "And I'd also like to continue what we started earlier."

Heat rocketed through me.

It had been real.

I was nodding before he even stepped back. "Uh... Right... Yes. Me too."

I couldn't believe this was happening. I was going to lose my virginity. My freak out moments earlier was nowhere in sight. Hallelujah. I just prayed my dick didn't fuck this up for me again by suddenly going on strike.

"You are real, right?" I whispered.

His forehead furrowed at my question, but he nodded.

"It was you, wasn't it? Earlier..."

"You think you could confuse me with someone else?" The amusement in his voice told me he knew I'd never mistake him for anyone else. I envied his self-confidence.

"No. Not at all," I said. The kiss replayed in my mind. Heat rose in me as if he had me up on the console table again with his hips wedged between my thighs. Then I remembered again how I'd left things between us. Fuck. "I touched you. Like… there." My gaze dropped to his crotch and back up again. "With my hand. I'm so sorry. I don't normally… I mean… I didn't… Shit. I'm so sorry. I don't usually, like ever, do things like that…"

He leaned in close again and my panicked words tumbled to a stop. "I won't say I wasn't surprised, but the way we were grinding before that, I considered the touch consensual. You asked me to kiss you, and I did. After that, everything else happened naturally. And, for the record, I wanted way more than a little pat. But I'd be happy to touch you back, you know, just so we're even."

His words lit up my insides like fireworks exploding.

"Really?"

He nipped at my earlobe, gently tugging it between his teeth. "Really."

Was swooning a thing real people did? Or was it just something that happened to characters in books? Because I was ready to fall into this guy and have him carry me away. Not because I was a damsel in distress, but because I was a man with goals. And, right now, I was closer to realizing one of my goals than ever before.

This was the best day ever.

But first I had to finish this shift.

"I need to work," I said as I took a step back from temptation. "Uh, is later okay?"

"Of course," he said with a nod.

As soon as he was on the other side of the counter again, my body slipped into the familiar routine of filling his order. When I set the drinks on the counter, I found Gage watching me. A sexy smile played over his mouth.

I'd kissed that mouth.

And I was going to kiss it again.

My cheeks heated at both the memory and the promise in his eyes.

"Thank you, Jake," he said. And I swore I'd never heard those three words sound so seductive before. "I think we'll be in town for a while," Gage continued as he gathered the three pints in his big hands. "And I have a feeling you and I are going to get to know one another very well."

I wanted to say I thought so too, but now that he wasn't close enough to muddle my thoughts, I remembered I wasn't the bold guy I'd pretended to be earlier. All my bravado was used up. Instead, I ogled him as he retreated to the table where his friends were seated.

My cheeks were blazing hot as all the naughty and seductive things I should have said to him whipped through my head. My face had to be as red as the hot sauce some of my regulars liked to add to everything they ordered, but I was incapable of doing anything about it.

"Oh lordy," Sally muttered again and wrapped her arms over her stomach. "You've gone and broken him again."

Chapter Eight

GAGE

"It's about time," Isaac muttered as he grabbed his wheat ale from my hand.

This bar might be new to me, and the cutie behind the bar was *definitely* new—if I ignored how I'd already had my tongue in his mouth—but the job wasn't. So, as I set the other drinks on the table, I scanned the room.

"So we're here to meet that same hellhound, right? The police officer?" Nelson asked. "The one we met a few weeks back?"

At least Nelson was looking better now that we'd been here for a while. He'd been a bit blurry around the edges earlier.

"Yes," I said, speaking as quietly as I could. "It's the same guy. His name is Van Clark. He's the Chief of Police here. He's the one who contacted us about those stolen magical artifacts."

"Do you think he'll help us?" Nelson asked, keeping

his voice just as quiet. We didn't need all these people hearing what we were saying.

"Hellhounds tend to see the world in black and white, but it's worth remembering this is his town. He may not want to upset the status quo by going after the wolf pack if it means the town is negatively impacted. Adrian has a good impression of the guy, and so far, our goals have aligned. It might be different if that changes. He might have different priorities than us."

"I haven't met a hellhound before. Well, other than that short interaction a few weeks ago. Is there anything I need to know?" Isaac tapped his fingers on the table. He always had so much damn energy.

"Hellhounds can tell if you are lying." This wasn't the first time I'd dealt with a hellhound, but the last one was before Isaac joined us. "They also can't lie themselves. Those are the most important things to remember."

"Cool." Isaac nodded.

I asked for honesty from my team, so I didn't think the no lying thing would be an issue.

"Our plan is simple: Check in with Adrian and his mate when they get back. Meet the hellhound again. Find out if he still wants our help and determine if he'll be helpful or not. If it doesn't work out, we run our own investigation without local support."

"So we're staying here for a while either way?" Nelson crossed his arms, looking irritated by the idea of being stuck in one place again. He was relentless in his quest to help me find a place to tether before I lost control. He was overreacting.

Honestly.

I would know if I was close to losing control.

My team just worried.

Really.

I should never have told them, but since I knew their deepest desires, it was only fair that I share mine. Unfortunately, everyone had blown the whole he'll-lose-his-mind-and-go-on-a-killing-rampage-if-we-don't-get-him-tethered-as-soon-as-possible situation out of proportion.

As it did every time I thought about my magic snapping, a familiar and unwelcome memory hit me. My father's red eyes glared at me. They blazed brightly as he swiped his long bloody claws at my neck. My heart twisted with a pain that never really went away. But I also remembered that moment hadn't happened suddenly. There had been signs. And I wasn't displaying any of those same signs.

I was fine.

It was on the tip of my sometimes-forked tongue to suggest this might be the place I'd been looking for my whole life, just to ease Nelson's ever-present worry, but I swallowed those words down. Because, what if this wasn't the place? I didn't want to get anyone's hopes up.

Instead, I nodded.

"It'll be faster if we work with him, but either way, we're here for a bit. We operate the same as always. Get a feel for the locals, track unusual behavior, ferret out the assholes who are behaving badly and deal with them, and move on to the next supernatural fuckup."

Nelson nodded, but he didn't look impressed. I ignored him and looked around the room again.

And if my gaze lingered on the very kissable bartender, so what?

It was reasonable for me to want more information about him. He had to be the guy who'd inherited the place recently, the one who'd been robbed. That robbery had led us to the trafficking ring. So I could argue—if anyone questioned me, which I doubted they would—that my interest was related to our current case.

Except, that wouldn't be the full truth.

The guy intrigued me. Even if he hadn't kissed me senseless earlier, there was just something about him that kept drawing my attention. I couldn't figure out what it was, but I was willing to go with it.

Besides, our continued and undeniable chemistry aligned nicely with my plan to take Jake to bed. Isaac would say using the word *bed* was old-fashioned, but let's face it, at my age I had no desire to hook up with someone in a cramped bathroom stall, even if it was sparkling clean, which they never were. I liked beds. They served a purpose. They let me be comfortable while I took my time with my lover.

And I *would* take my time with the very kissable Jake.

"What did you find out?" Nelson asked.

"Not a lot," I said. "But enough to make me curious."

He didn't need to know my curiosity was mostly centered on the bartender.

My gaze drifted back to Jake. With his seeming innocence and inherent sweetness, he wasn't my usual type. But he'd also been the one who'd demanded kisses earlier, so maybe he wasn't so innocent after all. And now that I'd decided I wanted him, I was looking forward to finding out who he really was. But my interest in him wasn't just sexual.

What was it the hellhound had said when we met with him a few weeks back? Something about the guy who'd been robbed not having a clue about the Eternal Magic and then hinting Jake wasn't a mundane. How could a supe not know he was a supe?

But when I'd watched Jake earlier today and seen how he interacted with the supes in the bar, I didn't think it was an act. I doubted he was as ignorant as Van believed, but I got the sense he didn't understand what was happening either. Something wasn't adding up.

When I'd read his desires a few minutes ago, his deepest desire seemed centered around his art—something about his painting—but the reading wasn't as clear to me as it should be, which had never happened before. And that intrigued me even more.

My intuition told me he wasn't the one we were here to investigate, though, no matter how messy his magic seemed, which meant I had to pay attention to everyone else and not just think about all the ways I'd tease him once I got him into my bed.

That'd just be a very nice side benefit of this case. I could see it so clearly. How his skin would glisten and pinken so prettily as I brought him to orgasm after orgasm before I finally sought my own pleasure in his body. Blowjob or sex, I wasn't picky. Although his hair was long enough I could grip it tight as he worked over my dick with his plump pink lips. Fuck, he'd look good like that, kneeling on the ground before me.

But that would have to come later.

Right now, I had other things to think about. So, after I found my gaze lingering on Jake for the third time, I forced myself to look away.

It didn't help that my senses had been going crazy since we walked through the doors. The energy emitted by mages and shapeshifters wasn't all that rare, but when you added in the sphinx and the hellhounds and the merman... And then, like a cherry on the top of a very unconventional sundae, there was Jake himself. He wasn't human, but I couldn't identify his magic either—even after reading the guy.

Well, let's just say this was not your usual supernatural town.

I'd never seen so many different types of supes in one room outside exclusive clubs in the city, where our kind were forced to co-mingle in hidden underground havens to escape the overwhelming number of humans who thrived in urban areas. In more rural places like this, supes tended to stick close to their own kind. Wolves usually stayed with wolves, mages with mages, and so on. But the eclectic mix at least partially explained the magic I'd tasted when we'd first arrived.

The other part—the energy embedded in the place itself—well, I still wasn't sure what to do about that. At least I'd had a bit of time to acclimate. But I continued to feel its enticing invitation, and no matter how I poked at it with my own magic, I couldn't see anything artificial about it. If it was a constructed lure, made specifically to trap me here, it was the most seamless piece of magic I'd ever encountered.

The situation made me cautiously optimistic.

It wasn't a feeling I was used to, but the longer I spent in Willow Lake, the more I wondered if Willow Lake was the answer to my most fantastical dreams. The ones I'd spent most of my life believing would never come true.

Fuck.

I'd just quit fantasizing about the bartender and now I was daydreaming about the town.

Letting my guard down or allowing distractions to rule my mind was dangerous and risky. The goblin's cohorts were a serious threat. I refused to let my team down, so I inhaled a long, deep breath and let it out gradually. Calm and focus settled over me again.

"So, are you going to tell us what happened at the bar a minute ago?" Nelson asked quietly.

"Just getting to know the locals," I said, not wanting to go into any details with so many people listening. My words should be enough to let him know there wasn't an immediate threat.

"Right," he said, like he didn't believe me.

I scanned the room again.

The troll, who Jake had called Old Thom, was huddled in the corner, curling his body around his drink. The succubus at the bar, having unbuttoned her shirt again, was stroking her forefinger along her cleavage. The bear shifter by the billiard table was grunting and huffing as he leaned over to make his shot.

A redheaded man, who was entirely non-magical, was flirting heavily with a shy minotaur. Every time the ginger brushed his hand over the minotaur's arm, the beefy guy's eyes fluttered shut for a moment like he was savoring the touch before he carefully stepped away and put space between them again.

Then there was the small raven shifter in a shimmery top and tight purple pants, who shared a mate mark with a massive wolf shifter. The smaller man was dancing to the music on the jukebox, putting on a sexy show for his mate, who simply stood and watched him, like they were performing an elaborate mating ritual.

And those were only a few of the people in here. Every time the door opened, more came in.

So much for having a quiet space to talk to the hellhound when he arrived; the place was filling up fast and most of these people would have enhanced hearing. There would be no private conversations here, which wasn't ideal.

Van had to have known the risks when he suggested meeting here. Had he hoped to rattle the thieves with our presence? While it was true that if they became anxious, they might make mistakes, he should have told me his plan. I didn't like getting blindsided by situations. Investigations tended to be messy enough as it was, and I firmly believed everything else that could be controlled should be.

Based on what I knew of the hellhound, I doubted Van would have suggested meeting here if the wolf pack we'd come to investigate hung out here too. But any of these people might have allegiances that weren't immediately obvious. I wished I could push out my magic like a blanket over the crowd and pluck everyone's thoughts from their head, but it didn't work that way. To get a read on a person's desires I had to focus exclusively on them, but even that wasn't as reliable as people tended to think… nor did it always speak to a person's actions.

Few people ever thought: *My greatest dream is to kill someone today so I can harvest their organs*. It was more like: *My greatest wish is for my dad to get matched with a kidney donor before it's too late*. The two thoughts could potentially lead to the same murderous outcome, but the wishes were very different.

It was almost funny how my thoughts went immediately to murder.

Maybe Davina and the others were right to be worried about my state of mind. I swallowed down my ale to wash away the dark thoughts.

I would never be known as the life of the party or even overly friendly, but I also wasn't typically such a pessimist. I was a realist with a bit of cynicism thrown in for flavor. I always had been. All my years wandering this planet had just reinforced my outlook.

My gaze landed on Jake again. There wasn't anything dark about him. He was almost too light for the likes of me. So why did I keep looking at him? Was he just a puzzle to solve? I didn't like messy things, and Jake seemed very messy to me. He wasn't unkempt at all, but his magic was messy, like he'd been wrapped in a thick invisible blanket. Muffled. Buffered. Hidden.

It made me want to study his magic until I figured out how to unravel all the tangles. That was the only way I'd be able to tidy it up again.

"Weird place, isn't it?" Isaac asked quietly as he tapped the side of his pint glass. Despite his earlier complaints about me being too slow to get it in his hands, he hadn't touched his drink. Normally he'd suck back wheat ale like it was water, but even he seemed to appreciate we shouldn't relax in Willow Lake just yet.

He left his mouth open a little, and his torso rose and fell noticeably. He was inhaling deeply but trying not to give himself away. Some supes didn't like strangers scenting them. Once again, I wished Adrian was here, but his last update said their truck had finally been repaired but they were going to be late to our meeting. Adrian's sense of smell was superior to any of the rest of us. Isaac was doing his best, but a centaur's senses weren't as sensitive as a wolf's.

"Are we going to talk about the troll in the corner drinking Witch's Milk?" Nelson asked as he turned his pint glass in his hands. He also hadn't taken a sip of his dark ale.

"I hate trolls," Isaac muttered with a shiver.

"Are we reporting the bar owner?" Nelson leaned forward, keeping his voice low, but his eyes kept straying to the pool table where the hulking bear shifter was bending over to make a shot. The big shifter wasn't my type, but the guy did have a nice round ass. "The SC would want to know about that."

Nelson's concern was valid.

Under normal circumstances, I'd demand a record of the bar's permits. A place needed to be registered with the Supernatural Council to serve food or drink with magical properties, and I didn't see the necessary permits on the walls. The documentation was supposed to be posted just like any fire or alcohol permit, although they were spelled so only other supes could read the notifications. But they weren't here. I'd checked. I knew Nelson and Isaac would have done the same. After all, I trained them.

Based on what Jake had said, and the casual way he'd admitted to serving the drink, I didn't think the kid—I grimaced, I shouldn't think of him as a kid, not when I was keenly interested in seeing him naked—even knew what he was doing or that he was breaking at least four different supernatural regulations.

Why the hell hadn't the hellhound in the local police confiscated the Witch's Milk after the grandfather died? What if Jake had served it to a human? And, more importantly, did he have more magically enhanced drinks behind the bar?

At the moment, it appeared Jake was just as haphazard with the care and monitoring of enhanced drinks as he was with the magical items that'd been left to him. Those same magical items that had been stolen. The ones we'd been hired to find. The ones Jake didn't seem to care about, if what Van said was true.

Seeing so many messy things tangled around this one person was enough to make me crazy. This inn was just one red flag after another, but we wouldn't get anywhere by busting the local bar owner on our first day in town, nor was that the case we were here to investigate. Still, I couldn't let this slide, either. No matter how cute the bartender was.

I'd have to ask Van how the magic-infused drinks were being monitored. I couldn't imagine him turning a blind eye to the situation without there being a system in place to protect his people—even the humans. The hellhound's innate moral compass wouldn't let him.

My decision to ignore the infraction a little longer had nothing to do with Jake. Or his cute as fuck face.

Nope.

If Davina was here, she'd be whacking me on the back of the head and telling me to smarten up about now. And maybe I should. It didn't matter how many times I told myself to focus on what we'd come here to do, the cute bartender continued to distract the hell out of me.

I had no idea why I couldn't stop myself from thinking about him. It wasn't like he was going out of his way to fall in my lap like the seductive succubus had. Based on our conversation and the way he stammered at my suggestions, I had the sense Jake didn't normally kiss random strangers or make plans to take them home later.

And, if I thought about the situation for more than five seconds, I'd probably also decide I shouldn't get involved with him until he had his shit figured out. It wouldn't be fair to him.

Of course, a little voice inside my head had to point out whatever I might do with Jake would be little more than a fling, so would it matter if he didn't know I was a super-natural being or understand what that meant? If I was any other kind of supe, it probably wouldn't. But most supes didn't want to get too close to a demon who wasn't grounded in a location. Untethered demons tended to go insane and kill people. And that risk tended to kill—pun intended—most people's interest.

Our current investigation didn't help the situation either. My team and I suspected a demon was involved with the trafficking ring we'd stumbled upon a few weeks ago. Because what was worse than having one demon in the area? Two demons.

But I wasn't prepared to listen to any of those reasons to stay away from Jake. It didn't matter if it was the right thing to do. My instincts were driving me right now, and everything in me was fixated on that cute bartender.

"Let's leave it for now," I said, answering Nelson's question. "I have a feeling there is more going on here than what we can see."

"Why would we do that?" Isaac's eyes took on a darker brown lustre, showing his centaur.

"Is this because you're attracted to him and want to get your dick wet?" Nelson challenged, holding my gaze.

"Holy shit, Nel." Isaac whistled and brayed out a loud laugh. "I can't believe you said that."

I stared at Nelson steadily. I didn't bring my power forward. There was no need. Nelson knew better than to ask me shit questions like that. Even if they were true.

"Okay, boss." Nelson averted his eyes after several long seconds. "I was out of line."

"As I said, there is something more going on here," I said. "When I tried to read the bartender, I couldn't. He was muffled somehow. It isn't natural."

"Is he casting a spell to disguise himself?" Nelson asked.

"No. I don't sense that kind of active spell work around him. I need to think on it a bit more. It's strange." I shook my head and glanced back at Jake. The guy was busy pouring drinks and looking everywhere in the room except at our table.

"A curse then?" Isaac grimaced. "Nasty."

"Possibly. I'm not sure yet," I admitted.

Nelson watched me carefully as I spoke. Then his eyes went back to Jake.

"So it's more than just sex," he said, mostly to himself.

After that, the three of us didn't say much. We pretended to watch the afternoon baseball game on the TV mounted on the far wall, but it was just a ruse to let us listen in to conversations. The chatter was a low hum around us, but I expected none of the supes were letting their guard down. Not today. Not after I'd confronted that troll.

Supes could see my horns, but most wouldn't know what that meant since there weren't a lot of demons wandering around anymore. In the past, I'd been mistaken for a lot of things, including a ram shifter in a partial shift. Davina had laughed her ass off at that one. But unveiling my power? That had been a mistake, so early in our investigation. But when the troll had attacked Jake, my urge to protect him had nearly overwhelmed me.

If it hadn't been for the being disguised as a fat cat on the bar, who knows what I might have done? The cat had met my surge in power with his own. It'd been a warning, no doubt about it.

Very few beings had the strength to negate a demon's power, but I suspected the cat could have if I hadn't backed down. I couldn't identify what kind of supe the being was, but I doubted the cat body was his natural form. It wasn't often that a supe surprised me, but the cat had. It was just one more thing I'd need to watch, and we hadn't even sat down with the hellhound yet to have a proper debrief.

And then there was Jake himself. He'd looked ready throw himself between me and the angry troll. It was such a stupidly misguided reaction that it distracted me before my demonic side could fully engage.

This little town was more complicated than I'd expected.

That was fine. We had time. I leaned back in my chair. We would stay here for as long as it took. And if I had to keep returning to the Willow Lake Pub for research purposes—my gaze coasted over to Jake, who was still busy behind the polished oak bar—well, that wouldn't be so terrible.

The pub door was thrown open just as someone hit a ball out of the park on TV. The thick oak door banged against the wall, and everyone jumped in surprise. A werewolf stomped inside the bar and lifted his head to sniff the air. His eyes glinted with a golden light when he spotted us. His face contorted in a menacing scowl that stayed on his face as he stalked through the room to our table.

Was this wolf from the pack we were here to investigate? Wouldn't that be convenient?

The wolf slammed his hands on the table, jostling our drinks. The smell of motor oil and grease clung to the man. Dirt and grime covered his hands, like he'd stopped in the middle of rebuilding an engine just to come and scowl at me. He leaned over and put his face right into mine.

"Who the fuck are you and what are you doing in Willow Lake?"

"You the alpha here?" I asked calmly.

Werewolves didn't scare me. Very few supes did. The guy had the energy of an alpha, but it wasn't as strong as I would have expected. His pack mustn't be very big. Maybe this wasn't the guy who'd stolen those boxes.

From the corner of my eye, I saw the strange supernatural cat jump onto our table. The creature settled himself amid the drinks like he had every right to be there.

"Answer my questions." The werewolf's eyes flashed gold, showing again how close his beast was to the surface.

"I don't answer to you."

The wolf growled. "Get the fuck out of my town."

I lifted an eyebrow. "Did you miss the part where I said I don't answer to you?"

"I'm serious. We don't need assholes in Willow Lake."

"Someone called you." I leaned back in my chair and glanced around the room. Most of the supes were watching. The bear shifter lifted his chin and narrowed his eyes at me. Not many supes could hold my gaze, so I was impressed. And now I also had a good idea who'd called the alpha.

"You threatened my…" The alpha paused. Alphas were driven to protect their packs, but this one seemed to struggle saying the word.

I let my demonic power rise. The ability to read people's greatest wishes came in handy in times like this. Angels, our traditional counterpart, read people's greatest fears. On occasion, people's wishes and fears were entwined so deeply that every part of their identity was revealed to me even though I wasn't an angel. That was the case with this alpha.

The wolf shook his head but didn't seem to realize I was poking around in there. He obviously hadn't been around any of my kind before, or he'd have realized what was happening as soon as my eyes changed color.

"You threatened my...my—" the werewolf tried again, "—my *town*, and now I'm telling you to get the fuck out."

"No." I reached for my dark ale and took a long slow drink. I'd seen enough to know the wolf wasn't one of the ones we were investigating, but I'd not allow him to bully me into obeying him either. The very idea of that happening was laughable.

Although I didn't look at Isaac and Nelson, I felt them bracing for a fight.

"Sit down," I said to the wolf, throwing a bit of my own power behind the command. "Then you can tell me why you're okay with a troll attacking the bartender but are getting mad when someone steps in to defend him."

The wolf shot a look at Jake, then at Old Thom.

"I was told some stranger was throwing his power around. The place reeks of unfamiliar magic." He rubbed his nose as if to emphasize his point. "And now that I'm close to you, I'm getting the same stink off you. I don't have to be a genius to figure out it was you."

"The troll pissed me off." I wasn't going to apologize for that. "But you can see he's still over there. Nothing wrong with him. Nursing his Witch's Milk. Interestingly, I don't see an SC permit, do you?"

The wolf winced and dropped into one of the empty chairs. Another ruckus at the door interrupted the wolf's answer. Ah, yes. The hellhound was finally here. The good-looking Black man in a police uniform marched over to our table.

"Well," Van said with a grimace, "I didn't think asking

you here was going to cause such a shitshow. The phone lines at the precinct have been blowing up all afternoon. What in the name of Magic is going on?"

"You asked them here?" The wolf gaped at the hellhound.

"Hellhounds are smarter than they look," the cat said, then licked his paw and started cleaning his tricolored face. He was still sitting in the middle of the table.

"This is only half my team. The rest will be here in a day or two, then we'll decide on our next steps." I met the hellhound's gaze and held it. I had every intention of proceeding with my investigation, but I wasn't going to tell the hellhound that. Not right away. Not until I understood more about his allegiances. But, with the way hellhounds detected lies through spoken words, I had to be careful about what I said. "We owe you a debrief. We'll keep looking for the rest of your magical items, but our focus has shifted a bit."

I didn't go into details. We could do that later, when we had more privacy.

"What job?" the wolf asked.

"This is Hayden." Van pointed at the wolf with his thumb. "And the cat on the table is Paws, if you haven't been introduced yet."

I recognized the names from Adrian's updates.

"What job, Van?" Hayden asked again.

Van straightened his shoulders. "I asked the Supernatural Council for help. We need to find the rest of those things Robbie's pack stole before they end up in the wrong hands, and I don't have the resources." He scrubbed his hand through his short black hair. "We were short staffed before Dot's arrest, and it's worse now. Dillon is helping out, but he's still learning the ropes and isn't officially on the payroll yet."

"I thought that was done. You found the boxes."

"Most of them," Van agreed. "But I'm guessing they're here about… everything else."

Based on that vague sentence, I figured Adrian had already filled in the Chief of Police. I remembered sending Van a short update when we'd first found the goblin's storage facility. He'd arranged backup for us that day. But I hadn't given the guy a thought since, not until we decided to investigate the local wolf pack more closely.

Hayden's shoulders dropped. "So this is still about Robbie."

Van reached over and squeezed the wolf's shoulder. "Yeah. If he's involved with any of this, we've got to stop him. We should have stopped him years ago."

That was what I wanted to hear. It looked liked the hellhound would be an ally.

Hayden nodded and closed his eyes, as if needing a moment to gather his resolve. When he opened them again, his eyes glowed with the strength of his wolf. Power rolled out from the alpha. He was stronger than I had first thought. "So you're part of Adrian's team?"

I nodded.

"I've got his truck back at my shop," Hayden said. "And we've met for beers a few times."

"Then you know what we found," I said, leaving my words vague. If he knew, he knew. There was no need to talk about the details here. Besides, our investigation into the trafficking ring was ongoing and I didn't have enough answers. I had no desire to have our lack of success broadcast all over town.

"Yeah. I know. That's why you're here, isn't it?" Hayden grimaced. "What do you need? I haven't talked to my brother in years, but I will do whatever it takes to protect Willow Lake."

"Are we okay to talk in here?" I asked, pointedly looking around at the crowd, none of whom were even trying to hide that they were listening.

"Yeah. It's fine. Even if we moved to the station, everyone in town would know what we said in no time. It's one of the joys of living in a small town."

That sounded like a problem, but who was I to argue with the Chief of Police? I glanced over at the bartender, wanting to signal for another round—I had a feeling this discussion might require more alcohol—but when Jake's eyes caught on mine, for a long moment I forgot all about the drinks.

I didn't understand it, but I felt a connection to Jake almost as strongly as I'd felt a connection to the land in Willow Lake. A strange fluttery sensation unlike anything I'd ever felt before flowed through me. And, in that moment, I knew I'd do whatever it took to protect both Willow Lake and Jake.

Chapter Nine

JAKE

"Are you okay, honey?" Sally asked as I wiped down the bar.

A few moments earlier I was sure I'd have to break up a bar brawl. And I wasn't the only one who thought that, based on how my older patrons and a few peace-loving couples, like Mercer and Oak, had scurried away when things started heating up.

How could I possibly stop a bar fight? Now that Mercer had left, I was the smallest person in the place.

I worried the bar rag in my hand and stared at Gage's table, where now Hayden and Van were sitting too. They were getting along better, but the whole situation was unsettling.

"Should I break them apart? I'd rather be pre-emptive than not," I whispered to Sally.

I didn't want to alienate the only guy my dick had ever

taken a liking to, but I would if I had to. I'd gone this long without sex; I could wait a little longer.

She peered over her shoulder at the group, then waved her hand through the air dismissively. "Nah. They'll be fine."

I wasn't convinced she was right.

"Are you sure?" I asked, trying not to look at Gage. "Something doesn't feel right…"

Sally got a strange gleam in her eye as she leaned toward me and nodded her head encouragingly, eyeing me like I was the most fascinating thing in the room. "Oh really? Tell me more. What do you feel?"

I rolled my eyes. "They're stirring up trouble. That's all."

That was not all, but that was all I was willing to say aloud. A busy Saturday afternoon wasn't the time to dissect how a figment of my imagination had suddenly walked through the door and was making everyone angry.

When Hayden Walker had burst through the door and his eyes landed on Gage, it was like a scene from an old western the way everyone quieted and swung their gazes back and forth between the two. Then Hayden sniffed the air before charging right over to them. And, for the record, I was never going to get used to the way the people in Willow Lake were always sniffing things. It was weird, but so much of Willow Lake was.

Even Sally had swiveled in her seat to watch as the mechanic stalked through the bar toward Gage. And all I could think was *no, no, no*. I didn't want my imaginary Mr. Horny Dude to be an asshole. I refused to lust after a jerk.

Because I was still lusting.

There was a lot of lusting going on. More lusting than I'd ever lusted before.

I was thrilled my body had finally decided sex might be nice. It fit in well with my new goals. But it needed to settle down a bit until I had time to do something about it.

My previously absent but newly awakened libido hadn't even lessened when Hayden slammed his hands on the table and looked like he was going to toss the table across the room and dive for Gage. If anything, my dick perked up at how calmly Gage sat there. Confidence and self-control were unbelievably sexy; I hadn't known that until now.

And then I swore I heard growling like he had an angry animal in his pocket. Of course, it *wasn't* growling. It was just… um… rumbling words? Yeah.

Hayden had leaned in close, pushing his face right into Gage's space. And it was like the whole bar inhaled and held their breath. Gage merely cocked one of his eyebrows and took a drink of his dark ale. Meanwhile, I'd almost marched over there and pushed Hayden away, which was crazy.

Hayden was a great guy. He'd been incredibly helpful over the last year. Yes, he was gruff and grumpy, but I always found him to be honest and supportive too. Without his encouragement, I might have closed the pub.

So why was I feeling compelled to defend the stranger against him?

I didn't understand any of this.

I thought my midnight painting sessions were stressful, but this was so much worse.

At least Gage hadn't looked like he was about to punch Hayden, the way he had with Old Thom.

Usually, I liked when Hayden was around—he had some innate leadership quality that made all the other patrons behave better—but I'd never seen the guy get so angry so fast before. And he'd been pissed. I may not have heard the words, but there was no mistaking his body language.

I really wished I knew why Hayden had acted that way. Did he know Gage and his friends? Were they trouble? I hoped they weren't trouble. Because I *really* wanted to explore this attraction I felt to Gage. It was such a novelty, it seemed wrong to let it go. And, as strange as it was, even though we'd barely met, he was the only one I wanted to get naked with.

It also didn't hurt that he was an exceptional kisser.

But given all the problems Gage and his friends were stirring up, my attraction to him probably wasn't healthy. Should I kick them out? My common sense told me I should.

I sighed.

Right. Me and what army?

Because if they didn't want to leave, I'd never be able to shove them out the door. My regulars were usually mellow and relaxed, so I hadn't worried about hiring a bouncer or any other kind of security. The few times something had happened, Hayden or Van or one of the others had stepped in to diffuse the situation or usher the problem outside.

But I had a feeling none of us had ever confronted a group of people like Gage and his buddies.

At least Van was over there now too. I hoped he'd sort things out for me. What could I say? I was a wuss.

"You okay, Jake dear? You look a little pale." Sally's brow furrowed with worry.

"I'm fine," I assured her, pulling my gaze away from the group in the corner.

I glanced around the bar. Shit. There were several more people than just a moment ago. My gaze dropped to the counter, and I frantically searched for evidence of a new drawing or painting. Usually when I lost time, I'd wake up to find I had an upset stomach and a newly drawn picture.

I didn't see anything. Good. And I wasn't queasy. Also good.

"Hey, Jake, can I get a drink?" a woman shouted from the other end of the bar.

I nodded and got to work.

The next time I glanced over at Gage's table, Van and Hayden were still seated with Gage and his friends. Based on the nods and sober looks on their faces, they were having an intense conversation, but they didn't seem ready to fight anymore so that was a relief. Sally was right. It'd be okay. Then Van gestured toward the bar and every single head turned to look at me.

I waved my hand awkwardly, then pulled it down quickly.

What was I doing? I was such a weirdo. I couldn't even smile and nod like a normal person. Nope. I had to wave, like a toddler waving to someone in line at the grocery store checkout.

My gaze caught on Gage's for a long moment and my pulse kicked up again. And, once again, my cock perked up and took notice. Why was my body betraying me like this? I wanted to die. Thank Cezanne for the bar counter in front of me so no one could see my erection. Whoever was sitting next to Gage nudged him with their elbow, drawing Gage's attention back to the conversation. I let out a long breath.

It wasn't normal to want to go over there and crawl into some strange guy's lap.

At least it wasn't normal for me.

I'd once viewed sex as a necessary milestone to get past, not something I felt passionately excited about. When I'd first started taking art classes after high school, I dedicated myself to losing my v-card and I still failed to get rid of it. The few times I attempted to have sex had been disastrous.

The first time, I thought if I got naked with another guy my body would respond—wow, had I been wrong. My dick was completely uninterested. The second time, to my horror, the guy I was with took my limp dick as a personal challenge. Spoiler alert: the guy was unsuccessful. The whole experience was awful and humiliating, causing me to swear off sex. I dropped out of the class we were both enrolled in, just so I never had to see him again.

But in the last year, my sex drive had suddenly woken up like a rabid beast. Was it enough? I hoped so.

I bet Gage never had problems like that.

Hell, maybe I wouldn't have problems like that either if I was with someone like Gage.

And what if the guy, who may or may not have horns, wasn't into men, or was already in a relationship, or wasn't attracted to me in particular? I knew I wasn't anything special.

Sure, he'd flirted, but had he been serious? Did he mean what he said about getting together later? My old roommate would have been disgusted by all my worries, but he was an expert at getting guys. I definitely wasn't.

And these were legitimate concerns.

How could a guy like Gage, all godlike and perfect, want to have sex with someone like me? What if as soon as we were naked, my dick went on strike like it had in the past? Was I ready to open myself up to that kind of mortification again?

But what if it didn't?

My heart pounded in my throat.

I jotted my phone number on a scrap piece of paper. It'd just take ten steps or so to get out from behind the bar and go to his table. I clenched the paper in my hand. Would his friends tease him about having the bartender try to pick him up?

Did they know we'd already kissed?

He hadn't asked for my number earlier. Did that mean he didn't want it? I had to find out, right? I was still trying to work up the courage to approach Gage when the doors slammed open *again*.

The din in the pub dropped away.

Good grief. What now?

Jeremy, a new guy to town, dashed inside. Adrian, his attentive boyfriend, was on his heels.

"Damn it, Adrian," Jeremy exclaimed. "We're late. I told you Nelson and Isaac wouldn't lie to me. They texted that things were starting and it's true."

He grabbed a chair at a nearby table and dragged it over to Gage's. As soon as he plopped down, he pulled out his ever-present notebook from his backpack—I'd never seen the guy without a pad of paper and a pen—and eyed the others.

"Okay. I'm here now. What did I miss?" His words were loud, and I heard them all the way across the room.

"About time you two showed up." The blond guy grinned at Jeremy and punched him lightly in the arm. Adrian, who'd now pulled over his own chair, swatted the blond guy's hand away.

Huh. They knew one another.

I liked Jeremy. He always had a welcoming smile and talked a lot. If Jeremy liked these guys, maybe they weren't so bad after all.

"Shit," Jeremy muttered. "We need drinks. I'll get them." He pushed his notebook and pen toward his boyfriend. "Take notes while I'm gone."

I glanced at the orders I had lined up. I was filling them as quickly as I could, but most of my regulars liked things that took time, like mixed drinks or draft beer. Draft was the worst because if I tried to go too fast, the drinks would be all foam. Very few people ordered easy things like bottled beer or coolers.

"Hey, Jake," Jeremy said as he bounced up to the bar.

"It'll just take a few minutes—" or a lot of minutes, "—for me to get to your drinks, but what can I get you?"

Jeremy scanned the bar. "Where is your usual server?"

"She couldn't make it today."

"So you're working alone?" He cast his gaze over the crowd. His eyes lingered on the table where his boyfriend was now chatting with the others. Then he turned his attention back to me. "I've worked in bars before. Can I help?"

"Oh, I couldn't ask you to do that. You're here to meet your… friends…"

Jeremy waved his hand through the air, dismissing my words. "Adrian is getting pretty good at taking notes. He'll fill me in on what's happening with Mr. Dimples and the others." Then he ducked around the end of the bar, like everything had been decided and he was now my employee for the night. "I'm pretty sure I know all the latest news anyway. Just had a touch of FOMO when we were running late, but it's fine now that I'm here."

"Mr. Dimples?" He wasn't talking about Gage, was he?

Gage, as if he'd heard what Jake and I were saying, glanced over and frowned at Jeremy, who snorted and wiggled his fingers at him in a little wave. *His* wave didn't look like he was a toddler, but it did feel mischievous.

"That's just what I call him. I couldn't believe it when I met him and saw his cute little dimple. He's such a badass dem—"

Sally squawked, cutting off whatever Jeremy was about to say.

Jeremy's mouth snapped shut. "Uh… Oops. I meant to call him a… a… um, demonstrably badass kind of guy. My mouth just gets tangled sometimes. You know how it goes."

Jeremy was lying to me, very poorly too. He'd almost said something else, but I couldn't figure out what.

"Do you know those guys well?" I asked quietly.

Jeremy grinned as his gaze bounced back to Gage's

table, and my eyes followed. "Oh, yeah. They're great. Adrian considers them family."

"Huh. Okay. Things got a little tense in here when they arrived, so..."

Jeremy waved his hand through the air, dismissing my concerns. "They're the good guys. Trust me. They saved my life."

That seemed a bit dramatic. After all, how often did a person get in a situation where they needed their life saved? He had to be exaggerating. But his endorsement swept away my lingering concerns.

"Okay. What do you need me to do?" Jeremy rubbed his hands together.

I tucked the piece of paper with my number on it into my back pocket and then Jeremy and I got to work pouring drinks, bussing tables, and making food. Now that I had help behind the counter, it was like everyone rushed over at once.

We were swamped with orders, but Jeremy still found time to talk. I didn't think he knew how to stop talking. I heard all about the paranormal romance he was writing. And then he started on some weird questions that I assumed were related to his book.

He put a pint glass under the lager spout and tilted it perfectly as he opened the tap. As he let the glass fill, his gaze wandered over to me.

"So... hypothetically speaking... do you think demons are sexy?"

Sally, who was still perched on her regular bar stool, waggled her finger at him. "Jeremy, you know better than to ask things like that."

Jeremy cast big puppy dog eyes at her, the picture of innocence. "I'm doing research. You know, for my book. My *paranormal* romance…" He spoke deliberately and nodded his head in an exaggerated way, as if trying to get her to agree. She narrowed her eyes.

What was up with tonight? Was there a full moon? Tired of the weird tensions in the bar and not wanting Jeremy and Sally to get into it next, I decided to just humor him.

I shrugged. "I don't know much about demons."

"Well, you know about the stereotypical demon, right? All dark and brooding with a propensity to scowl." He was looking at Gage's table as he spoke, raising his voice a little as he said that last bit.

Was that some kind of inside joke between friends? The guys at the table must have heard him because they all turned to look our way. Gage's eyes found mine. It was almost like he wanted to hear my answer, which was silly because it was such a fantastical question, right up there with asking if the moon was made of cheese.

"My mom kept all that stuff away from me when I was growing up. I didn't learn about things like that until I enrolled in art classes, and by that time I had a lot of other things to think about. I only really know what we talked about in my art history class."

Jeremy's mouth dropped open. He set the full pint on the bar counter and turned to me. I was pouring a round of shooters for the guys at the pool table. "Any of that being…?"

"I don't know. Paranormal stuff. Mythology. Religion. My mother considered it all unacceptable. The only time I brought a book about magic home from the library, my mom freaked. It was easier just to stick to stuff that didn't bother her."

"What?" His question came out more like a screech. His eyes bulged in disbelief.

"You... You mean you've never seen *Willow* or *Ladyhawke* or *Hocus Pocus*? You never read *Inkheart* or *The Chronicles of Prydain* or... or...?" His mouth kept opening and closing like he could go on and on and on.

I shook my head. "Nope. I don't think I missed out on anything. There are a lot of books and movies that have nothing to do with magic. I watched a few things when I lived away from home for a bit, and again when I moved to Willow Lake, but..." I shrugged. "I don't think it's really my thing."

"He doesn't think he missed out on anything. He doesn't think it's his thing," Jeremy muttered like he couldn't believe I'd said such things. He waited until I set the bottle of tequila on the counter, then he lunged for me, pulling me into an embrace. "I'll help you. I promise."

As he hugged me tight, a strange tingling sensation pulsed along my skin wherever Jeremy's skin met mine. I didn't know what it was, but it felt... good. The sensation seemed to sink into me. A lightness filled me as an intense feeling of happiness flowed through me.

Was I so touch starved that a hug from an acquaintance would have such an impact on me?

I blinked away tears. That's when I noticed an unusual white light pulsing around us. It almost appeared to be coming from Jeremy. Shit. I couldn't have another hallucination now. I had a bar full of people to take care of. I snapped my eyes closed and pretended everything was normal. I patted his back awkwardly until he released me, then I pointedly ignored the unnatural glow.

Jeremy sucked in a deep breath, then bounced around a bit like he was prepping for a boxing match. "We'll get you through this."

"I'm fine." I laughed and nudged him back to the beer taps. "Just pull some more pints."

Then he glanced down at his hands, which still had that freaky white glow to them.

My hallucination was incredibly vivid.

Except the last time you thought you were hallucinating, you weren't... the stupid voice inside my head pointed out.

People don't glow, so fuck off. Great. Now I was arguing with the voice in my head.

I kept my face as neutral as I could.

"Holy fuck!" Jeremy squealed and flapped his freaky hands. "Do you see this?"

"See what?"

"I'll be right back," Jeremy shouted at me as he shot out around the counter and headed for Gage's table. "Adrian! Look!"

Jeremy's boyfriend jumped up from his seat and closed the distance between them. Judging by the look on the guy's face, I'd swear he was ready to murder someone. But then Jeremy shook his still glowing hands at him, and the man's face changed. He looked... proud? Adrian picked up Jeremy and swung him around in a circle. They were laughing and carrying on like Jeremy had just achieved something spectacular.

I had no idea what was going on.

"You okay, Jake dear?" Sally asked.

I tore my gaze from Adrian and Jeremy to find Sally staring at me. She wasn't the only one. At least half the pub was eyeballing me. "Of course. Why wouldn't I be?"

Lately, her questions had become increasingly probing, like she knew something was going on with me. I ignored the speculative gleam in her eyes and poured more drinks. Jeremy came back a few minutes later and got to work, but it didn't take long for his mind to wander again. I wondered what a typical conversation was like between Adrian and him. It had to be wild if he was like this all the time.

"So… my book is about paranormal stuff. But let's say one of my heroes was magical but didn't know it. At what point in a novel should the clueless hero be shown he's actually magical?"

"I don't know. I suppose it'd depend on what else is going on in the story. It could be anywhere really… I don't know that there is just one way."

"Mm hmm," Jeremy hummed. He thought things over for a bit, then he wiggled, and I knew he had just come up with another oddball question for me. "Do you think a small town with lots of magical beings would feel different?"

"Every town has its own energy, doesn't it? Look at Willow Lake. It isn't like any place else I've been. It must be all that fresh air sweeping down from the mountains. It's invigorating."

"Ha!" Jeremy let out a choked laugh. "Yeah… That must be it."

Sally leaned forward and waggled her finger in Jeremy's face again. "That's enough."

He pouted but didn't argue with her. I still didn't understand why Sally cared what we talked about. It was just a bit of fun. When he didn't ask any other questions, I was a little disappointed. The conversation was a lot different from what I talked about with Alice when she worked, but it was entertaining. And he was great with the customers and the work in general. I hoped he'd be interested in picking up some shifts on a regular basis. It'd be a relief to have some backup staff.

And I liked Jeremy, even if he was a bit strange.

Chapter Ten

GAGE

It still seemed strange to me that we weren't relocating to a place where we could talk more freely about the case and what had ultimately brought us to Willow Lake again, but it looked like that wasn't what was happening. Van had settled into his chair across from me and didn't appear to be interested in moving any time soon.

"I need more information about who these people are," Hayden, the alpha wolf shifter, said to Van as he gestured to us.

"We need information too," Isaac said. The centaur was leaning forward with his forearms on the table, a picture of eager interest.

Nelson was more circumspect. He was leaning back with his arms over his chest and his eyes partially closed, but I knew he was alert and paying close attention. His face was blank.

"Alright, fine." Van nodded. He pointed at me.

"That's Gage Stewart. Demon. He's the lead on a team sanctioned by the Supernatural Council to undertake investigations."

The wolf shifter studied me, but eventually he nodded. "Gage Stewart. Sure. I've heard your name."

I dipped my head in acknowledgement. I doubted the wolf was much older than his late thirties or early forties, so a hell of a lot younger than me, but I wasn't surprised my reputation had reached him. I hadn't always gone by that name, but I'd been using it for a couple of centuries now.

"You already know Adrian," Van said, nodding to the wolf. "And I don't know the rest of his team. Only met them once." Then he faced me and pointed at Hayden. "I know I already told you his name, but this is the Willow Lake alpha who doesn't think he's an alpha."

"Fuck off, Van," Hayden muttered in a weary tone that suggested this was a long-standing argument between the two.

Isaac and Nelson introduced themselves quickly, offering nothing more than their first names.

"The wolves we're having problems with used to be part of the pack here, but they severed ties with Willow Lake and formed their own pack about twelve years back," Van started. I knew most of this because Adrian had at least managed to tell me that much in his very short and chaotic debriefs. "It's Hayden's brother Robbie who pretends to be the alpha to those other wolves."

Okay. That was good to know.

"Other than the robbery, have they done anything else? Are they dangerous?"

Van winced and shot a look at Hayden. "Why don't you go grab us another round?"

Hayden scowled and crossed his arms over his chest. "Just say it."

Van's jaw tightened, but then he gave a short nod. "It was never proven, but we believe Robbie was involved in his parents' deaths. He wanted to be alpha. More recently, he sent his men after Dillon, who I think you've met. They tried to kill him and Ash, Jeremy's friend. We think it was because he was angry Dillon left his pack. We haven't been able to prove any of it, though. He engenders enough loyalty—or perhaps it's just fear—that people willingly take the fall for whatever happens."

We all sat in silence for a long moment.

"So he is dangerous when he wants something or when things don't go his way," I summarized.

"Sounds like a toddler when you put it like that," Isaac said.

"A very deadly toddler," I agreed. "And he wants something from this place, so he should be considered a danger to this place and its people." My gaze fell on the cute bartender again, who had already been targeted by the asshole wolf pack at least once when they robbed him. Would they come back for more?

"I wish I believed my brother wouldn't endanger anyone," Hayden said, glancing toward Van as he spoke. "But we know that isn't the case."

The alpha wolf rubbed his eyes. Some of his angry mask cracked, and I saw the hurt beneath. He'd discovered his brother was a murderous asshole over a dozen years ago, but the pain was still there. I suspected it always would be. My magic itched under my skin, as if begging to slip out and fix everything that was wrong, but I couldn't. Even though I knew what it felt like to be betrayed by someone you should have been able to trust.

"And the owner of the inn?" Nelson asked. "Is that him behind the bar?"

Everyone but Adrian looked at Jake, who was laughing at something Jeremy had said. Adrian was busy scribbling in the notebook his mate had shoved at him, dutifully trying to keep up with everything that was said.

Fuck, Jake was gorgeous when he smiled. Yes, he was attractive even when he wasn't smiling, but there was something special about seeing joy light up his face. It did something to me. I could sit back and watch him laugh all night long and be thoroughly charmed.

"Yes. That's Jake," Van said quietly.

"The guy who doesn't know he's a supe?" Nelson prodded. "Is he still refusing to help with the investigation? Because that sounds shady as hell. Are you sure he isn't working with the wolves?"

The cat, Paws, turned to Nelson and hissed at him. Then he sat facing Nelson with a glower on his little feline face. Davina would think the creature was cute. She was always showing me pictures of random cats on her phone. Her favorites were the ones that looked pissed off at the world, like Paws did right now. But I remembered the power the creature had summoned. We did not want to make an enemy of this cat.

"Yeah, it's complicated," Van agreed, as he scratched the back of his neck.

"I'm confident he isn't working with Robbie," Hayden

said. "I don't pick up any signs of deceit from him. His scent is confusing, but I've never sensed any lies."

Adrian looked up. His hand was still poised over the notebook. "I agree with Hayden. I've been watching Jake since coming to Willow Lake. I don't think he's involved."

"Okay. Here's the quick version of where I think we sit at the moment," Van said, leaning forward almost as much as Isaac. "The werewolf pack that robbed the inn has been keeping quiet, but we all suspect they are biding their time. And, after going through the boxes you already recovered, we think there are still some boxes missing. Two. Possibly three. I think that asshole alpha is looking for another fence to sell the stuff he stole."

"What's missing?" I asked. It was possible those missing items included something that would help them make Babette's cages almost unbreakable. When we'd found people locked up in her warehouse, I couldn't free them by myself. A powerful magic had been used to secure those cages. Finding the boxes would actually be a relief, because if we found an object that changed those locks, I could destroy it. It was a much more comforting thought than believing the people we were hunting could channel enough magic on their own to contain even me.

The hellhound frowned. "We don't know. We think it is all magical artifacts, but we don't have a list of what's missing."

"And Jake is still refusing to help you?" I asked Nelson's question again, as everyone's gaze drifted back to the cutie at the bar. When I'd read his desires earlier, I hadn't picked up anything problematic. Could he have fooled me? Uncooperative robbery victims raised a lot of red flags.

"It's a little more complicated than that." Van scrubbed his hand through his short, cropped hair.

"He still doesn't know about supes, does he?" I asked with a frown. That complicated things all right, but it matched what I'd concluded on my own. "I thought as much, based on how I've seen him interact with people today."

"We knew he was a supe when he moved here. His grandfather was trying to ease him into the magical world gently, but the old man died before he could. Now it is up to us, but we haven't had much luck there either. For some reason, he isn't seeing past Mother Magic's curtain," he said, using the anthropomorphic term many supes used to describe the Eternal Magic that permeated the world. "Then just before the robbery, we discovered he's an oracle."

Isaac whistled as if impressed, but Nelson tensed. I understood Nelson's reaction better than Isaac's. Oracles were dangerous, both to themselves and others. Secrets weren't sacred if an oracle was close.

And worse? Didn't these people understand how vulnerable Jake was right now? Oracles needed to be tethered as much as demons, whether to a place or a person or both. It was how the Delphic cult originated in ancient times. If an oracle's connection to this world was weak, they'd ultimately lose themself in visions of the future, forgetting to eat and sleep and all the other things a human needed to survive. If the situation wasn't corrected, the oracle would die.

Unbidden, my magic surged and reached for Jake, ready to encase him in protections and wards. I barely managed to yank it back, although my magic and I were in agreement. Jake needed to be protected.

Why hadn't Van mentioned the inn owner was an oracle the last time we met? What other dangerous secrets was the hellhound keeping?

Chapter Eleven

JAKE

Throughout the evening, despite how busy we were, I kept sneaking glances at Gage.

I was hyper-aware of the piece of paper with my phone number in my back pocket. Actually, I was hyper-aware of everything related to Gage.

My earlier reaction to him had been driven by my newly discovered lust, but now that I'd had a chance to think things over with a slightly cooler head, I decided I was still okay with the whole let's-have-sex plan. He was a safe option, even if he had that whole dark and mysterious thing going on. He was safe, mostly because my body had reacted to him, but partly because he wasn't from here.

If we did try to have sex and things didn't go to plan—because I couldn't count on my body not betraying me again—we never had to cross paths again. He would be moving on, going back to wherever he'd come from, and I'd be here. My chest tightened at the thought of not seeing him again, but it was for the best. After all, if I couldn't get my hallucinations under control, I might not be in Willow Lake much longer either.

I swallowed and let my gaze linger on him. His broad shoulders filled out the breadth of his black dress shirt beautifully. His horns glinted under the lights every time he nodded or tilted his head as he talked with the others. Even his jaw was sexy. I wanted to trace that sharp edge with my fingertips… or maybe my lips.

I squished up my nose. What was wrong with me? First, I'd wanted to lick his dimple and now his jawline. Why did I keep wanting to stick my mouth on him? I'd never had an oral fixation before. Could you develop one as an adult?

That was just one more thing for me to look up on the internet tomorrow.

Right after I read up on demi-sexuals again. Maybe I was Gage-sexual. Was that a thing? Because my libido was fixated on him.

I brushed my fingers over my lips and swore I could still feel the way his lips had moved over mine and how his hips had felt, wedged between my thighs. I wanted to feel that again…

"You okay?" Jeremy asked, startling me. "You look a little flushed."

I jerked my fingers from my lips. "Yep. Just fine."

Jeremy looked over at Gage, seemingly aware of who I'd been staring at. "I suppose he is handsome, if you like dark, powerful, and slightly unhinged."

I focused on yanking the freshly cleaned pint glasses from the dishwasher and stacking them on the shelf.

"Do you want to meet him?"

"Oh, uh… I did already."

"You know…" Jeremy said with exaggerated slowness, as he sidled over to me and bent his head close to mine. "I think he is a little lonely. Would you be interested in going on a date with him? It'd be fun." He watched my face carefully. Whatever he saw had him nodding and smiling. "It's decided. The four of us will go out somewhere together."

"I don't really go on blind dates…" *Or any dates at all.* Although I would love to spend time with Gage, some selfish part of me wanted it to be just the two of us. Alone.

"I didn't date a lot either, until Adrian. Sometimes the heart wants what the heart wants and nothing else will do. I'm sure we can come up with something fun to do to take the pressure off it being a *date* date…" He tapped his finger to his chin. "What do you think about line dancing or karaoke?"

I ducked my head down to hide my horror. "I'll think about it."

If I had to go on a double date—and Jeremy struck me as someone who'd badger me until he got his way—I would prefer not having to do anything embarrassing.

What I'd really prefer was to slip Gage my number later when Jeremy wasn't looking. If he was interested, we could do something with just the two of us. And, if I was super lucky, it'd involve very few clothes and a flat surface.

Or maybe I'd just dream about giving it to him while avoiding their table and staying safely on my side of the bar like I had all night long.

That seemed more likely.

Honestly, I was lucky Jeremy had volunteered to help me tonight, because he'd taken over delivering drinks to their table. If it'd been left to me alone, they wouldn't have had any service because I'd be too self-conscious to do it.

And how was I going to turn this business around if I shied away from customers?

Then, suddenly, everyone at Gage's table stood up.

I hadn't found the courage to approach Gage yet, and now he was leaving. Every eye in the place was on them. There was no way I'd make my move now when everyone was watching. I'd finally found someone I was attracted to, and I still couldn't get things to go my way. How typical of my life.

Van approached the bar and gave me enough money to pay for everyone's bill and more. "Can I show these folks around the place? They're private consultants. Thought we'd try to track down more of those things that were stolen."

I frowned as I rifled through the cash register for Van's change. "That really isn't necessary. I don't even know what's missing." I glanced down and my cheeks heated. "And I can't afford to hire people like that. That stuff is long gone. I don't need it, so I'm happy to just forget all about it. Besides, I don't want anyone else getting hurt looking for things I don't care about. Ash is looking better now, but it could have been so much worse." I shivered at the memory of him in the hospital after he'd been shot during an attempted robbery here. He'd been so pale as he slept. I never wanted anything like that to happen again. Not under my roof.

The dark-haired guy who'd come in with Gage scowled at me. Had I said something to piss him off?

"You don't need to pay for anything, okay?" Van said as he rapped on the bar with his knuckles. Then he waved away the change I held out to him. "Keep it. So, is it okay if we look around?"

"I don't want anyone to get hurt." I whispered. "Can't we just... I don't know... Forget about it?"

Hayden stepped up beside Van. His eyes had an unusual softness to them as he reached over the bar and cupped the back of my neck in his warm palm. This wasn't the first time he'd touched me like that, but I was always surprised at how nice it was. How safe it made me feel.

I felt the weight of everyone's gaze.

"We'll be safe," Hayden said as he held my gaze. "But we need to find all the people involved with what happened."

I swallowed hard and glanced between him and Van. They both met my gaze steadily.

"Can we look around?" Van pressed.

My shoulders dropped a little in defeat and Hayden squeezed my neck a little like he approved of my decision even though I hadn't spoken yet. I sighed. "Yeah. Okay, I guess. Just... I don't want any trouble, okay?" Renoir knew I had enough of that already. I didn't need to invite any more problems into my life.

"Agreed," Van said with a curt nod. "Are the keys for your grandfather's suite still in the same place?"

"Yeah..." I said as I curled my fingers around the money I hadn't shoved in the tip jar yet. "Do you remember the combination to the lock?"

"I do. Thanks, Jake."

Should I warn Gage and his friends about the suite? Van and Hayden had already seen it, which was bad enough, but now even more people would be traipsing through there. The rooms were bursting with weird shit that was only suitable as props in a creepy occult movie. I should have cleaned them out ages ago but a little voice in my head always stopped me.

When some stuff had been recovered from the robbery, I hadn't even opened the boxes the police had returned. I just dropped everything inside my grandfather's suite and got out as fast as I could. Now Gage and the others would see all that mess and all the bizarre occult-ish things my grandfather had collected.

I wanted to explain and make excuses, but what would I say? If any of them saw inside my own room bursting with all my black-and-white paintings, it'd look just as crazy.

"Alright then," Van said. "I'll put the keys back when we're done."

"We'll take care of everything," Hayden said as he released my neck. Then he glanced at Sally, who was still perched on her regular bar stool. "I'll see you Monday, Sal, for your new tires. They came in this afternoon."

"While Buddy works on my car, I might need you to look at my spark plugs too. If you know what I mean," Sally winked at him and let out a little giggle.

"We'll have to see about that," he said lightly, but I didn't think he took Sally's flirting any more seriously than I did.

Adrian and Jeremy were whispering to one another across the counter a few feet away.

I called Jeremy's name to get his attention. "Things are quieter now. I can handle it on my own."

"Are you sure?" Jeremy looked conflicted as he watched Van and Hayden lead the others to the door.

"Of course. Thank you for your help." I grabbed a handful of bills from the till and everything from the tip jar too. "Here, take this as payment for tonight. And... I would love to hire you to cover some shifts. If you're interested..." I pushed the words out. I tended to be socially awkward in unfamiliar situations. This was one of those moments.

Jeremy smiled. "Aw, thanks, Jake. I promise I'll think about it. I'm not sure how long I'll be in town, but it might be nice to pick up some shifts while I'm here."

"Just let me know."

"Hey, give me your phone and I'll add my deets."

Jeremy reached out and wiggled his fingers for me to pass over my phone. I wished it was Gage doing that instead. I unlocked the screen and passed it to him. He typed into my phone with surprising speed.

"There. I've just sent myself a text from your phone, so we're good. I added Ash's info too, since you didn't seem to have it." Jeremy grinned as he returned my phone. "I'll be in touch soon about setting up some movie nights to fill in some of the gaps in your education. Oh, and we should start a book club too. Not right away though. I need to come up with a list of books and movies and TV shows first. I think we'll need to work up to some of my fave mpreg stories, but that's okay. I'll figure it out. When we finally get to magical jizz, you'll be ready for it." He rubbed his hands together. "This is going to be amazing. You'll see."

"Uh… okay?" I had no idea what half of that meant. Had I agreed to all that? I didn't think so, but Jeremy didn't seem to care.

Then Jeremy and Adrian followed the others to the door. My grandfather's strange cat wove between their legs.

Gage approached and stopped where Hayden had stood just a moment earlier. The steady and heated way he eyed me had my blood warming again. He didn't glance at Sally who was fanning herself beside him, nor did he acknowledge his friends who were waiting for him. His focus was entirely on me.

Impulsively, I grabbed the piece of paper with my phone number from my pocket. I shoved the wrinkled paper at him. He lifted one eyebrow but took it from my trembling hand. He cast his gaze over it, then smiled.

"I wasn't sure if you wanted it, but…"

"I do," he said quietly. Maybe it was wishful thinking on my part, but I swore his tone was intimate and full of promise. A shiver danced down my neck at his words. They were just normal everyday kinds of things people said to one another, but my body was reacting like I'd been propositioned. "I'll see you soon, Jake."

"You're coming back, right?" My question sounded breathless. Heat blazed across my cheeks.

"Soon," Gage agreed. His gaze fell to my lips for a moment, making my breath hitch. Then he met my eyes again. "Very soon."

Then he turned and left with the others without looking back.

As soon as they were out of sight, everyone in the pub seemed to exhale all at once. My heart was racing. I wanted to chase him and beg him to stay.

I didn't know him, so why did I feel like I was already missing him? I shook my head to shake loose the unusual feelings. One of my goals was to turn the pub's finances around. I wouldn't do that by daydreaming about some random stranger.

Even if the stranger didn't feel strange... or random.

I straightened my shoulders and tried to get my thoughts back where they were supposed to be. People were waving at me for more rounds, and I got to work. Laughter and conversation bubbled up around the room and soon it was like any other Saturday. Was that because the Chief of Police was gone? Or was it something else?

Willow Lakers were weird, so it could be anything.

Chapter Twelve

JAKE

Long after Gage and the others had left, I continued to watch the door, waiting for him to return.

He didn't.

And the longer he was gone, the more I was sure I'd misremembered the entire day. Having the guy from my painting come into my bar was not only improbable, it was impossible. Gage simply had similar features.

Yeah. That's what happened.

I was attracted to a real person, not an imaginary one. What a relief. Except I was still itching to get upstairs and pull out the paintings I had hidden under my bed to confirm my mistake. Just because.

So, when closing time came around, I didn't waste any time announcing last call. Only a few people lingered over their drinks, and I didn't think they'd stay long. Perfect. The end couldn't come fast enough.

I shuffled around the room, clearing away empties and

wiping down tables. My feet ached from working at the bar all day and night. I hoped Alice's date went well, but if she ditched me next week too, I'd have to hire a third person for the pub.

Hopefully Jeremy would take me up on my job offer. On weekdays I only opened the doors at four, but on Saturdays we were open from eleven in the morning. It made for a long-assed day. Between looking after all the drinks and the food orders, I was exhausted, even though Jeremy had helped for a few hours.

After the last of my other patrons left, Sally paid her tab but made no move to leave. She rested her elbows on the bar and cast an assessing eye over me. "Well, honey? You know you can talk to me, right?"

I suppressed a sigh and pasted a smile on my face. It was the same fake smile I'd worn a lot lately. "Everything is good."

"Uh huh." Sally didn't sound convinced. "Wanna try that again?"

I wiped the same part of the counter I'd just done.

"Are you sleeping at all?"

I stilled. What had she noticed? "Of course."

"Oh, honey. You suck at lying." She reached over and patted my hand. "I think we should play poker some time."

I snorted and moved away to grab the highball glasses from the dishwasher.

"Is it because it's coming up to the anniversary of... you know what?"

My gaze snapped over to the calendar hanging on the wall. She was right. It'd almost been a year since my mother had died. Almost a year since I discovered I had a grandfather. Almost a year since I moved to Willow Lake to get to know my only living relative, only to lose him too, just a month later.

Sally squeezed my hand. "I guess it wasn't that. I'm sorry, sugar. I didn't mean to bring up bad memories."

I shook my head. "It's fine. I'm fine. Nothing to worry about."

A frown pulled at Sally's face. She didn't have a lot of wrinkles, but I always had the sense she was older than she appeared. Right now, as she eyed me, her concern made her seem even older. "All right. I'm not going to push. But I'm here if you want to talk."

"I know. Thank you."

She tugged on her bright pink denim jacket and then gathered up her matching bedazzled purse. "And it doesn't matter what it is. Believe me, you can't shock me."

Somehow, I doubted that.

And then she was gone, and I was blissfully alone. Finally.

I watched from the shadowy threshold as she drove away. I pushed the button to activate the gates at the end of the driveway as soon as her car was clear. My grandfather had always insisted the gates be shut at night, but tonight was the first time in five months I'd bothered with it.

As soon as the gates were closed, I slumped against the wall. I should finish cleaning up. Mop. Wipe the rest of the tables. Scrub the kitchen. Clean the bathrooms. Stack the boxes of empties. That's what I did every night.

But maybe not tonight.

With it being Sunday tomorrow, the bar would be closed. And even though I had a few things going on, there would be time to clean up in the morning. My drop-in painting meet-up group didn't start until the afternoon. And on the off chance I slept late—*please, let me sleep late*—I should still have a bit of time before people started arriving for my weekly potluck.

I knew I shouldn't hold a potluck at the inn, what with health codes and all that, but no one seemed to care here, and it was only the locals who came. It was one of the perks of small-town living, I supposed.

Yep. This was my life: potlucks and painting with women old enough to be my mother.

I knew local octogenarians with more interesting social lives than me.

Whatever.

At least I had time for my art in Willow Lake. And, thanks to my grandfather's bequest, I didn't have any debt. I didn't have any excess either, but maybe living like a lethargic eighty-year-old wasn't a bad thing when I didn't have any money.

I checked the lock on the bar door one more time. As I did, I stole a peek at the empty parking lot. I was truly alone. Nothing moved in the shadows and no horse-people trotted by, which was even better.

The short, narrow corridor connecting the bar to the hotel was dark. The inn wasn't exactly a highly sought after destination resort, so we never had many guests. But tonight, I was the only person here, so I followed the familiar route to the lobby without bothering to turn on a light. I wanted the dark, so I could confront my secrets with only the shadows for company.

No one had stayed at the inn for weeks, which meant

the inn had been locked up tight every night for quite a while. We hadn't even had any inquiries. I bet the last person had left a scathing review somewhere on the internet. To say they'd been unimpressed with the accommodations would be an understatement. They complained about everything from the towels not being fluffy enough to hearing an animal howling outside in the middle of the night.

I paused... Huh... I'd been alone in the inn last night too. So, if my kiss with Gage was real, how did he get inside this morning before I unlocked the doors? Had I forgotten to secure everything last night?

All I wanted was to get upstairs, but it looked like I'd need to detour and check all the locks. I sighed as I made the familiar circuit on the main floor, stopping at each door and window. I navigated through the space in the dark with ease. I knew where all the worn-out furniture sat. I could picture everything in my head, right down to the most threadbare spot on the sofa and the water stains on the coffee table.

The public rooms, which opened onto the foyer, were kept clean and tidy, but they were showing their age. The other offices and rooms with doors, though? I never went into them. I'd gotten so used to ignoring them, I tended to forget they were even there.

My room and my grandfather's suite were on the second floor with the rentable rooms. I suspected my grandfather's suite had once been two separate rooms, given the unfinished state of the threshold connecting the two spaces. The haphazard state of repairs and renovations was a recurring theme in this place, so it wasn't surprising that only three of the remaining six rooms on that floor were fit for paying guests. None of them—even the rentable ones—were fancy, but I supposed they had a certain antiquated charm.

The top floor, though, that was a real mess. No one went up there. Ever. I'd only poked around those rooms after my grandfather passed and they freaked me out. The long deep gashes in the walls reminded me of massive animal claw marks, and the ceiling in one room was spattered with something brown-ish that I feared was dried blood.

No.

It was better to pretend the top floor didn't exist. It made the hair on the back of my neck rise just thinking about it. I hated it up there. But leaving all those rooms to deteriorate wasn't good for business either. If I wanted to turn this business around, I really needed to do more.

However, despite having my list of shiny new goals, I didn't care about any of that tonight.

Okay. That was a lie. I actually didn't care most nights. I liked having the place to myself. No wonder the business wasn't growing, when I felt happier at the idea of not having to deal with strangers in my space. I really needed to adjust my attitude if I was serious about building the business for my successor.

But that was tomorrow's problem.

Tonight, I was relieved the hotel was peaceful and empty, well, except for my grandfather's cat. Although now that I thought about it, I hadn't seen Paws return from touring the place with Gage and the others. It'd be strange for him to leave the inn at night—that cat seemed to expect a pampered life more than most animals—but what did I know? I'd never had a cat before. Maybe they were all like that.

I trudged over the familiar route to my room. I knew which steps protested and squealed under my footsteps. I knew where to step to avoid stubbing my toe on the console table in the hallway. I knew how my key sounded as it scraped in the lock on my door.

As soon as I stepped inside, I locked the door again. The click was reassuring.

The familiar scent of paint greeted me. Over the last year, this hotel room had become my home, but right now I didn't find comfort in it.

My first task was to secure the curtains again. I'd opened them this morning, hoping the morning light would energize me, but now I needed the flimsy mental security having them closed would provide.

It didn't matter that I stayed on the second floor, I needed to know no one could see in. At all. Not even a little bit. As I tugged the curtains closed, I peeked out at the darkened landscape. Nothing moved out there, but my heart still thundered in my chest like I was being chased by a pack of rabid dogs.

Ever since Gage had left the bar earlier, all I wanted to do was shove everyone out the door and come back to my room. But now that I was here, I hesitated. Did I really want to see those paintings again?

I wiped my sweat-drenched palms on my jeans. Then I flicked the light switch. I blinked under the intensity of the light. I painted at all hours, and I hated the yellowish tinge the original bulbs had cast, so I'd replaced them all with the brightest, whitest bulbs possible. Normally the brilliant light invigorated me and made me want to paint.

Tonight, that unforgiving brightness highlighted every secret I had stashed away.

My gaze darted over the black-and-white canvases in one corner of the room, and then the other. I always made sure to put my colorful paintings facing out where I could see them, with the others tucked away behind them. But there were so many of the black-and-white ones now it was becoming impossible to hide them all.

Then I eyed the bed.

Even from this angle, the canvases under it were visible. Stacks of them.

Then I was moving.

Kneeling.

Tugging out my hidden works.

My breath hitched when the first one was revealed. It was exactly as I had remembered. It was the exact likeness of that man—*Gage*. Including the horns.

I hadn't mis-remembered anything.

"Oh no, oh no, oh no."

Then I pulled out the others.

I gulped as I scratched the back of my neck. I hadn't seen them all lined up like this before. I just painted them, then shoved them under the bed. But looking at them now, I realized they were almost like a graphic novel. And, worse yet, it looked like a love story.

For each image I had painted of this man alone, there was another of the two of us together. Sometimes we were naked, in what could only be described as pornographic situations—at least my mother would have thought so.

She'd always hated when I had to take figure studies in art school. She especially hated when I drew nude women.

She was such a prude, I often wondered how she'd ever become pregnant with me. But she was incredibly supportive when I came out to her, so there was that. Of course, she laughed and said it relieved her to know I wouldn't be showing up with any surprise babies, since she was too young to be a grandparent.

But I didn't want to think about my mom tonight, not when I was face-to-face with... *this*. Whatever *this* was.

And then I remembered the way that man—*Gage*—had touched me. The way he'd brushed his warm strong fingers along the place where Old Thom had hit me with the bottle cap. The way my body had responded when he kissed me. The way his whispered words ignited a part of me I didn't even know existed.

For the first time ever, I wanted someone. A stranger. It was more than mere interest or arousal: I ached for him. How could meeting one person change my whole life? We hadn't even said more than a handful of words to one another.

I didn't understand any of it.

And it scared the shit out of me.

I just wished being scared wasn't becoming the norm.

Chapter Thirteen

GAGE

Birds were noisy bastards. Particularly at dawn. I groaned and willed myself to fall back asleep despite all the squawking and chattering.

After a few minutes, I reluctantly gave up.

Last night, I'd originally planned to detour back to the pub when we finished the tour of the inn, but Van had had other plans, insisting we review his case files. Unfortunately, the case took priority over my seduction plans. So we'd ended up at the police station instead.

Although I'd only agreed to leave the inn after Paws had agreed to watch over Jake. Van said the cat didn't always stick around, but he would if he made a promise. I had to trust Paws would do as he said. I hated to think how vulnerable Jake was alone in that building, but the cat was powerful enough to take care of any problems.

Then it took an obscenely long time to review the police files, some of which were more than a decade old.

Sure, it was important to understand what we were up against, but did it all have to happen in one evening? The same evening I'd planned to finish what I'd started with the cute bartender? By the time we'd parted ways with Hayden and Van, the main gates to the inn were closed and the lights were all off.

I'd lain awake too long after climbing in bed, thinking about the strange magic, the bold guy, and that kiss, to get up this early. Was it even five thirty yet? I groaned again and pushed the covers off. I didn't bother looking at the time. I was awake, so it didn't matter.

I wasn't ready to face my team, though.

I couldn't stop myself from moving to the cabinet beside my bed where I kept my research. I retrieved the most current box of maps I'd been using. I set the box on my bed, then removed the lid. The document sitting on top of the heap was my first priority. I unfolded it and spread it out across the comforter. This map was one of hundreds, or perhaps even thousands I'd used over the years. I took a plain pencil and updated the drawing with the approximate location of our campsite. Then I drew another circle around the town.

My palms grew sweaty as I reached for a second map, which was the one where I'd carefully marked out all the locations where demons had tethered. I wiped my hands hastily over the cotton sheet before gently unrolling the ancient map. Some long-ago magical map makers had surveyed ley lines all around the world and that's what I used as the basis for my work. I'd replaced it a few times over the years, and this version would need to be replaced soon too. The paper was yellowed, the ink was faded, and the fragile edges were starting to rip and crumble.

I'd memorized the locations of each demon stronghold long ago, but I let my gaze drift from one to the other in a nearly ritualistic pattern. Then I let my gaze settle on Willow Lake, or my best estimation of where Willow Lake would be if it was populous enough to show on a map of this scale.

My eyes caught on the spot, and I swallowed.

"No wonder the energy of the place is so…" I let my sentence trail off, not sure what the right word might be. I checked the location again. There were ley lines running through the area. A lot of them.

My heart thudded hard in my chest as I studied the other demonic sites. They too were all found where ley lines crossed. I knew that… of course I did. I'd devoted my life to finding a place to tether. Ley lines were an obvious place to start. But this was the first time I'd been to a spot where I'd felt the essence of the place so strongly.

"Could Willow Lake be mine?" I whispered.

Or was it a false lead like so many others?

I stared at the map for a long, long time. Then, reluctantly, I carefully returned my maps to their spot in the built-in cabinet beside my bed. It was still early yet, so I pulled out a paperback I'd been reading. I flipped through a few pages, but it wasn't holding my attention. I tossed it aside.

All I could think about was that damn magic in Willow Lake and that sexy man who'd kissed me.

The questions about Willow Lake, though, those could change my life completely. Could this be *my* place?

Demons didn't get scared or nervous, but the unfamiliar, almost painful pressure in my chest felt a lot like what I imagined anxiety would feel like.

I sat on the edge of the bed and let my demon form wash over me. My limbs lengthened and my vision sharpened. The biggest change, though, was my wings, which unfurled behind me and fluttered softly in the quiet of the room. Once in this form, I couldn't stand in here or squeeze through the narrow doorways, but I could still sit on my bed. This was one of the few places I regularly allowed my true form out. A rush of power surged through me with the change, but it was all neatly contained and controlled.

"See?" I whispered. "Everything is fine. Just as it should be."

I closed my eyes, not needing to see the little details my improved eyesight would give me. My hands with their long, thick claws rested on my thighs in loose fists. As I breathed in deeply, then exhaled, my forked tongue curled and uncurled in my mouth.

"I am in fucking control, damn it. I am in fucking control," I muttered over and over.

I wasn't convinced meditation worked for my kind, but Jeremy had suggested it and he nagged me until I gave in and agreed I'd try it. Ever since Adrian had told him about the deadly promise I'd demanded from my team, he'd been determined to stop my end from happening.

I could pretend he was worried about me, but I knew his primary concern was for his mate. Jeremy didn't want Adrian to be forced to kill me.

So, to protect myself and, more importantly, my team,

I was willing to do anything that might delay the inevitable, even meditating and chanting personal fucking mantras. I couldn't afford to be proud or dismissive. Pride wasn't helpful. Just ask my father. Oh, right, you couldn't because he was dead. Perhaps if he'd done something like this, things would have turned out differently for us all.

After I finished, I let my demon form fall away.

Now what?

Maybe I should try sleeping again. I had the feeling this was going to be a long day.

I stretched out over the covers and closed my eyes. My eyes snapped open. This wasn't working.

I didn't want to fall asleep wondering if this could be *my* place. Magic only knew what the hell that would do to my dreams, so I pulled up a memory of the quirky man who'd demanded kisses from me. It'd been a long time since I'd taken anyone to my bed, and the prospect of seeing him again gave me something to look forward to. I wanted to demand my own kisses next time. I wanted his lithe body under me. I wanted him moaning my name and begging for more.

I settled back and let the fantasy distract me.

When I emerged from my bedroom at the back of the RV some time later, Nelson was already up and in the kitchen area, waiting for me with coffee brewing. The others might choose to sleep in tents at night, but most of the RV was available to everyone on the team any time they wanted it. The only place off-limits was my bedroom.

"You're up early," I said.

"The damn birds woke me," he muttered in disgust.

I grunted in agreement as I poured my coffee.

Nelson made the best coffee. It was as dark and strong as his magic. When I reached the bottom of my mug, Nelson cleared his throat.

"We need a plan," he said.

"You already have one, don't you?"

He shrugged. The shadow jumper always had a plan. I figured it had to do with his magic. When you lived in the shadows, you needed to know where those shadows were and how to get to them. Sometimes he took too many risks with his own safety, but so far, he'd always come through.

"Let me get another cup and you can tell me about it."

As soon as I was back at the table with a fresh cup, I nodded for Nelson to begin.

"The way I see it, we have three problems. One is to confirm the extent of the wolves' involvement with Babette's operation. The second is to figure out what's happened with the rest of those boxes and get the stuff back where it belongs. And, lastly, we need to help that bartender. If someone has messed with his magic, we can't leave him like that."

I nodded. "Okay. I agree."

"The first two are linked and I figure the best way to find out more is to do some recce." He paused for a moment and met my eyes. I knew whatever he was going to suggest I wouldn't like. "I'll go to the wolf pack and look around."

"It's too dangerous." I set my coffee down harder than I planned, but what he was suggesting was risky, even riskier than his norm. "They'll be able to scent you even if they can't see you."

"I've been working with Teague and Adrian. Teague's

come up with a scent blocker strong enough to fool Adrian's wolf. If I can hide from him, a wolf who knows my scent, I can hide from any wolf."

"What if it wears off? What if it rains or you sweat?" I crossed my arms. "I don't like it."

Nelson's mouth twitched. He was usually the stoic one, the one who didn't like to reveal his feelings. Seeing his mouth move even that much told me he appreciated my concern for him more than he would ever admit out loud. "I knew you wouldn't, but it's the best we've got. If it helps, the forecast says we're in for a sunny day but only moderate temperatures."

"It'd be better if I went to the wolf pack. I can transport myself in and out before they even know I'm there, and I'm strong enough to defend myself against the whole pack if I need to."

"Nope," Nelson shook his head. "You need to help that bartender. I saw how you two were eyeing one another up. I might have misspoken when I said what I said about you and him last night, but it is obvious you're attracted to him. You have an edge in dealing with him that the rest of us don't. He needs help. You are the best person to do that."

I didn't say anything. Did I want to reconnect with Jake? Absolutely. I'd spent most of last night thinking of all the ways I wanted to touch and taste him. I had already decided I would see him today. I just hadn't expected Nelson to point me in Jake's direction and say *go*.

"Help him, Gage. It's what you do."

"It was strange," I admitted. "When I touched him, I

couldn't sense the nature of his magic. With him being an oracle, it should have been prominent, but it wasn't."

"You've helped all of us. None of us would be where we are without you." Nelson's fingers tightened around his mug. It was the only sign he was remembering how the two of us met. "You're attracted to him, sure, but I bet you are also itching to help him."

I wasn't surprised he'd noticed my interest in Jake— both his problematic magic and the man himself. I'd been drawn to him, right from the start, and my reaction wasn't typical. Not for me.

It'd led me to impossible, crazy thoughts in the middle of the night.

Thoughts that sounded a lot like *was Jake my mate?*

I wasn't ready to admit that one aloud yet, but I couldn't ignore my unusual fixation on the guy. If he really was my mate, I had to think carefully about what that might mean for me. A single person wasn't enough of a tether for a demon, and if I became the tether for his oracle powers and I snapped... he would be in a worse situation than he was now.

"Did you talk this over with the others?"

He nodded.

"Because you know the drill. Once I commit to helping someone, I doubt I'll be able to stop." My demonic nature made me a good investigator, but it also made me a liability when I became fixated on someone or something. If Jake didn't offer me anything in return for my help— and without knowing he was a supe or what that meant, why would he?—it would deplete my magic to fix his, which would leave my team weak. They were already vulnerable enough with Davina and Teague still away.

"We talked. We all agree. We aren't expecting any confrontations right away while we're gathering information. There should be time to replenish your magic before anything happens."

I nodded. Then my thoughts drifted back to the strange way I was drawn to the magic in Willow Lake. Going to town to help Jake was a good excuse to explore the magic there too.

"Fine. I'll check on the oracle, but I want regular updates." I stared at him until he nodded. "Take one of the bikes. Have Isaac drop you off and he can stay close. The minute something doesn't feel right, get out of there. Both of you."

"You want me to ride bitch," Nelson said slowly. "Behind Isaac."

"Don't be so sensitive. Unless you want to take the Pink Lady. I don't think she'll be quite as agile on the backroads, but…"

Nelson grimaced. "Fine."

The shadow jumper opened the door and emptied his coffee mug on the scrubby plants outside. Then he set the cup in the tiny sink before turning to me.

"You need to be careful too. I think you need to help the bartender, but we don't know what's going on with him."

Just as I'd done with him, Nelson held my gaze until I agreed. Then the shadow jumper left to wake Isaac.

I leaned back and went over what I knew. If Davina

was here, we could talk to any of the ghosts at the inn, because I suspected that old pack house had more than a few hanging around the place. If Jake's grandfather was there, even better. And, if he wasn't, Teague could summon him.

I glanced at my phone, but I hadn't had a new update from either of them yet. How long did it take to banish a ghost anyway? Shouldn't they be wrapped up at the morgue by now? I re-read their last update when they'd said they still needed a few days. That was yesterday morning.

I rubbed my chin. Nelson was right. We needed to gather information.

What Nelson didn't know was that my interests went beyond Jake and the wolf pack. I wanted to know everything about Willow Lake. I should have told everyone about my suspicions as soon as I sensed the magic here. I didn't allow secrets on my team, but it felt too early to talk about the way Willow Lake was calling me. Davina, my second, would have known I was holding something back. She'd been with me the longest of anyone.

It seemed premature to even be thinking about it, but what if I bonded to Willow Lake and my team didn't want to stay here with me? They had become my family. I needed them as much as I needed an anchoring place. I'd bound them to me and they'd all come to me willingly. But staying in Willow Lake would change everything about how we operated.

Tethering would limit how much I could move around. Adrian might stay. He had a mate now, and Jeremy didn't seem like the kind of man who'd enjoy living out of a tent for too long. For the others, though? The one time I'd released someone from their deal with me, everything had gone wrong. Abigail withered, and just six months later she was gone. Although she swore her illness wasn't related to our broken bond, I wasn't convinced.

If Teague had been with me then, he'd have been able to tell. Unfortunately, I didn't find him until nearly a century after Abigail's death. The idea of trying to release someone again made me cold and sweaty all at the same time.

Or, I would if demons felt nerves.

If it came to severing the ties I had with my team, I'd need to figure out what went wrong last time. I couldn't watch anyone from my family die again. Never again. But, even if I did develop a safer way to do it, breaking our magical connection would still be painful, for all of us— well, except perhaps for Adrian, who had his mating bond already in place.

I swallowed down the last of my coffee. The bitter liquid didn't help settle me this morning. There were too many unknowns. This job was becoming more complicated by the minute. As if tracking down someone who trafficked supes wasn't complicated enough already.

I wiped my hand down my face and set my worries aside. I had work to do.

I'd seen a flyer on a bulletin board at the pub last night about painting in the park this afternoon. From what Van and Hayden had said, Jake was an artist, so I was betting on him being there. It was a place to start.

I grinned, then a strange effervescent sensation bubbled up inside me.

A demon's stomach never fluttered in anticipation, but something unusual was happening. I forced the feeling away until my stomach was absolutely, one-hundred percent flutter free at the idea of seeing Jake again.

Chapter Fourteen

JAKE

Winslow Park was situated on a considerable stretch of land along the north side of town and held most of the community's recreation areas, or at least the ones that weren't connected to the lake. The flatter areas of the park were filled with sports fields, a golf course, and parking lots, but where my fellow painters, who were all older ladies, and I chose to set up was on a slope overlooking the town.

If I climbed a bit higher to the crest of the small foothill, I knew I'd see the mountains to the west. They were gorgeous, and I'd painted them several times since moving here, but today I wanted something different. Something I could touch if I wanted. Something I could prove was real.

So I'd set up my easel facing south toward town.

The brightly painted buildings in town were a riotous bouquet from this view. To the left was the motel with its chaotically colorful finishes. It was certainly a memorable landmark, and I hoped it attracted more guests than my inn because it'd suck if both our businesses were struggling.

Along the main street, the businesses were an explosion of vivid rainbow colors. The apartment complexes to the west of downtown were varying shades of blue and yellow. And in the distance, every house in the new residential area was a dollop of bright, undiluted color like the paint on my palette. Not one of them was beige. Even the only brown house, which was where my friend Alice lived with her parents, was a rich, vibrant brown.

When I'd first moved to town, I found the place garish and uncomfortable. I couldn't believe no one commented on the crazy colors, but perhaps they'd all just lived here long enough to become immune. No one seemed to care if their house clashed with their neighbor's. It was like the residents of Willow Lake had collectively decided consulting a color wheel to look up complementary, analogous, or even tetradic color schemes was for cowards.

Today, however, I embraced all that color. I needed it.

I refused to squeeze even a drop of white or black paint onto my palette.

Using my fattest paint brush, I filled my canvas with yellow. I never used yellow to underpaint, but today I wanted brightness. I wanted sunshine. I swore this was going to be the happiest, most cheerful painting I'd ever done. It was going to be a freaking joy to behold.

Sinking into my art, I lost track of everything around me.

Most of the ladies, I'd discovered in the months since I'd been organizing this meet-up, just came out to chat and occasionally do a sketch or two. I learned to only half-listen to their chatter, especially when they complained about hot flashes and other things I really didn't want to know about.

Today, they were excitedly chattering about Mrs. Jennings' newest bakery offerings. They seemed very knowledgeable about people's personal preferences, which I found odd, but it was a small town, so that might explain it. The ladies cackled about how Dillon liked things hot and had cleared out all the new cinnamon heart creations before Van even saw them, how Hayden had been drawn in by the smell of the new meat pies, while Weston, who usually complained about the low salt content, had apparently been thrilled with the new salted caramel options.

Why this was discussed with such enthusiasm, I had no idea.

I focused on the view instead.

The Lister Apartment Complex was the first building I sketched onto my painting. It'd anchor my drawing on the right and set the scale for the rest. I roughed in the perspective lines and rough shapes through the wet yellow paint. From this view, two sides of the building were visible.

"Four windows across there," I murmured as I counted. "And on the other side, another one, two, three…"

I squinted at the building.

Something was hanging out of the window on the top floor. It was similar to a tree branch, except it was green and undulating like a tentacle. My stomach lurched. No, no, no. I would not allow myself any hallucinations today. Nope. No way.

As if to prove me wrong, another tentacle-like thing wiggled out of the window and wrapped around the first one. A fine mist seemed to sparkle in the air around the writhing tentacles.

"Oh!" Daphne Rivers, who was to my left, gasped and pointed in the direction of those tentacles that couldn't be tentacles.

She had a few sons about my age, including Simon Rivers. He was a bit of an odd duck—always acting like he had a guilty secret—but I wasn't in any position to judge. I knew him better than the others because he was one of the few guys my age who came into the pub regularly. He was a good-looking guy and, for half a second, I'd thought about asking him out, but I couldn't summon enough of an attraction to risk going on a date with him. I didn't want to initiate something I couldn't carry through on.

In the end, I decided keeping things platonic would be better. If my interest in him had been a fraction of what I felt with Gage, things might have been different. Although, I couldn't imagine trying to date one of Daphne Rivers' sons. Based on the stories she told while painting, I knew she was insanely protective of them all.

"Sally must be visiting Henrietta and Gary again. Meow." Daphne's meow was so much like an actual cat that I glanced around for a stray. She sounded more like a cat than Paws did.

The other ladies giggled and watched the non-tentacles.

"What was that?" I made myself ask.

Daphne adjusted her straw hat. Her cheeks were flushed. "Oh, nothing, dear."

I got the sense she was lying to me in the same way an adult dismissed a question from a curious child about a complex adult topic. Fine. Whatever. I didn't need to know.

I sketched in more windows.

I did not include any tentacles.

Beside her, Gloria shook her head, and wisps of her long gray hair came loose from her ponytail. "I don't know why they can't just accept they are better together," she muttered just loud enough for me to hear. "Those three are meant to be a throuple. I can't believe they make that poor succubus go to the bar to feed regularly when they should just invite her to move in. Everyone would be happier. They don't live with their consortium anymore. They shouldn't be so scared about challenging traditional views."

Again with the succubus thing? And what was a consortium?

Before I could ask about that—although I wasn't even sure how to phrase such a question—Vanessa, Alice's mom, waved her chubby hand at me.

"Oh, Jake dear?" she said. "Can you come here? I have a question."

I set down my paintbrush and crossed the grass to where Vanessa had set up her gear. She sat under a brown beach umbrella on a lawn chair that was too tall for her small body, so her feet dangled. In a town where so many favored bright colors, Alice and her mom were the exception. Everything they owned was brown, usually in the same shade as their shaggy dark brown hair. The light under the umbrella was muddy and dull. Vanessa tilted her head up to me, so, although I couldn't see her eyes behind her dark brown sunglasses, I knew she was looking at me.

"You've done a great job of capturing the shape of the tree," I said as I considered her painting.

"Thank you, dear. But what about this branch? I just can't seem to get it right." She pointed at the tree in question. The branch was coming straight toward us.

"Hmm... Yes. I can see the problem. Foreshortening can be challenging, but at least with a tree it's easier to fudge than if you're drawing a human figure," I said. I started describing a few techniques. I was pointing right at the tree when something shimmered underneath it.

My chest squeezed as Mr. Horny Dude—Gage— appeared out of nowhere. My stomach tightened and I thought for sure this morning's breakfast was going to make a reappearance too. He saw us, waved, and started walking toward us. Sunlight caught on his horns, making them shine like they'd been dipped in iridescent glitter.

Except people didn't just suddenly appear out of nowhere. Even if I'd hoped all my interactions with the man yesterday had been real, this was *not* real.

Vanessa jerked her head around and stared at me.

"Well, look at that," Vanessa said. "Do you know him, sugar?"

"Him? Him who?"

Vanessa pointed at Gage. "That man."

My stomach flipped, then flopped. Vanessa saw him too? I cleared my throat and pasted a brittle smile on my face. "Oh! Ha! Him? I met him last night."

"Did you now? And what do you know about him?"

He has horns. No. I couldn't say that. *I have approxi-*

mately ten million paintings of him in my room, give or take a thousand. Nope. Couldn't say that either. *I want to lick his dimple.* I'd sound like a creep. "He drinks dark ale."

Vanessa snorted. "Are you sure there's nothing more? You don't happen to notice anything else? Maybe…um… in his hair or something?"

"Nope. Nothing at all."

My heart pounded. She wasn't talking about his horns because his horns didn't exist. Then my fingers tingled as I grew dizzy. I recognized the signs, and panic sprinted through me.

"No, no, no…"

I couldn't have one of my possessed painting episodes. Not now. Not in front of everyone… But it was too late.

"Jake dear? Is everything okay?"

But I didn't have time to answer before my vision blurred and darkness enveloped me, pulling me under.

Chapter Fifteen

GAGE

I had parked the Pink Lady in the lot at the bottom of the hill at Winslow Park, but when I spotted where the painting group was set up, I decided to take a short cut and jump through a portal to get closer instead of walking up. It was just my luck to appear precisely where Jake was looking. The guy's eyes had nearly popped out of his head with how wide he'd opened them.

The brownie Jake was standing beside giggled glee-fully at my appearance. She spun toward Jake to see his reaction. After all, usually all it took was one glimpse through our natural glamour and a mundane would see everything in the supernatural world.

Exposure happened in a lot of ways, like if a shifter was seen changing forms, or, in this case, a man appearing out of nowhere. Shit. I couldn't believe I'd made such a basic mistake. But I hadn't expected Jake to be looking at that lopsided tree at that exact moment.

I shot out my magic and confirmed the others on the hill were all supes. No harm done there at least. I just needed to check on Jake.

Jake shook his head and turned back toward the painting in front of the brownie and talked to her like nothing had happened. Of course, his flushed cheeks gave away his discomfort. Interesting. Could he see my horns or not?

Then Jake's eyes seemed to roll back in his head and his body stiffened.

"What's wrong with him?" I ran forward, closing the distance between us.

Jake, without looking, unerringly grabbed the brownie's paintbrush and palette from her hands. He pushed the brush into the mound of black paint and lifted it toward the canvas.

"Oh, heck no," the brownie shouted and grabbed her painting. She darted away from Jake and his black paint, taking her canvas with her.

Jake took slow lumbering steps toward another easel. No one came forward to claim the piece or stop Jake from using it, so I followed behind. The painting was a lively work of the town below. Was it Jake's? It'd be a shame to lose it. In a flash too fast for a human and even most supes to follow, I grabbed a blank canvas from the small stack at the base of the easel and switched it with the townscape.

The paintbrush hit the canvas the moment I set it in place.

With each push and pull of his arm, Jake applied more and more black paint even though his eyes were vacant as he stared unblinkingly ahead. Then he added dots of white here and there, followed by an unpredictable mix of fine lines and exuberant strokes. I watched, mesmerized, as an image emerged through the black. The ladies he'd been painting with gathered around too. No one spoke.

By the time Jake stilled, a dismal scene had emerged. The subject matter was all too familiar, and yet I knew this painting didn't reference the past. Oracles only foretold the future. Just a few weeks ago, we'd discovered a storage facility filled with imprisoned supernatural beings. The scene on this painting was strikingly similar, confirming that although we'd stopped one arm of the trafficking operation, we weren't done yet. I had suspected as much, but I'd hoped I was wrong. This message from the oracle told me I wasn't.

Jake's body convulsed then. Before I realized what was happening, he had spun away from the painting. He bent over and threw up, all over me. Warm runny vomit soaked into my pants and covered my shoes. I gagged but managed to calm my stomach before I emptied my breakfast too.

The women all squealed and took a step away from us.

Jake staggered. His eyes rolled back in his head again and his whole body went limp. I swept him into my arms before he fell.

"You." I pointed at the brownie. "What's your name?"

"Vanessa," she said. Her eyes didn't meet mine, but that wasn't anything knew. Most weaker supes avoided making eye contact with a demon.

"Vanessa, you are responsible for gathering Jake's supplies and getting them back to his place." I glanced at the painting Jake had just finished. I wanted to take it with me, but I didn't think I could manage it and Jake too without the paint being rubbed or smeared. The message from the oracle was too important. And if what he'd painted was true, then we needed to make sure this vision was safe so we could study it for clues. I should have set Jake down and protected the painting, but that wasn't going to happen. I could blame it on my demonic nature's fixation on him, but it didn't change the facts. Nothing would stop me from protecting Jake above all else. "And that painting. Make sure it is handled with care and protected."

The woman nodded. "Yes, my lord."

My lord. I frowned. Such an old-fashioned way to address one of my kind. The whole *lord of darkness* reputation had always rubbed me the wrong way.

"Call me Gage," I corrected her.

Her head bobbed.

"Where does Jake live?" I suspected he stayed at the inn, but I needed confirmation before I started wandering all over Willow Lake with the unconscious oracle in my arms.

"At the inn, my lord. He has a room on the second floor."

I sighed. Clearly, she wasn't going to stop that *my lord* business like I wanted. Jake moaned in my arms.

"Do not fail me," I said to the brownie, pushing a bit of my power into the words.

She shuddered under my threat. I almost hated myself for it, but this was too important. She and everyone there needed to understand the severity of the situation.

Then I opened a portal and stepped through it and into

the pub. Since I'd spent the most time there the night before, it was the easiest place to form the portal connection. I'd expected my magic to protest being used without a deal in place, but it didn't. That was curious. I pushed out my magic to check my surroundings. The pub and the inn were empty; not even the cat was there. The door leading into the inn was propped open, and I carried Jake through it and into the foyer. I hadn't been shown Jake's room the night before, but I suspected it was the room I'd seen him exiting the day before. I climbed up the stairs toward the door, hoping I was right.

Sure enough, as I entered the hallway, the scent of paint tickled my nose. I'd caught the scent briefly yesterday too, I realized now. I just hadn't understood the significance at the time.

The door to Jake's room was locked, but few things could keep out a demon. An old metal lock was not one of them. I let magic flow from my fingers. The lock clicked. The doorknob turned in my hand and the door swung open. I stepped inside just as Jake's eyes shot open. His gaze darted frantically around. He gasped when he saw me and then again when he saw where he was. He wiggled and struggled in my arms.

"No, stop," he cried out. "Don't look."

But it was already too late. I gaped at the dozens of black-and-white images around the room. I couldn't believe what I was seeing, especially when more than half of them were of me.

Chapter Sixteen

JAKE

"Oh no," I moaned. I wanted to curl up and hide, maybe move to another place far, far away. Like South Africa or Borneo. Okay. I had no idea where Borneo was, but it had to be better than being here.

I reeked of puke and my clothes were wet. Those two ideas together made me feel queasy all over again. I didn't usually puke on myself, even when I wasn't aware of what I was doing. Yep, today was an extra special kind of day. How fucking wonderful.

Gage was cradling me like an overwrought damsel in distress as he carried me deeper into my room, where he'd see all my crazy paintings. Until last night, the paintings had been at least partially hidden, but I'd pulled them all out before going to sleep, including the ones under my bed, and I hadn't put them away yet.

No one ever came into my room, not even my grandfather's creepy cat. So I hadn't worried about it. What a colossal fucking mistake that had been.

Why did this have to happen today?

As Gage gently lowered me to my messy bed, my eyes caught on the guy's clothes. They were wet and...

"Oh no," I moaned again. "I puked on you, didn't I? I am so sorry."

It didn't matter how much he'd flirted with me yesterday, my plan of asking Gage out for coffee or *more* died right then and there. A little gravestone marked the place where that idea used to live in my head.

"Are you okay?" Gage smoothed back my sweaty hair where it was plastered to my forehead. "Would you like a shower? I can wait here to make sure you're okay."

"I'll be fine now." At least until the next time this happened. I stifled a yawn. "I just need to sleep for a bit..."

"You should change your clothes at least."

"And brush my teeth. Yeah, that'd be good." I nodded and struggled to sit up. Sometimes I powered through after one of my painting episodes, but lately I was often completely zapped. Today it was like bad luck had smacked me with a baseball bat and just kept on hitting, because on top of all the other shit that'd happened, I could barely muster the energy to lift my head off the pillow.

Little insidious thoughts curled sluggishly through my head, reminding me these bouts of illness and fatigue were increasing in severity and frequency. I couldn't keep functioning like this. I wondered if taking vitamins would help. Nothing else seemed to.

Gage helped me stand and guided me to the sink in the

corner of the room. I stood in front of it and stared at the deep chip in the porcelain by the tap as I tried to gather the willpower to clean up.

"Let me help," Gage murmured. He reached around me and grabbed my toothbrush. He squeezed toothpaste onto the bristles, then handed it to me. I stared at it. "Brush your teeth, sweetheart," he said gently.

Huh? Had he really called me sweetheart? Why hadn't he just dumped me in my room and run far, far away? He wasn't acting like he was disgusted by me, nor did he seem put off by me obsessively painting someone who looked just like him. I'd have to think about that later. Right now my head was too fuzzy.

After I finished brushing my teeth, Gage turned me so we were facing one another. My yawn erupted before I could stop it.

"Sorry," I muttered. At least my breath was minty fresh now, so yay.

"Are you feeling better?"

Gage brushed a finger over my cheek. Hmm… that felt nice. I'd liked when he touched me yesterday too. I leaned into the caress.

"Do you need help with your clothes?"

My eyes popped open at that question. "Uh, what?"

"You're very tired, but you should at least take off these dirty clothes before you lie down to sleep."

I blinked as I replayed Gage's words. Yeah. Okay. That made sense. Everything seemed to be in slow-motion as I fumbled with the hem of my T-shirt. It seemed like a monumental effort to pull it up. If it wasn't too dirty, I could just leave it on. I looked down at it. Nope. It was disgusting. I just needed to…

"I promise not to do anything but help," Gage said softly. The air seemed to flutter at his words. "Is that okay?"

I stared up at Gage. Almost everyone was taller than me, so that wasn't such a new thing, but having Gage's impressive body standing so close did things to me. He made me feel safe and protected. His horns didn't detract from those feelings at all. I had an unshakeable conviction that Gage was capable of handling anything life might throw at me.

Huh.

I trusted him. Even if he was a stranger. How odd.

"Can I help?"

Right. He'd asked that before. I nodded.

My T-shirt went first. Gage set it beside the sink. Then he reached for the button on my jeans. My pulse quickened as Gage's strong, thick fingers slipped between the waistband on my jeans and my skin. Then he was kneeling on the floor in front of me. His head was level with my hips. And my pants were open and being tugged down my legs. Holy Mother of Oils and Acrylics.

"Lift your foot," Gage commanded.

"Fuck," I whispered. My cock was fully hard, even though my body had about as much energy as a stack of bricks.

Gage winked at me. "Later, sweetheart. Let's get you cleaned up and into bed so you can sleep first."

My cock jerked at the flirtatious suggestion. My underwear had a wet spot that had nothing to do with my post-painting puke fest. I should be embarrassed about my obvious arousal, but I wasn't.

This was a moment worthy of celebration. I was actually hard with another person in the same room and everything. So stiff and erect that my underwear was actually tenting. I hadn't even known that was a thing; I'd always thought it was an exaggeration. But there it was. My cock. All hard and eager. With another person in the room. I wanted to jump for joy.

Or, you know, fall into bed and sleep.

Because the rest of my body clearly had a different agenda from my cock.

I lifted my foot as instructed, then Gage slipped off my shoe, my sock, and then my pant leg. We repeated everything with my other leg. Then I was standing in front of this unbelievably sexy—but horned—man in nothing but my underwear. I didn't even cringe too much when he saw the undies I'd put on today. They had little paint palettes with wings on them with the words *I'm winning with flying colors*. I mean, I wasn't winning at life or anything at all, but I'd always figured a little positive messaging, even on my underwear, couldn't hurt.

I swayed toward Gage. I'd felt a magnetic pull to him yesterday too, but today it was like a current was pushing me toward him and I was helpless to resist.

"Easy now," he murmured. He jumped to his feet and grabbed my narrow hips in his strong warm hands. His thumbs rubbed little circles on the skin right above my underwear as he steadied me. He led me over to the edge of my bed and helped me sit like he was scared I'd collapse at any second. And he wasn't wrong. My legs were wobbly, and my head felt foggy.

When he stepped away, I whimpered just a little, but he wasn't gone for long.

"Almost done," he whispered. "Let's just get you cleaned up a little more."

Then he drew a warm wet cloth over my skin. I gasped in pleasure.

Holy shit.

Why did that feel so good?

I sat, enthralled by the sensation, and watched Gage clean me. Shockingly, my cock was *still* thrilled about what was going on and was happy to let him know all about it. It bobbed and jerked with each gentle stroke of the cloth.

"There," he said when he finished. He tossed the dirty cloth to the sink, and I was absurdly happy he didn't walk away again. I didn't know why I was being so clingy, but it was like all my normal self-preservation techniques had been obliterated under the weight of my fatigue. "Now, let's get you into bed."

I wanted to nod enthusiastically. I wanted to grab Gage and pull him down to the mattress too, but as soon as he pulled the covers over my body, my eyelids became detestably heavy.

"You didn't come back last night."

"I'm here now," he said.

"Don't leave," I murmured. I was ready to have sex. As soon as possible. Since he hadn't run away because of the puke, I was eager to capitalize on his lack of self-preservation. I couldn't do that if he left. "Just need an hour or two."

"I'll be here when you wake." Gage's lips brushed my forehead.

Chapter Seventeen

GAGE

As soon as Jake's breathing settled into the steady and even rhythm of sleep, my gaze strayed to the strange assortment of paintings littering his room. Any concerns I'd had about my attraction to Jake, or the strange pull Willow Lake had over me, evaporated. The oracle's message was clear: Destiny had called me to Willow Lake and to Jake.

Who was I to turn my back on a message from the Eternal Magic?

When I was sure Jake was deeply asleep, I opened a portal to the Pink Lady. I'd never stripped off my clothes, showered, and dressed again so quickly. Then I checked my phone for any messages from my team.

Last night Adrian had volunteered to interview some of the older locals to get more anecdotal descriptions of the wolves in the hills from when the bastards had lived in town. He hadn't messaged me yet with any information. I wondered if he'd taken his almost-human mate, Jeremy, with him.

I found Jeremy's endless barrage of questions disconcerting, but many others found him cute, which was surprisingly effective in getting people to open up, even the old guard supes. I wasn't above using any means necessary to get answers, even sending the persistent and guileless Jeremy into interviews. Nothing had come in from my people in the city either, but there were messages from both Isaac and Nelson. They had both just sent a number "4" through text, which was our code that things were going fine.

Good. I'd promised Jake I'd be at his side when he woke. A demon never broke a promise.

Rather than opening another portal, I drove the motorhome back through Willow Lake to the inn. Having seen the oracle's messages in the paintings about me staying in Willow Lake, I studied the small town with heightened interest.

The town was unlike anywhere else I'd visited, and I suspected it had to do with the substantial number of supes who called it home. The lights in all the store display windows sparkled a little brighter, each intersection provided a picturesque view of the lake, and almost everyone, from the people in other vehicles to the pedestrians on the street, waved at me as I passed them. There wasn't an overt use of magic like you might see in gated mage communities, but the place was almost like a scene from one of those predictable and disgustingly sweet holiday movies Davina liked to watch in December.

But a demon was not the kind of person you'd expect to find in a small-town holiday movie.

Had the Eternal Magic made a mistake?

Still, I couldn't deny how right it felt to guide the motorhome between the grand gates into the parking lot at Jake's inn and park my home close to his. The large, gravelled space was empty except for one other vehicle. Vanessa, the brownie from Jake's painting group, stood beside a dark brown sedan with her hands clasped in front of her. She dipped her head slightly in respect when I descended the motorhome steps.

"Everything is here, my lord," she said. "Except his car. I didn't see his keys with his painting supplies."

I nodded. "I will collect the car later. The painting is what is most important."

"Of course, my lord. I have it here." She opened the back door of her car and gestured toward both of Jake's paintings, the colorful one and the black-and-white one, which she'd propped up on the back seat. "I was going to put everything inside, but the doors to the inn are locked."

"I have the key," I lied.

People tended to get anxious when they discovered how easily locks succumbed to my magic. Although even a mundane human could get inside most locked buildings if they really wanted to. Locks were more of a suggestion than anything else.

"Of course, my lord," she said demurely. Then she reached in and grabbed a basket from the floor. "Please, my lord, will you accept this?"

I eyed the cellophane wrapped basket with its bottle of wine, a selection of chocolates and nuts, and what appeared to be a handcrafted metal ornament in the shape of a goat. The petite goat, I knew, was meant to represent my demon. Insulting, but true. When I didn't immediately accept the gift, Vanessa glanced up before averting her eyes again. "Please. It is freely given."

People had given me offerings in the past, usually after a negotiation when someone regretted what they'd done and wished to be free of their obligation to me. Sometimes I found them acceptable, but usually I didn't. But to have someone offer a gift without negotiating? That was odd. It implied a relationship, and few people wanted to be linked to one of my kind.

Although that wasn't entirely true, was it? I had vague memories of my grandfather receiving gifts regularly. I'd always suspected it was another way to bind a demon to a place. By giving offerings, the local townsfolk were basically stockpiling the demon's good favor, ensuring that if something should arise, the demon would then be able to act and use their magic in defense of the town without having to negotiate first.

That this woman, who clearly didn't feel comfortable with me, would come with such a gift was humbling.

"Of course," I murmured and took the basket from her.

She smiled and some of the tension in her body appeared to loosen. She carefully pulled one of Jake's paintings from her vehicle and passed it to me. Then she retrieved the second one.

"Is it normal for the doors to be locked?" I asked as we carried Jake's paintings, his supplies, and my new basket to the inn.

"The inn doesn't get much business," Vanessa said, like that explained everything.

I'd suspected as much, so I nodded my understanding. I stood between Vanessa and the door so she wouldn't see my hand was empty as I touched the lock. With a little push of magic, it clicked open.

Was his lack of business because of the location or because he kept the doors locked? Was it his low season? That seemed unlikely since it was summer, but would a place like Willow Lake actually have a high season?

I knew nothing about the hospitality industry. But it seemed a shame to have all these rooms and facilities with no one using them. The place was run-down, so I suspected the inn wasn't doing well. And last night Jake had mentioned he didn't have the money to hire a consultant.

Was he struggling financially? I could help with that...

Casting my eye around the place with that thought in mind, I saw a lot of areas that needed improvement. The old building was worn, but it held a lot of potential—good bones, as they said on those decorating shows Isaac liked to watch on his laptop. If I stayed in Willow Lake, I would need to do something to keep busy. My days of travelling from job to job in my motorhome would be over.

How strange that I didn't find the idea of such a massive change unsettling.

Which brought my thoughts back to the inn.

Would Jake be open to an outside investor?

"Is the potluck still on for tonight?" Vanessa asked as we set the gift, the gear, and the paintings by the empty registration desk.

"What potluck?"

Vanessa glanced at my face in surprise before hurriedly dropping her gaze to the ground again. "Every Sunday night, Jake opens the dining hall, and we have a community potluck."

I almost asked her to repeat what she said but I had heard her well enough. The idea was just so foreign. Was this what people did in small towns? It seemed a little too Mayberry. My first impulse was to say the potluck was cancelled, but I still had a job to do, and an informal gathering would be a great opportunity to observe people.

"He started it after his grandfather died," Vanessa explained when I didn't say anything.

"Right," I said. "What time does it start?"

"People start arriving around four or so."

I glanced at the clock on the far wall of the foyer. That was still a couple of hours away. Jake had thought he'd be awake by then, so that should be fine. I nodded. "Yes. That would be acceptable."

"See you later, then." Vanessa smiled happily, although her gaze only travelled as high as my shoulder. She had a bounce in her step as she made her way back out.

As soon as she was gone, I locked the door again. I'd open it later. For now, I wanted to check on Jake and, hopefully, get a better look at some of his paintings too.

I grabbed the two paintings he'd been working on in the park. I'd come back for my basket and his supplies later. These paintings were too important to leave unattended—even the colorful one, because I suspected Jake loved it more than the other. It was something he'd created because he'd wanted to do it, not because the Eternal Magic had forced it on him.

My footsteps were silent as I stole through the inn to Jake's room. I paused for only a moment outside his door.

I'd told Jake I'd be there when he woke, so it was acceptable to go back in the room, right?

Right.

I slipped inside, taking care to keep my steps light so as not to disturb the still sleeping Jake. He was hugging a plump pillow to his chest and had kicked the blanket off his feet. I took a moment to admire him. His dark hair was in disarray. His typically pale cheeks were flushed in his sleep, and the dark depressions under his eyes didn't seem as harsh now as they had earlier. But it was obvious he wasn't well and hadn't been for a while. I missed seeing his dark brown eyes and the way they always seemed to be watching me, but it pleased me that Jake had fallen asleep in my presence. It meant he trusted me.

Or that he was exhausted.

Given the number of paintings in the room, I doubted he got anywhere near eight hours of sleep each night.

I set the new paintings against the foot of the bed, the only place with free space. The disordered chaos in the room made my eye twitch, but this was Jake's space, not mine. Obviously, he preferred it this way, although I had no idea why.

To distract myself from giving in to the impulse to tidy his space, I took in a deep breath and tasted the air.

What struck me first was that I still couldn't get a clear feel for Jake's magic, even though I knew what it was, and I'd seen him access it. With that knowledge, it should have been easy to identify, but it wasn't. Whatever I could sense of his magic was muted and faded. How was that possible when he'd obviously had a lot of visions in here? The place was filled with paintings.

Based on my observation of his behavior in the park, I doubted the colorful ones were products of his oracle abilities. And that matched with what I saw in this room. The paintings with color were remarkably bright, a sharp contrast to the others, making his single-minded resolve to ignore his oracle side when he was conscious obvious.

How many other things did Jake ignore?

Probably a lot.

Given his reaction to having me in his space, I doubted he'd be happy about inviting even more people to view his work. But with enough analysis, we should be able to determine if his visions covered a specific geographical region. Which meant Van and Hayden needed to see them, if only to identify any local people or places.

Which brought me back to my other question: Why didn't Jake know he was an oracle?

According to Van and Hayden, Jake didn't know about the supernatural world. I suspected they believed that because Jake pretended it didn't exist. Which then begged the question: What did Jake think was happening when he created these paintings or when he saw other supernatural beings? Because obviously he *could* see under the glamour, and he probably had for a while.

Unfortunately, the paintings themselves didn't hold any answers to Jake's reasons and beliefs.

I stared at the canvases. It would be so easy to flip through them and see what other messages the Eternal

Magic had for us, but my conscience rebelled at the idea. This was Jake's sanctuary, his sacred space. If he'd lived in ancient times, he would have a temple built just for him. He'd be surrounded by disciples. People would travel from all over just to ask for his guidance. Warriors would protect both him and his sacred space.

This wasn't ancient times, but I could be that for him. I could dedicate my life to him.

His warrior.

Jake's warrior.

The idea appealed to me more than I would have expected.

I moved a stack of empty canvases off a chair beside the bed and sat down. Since I refused to look at the paintings, I turned my attention to the sleeping painter.

It was clear Jake's supernatural magic was starting to overwhelm him. Throwing up and passing out every time he channeled a vision would work against him too. His survival instincts might have driven him to host the potluck every week. It was a way to bind himself to the present. But that weak connection wouldn't be strong enough to balance his magic for long. He needed a better anchor, like a mate.

My pulse picked up at the thought.

How strange. Ever since I'd come to Willow Lake and met Jake, I'd been suffering through a strange assortment of sensations. My reaction at the thought of mating with Jake was almost as bizarre as the weird fluttering sensation I'd felt earlier when I decided to see Jake again.

Was it connected to finding my fated mate?

Because I couldn't deny that's what he was.

Given the paintings Jake had done of the two of us together, I couldn't pretend we weren't destined for one another. That had to be why I was so drawn to him and why Jake had painted my likeness over and over again.

I leaned back in the chair.

That complicated things and made them pretty fucking simple all at the same time.

I'd known as soon as I stepped onto the ground in Willow Lake that this place would change me. I just hadn't realized *everything* about my life would be flipped upside down. And I wasn't the only one whose life would be impacted.

My team had been with me a long time, but I couldn't predict how they would react to this news. Once again, my chest ached at the thought of my team, my family, leaving me. The inn appeared to have lots of unused space... Could we convert it into a home for all of us? Would they want to stay here? Would having them here make Jake uncomfortable? After all, I'd chosen my team for a specific reason, and it wasn't for their social skills.

My thoughts were presumptuous, considering Jake didn't even know he was an oracle or could have a fated mate, but I didn't get to where I was by sitting back and coasting through life. The Eternal Magic kept me humble —she dictated my need to tether to a place and she chose my fated mate—but I seized every bit of control over my life I could. I refused to feel vulnerable or lost again, and if I could stop other people from feeling that way, then I did that too.

But I couldn't control Jake or our potential mating. If I rushed this, I could lose everything. I clenched my hands into fists, fighting the desire to gather him close and never let him go.

Jake stirred in the bed. He stretched and groaned and then his eyes fluttered open.

Okay. It was time to have a candid conversation with my mate and hope I didn't screw everything up. Sweat beaded along my hairline and my palms felt clammy.

I'd grown up being told demons were never unsure, that uncertainty was a species trait we just didn't possess. What a fucking lie.

It made me wonder what other lies I'd been told.

Chapter Eighteen

JAKE

Before I even opened my eyes, I knew two things. First, I was in my bed at the inn. Second, I was not alone in my room.

Then I remembered everything else... Well, most of it anyway. Enough to know I wished I could just fall back asleep, wake up alone, and continue living my life like nothing had happened. Call me an ostrich. That would be fine.

But my secret was out, and, just like Pandora, the one Greek myth I remembered, I doubted I could push it back into its box.

"Jake?" the deep sonorous voice that could only be Mr. Horny Dude asked. "You awake?"

I pulled my blankets over my head.

"Are you okay?"

"Yeah?" I whispered. I was physically fine, although the rest was to be determined. I sighed. This moment of reckoning had been coming for a long time. If my secret hadn't been discovered by Mr. Horny Dude, then it would have been some other well-meaning Willow Laker. Sally came to mind—she'd been really nosy lately—or maybe Alice. It was just my luck that it had to be Gage.

"I'll just step out so you can have some privacy to shower and get dressed. I'll be in the hallway when you are ready." He paused. "Then I think we should talk."

Oh right. I was almost naked because I'd puked on the only guy my dick had ever taken a liking to. Fan-fucking-tastic. How had I forgotten that little gem? And having the I-think-we-should-talk talk before we even started dating seemed unfair. Shouldn't I at least have the memory of a date to soften the conversation to come?

I didn't open my eyes or move until I heard the door close behind Gage and I knew I was alone. Then I forced myself to crawl out of bed. It didn't take nearly long enough to make myself presentable. Even stripping my bed and putting on fresh sheets didn't waste enough time. Gage was leaning against the wall across the hall from my room when I finally opened the door. I froze in the doorway.

I'd known he'd be waiting for me; I just didn't expect him to be waiting right there in the hallway. A strange sense of déjà vu swept over me. It was just like the day before, when I'd seen him in this same hallway and assumed he was something my brain had dreamed up. My gaze flitted to the console table, then back to Gage. His lips twitched, like he knew what I was thinking. As I scrambled to close the door on my atrocious paintings, Gage cleared his throat.

"I would like to talk to you about your work." He motioned toward my room.

"Nope," I said, popping the 'p.' I checked that my room was locked. "Thanks for bringing me home. I'm okay. You can go now."

"Jake."

Hearing his rumbly deep voice say my name made me shiver in the best of ways. I'd have thought my acute embarrassment would have slain any lingering hopes of sexy times with the guy. Apparently, my cock hadn't gotten the message.

"Gage." I said his name in the same tone he'd used, as I walked past the guy.

A huff of irritation followed me down the hallway. He trailed after me all the way through the inn. I opened the locks on the front door and then retreated to the dining hall and kitchen. People would arrive soon for the potluck, so I should check if anything needed to be moved or cleaned or fixed before they arrived. Sure, I'd already done this same routine this morning after I'd cleaned the pub, but that was irrelevant. Gage leaned against the stainless-steel counter in the kitchen and watched me putter around the room.

My heart pounded as I realized this was the perfect opportunity to talk to him—not about my paintings, but about other stuff. Sexy stuff. We were alone. No one would arrive for the potluck for a bit. And my body's excitement at being close to Gage was back. I couldn't believe I was aroused. Again.

"You know," I said, as I wiped the center island in the kitchen for the second time, "I was thinking of asking you for coffee."

Hey, look at me rocking my ostrich routine! Excellent. Go me. If I ignored everything else that had happened, maybe he would too. Fingers crossed.

Gage grinned. "Is this you asking me now?"

My cheeks were blazing hot. "And if I was?"

Then he straightened and closed the distance between us. I glanced up at him. Man, he was tall. Even without the horns.

And then when you added in the horns...

I stared at them for a long moment before forcing my eyes back to his face. He was staring at me intently. I really wanted to kiss him again, but it sort of felt like it'd be for the first time, since I hadn't known the first time was real. He wouldn't have come this close if he wasn't still interested, right? I licked my lips.

I tried jumping up on the counter so my mouth would at least be at the same height as his. Seeing what I was trying to do, Gage wrapped his hands around my waist and lifted me like I weighed nothing at all.

His face was closer to mine now. Yes, it was so much better this way. I opened my legs and without any hesitation he stepped between them, just like he had yesterday. Oh. My dick liked that. I was hard, harder than I'd ever been before. And it was all because of this man.

Then we leaned toward one another until the heat of our breath mingled between us.

"Jake?"

"Kiss me," I whispered. I'd said the same thing to him in the hallway yesterday, but this time my heart was pounding and every nerve in my body felt coiled and ready to jump at the slightest touch.

And then his mouth met mine.

I forgot all about how embarrassing today had been, how I'd puked on him, and how he'd seen my crazy paintings. But I didn't forget about how he'd helped me, how he'd stayed with me while I slept, or how he hadn't run away yet. Everything about this man called to me. I wanted to know everything about him.

I wanted to pretend I wasn't going crazy—just for a little while. Pretend I could be normal and have a normal relationship and a normal everything else too.

His hands were hot and heavy against my hips as he slid me forward until my body was pressed right up against his. I wrapped my arms around his neck, needing to feel him even closer. My fingers slipped into his silky hair. I loved the way his lips moved against mine like they were teasing me. His tongue was like a cautious explorer. The sensation of that warm and wet intrusion made me groan. I opened my mouth wider, inviting him in deeper. I hadn't been sure about having a tongue in my mouth before, but *fuuuuck*…

I arched my back, needing to feel more of him pressed against my body. My legs wrapped around his hips. His erection was a tantalizing hardness against my own. I wanted to feel it, wrap my hand around it. I'd had a lot of recent practice pleasuring my own dick. Could I do that for him too? I wanted to. I wanted that and more. My fingers clenched in his hair, holding him close.

"Yes," I murmured against his lips when his hips rocked against me. I scrambled to adjust my position, needing more pressure. I didn't want any space between us. My hand slid along his silky hair…

My fingers collided with something hard. I froze. What the fuck was that?

I gasped and pulled my hands away. I leaned back on the counter and stared at the top of Gage's head... at his horns, specifically. My hallucinations should not be tangible. Maybe there was an easy explanation.

"Do you have implants?"

"No."

Gage eyed me with interest. His lips were wet from my kisses, and I wanted to dive right back into exploring his mouth, but something was terribly wrong with me. I shouldn't get involved with anyone when I was not well.

"You can see my horns, can't you? Did you feel them too, just now?" Gage asked, apropos of nothing.

I sucked in a sharp breath at his questions. Spit caught in my throat, and I sputtered through a cough. "What?"

"My horns," Gage said as he reached up and stroked his hand over one of the long, dark horns that curled back over his head.

Please let this be a dream.

"I don't know what you are talking about." My eye twitched and I struggled not to look at Gage's hand... or his horns. I pushed him away and jumped off the counter. I grabbed the rag I'd been using a minute ago and wiped it over the place where I'd been sitting.

What had I been thinking? People prepped food on this counter. I shouldn't have put my ass on it.

"Next you're going to say that there were tentacles coming out of one of the apartment buildings today."

Gage studied me. When he spoke, his voice was soft.

"Jake, did you see tentacles coming out of a building today."

I tossed the rag toward the sink and spun to face the man. I crossed my arms and scowled at him. "You're crazy. Do you hallucinate? You should see someone about that."

"Is that what you think they are? Hallucinations?" Gage rubbed his chin. "That explains a lot."

"I think you should leave." I pointed at the door. Sweat slipped down the back of my neck. Had I imagined this whole interaction? Fuck. After watching Gage in the pub yesterday, I'd been so sure he was real, but that didn't explain those horns. Did that mean it was *all* an illusion? Had *everything* yesterday and today been one gigantic dream? Because when my hallucinations started justifying themselves, that was a problem, right?

Shit.

"I realize this must be frightening, but you aren't seeing imaginary things," Gage said gently.

He shifted like he was going to move toward me or reach for me or something. I took a step back and shook my head.

"What you are seeing is real," he continued. "The two horns on my head. Those are real. The calico cat who speaks English. He's real. The tentacles sticking out of that building today? I suspect those were real too."

I didn't say anything, and I could barely see through the spots dancing in front of my eyes. At least *those* weren't a sign from my broken brain. No, those spots were because I was hyperventilating.

At least I wasn't puking.

"Hush, now," Gage murmured. This time I didn't retreat when he approached. "Can I touch you?"

When I didn't say no, he rubbed my arm but didn't pull me into a hug. I wasn't sure if I should be disappointed or not, but I kind of was. Even if he was the one who was freaking me out, I wanted to be comforted by him.

"I've got you," he soothed. "You're going to be fine."

I snorted. I was *so* not fine.

"You should have been able to see those things all your life, but the reason you couldn't is because your senses were blocked."

"Right," I scoffed. "Because everyone has a talking cat and knows people with horns."

"Most humans can't see magic unless they are exposed to it, but you aren't like most humans."

"Then what am I? An alien?"

"Most of the people in your pub last night are supernatural. And those ladies you were painting with today? They are too. And so are you."

I blinked. Gage sounded so sincere.

"I don't believe you." My blood rushed so hard and fast through my veins I felt my pulse in my throat and heard the blood thundering in my ears.

Gage slowly dipped his head down, tilting those horns toward me. "Touch my head, Jake. My horns are real. They aren't a figment of your imagination."

"Unless your entire body is," I muttered, but I still couldn't resist reaching for Gage's head. My fingers collided with a very solid, very real horn. The satin-like texture over the hard length of it surprised me as my fingers danced over the surface.

"I'm real, Jake." He looked me straight in the eyes. Standing so close, touching his head, suddenly felt too intimate. Even more intimate than waking up to find Gage in my room.

I swallowed and jerked my hand away. "I don't understand."

"Supernatural beings have always existed alongside humans. The Eternal Magic, or what some call Mother Magic, hides us with a natural glamour to protect us. Whenever too many mundanes realize we exist, they tend to come after us with weapons. We must be careful about who we share our secrets with, or it could hurt us all."

"You're saying I shouldn't be able to see you. So why can I?"

"When someone—a human—sees under the glamour, then they can see everything."

I hugged my stomach. "What does that mean?"

"Like if you saw a werewolf shift from their human form to their wolf one."

"So I can see all you magical people because someone made a mistake."

Gage grimaced. "Not exactly."

"You aren't making any sense."

I rubbed my forehead. The same place Old Thom had hit me with the bottle cap last night. I didn't think I'd been hit that hard, but it was starting to ache again. Gage gently pulled my hand from my forehead and brushed his thumb over the spot. Just like last night.

A strange pulse of... *something*... throbbed through the air. Was that something supernatural? Was it coming from Gage?

"Oh, I see," he muttered, more to himself than to me.

Then there was a tugging sensation in my head. Red filled Gage's eyes as the oppressive feeling intensified. What was he doing? Cursing me? If magic was real, curses had to be too, right? I tried to pull my head back, but whatever he was doing to me held me in place like an invisible chain was linking something in my head to his fingers. Gage fisted his hand, then yanked it back. My head snapped forward.

"Yes, I've almost got it," Gage said. I swore he hissed when he spoke, as his tongue—oh, wow, was his tongue actually forked again?—curled over the words. He put his hand up against my forehead again, made another fist like he'd grabbed hold of something, even though I couldn't see anything in his grasp, and then jerked his hand away fast.

I cried out as my body jolted. Something shattered. Nothing I could see or hear, but there was an intangible *something* there one minute and gone the next.

"What the fuck?" I stumbled back.

"It's gone." Gage extended his hand, and smoke curled up from his palm like he was holding a burning piece of paper. Except nothing was there.

"Was that some kind of parlor trick? What's next? Pulling a rabbit out of your horn?"

Gage lifted his eyebrow, then barked out a laugh.

"Right. I'm hilarious," I muttered.

I brushed my fingers over my forehead again, surprised at how good I felt. Whatever Gage had done, it'd eased my headache. My head was clearer than it had been in a long time. I pushed my fingers into the spot where my headache had been throbbing just a moment earlier. "What did you do? I bet you'd make a good living on a miracle cure tour."

"You were cursed. Not very well, mind you, but still cursed," Gage said. "I didn't recognize it immediately because it's old and starting to deteriorate. Whoever did this was an amateur and didn't know how to weave a proper curse, which is good for you. If a more skilled practitioner had cursed you, it would have taken a lot more time and effort to remove it, possibly even a coven of mages."

"There is a *proper* curse?" I asked as I slid down the wall until I was sitting on the floor.

A little smile tugged at Gage's mouth at my question. "Perhaps well-executed would be a better description."

I stared straight ahead as I mulled over what else he'd said. "So curses are real. Someone put a spell on me. That's messed up. Who would have done something like that?"

"Spells are different from curses," he explained. "The curse might have something to do with stifling your oracle abilities. I'm guessing as the curse degraded, more of your natural gifts pushed through."

"I'm not an oracle." I scrambled to remember what that was. I really should have taken that Ancient Art History class in art school. "I don't even know what that is."

"Right. I guess we haven't talked about that yet." Gage sighed and crouched down in front of me. "An oracle is someone who passes along messages from the Eternal Magic. They are visions of the future. Prophecies."

"Yeah, I'm definitely not that," I argued.

"Those black-and-white paintings in your room tell a different story."

Well hell, didn't he just have an answer for everything.

"If I'm an oracle, what are you?"

"I'm a demon."

"Like Lucifer and God and the bible and everything?" I cringed. I didn't know much about any of those things, just what I'd learned in my art history classes. My mother had been adamant nothing like that would ever be discussed in our house. Since I was home schooled after I turned seven, I didn't have the opportunity to find out much until I was an adult. I'd always just thought demons and angels were symbolic.

Apparently I was wrong.

Gage rolled his eyes. "No. Humans have perverted and warped the history of demons and angels both. Just like they have with every other supernatural being. Think of it like playing Telephone. Occasionally, a tiny bit of the truth survives, but most of the message is nothing like how it started. We were once universally known as daemons and considered neither inherently good nor inherently evil. Later, our name modified slightly to *demon* and became associated with evil." He shrugged, like it didn't bother him one way or the other.

"Okay," I said slowly as I mulled over what he said. It made sense. And, weirder yet, I believed him.

My brain had stumbled over the whole demon thing—helpfully supplying images of medieval art where a gigantic devil was stuffing his mouth full of bleeding and mangled people—but my heart and my gut said Gage was trustworthy. And if my oracle alter-ego had painted all those images of him, that had to mean something too, right? Like if he wasn't trustworthy, those pictures wouldn't make him so appealing. I'd never created an image of him I found disturbing or grotesque. Of course, that meant accepting the oracle thing was true... well, and that supernatural creatures existed too.

"It is a lot to take in, but you being an oracle is important," Gage said. "Those paintings you didn't want me to see? Those are messages. Visions of the future."

I frowned down at my hands. "I'm just an ordinary person. I'm not an oracle. Believe me. You've made a mistake."

"Those paintings don't lie. Didn't you wonder what they were? Why you were painting them?"

"Of course," I retorted. "They're... Those paintings are horrible. Awful. Some kind of strange manifestation of my... my..." I wiped at my damp eyes.

"Your what?" Gage asked gently.

"I'm losing my mind. It's all part of it." I whispered.

"You really aren't. Someone should have talked to you about this as soon as they realized what was going on." He sounded angry as he clenched his hands into fists. "Instead, they let you flounder in your confusion. Fucking assholes."

"Who should have? What are you talking about?"

"You are magic. Just like me. Just like the succubus who sat at your bar last night. Just like the alpha who runs the mechanic's shop. Just like your Chief of Police."

My eyes bulged. "All of them are... Everyone is..."

"Supernatural. Yes."

"Oh..."

"And you're supernatural too." Gage looked me straight in the eye as he spoke.

"Have you seen those paintings? They are awful. There is no way those are messages." But even as I said it, I wondered if I was wrong. I remembered the déjà vu I'd felt when Alice told me she had a date with Buddy. I remembered the relief I'd felt when I'd been able to paint over the painting the other night of the headlights going down the road, right after I'd seen the exact same thing from my window. And all those pictures of Gage and me…

Did that mean we would actually do those things together? Like all that sex?

Heat bloomed over my face.

"How can I be sure?" I whispered.

"I know they feel personal and private to you, but those messages need to be shared, for your safety and the safety of the people you know. I think talking to people about your visions will also help you."

"What do you mean? They're just weird paintings of weird things."

Gage sat down beside me. Our arms rubbed. I had the urge to rest my head on his shoulder. Fuck it. Why not? If there was any time to accept that I didn't have my shit together and might need a little support, it was now. I leaned over and settled my head on him. He stilled for a moment but didn't shake me off. He wrapped his arm around my shoulders. I sighed and pressed in closer. It was nice to sit with him like this, despite all the crazy shit he was saying. For the first time since my grandfather's death, I didn't feel alone, and I didn't want this feeling to end.

"You might not remember this, but I was told that just

before the robbery you drew one of your pictures. That's how Van and the others knew Dillon was being chased through the woods."

I froze. I knew what night he was talking about. I'd been working behind the bar like normal, and then I lost time. I came to just in time to run to the bathroom and puke. I'd been sure I'd had one of my painting episodes, but when I returned to the bar, I hadn't seen a drawing. No one said anything. No one acted weird, or at least not any weirder than normal. Alice sent me upstairs and told me to get some rest. Even though I felt like shit, I was so fucking happy about having a stomach flu. Oh, the lies I told myself.

Shit. That meant everyone in Willow Lake knew my secret.

Did that mean I wasn't crazy?

I didn't even know anymore.

"He was being chased?"

"Van said if Ash hadn't found him, he might never have come out of those woods alive."

"Like someone was trying to murder him?" I couldn't believe it. A murderer? Here? The people in Willow Lake were quirky, not evil. "Why hasn't anyone talked about that? Is the would-be murderer behind bars? Who was it? I hope it wasn't one of my regulars."

"What I'm trying to say is that it's possible your other paintings are important like that too."

"You didn't answer my question," I pointed out.

Gage gently took my shaky hand in his warm one.

The connection felt good. It grounded me when everything else had sent my thoughts spinning like I was on a merry-go-round, and not one of those new safe ones either. No, my mind saw one of those old ones that hurled kids out in every direction once it got going.

"I just got here, remember," Gage said. "Some of these questions you'll have to bring up with Van or Hayden."

"They are supernatural too? Shit. I guess you said that already, didn't you? The mechanic and the Chief of Police..."

Gage nodded. "Like I said, most of your patrons are. Van is a hellhound and Hayden is a werewolf."

"So they turn into crazed animals during the full moon or something?" I vaguely remembered one of the other art students constantly drawing beasts under a moon in his sketch books. Had those been sketches based on real life? I never would have guessed.

"No. Not quite. Like with demons, human pop culture got a few things wrong." Gage laughed. "Most supes—"

"Supes?"

"That's just a short name for supernatural beings," Gage explained. "Most supes have the ability to change their bodies in some way. With Hayden, as a werewolf, he can transition into a wolf-like creature. He still retains his thoughts and his ability to speak, but some of his senses become sharper and he is stronger."

"Do you have a different form?" I thought I already knew the answer to this, just based on the paintings I'd done of him, but I wanted to know for sure.

"Yes. My skin and eyes become red, my body grows both taller and bulkier, and I have wings—"

"Can you fly?"

"Yes, but I haven't for many years. It is too risky. Too

many humans might see. And, like I said, once a human sees under the magical glamour we are born with, then they see everything."

"That'd suck. To be able to fly, but you can't because humans are idiots," I said. "So... that glamour thing you talked about... that hides your horns?"

He nodded.

"Can I see you? Like demon you?" I widened my eyes. "I mean, is that intrusive? Too personal? I didn't mean to pry."

Gage just grinned. "I'm glad you wish to see my shifted form, but perhaps not today."

"Yeah. Okay," I said. "So what does a demon do? Besides fly. Like, do you have other powers or something?"

"Yes, I suppose I do. Adrian's little almost-human has asked this same question many times. He is a strange creature." Gage paused, as if unsure how to begin.

"If you don't want to say, that's fine." I thought about asking about Jeremy being almost-human—because what did that mean?—but I was more curious about Gage.

"Ask me your questions."

"I don't even know where to begin. My mother hated anything to do with magic... Huh. She must have known about all this, hey?"

"I expect so," Gage said carefully.

"I don't know what to ask. What are some of the myths about demons?"

"The most common one is that we try to steal people's souls."

"And do you?"

Gage shook his head. "I make deals. It's the only way to use my powers to help others without depleting my own magic. Magic is all about balance. Every time someone uses magic, there is a cost. It's like when you have your visions. Right now you suffer because there is no balance. I'm hoping we can correct that. But, no, I don't collect souls. That's just a lie humans tell."

Okay then. "And your friends? What are they?"

"Adrian is a wolf shifter, Isaac is a centaur, and Nelson is a shadow jumper."

"Centaur. That's a creature who is part horse and part man, right? Is that why his laugh sounds like a neigh?"

Gage snorted. "Best not to say that to him. He may not look it, but he can be a bit sensitive."

"Wait... Did he run by here the other night?"

"He did," Gage said with a nod. "The first night we arrived."

If that had really happened, what else had I seen and tried to dismiss? I thought back over all the bizarre things I'd seen or heard over the last year. There were a lot of them. I suspected magic had a lot to do with it. "Are you sure I'm not dreaming this whole conversation?"

"I'm sure," Gage said, taking my hand in his and rubbing gentle circles over my palm. "But that's enough for now."

"I get the sense there is more you want to tell me," I said.

"There is, but it can wait. I don't want to overwhelm you with everything all at once."

Ha! Great. That didn't sound ominous at all.

Chapter Nineteen

JAKE

I couldn't help but stare at people as they arrived for the potluck.

It was amazing how Henrietta Jenning's body seemed to undulate under her dress as the tip of a tentacle peeked out from under her hem before disappearing again. Then there was the way Van's eyes flickered like fire. And those weird lines on Weston's neck, were those gills?

I'd seen all of that before, obviously, but now I allowed myself the freedom to stare at those quirky things and acknowledge they weren't created by my imagination. I wasn't going crazy. It was a heady experience.

And everyone else was watching me just as closely.

I found it equally strange how many people arrived with a gift for Gage. They'd shuffle up to him with their heads bowed and hold up a gift basket or an expensive bottle of whiskey or some other generic but attractive gift. When he accepted them, they flashed a relieved smile, then scurried off to their friends again. Then he'd carefully carry it into the foyer where he set it behind the registration desk with other similar gifts. He was getting quite the collection.

Jeremy, wearing an infectiously friendly smile, was tugging his boyfriend over to where I was standing with Gage.

"Thanks again for the help last night," I said, trying to casually study Jeremy and Adrian for signs of their magic.

"Happy to help," Jeremy said to me, then he turned to Gage. "Did I just see someone offer you a present, Mr. Dimples?"

Gage's eye twitched at the nickname, but he didn't complain. "Yes."

"Why? Oh my God, is it your birthday? How did they know when I didn't?" He turned to his boyfriend. The light coming in through the dining room windows vividly showed the strange tattoo Jeremy had at his temple and the colorful patch of hair beside it. His boyfriend had the same markings. My grandfather had had a colorful lock of hair in nearly the same place. And come to think of it, other Willow Lake couples wore matching marks too. Was it a supernatural thing? Were they significant? "Adrian, you're supposed to tell me shit like that." He elbowed his boyfriend before turning to Gage. "So, how many candles should I put on the cake? A hundred? Five hundred?" Then he covered his mouth and eyed me, like he'd said something he shouldn't.

"He knows," Gage whispered very quietly to Jeremy.

Jeremy let out a relieved sigh. "Thank God. Paws would skin me alive if I'd been the one to spill the beans."

Then he turned to me. His eyes were gleaming, and he had a wide, excited smile on his face. "We have so much to talk about. So many questions to ask you. Like, how do you feel about snakes? In Delphi—"

"And it isn't my birthday," Gage interrupted Jeremy, drawing his attention off me.

But now that the question had been raised, I was curious too. And I really didn't want to be interrogated by Jeremy. So, just how old was he? People couldn't live to five hundred, could they? Yesterday I would have thought the answer to that question was obvious. Today I wasn't so sure.

"How old are you?" I asked.

Jeremy's face lit up with excitement. He leaned close.

"Older than you," was Gage's only answer.

"Hmm…" Jeremy tapped his lip. "Were you around during the construction of those massive abbeys in medieval times? With your wings, I bet you'd have been popular when they had to do stuff up three hundred feet in the air."

"Did you really just ask me if humans hired a demon to build a cathedral?"

"Well, when you put it like that…" Jeremy muttered.

"I've never worked in construction," Gage said, as if that might still need to be clarified. He looked like he was regretting drawing Jeremy's attention.

"Fine. Don't tell me." Jeremy frowned at Gage. "You know… I've always wondered if you have a secret demon name like in the paranormal books I read. If I figure it out, will you be at my mercy? Could I command you to answer my questions?"

Now it was Gage's turn to frown at Jeremy. "What do you think?"

"Why does pop culture get everything wrong?" Jeremy muttered to himself as he pulled a small notebook from his back pocket and a pen from behind his ear. He flipped open his book to a blank page and looked expectantly at Gage. "So… what's up with all the gifts then? Oh, oh, oh… are you guys mated? Are these like wedding presents?" Jeremy eyed us with undisguised curiosity. "Do you have mating marks hidden somewhere?"

"Mating marks?" I asked.

"Yes." Jeremy grinned as he stroked his hand over the strange tattoo and stripe of pastel green hair by his temple. "When two supes love each other very much, the Eternal Magic whacks them with the magical mating stick. And then they get awesome things like matching tattoos and a long life together."

There were a lot of things I didn't understand about what he just said. I looked at Gage for help. He sighed.

"I hadn't planned to talk to you about that yet. You already have enough to think about."

When I stared at him, waiting for an explanation, he just nodded.

"Okay." He rubbed his forehead. "Here is the short version. Fated mates are two beings who are destined for one another. The Eternal Magic will eventually bind their life forces together. With Jeremy and Adrian, for example, Jeremy's life span was extended to match Adrian's much longer one and, providing nothing unforeseen interferes, their lives will be entwined until their natural deaths."

Had Jeremy been joking when he suggested Gage and I

could be that to one another? Because there was no way. Gage was… well, Gage. Sexy. Strong. Powerful. People probably flung themselves at him on the regular. Fate or the Eternal Magic or whatever you wanted to call her wouldn't saddle someone like him with someone like me. I was happy to be a temporary diversion for him, but the idea it could be more was laughable. I glanced back at Jeremy.

"Nope. Not mating gifts," I said with certainty.

"They are offerings," Adrian said. "Right, Gage?"

"Offerings? Like when people leave offerings at altars and stuff?" Jeremy's mouth dropped open. "Holy shit, Mr. Dimples, are you starting your own cult?"

"No." Gage's flat denial didn't deter Jeremy, who whistled to himself and scribbled something in his notebook.

"I really need to research this," Jeremy said when he finished. "How is the Wi-Fi here?"

"You can do that later," Adrian said.

"Fine," Jeremy muttered. "So what's the plan? I've never been to one of your potlucks before, but Ash and Dillon mentioned this was the place to be on a Sunday afternoon."

"No plan. Just food and eating and…" I shrugged.

Sally sidled up to us, having just placed her plate of fresh oysters on a tray of ice. She brought the same thing every week, and it was a bit of a running joke with the others since they were considered aphrodisiacs. I suspected the joke was connected to the nickname my grandfather had given her.

"Jake, honey," Sally said. "Is there something you need to say? Or ask? Or announce?"

I shook my head. "Nope."

"Oh, I just thought…." Sally's forehead wrinkled. She glanced at Gage, then back to me. "Are you sure?"

Gage leaned over until his lips were almost touching my ear. The warmth of his breath tickled my neck. I shivered at the delicious sensation.

"She's asking if you know you are an oracle and can see under the glamour," he said quietly.

My gaze snapped to Sally, then back to Gage. "She isn't…" I dropped my voice to a whisper. "Human?"

Gage shook his head. A pulse of something—a magical power maybe?—surged up around him as he glanced around the room. Then he met my gaze again. He gently took my hand in his. He brushed his thumb over my palm as if he was worried I was about to freak out and he wanted to soothe me.

"What?" I asked. "Just say it."

"No one here is."

"Is what?"

"Human," he said.

"No one?" My voice squeaked and was way louder than I intended. Were my eyes bulging? I was sure they were as I gawked at the people who'd taken me under their wing after my grandfather died. And now they were all looking in my direction.

The sensation of something—sure, let's call it magic—ratcheted up.

"Heya, Jake, it's okay," Jeremy said as he wrapped his arm around my shoulders. "It feels kind of awesome too, am I right? I bet you didn't think I was one too. But I am. I'm a newbie, but I'm super excited to be a part of the supe crew."

"Wow."

"Right? So cool. And can you feel that pressure or tingling or energy? It manifests in a lot of different ways, but that's magic."

It was one thing to hear Gage talk about magic; it was another thing altogether to hear Jeremy talk about it. Gage was big and powerful and horned. Of course he was super-natural. But Jeremy? Jeremy looked and acted like a regular, normal nosy guy.

"You look freaked out. Don't be. They're a friendly bunch." He squeezed my shoulder. "But, if it helps, just envision everyone's tummy glowing like a Care Bear as they unleash their power. Wait, do you know about Care Bears?"

"Like that cartoon on TV? My old roommate watched it when he was hungover." I surreptitiously glanced around again. "Was that show inspired by supernatural people? I don't see rainbow beams shooting through the room…"

Jeremy laughed like I'd told the best joke.

"Jeremy," Gage said, sounding like he was repri-manding the friendly guy. "Jake doesn't have to talk about this with anyone. It's his choice." Then he turned his atten-tion to me. "Although, if you are up for it, you might want to chat with Hayden and Van. I can go with you. But if you don't want to do it today, it can wait."

"I… uh…" I swallowed.

Gage had said my pictures might be important. If they were, I should show them to people, right? Because I had no idea what they meant. But after hiding them for so long, I felt queasy at the thought of letting people look at them.

What would they think of me?

Hayden stalked over to us. "What's going on?"

An eerie quiet stole over the room as everyone else seemed to lean in to listen to our conversation.

"Gage thinks I'm an oracle," I blurted.

Based on the gasps and squeals around us, I knew the whole room had heard. A bunch of people pulled out their phones. Their fingers tapped rapidly on their screens. They weren't texting about me, were they? The way people were eyeing me, though, I knew I was lying to myself. But why would anyone care about me?

Hayden narrowed his eyes in Gage's direction. Then his irises seemed to flash with some unnatural light. I gaped.

"That's just his wolf coming to the surface," Gage said in a bored tone. "Nothing to worry about."

"You told him?" Hayden's question came out like an accusation.

Gage shook his head. "He's been seeing under the glamour for a while now and decided he was going crazy. I thought having a conversation would help."

"We didn't think he'd have that kind of reaction. We should have thought of that." Hayden dragged his hand down his face. "Van, get your ass over here. Everyone else, Jake knows and has known for a while. So give the boy some room to breathe."

"When?" someone in the back of the crowd asked.

"Yeah. When did he first find out?"

"Was it at the painting class today? Someone said something happened."

"Ah, man, I had tomorrow," someone else complained.

"What are they talking about?" I asked.

Hayden's cheeks darkened and he glanced away. "Ah, there may have been a bet going."

"A bet?" The demon's power rumbled through those two short words.

"Knock it off," Van muttered. He scowled at Gage until the power surge ebbed away. When it was gone, Van nodded. "Yes, okay. The locals had a bet going about when Jake would realize his legacy. Answer the question, Jake, so the others will leave us alone. Then we should talk."

"What do they want to know?" I asked.

"When did you first see something supernatural?"

"I… uh… I don't really know." I rubbed my forehead. The spot where Old Thom had hit me with the bottle cap the day before was aching again. Why was my head bugging me now? I'd felt so good after Gage had removed the curse or whatever. But every time I tried to access memories, I hit barricades.

"Is your head bothering you still?" Gage asked. He pushed my fingers out of the way, replacing them with his own. A soft pulse of warmth blossomed under his touch. My eyes fluttered closed for a moment.

"That feels good." I hummed.

"Did you know he could do that?" Jeremy asked someone, probably Adrian. "I thought the only one on the team with healing mojo was Teague."

"I don't sense anything wrong," Gage said, ignoring Jeremy. "But some memory loss may be a symptom of the curse as it tried to hide magic from you. At this point, it is likely permanent, but we can consult with a coven."

I shook my head. I hated that I'd apparently lost some memories, but that didn't mean I wanted more people messing with my head. I tried to think about my first freaky experience. "I guess I saw a few things when I first got here, and then it seems like I saw more and more all the time. I just found out about what it all means today."

Someone in the back of the room groaned. "Shit. Now what do we do?"

"He found out about magic today. That's your answer." Yep. That was my grandfather's cat talking as he sat on the floor in front of me with his tail twitching back and forth.

"Shut up, Paws," someone shouted. "You're just saying that because today was your day."

Paws hissed and then started licking his calico fur.

"You've got your answer. Go on now," Van said, speaking in a way that oozed authority and a don't-piss-me-off attitude. "Jake? You ready for this?"

I nodded. "I guess you want to see my paintings, hey?"

"Can I come?" Jeremy asked.

"No," Van, Hayden, and Gage all said in unison.

"Fine. Sheesh," Jeremy muttered. Then his phone pinged, announcing a message. When he read it, he grimaced. "Shit. We need to go pick up Ash and Dillon. Their truck, the one we borrowed to look at trailers—" he shuddered when he said the word trailer like it inspired horror, "—it quit again."

"Do you need to borrow a car?" I asked, then realized mine wasn't there. It was still in one of the parking lots at Winslow Park. I'd have to retrieve it later.

"Thanks, but Hayden is lending us a beater until Adrian's truck is fixed." Then he caught my eye. "But we'll talk later, m'kay?"

After Adrian and Jeremy hurried out the door, Van motioned for me to take the lead and I realized Van, Hayden, and Gage were waiting for me. My heart beat faster and faster the closer we got to my room. By the time I opened the door, my breath was sawing in and out like I'd run a marathon. My hand shook as I waved them inside.

"Hold on," Gage said as he rushed to gather the pieces showing him alone or with me. He set them aside. "You don't need to see these."

"Shit," Hayden said when he saw how many paintings remained. He rubbed at his mouth. "This is more than I had guessed."

Van nodded. "Best way is probably just to start at one end and go through them one by one."

"It's… just the black-and-white ones," I managed to say. "The others are just mine. No… uh… messages from beyond or whatever."

"Makes sense." Van stood in front of one of the paintings and stared at it. Hayden followed him.

Gage went over to stand by the others.

They were staring at an image of two people at an outdoor market. The table in front of them was littered with various junk objects. Actually, those figures looked an awful lot like Jeremy and Adrian. They were lifting two boxes. Peeking out of one of the boxes was a weird little statue I was sure I'd seen in my grandfather's rooms at some point.

It'd been a while since I painted it, so I'd forgotten about it. Seeing it again, I was sure I could paint over it now, but Gage and the others were staring at it like it was important.

"That's Adrian and Jeremy," Gage said, confirming my suspicions.

I pointed at the statue in the box. "Do you see that? It looks like something my grandfather owned."

"The Jahaller?" Gage looked at me sharply.

"I don't know what you just said but if that's what it's called, then yeah."

"Did you talk to it?"

"No... I..." I shook my head and rubbed the toe of my shoe over a stain in the old blue carpet. "I think it might have said something. Maybe? Once? My grandfather's suite freaked me out, so I didn't go back in there. Is it a talking doll or something?"

Hayden made a whimpering sound.

Van's Adam's apple bobbed as he audibly swallowed.

"What? What did I say?"

"A Jahaller is a supernatural being. A living magical creature. But their kind can only survive on magic and interaction with magical beings. If he was isolated from magic and ignored, he would have starved." Gage grimaced. "Without magic, they slowly die and turn into statues."

I clutched at my throat as horror flooded me. "I killed someone?"

"It takes a long time," Van said quietly. "And Paws seems to think the ward on your grandfather's suite should have been enough to sustain it. But once it was stolen..."

I sank onto the edge of my bed. "That's why you were all so concerned about the robbery."

"We found him. That's what's important," Van said.

"Is he okay?" I held my breath as I waited for an answer.

"He will be."

"Are there more creatures like that?" I whispered.

"Probably not," Van said. "But we can't know for sure. Your grandfather owned a lot of magical artifacts. Well, I guess everything is yours now. Some of them are quite powerful. The magic in most will be inert until activated through ritual, but whatever was stolen, we want to get them back. No one wants any of those things falling into the wrong hands."

"You mean like someone who isn't a supe?" I asked.

"Yes," Van agreed. "Or a criminal, or even just someone with bad intentions."

"Looks like his visions are fairly accurate and realistic," Hayden said to Gage. "When we first realized he was an oracle, I feared we wouldn't understand the messages he was giving us."

"Where is the one he painted today?" Van asked.

Gage pointed to a painting by the bed. We all turned to look at it.

I hadn't seen what I painted today. By the time I got myself under control, Gage had already brought me back to the inn. And when I'd woken earlier, I had other things on my mind—namely Gage. My stomach twisted as I eyed the picture. It showed a shadowy scene of people in cages. Stacks and stacks of cages.

"Shit," Van muttered. "There are more of them."

"Yeah…" Gage agreed. "It isn't good. There aren't enough details to pinpoint a location and none of the bastards running the place are shown."

"Are you sure this is from today?" Hayden asked.

"I saw him paint it."

"Could it be a scene from the past?"

Gage shook his head. "I don't recognize any of those people."

"Fuck." Hayden pushed his hands through his hair.

"What do you mean? You've seen something like that before?" I asked.

Gage grimaced. "Yes. When we found the person who was trying to sell your stolen artifacts, we discovered she had a warehouse full of imprisoned supes. We freed them, but we suspected her warehouse was part of a larger trafficking ring." He motioned toward the painting. "It looks like we were right."

No one spoke for several long minutes, then they moved on to the next. I staggered to my bed and sat on it. I wrapped my arms around my stomach and hunched down as they discussed each painting. If I'd talked to someone, like my grandfather when he was still alive, or even Sally or Alice, I would have known about this long before now.

"Hey." Gage sat on the bed beside me. "It's going to be okay."

How could he be so relaxed and understanding about this? How much harm had I done by trying to pretend my black-and-white loving alter-ego didn't exist?

My phone pinged, announcing I had a message. The only messages I ever received were from Alice asking about her shifts. I just didn't have friends who texted… or any friends at all, really. It was probably spam.

I sighed as I pulled my phone out and unlocked the screen. It was from someone called *SuperAmazingWord-Wizard*. Who on earth was in my contact list under that name? Unless that's what Jeremy called himself when he put his details in my phone.

> SuperAmazingWordWizard: Jake is part of the Supe Crew now. *clapping emoji*
>
> FireFingers: Damn it. *frowny face* We're missing everything. Are you on your way? And who else have you included? I don't recognize the number.
>
> Me: Uh… this is Jake. Who is FireFingers?
>
> SuperAmazingWordWizard: *laughing emoji* That's Ash.
>
> FireFingers: Really, Jeremy? FireFingers?
>
> SuperAmazingWordWizard: It's better than half-pint, isn't it? Or lil' bit?
>
> SuperAmazingWordWizard: And, yes, we're almost at your place, but I wanted to ask you a question before I forget. So I thought I'd better text. What do you think about Leif as a possible name for my naked Viking werewolf? Is it too close to leaf or leaves? I mean, he's a werewolf, right? So he's not a vegetarian. And his parents weren't hippies. He doesn't have any siblings called Stream or

Pebble. Or is the Scandinavian pronun-
ciation of Leif nothing like leaf?

FireFingers: Did you ask Jake if he wanted
to answer all your crazy questions?

SuperAmazingWordWizard: Rude. We
bonded the other night over slinging
drinks. There is no escape now.

Me: It's okay.

SuperAmazingWordWizard: Hey, speaking
of my inner circle... Does anyone have
Simon's contact info? I think we should
invite him into this loop too.

FireFingers: Simon? The guy who always
runs away and hides? I mean, he seems
nice enough, but don't you think you
should get to know him before you
throw him into a group chat?

SuperAmazingWordWizard: We're
awesome. He'd be happy to be
included.

FireFingers: I don't have his info.

Me: I don't either.

SuperAmazingWordWizard: I'll find out.

And then the messages just stopped. Neither Ash nor I
had answered his question about Leif as a name for his
werewolf character. I wasn't sure if he even wanted our
opinion, or if he just liked dumping out all the thoughts in
his head.

I read the messages again.

My mother hadn't allowed me to have a phone when I

was growing up, and as an adult, I pretty much kept to myself, so I'd never had friends who texted before. Was this normal? I doubted it. I got the sense Jeremy had suddenly decided to make it his mission to adopt all the strays in Willow Lake. Ash wasn't a stray, but he hadn't really fit in with the other locals either, not until Dillon showed up.

Should I respond again? Let Jeremy know I could ask Simon's mother for his contact info. Daphne was in my painting group, so I had her number. Except if I asked her for her son's number, she'd probably think I was going to ask him on a date. So, nope. That didn't sound like a good idea. Jeremy could get Simon's number on his own. They'd probably be here for the potluck later anyway. Daphne loved to bring fish casserole experiments. They were inevitably always beige and lumpy and rather unappetizing.

"Is everything okay?" Gage asked.

Then I remembered everything that'd been happening before the texts came in. With Gage at my side and after receiving those weird messages from Jeremy, things didn't seem as bleak as they had a few minutes ago.

I wasn't losing my mind. Van and the others would use my paintings to help people. I might be on my way to having friends. And a sexy man had kissed me. Things were looking up.

"Yeah." I nodded. "I think I'll be okay."

I hoped I hadn't just jinxed myself.

Chapter Twenty

GAGE

The dining room was a cacophony of loud conversations, laughter, and music when we returned to it. We'd just finished a cursory review of all the paintings, but I knew we'd have to go through them again. Van had texted his team at the police department to move forward with a few lines of inquiry, while I had sent off similar updates to my contacts at the Supernatural Council and my own team.

People swarmed Jake, offering hugs and advice. A few even asked for a reading, as if someone who hadn't known about his magic until a few hours ago would have suddenly mastered it. I hated stupid people. My scowls were enough to have most of them rethinking their requests, often eliciting spluttering apologies, but a few misguided individuals were persistent.

Jake turned them away with blushes and shy smiles, explaining he couldn't do that. But I suspected, without the curse impeding his magic, he'd get more proficient soon.

All he needed was confidence and practice. He stammered when he talked to people about his abilities, and I suspected he didn't really trust what was going on yet. The poor guy looked like he wanted to run back upstairs and hide in his room.

Luckily, some of the ladies from Jake's painting group had taken over getting the potluck organized while we were upstairs, so it wasn't long before everyone was encouraged to dish up their plates. Nothing was better at distracting a group of supes than food.

Long rectangular tables along the wall by the kitchen were laden with all kinds of dishes. Supes ate a lot, but I didn't think anyone would go hungry today, even if they were acting like they hadn't eaten in days. It was chaos.

Almost as chaotic was the surplus magic tingling through my blood. With each gift I received from the locals, my magic sang just a little louder. All this goodwill was unbalancing my magic, but… in a good way? Each present was like an open negotiation. The details hadn't been finalized yet, but the deal had almost been completed. I'd received payment for something I hadn't done yet.

Part of me felt off-kilter at all these unfinished deals, but my magic felt… joyful. That was the only word that came to mind.

"Where are the extra napkins?" a woman shouted from the kitchen.

"I'll go grab some," Jake called back to her, then he turned to me and patted me on the chest. Around us, a few of the ladies tittered at the display of affection and I suspected there would be a new bet about our relationship starting up soon. "I'll be right back, but you should get some food while you can. It goes fast."

Jake darted into the kitchen to retrieve more napkins while I grabbed two plates, one for him and one for me, and got in line. I felt absurdly pleased at the idea of providing food for him, even if it was just dishing up from a buffet. Balancing a handful of utensils and the two plates, I found it unexpectedly tricky to add everything I wanted to our plates. Ahead of me, a young woman was managing to do the same thing with three plates, presumably for her kids who were circling around her legs and scurrying in and out from under the table. It was impressive. I was also surprised to see a supe with so many children. That was a rarity.

"Help the nice demon, Simon," a woman commanded from ahead of me. I recognized her from the group of ladies who'd been painting with Jake earlier.

The dark-haired man in front of me stiffened.

"Go on. I raised you to be a good boy, didn't I?" The woman glared at the man, who was presumably her son, and motioned toward me.

The man, Simon, pivoted to face me. He swallowed audibly when he saw who he'd been tasked with helping. His one hand moved immediately to grasp at something in his hoodie pocket like he was worried I'd pickpocket him.

"Uh… Help?" he asked, almost like he was asking for help, rather than offering it.

If I was staying in Willow Lake, I supposed it made sense to get to know the locals. This was a start. I eyed the young man. He was probably around the same age as Jake.

He cowered under my gaze. His eyes took on a very feline appearance and the tips of his ears tufted up like a cat's.

"Can you scoop some of that onto my plate?" I nodded toward a lumpy creamy casserole.

Simon gulped and looked at the casserole I'd indicated. His nose wiggled as he smelled the dish. Then he glanced quickly at his mother, before looking at me. He gulped again, like he needed to gather the courage to talk. Then he subtly shook his head and squished up his face.

"Maybe this one instead?" He pointed to a different casserole.

I shrugged my indifference.

Simon had just dropped a spoonful of mystery casserole, with a very shaky hand, onto one of the plates when my phone pinged. With no space on the buffet table to set down the plates, I tried to balance them in one hand while I fished my phone from my pocket with the other. That was even trickier than dishing up our plates.

I didn't need to swipe into my phone to see the start of the message.

Nelson: Get to the inn. Tell…

The ominous sounding message was cut off. Nelson never sent unnecessary texts. Something must be going on. I stepped away from the table and set the plates down on the nearest bare surface and opened my messages to read the rest.

Nelson: Get to the inn. Tell the hellhound.
Something is happening.

Fuck. I scanned the room for threats. No one was acting sketchy. I didn't sense anything suspicious. I flagged Van over as I replied to Nelson.

Me: Already here. What's going on?

The pause stretched longer than I liked. Was he back with Isaac now? Was he safe?

"What?" Van demanded when he reached me. He'd abandoned his own plate of food along the way. He looked every bit the police officer who knew he'd need to spring into action.

"I don't know," I said and showed the hellhound my message from Nelson.

Fire danced in Van's eyes when he finished reading it. His fiery gaze slid over everyone, looking for threats. The faint scent of smoke curled through the air around him as his hellhound's fire surged through him.

"Where is he?" Van nodded to the phone.

"Out at the pack lands. Doing some recce."

When the phone pinged with a message, we read the screen.

Nelson: Bombs.

Fuck.

Van ran to the fire alarm and pulled it. The warning siren shrieked over the laughter and chatter. The sickening scent of fear exploded through the room.

"Everyone out." My voice burst out of me. I pushed my demon form to the surface and pushed power into my words until they became a command no one would ignore. "Get out! Now!"

Around us, shifters of all shapes and sizes shimmered as they took on their animal forms. Generally, our non-human form was the strongest and most able to withstand an attack, so I understood why they shifted. Simon, who'd been in the buffet line with me, shrank down into a house cat. His tail was puffed up like a feather duster as he bolted away, leaving behind only the acrid smell of his fear.

The woman with the three kids had dropped her plates. Broken glass and food splattered across the floor. She had the wrists of two children gripped in her hand and was reaching under the table for her third.

Where the fuck was Jake? I scanned the room. He wasn't there. Fuck. Was he still in the kitchen? My heart pounded in my chest like it was trying to break free. My demonic magic surged through me, but I needed to find Jake before I unleashed it.

"Jake!"

People ran, pushing at one another, knocking over anyone who was smaller in their rush for the French doors at the back of the room. The woman with the kids ran deeper into the building, ushered that way by some of the other locals, and I hoped they were going to the front door. But what if they panicked and got confused? It was a straight run to the door, but people didn't always act rationally when they were scared.

Under other circumstances, I would have gone after them, but not now. I had to trust the locals would get the woman and her children to safety. They knew this place better than I did. They would be fine.

But Jake still hadn't returned.

Where was he?

I had to find him. I had to get him out. The little oracle could *not* be injured. I wouldn't allow it. I pushed through the panicked people toward the kitchen.

"Where is the fire?" Jake rushed out of the kitchen brandishing a fire extinguisher.

I didn't have time to explain. I yanked the extinguisher from his hands, grabbed him, and threw him over my shoulder, holding his legs tight to my chest. Jake twisted and struggled in my arms. I ignored him and ran for the closest set of French doors.

"Stop. We've got to—" he shouted.

Boom!

Anything he was going to say was blown away by the force of the explosion. The wall of windows covering the full length of the dining room shattered. Glass flew at us like shrapnel. Jake cried out. I dropped low to shield us behind the tables, but it was too late. My body was already cut and battered, which meant Jake was injured too.

Fuck.

My demon energy, ignited by fear and anger, whooshed through me like a burning match thrown into a puddle of gasoline. All the energy from those presents, which my magic had identified as unfinished negotiations, snapped into place and I threw out a portal the size of the room—I'd never created anything so large. The force of my magic shoved whoever was still in the room into the portal and dumped us on the other side of the road by the lake. I hadn't even thought about the destination, but my magic had sorted it for me. With a portal that size, I couldn't carry too many people too far, and this location was better than other places it could have chosen.

As soon as we were all clear, the portal snapped closed on a pop.

I staggered, weak after expending so much magic. Any surplus energy I'd felt earlier was gone. All those open negotiations were now closed and sealed. But Jake wasn't safe yet. I couldn't stop now.

I cast my gaze over the group I'd scooped up as I searched for a place on the shoreline where I could set Jake down. I didn't want his wounds to become any more contaminated than they already were from the bits of wood and glass. The last thing he needed was dirt or sand in his cuts.

None of the people I'd taken through the portal were standing. I hoped that was because of the way I brought them here instead of their injuries, but I doubted they were all lucky enough to have escaped unscathed. The sounds of crying and screams of pain rose up around us. The scene shook me to my core. I hadn't heard anything like it since the last supernatural war.

I'd hoped to never hear anything like it again.

Over at the inn, Van guided an elderly man and woman out of the front door and pointed in our direction. Then the hellhound disappeared back inside as the couple hobbled toward us. The man was bent at his waist with a bleeding gouge on his forehead. Blood coated the side of his face and his shirt. The woman had her arm around him, trying to help him, but she didn't look in much better shape.

Someone raced over to help them.

Good. Because I had my hands full with Jake.

Spying a boulder, I walked stiffly toward it. The tears on my skin pulled with each step, but I'd survived worse. Nothing was fatal. Then I eased Jake down beside the boulder until he was on his feet. He swayed and grabbed at my arms to steady himself. Ignoring my own pain, I bent until my face was at the same level as his. His eyes were glassy.

Was he having a vision? Was he concussed? Was something else wrong?

When he'd painted his vision at the park earlier, he'd moved like a zombie until he found a place to draw out the message from the Eternal Magic. He wasn't acting that way now, so I suspected he was just in shock.

"Jake? You're going to be okay. You hear me? I'm going to check you for injuries before you sit, but first tell me where you hurt the most."

Jake shook his head and cast his gaze around like he couldn't figure out where he was. Then he saw the inn. "How did we get here?"

"I opened a portal," I said. Most humans understood terms like that from movies about magic. Jake looked just as confused as he had a moment earlier. "It is like a magical doorway between two places. In this case, between the dining room and here."

"Others are still inside," Jake said as he lurched toward the inn. "I saw Van…"

I wrapped my arms around Jake's waist. He felt so small and fragile against me. My arms shook as I realized how close he'd come to being killed. I pressed my face to the top of his head and breathed in his scent. It was laden with the stench of smoke and ash, but his unique scent was still there. He was still warm with life. His heart still beat steadily. He was alive and I vowed to keep him that way.

"He's just making sure everyone is out," I choked out, emotions I didn't fully understand making my voice rough. How had this man become so precious to me so quickly?

I should have been helping Van. I knew that. Sure, it was hard to kill a hellhound, even with a bomb, but demons were even more resilient. But I knew if I left to help, Jake would rush in right behind me, and I couldn't let that happen. Oracles weren't built for fighting or war.

My every instinct was screaming at me to shift into my demonic form, wrap my black wings around his body, and never let him go.

Instead, I eased Jake around to face me, then I set my hands on his shoulders and studied him. His face was even paler than normal against his dark hair. His gaze wandered around from one thing to the next, like he couldn't focus on anything at all. He swayed on his feet, and I half expected him to collapse at any moment.

Theoretically, Jake's injuries should be minor cuts along the backs of his legs. With the way I had been carrying him when the bomb exploded, his torso should have been shielded by mine. But what if something else had happened? Something horrible. If the glass hit a main vein or artery... I didn't smell a lot of blood, so I didn't think that was the case, but... What if?

I blinked away the stinging in my eyes.

"I need to check you over."

Jake's forehead crinkled in confusion. He reached for my face with a trembling hand. "You're bleeding."

"I'm fine. Demons are pretty hard to kill." Even as we

spoke, the faint ping of glass hitting the ground told me my body was healing. My magic was rejecting the jagged pieces of glass and pushing them out.

"It was so close to your eye…" Jake brushed his hand over my cheekbone, one of the many places where I'd been struck. His hand came away coated in my blood. Tears welled in his eyes. "Are you sure you'll be okay?"

"Yeah," I said softly. "Even the scars will be gone in a week."

"Was anyone injured?" Jake sucked in a ragged breath. "Or… killed?"

"I don't know." I tightened my grip on Jake's shoulders and brushed a kiss over his forehead.

He bit his bottom lip and squeezed his eyes shut. When he opened them again, his eyes seemed clearer. His mouth was pinched, as if he was forcing himself to ignore his pain. "We need to help the others."

"Let me help you first."

When Jake didn't argue, I took that as permission. The front of his body, like I had suspected, was fine. The blood on the back of his jeans, though, made my hands shake with a mix of anger and fear. What was that fucking mantra Jeremy wanted me to say again? It was supposed to help with my control, but I didn't think it was up for the task today. I took a deep breath and released it as instinct overrode logic. It was like the Eternal Magic was guiding my actions, just as she had when I'd created the bonds with my team.

I had to help Jake. There was no other option.

The tips of my fingers on one hand transformed into the black talons of my demon form. I swiped one wickedly sharp claw across my other hand. A line of black blood bubbled up and pooled in my palm.

A tiny inner voice whispered I shouldn't do this.

I silenced it.

The magic in my blood would not have responded if Jake wasn't meant to be mine. This just confirmed what I knew when I'd first seen Jake's paintings of us together. We were fated mates. If we weren't destined to be together, my blood would have remained red, like anyone else's.

But it wasn't red. It was as black as oil, filled with the power of my demon form.

Thank Magic, because that meant I didn't need to negotiate with Jake before I healed him. I could heal myself without upsetting my magic and now I could heal Jake too, because my magic recognized him as an extension of myself.

With unsteady hands, I swiped the black blood over each cut and abrasion on Jake's body, pushing it through the rips in the denim of his pants until I found and touched all the gashes and holes in Jake's precious skin.

"Whoa," Jake murmured. "What are you doing? It feels... I don't even know. Weird."

"Just let me help you," I said.

Satisfaction and relief warred within me as Jake's body expelled the glass and debris like my body had. I'd need to have a talk with Jake about what I'd done, but I didn't regret it. The sharing of my blood with him wouldn't harm the oracle. It wouldn't bind us together. Not truly. At least not on Jake's side.

And for me?

I'd never felt happier to enter into a one-sided deal. Jake was the only one I'd ever be able to do this for. I'd made my choice. I'd chosen Jake. And he would be the only person for me from now until the end of my days. Jake might choose to accept the bond, but even if he didn't... I would accept his decision. Eventually.

My team would be horrified by what I'd done, particularly since Jake's injuries hadn't even been life-threatening. I'd have to explain that I didn't feel any strain on my demonic powers. Hopefully that would appease them. I couldn't see Jake bleeding and not do anything about it.

"There now," I said as I stood. "Do you feel better?"

"Much." Jake twisted to look at the backs of his legs. "What did you do? When did you grab a first aid kit?"

"No first aid kit." I shook my head. "Just a perk of being a demon."

"Thank you." Jake's gaze held mine for a long moment, like he suspected there was more to it but wasn't sure how to ask.

"You should sit. You lost a lot of blood." I guided Jake to the boulder. I sat down and pulled him into my lap, still needing to feel him, to confirm he was healthy and safe.

Jake's eyes drifted back to the inn. "What do you think happened? Was it a gas leak?"

"It was a bomb."

Jake, his eyes bulging, squirmed out of my arms and jumped to his feet. He spun around to face me. "Did you say bomb?"

"Yeah."

"What...? How...?"

Then Van emerged from the inn, walking behind the

young woman with the three children and Simon, who was still in his cat form. They all appeared unharmed, thank Magic. At the same time, Hayden came around the side of the inn with the shaken and bleeding people who'd escaped the dining room through the doors to the back garden just before the blast. Neither Van nor Hayden returned to the building, so I assumed these were the last of the survivors.

Their arrival distracted Jake from asking any more questions. That was good because I didn't have any answers to give him. Not yet. Speculations based on Nelson's brief texts weren't definitive. I needed concrete, actionable information.

The oracle trembled and let out a shaky breath as the group staggered across the expanse of the parking lot toward the shoreline. He moved to intercept them, but a few shifters rushed over to help, getting to the survivors before Jake managed two shaky steps. Ash rained down on us until everyone and everything was coated in dull gray residue. The stench of blood and smoke and fear filled the air.

"Jake, come here, sweetling," I said softly, extending my hand to him. He didn't notice the little endearment that'd fallen from my lips. He was still staring at the chaos around us. "The first responders are almost here. They'll have questions."

"I don't have any answers," Jake said, turning to look at me again with watery eyes. "What can I tell them?"

"Let's just wait until they come over and see what they want to know."

Just as fire engines and police vehicles careened up to

the inn, another deafening blast rang out from the far side of the building. The air crackled in its wake. I grabbed Jake and wrapped my arms around him, then spun us around so my body was between him and the explosions.

The earth under our feet shook. I glanced over my shoulder to see more black smoke blooming like an ink stain across the blue sky. Dust and debris sailed through the air high above the inn. Van, Hayden, and the others close to the building had been thrown forward. They were sprawled out over the gravel parking lot. That was not a normal bomb. The bastards must have used magic to enhance it.

Before they made it to their feet, a third boom echoed through the air.

The building swayed, almost as if each board rippled under the concussive force of the blast. Everyone stared.

But the building didn't collapse. Not yet.

Chapter Twenty-One

GAGE

"What the ever-loving fuck was that?" Jake choked out in the aftermath of the latest blast.

If Nelson hadn't warned us...

I pushed the unhelpful thought away as I cast my gaze over the scene.

It wasn't in my nature to sit back and watch others struggle. The only thing making me hesitate was that I'd need to let go of Jake to do it. I slowly counted to ten before loosening my grip on him. All the blasts were happening behind the building, so he should be safe where he was.

"Stay here," I ordered him.

He didn't agree, but he didn't argue either.

I dashed forward to assist the people who'd been knocked off their feet. With each step away from Jake, my instincts screamed at me to get back to him, but I forced myself to move. I ran toward the woman and her children first. The kids were screaming and crying, and the woman was shaking so badly I feared she wouldn't be able to walk. As I rushed forward, Simon, still in his cat form, was slinking toward the shrubs by the lake with his belly low to the ground. His ears were pressed back, and his tail was still puffed up.

Then I heard hurried footsteps behind me; Jake had ignored my order. I was torn between being satisfied he was only a few steps away from me, so if something else happened I'd be able to reach him quickly, and being angry he was moving closer to the bomb site.

"No way am I sitting on my ass while people need help," Jake said when he caught me looking at him with a scowl on my face. "Now, get over there and help Esther and her baby while I help her other little ones."

With the possible exception of Davina, no one told me what to do. People might make suggestions or offer comments, but I was not a follower. Even with Davina, I'd never felt compelled to obey. But with Jake's command, I found myself moving to the young woman he'd indicated.

I checked her for injuries, not that I could help heal her or anyone else now, not without a clear exchange, but I didn't want her to suffer, even if I couldn't offer a new deal to her, or anyone else right now either. People tended to look poorly on those kinds of contracts once they were no longer confused and in shock. What I'd done for Jake was only possible for my mate.

Luckily, no one had sustained any life-threatening injuries, so it wasn't a big concern.

Without a deal, healing this many people, even their minor injuries, would just deplete me. That'd leave me weak and incapable of protecting my team… or Jake. I'd feel bad if any of these strangers died, but my family was my priority. Especially Jake.

I needed him safe. I needed him alive. I needed to be strong for him.

It sounded selfish, but this situation had made one thing clear: if Jake was harmed, whatever control I had over my demonic side would shatter.

Despite what my team thought, I'd always believed my day of reckoning was years away, but now… after only knowing Jake for a day, I knew everything had changed. All it'd take to break me was having something dire happen to him.

I'd never survive without him. My team would have to put me down.

I'd lived for centuries, almost two millennia. And suddenly, after only one tiny, miniscule day, my entire life had changed. How had I become so attached to him in such a comparatively inconsequential amount of time?

I wanted to grab him, use the last bit of my weakened magic to open a portal, and take him to another place. A safer place. A world away from here with its bombs, rogue werewolf packs, and other supernatural assholes.

My need to help these people warred with my need to protect Jake. Still, I scooped the young woman and her baby into my arms and carried her across the road as Jake wished. He was right behind me with her other small children. As soon as I set them on the ground, Jake's painting ladies swooped in and fluttered over the crying young woman and her family.

After all the survivors were safely deposited by the

lake shore, I sought out Van. Hayden and Jake were right behind me. Just as we arrived, an old boxy car rushed toward us. I turned to grab Jake again, ready to pull him out of the way, but the car jolted to a stop before it hit us. A man with messy brown curls exploded out of the car and sprinted to us. His eyes were pinched and his face ashen as he took in everyone.

"Van, thank Magic you're alive." The man threw himself at the police officer.

"Hey, Doc," Van said, rubbing him on the back like he wasn't sure what to do with an armful of frantic man. "I'm okay, but I'm glad you're here. There are a lot of people who need you."

"Right. Of course." The doctor nodded and pulled away from Van. Then he patted Van's body, as if needing to check for himself that he was truly unharmed. "You're sure you're okay, though?"

"I'm sure," Van said, shoving his hands in his pockets after the doctor had finished his impromptu assessment.

A professional mask slid over the doctor's face once he knew Van was safe. "Okay," he said. "What's the situation?"

We filled him in quickly, then he returned to his car for his medical bag and got to work. As soon as the doctor was tending to the injured, Hayden eyed Van with a speculative gleam in his eye.

"You and Xander, hey?" the alpha werewolf teased.

"Fuck off," Van said. "It isn't like that. Doctor Roberts is a friend."

Since a hellhound couldn't lie, I guessed he was telling the truth. But I suspected if I looked into his heart, I'd find

221

he wished things were different. But I didn't care enough about the police chief's love life to invade his privacy like that.

"Anyone else still in there?" I asked Van, nodding toward the building.

"I didn't sense anyone there." The hellhound shook his head. Blood coated the side of his face, but it appeared his injuries had already healed, just as mine had.

"And around back? Anyone still need help?" I asked Hayden, who'd just come from there.

"This is everyone," Hayden said.

The line of Van's throat worked as he swallowed hard. "You come across any fatalities?"

We both shook our heads.

"We should check, though," I said.

"I think the firefighters are doing that as they work to contain the blaze. The last I heard, they hadn't found anyone either," Van said.

"Thank fuck," Hayden said, voicing the same relief we all felt. Then the werewolf scowled and pointed at the building. "What the fuck was that?"

"Bombs," Van and I answered at the same time.

"All I smell is brimstone and ash, which I'm assuming is thanks to the demon." Hayden didn't look like he believed us as he lifted his face and inhaled deeply. "Yeah. Okay. I can smell the explosives now."

Hayden was still cursing and wiping his nose when Jake edged closer to me as if seeking the support only a mate could offer. Mate. Right, I hadn't even told him of my suspicions about what we were to one another. Or that he needed a tether. Or about my demonic side needing a place to anchor.

Right now, he was drawn to me by instinct, but he wouldn't understand why.

I should explain everything to him before things progressed any more than they had, give him the opportunity to reject me. It would be safer for him if he did. He could find someone else to use as his tether.

But I was an asshole, because I couldn't resist the urge to have him in my arms when he was so close... not after I could have lost him today. As soon as he was in my arms again, protected by my body in case anything else happened, my magic enveloped him, and my nerves settled.

"Do you think there are more bombs?" Jake's back was to my chest as we both stared at the inn. "Or is this one of those things that only come in threes?"

"Hard to say." I tightened my grip on him in case he was thinking of looking for any leftover bombs himself. Although... that was exactly what I should do. I knew it. But I couldn't bear to leave him out here, exposed, unprotected, vulnerable.

"I can't believe someone bombed my inn." Jake vibrated as anger seeped into his earlier fear and shock. "Who does something like that?"

"We'll have some answers soon," I said as I saw Isaac's bike racing down the road toward us.

Nelson clung to Isaac's back. The back tire swung around as they stopped. Nelson jumped off and ran for me with Isaac right behind him.

"Did you get the message in time?" Nelson panted.

"I think so," I said. "There were some injuries, but I haven't heard of anything life-threatening."

"Fuck, man. When we saw the black smoke in the air…" Isaac braced his hands on his knees like he was trying not to throw up. "But everyone is okay?"

"Everyone got out. Thanks to Nelson's message." I turned to the shadow jumper. "Tell me what happened."

"Here?" Nelson asked.

"These people deserve answers. Depending on our next steps, I'll probably call on half of them to help anyway," Van said, but Nelson still looked to me for confirmation. I nodded.

If the Chief of Police didn't care if all the supes who were scattered across the shoreline listened to our conversation, I didn't either. In fact, I hoped someone would tell those bastards they'd pissed off a demon. They deserved to live in fear from this moment forward.

"That pack, man." Nelson shook his head. "The alpha is fucked up and the wolves are just happily following him like they can't see how messed up he is. But I don't know how anyone could miss it, so I suspect they are all complicit and accepting of what he's doing."

"So it *was* the wolves who did this?" Van shot a quick glance at Hayden.

Nelson nodded at the alpha werewolf. "Sorry, but yeah. I didn't hear anything about it until just before I texted. It sounded like a small group of pack enforcers were sent in to rig the explosives. A need-to-know situation. I was just about to leave when they pulled into the yard in a rush. Decided to stay and see what was happening. They were taken right in to see the alpha and the first thing they said was they'd finished the job. I got the impression the bomb hadn't been the alpha's idea, because he got on his phone, telling whoever answered his call that the threat had been dealt with." Nelson rubbed at his eyes. "Fuck. I thought they'd already detonated it. Thought I was too late."

"You did good," I said as I reached forward and gripped Nelson's shoulder to steady him.

We all studied the inn for a long moment as we let that news settle over us. The building was standing. From this side, nothing looked amiss, but we really needed to check the other side. Black smoke spiralled up to the clouds and bits of ash fell from the sky. So far, there hadn't been a fourth explosion. Then again, there had been a long break between the first bomb and the second, so it was possible there were more undetonated ones hanging about the place.

Hayden's shoulders sagged. "What the fuck is he thinking?"

Nelson glanced at Jake, then at me. He lifted his eyebrow.

"He knows," I said.

Nelson nodded, then started talking. "News got out about there being an oracle at the inn. Something about the oracle having a vision the night of the robbery and causing problems for them. I got the sense someone, not necessarily the wolf pack, thought Jake needed to be stopped before his visions interfered with more of their plans." Nelson shot an apologetic glance at Jake.

"Someone wants me dead?" Jake gaped.

My power rose and filled my body before rolling out

through the air. Except for Jake, everyone, even Van, bowed their heads to me. "No one will touch you."

"How did they know?" Jake grabbed my arm. His grip was so tight his knuckles were turning white. "I only found out I was an oracle a few hours ago."

"But everyone else has known for a while," I reminded him. "Ever since the hellhound was found in the woods."

"Wasn't that weeks or more ago?" Nelson asked. "Why wait until now?"

Dread skated up my spine like an ice-cold blade. "Jake had a vision today. About more caged people. We need to find out who saw his latest painting."

"No way. It wasn't one of my painting ladies." Jake shook his head. "They wouldn't hurt me or their friends and family. They were all here, for pity's sake. With their children."

"Then they told someone about it, someone who still talks to Robbie," Van said. He scrubbed his hand over his face. "It means Robbie has more contacts in Willow Lake than we thought." He narrowed his eyes and looked toward the hills west of town where the wolf pack lived. "Someone has been feeding him information. Someone knew people would be at the inn today. This attack wasn't only about hurting Jake. They were trying to hurt a sizable section of our local supe community."

"We need to stop him," I said. "We were lucky this time. We can't count on luck saving us again."

Chapter Twenty-Two

JAKE

"I need to see what happened," I said, pushing away from Gage's embrace.

Being wrapped in his arms was unbelievably calming, but this was not a calm moment. My inn—my *home*—had been bombed, for fuck's sake.

Bombed.

Who did shit like that? If *Little House on the Prairie* reruns—which was one of the few shows my mom had encouraged me to watch when we still had a TV—had taught me anything, it was that small towns might be plagued with gossip and the occasional hurt feeling, but ultimately people cared about one another and wished one another the best. Sure, old television shows weren't real life and Willow Lake was undeniably weird, but bombs still didn't fit here. They just didn't.

The longer I stood on the lake shore, which was beginning to feel like an eternity already, the more my anxiety grew. Gage stayed close to me, and Van went to question my painting ladies while his deputies fanned out to take everyone else's statement. Given the look of frustration on everyone's face, I doubted anyone had seen anything helpful.

Even Hayden, Isaac, and Nelson had wandered off to circulate through the bedraggled groups of survivors, checking on everyone and helping the paramedics who were triaging people. Hayden's presence seemed to have the most impact. Everywhere Hayden went, he touched people as he spoke soft words of support and encouragement. Whoever he spoke to appeared instantly calmer. Was that a supernatural thing? Something to do with his magic?

I wished I knew.

Gage had told me about magic this morning, and I hadn't had enough time to make sense of everything. But now I saw extraordinary things happening all around me. Like when Carter Jones ambled toward the thickest part of the trees and bushes until he was nearly hidden from view. Then the air around him shimmered and suddenly a gigantic bear—the animal kind, not the human kind— appeared where Carter had been. A moment later, there was more shimmering and then a human-shaped Carter was there again. He stepped out of the foliage looking better than when he went in.

I gaped as others did the same thing.

Were they healing themselves like that? That was pretty wild.

Ha. Wild.

Like a *wild* animal.

I might be losing my mind.

It was a familiar feeling, one I'd hoped was behind me.

But people were already looking a lot better than they should in such a short amount of time. I had expected more people to be thrown into ambulances and hauled away, but it appeared supernatural beings were a hardy and resilient bunch. No one had been rushed away yet.

Thank Warhol for that.

After the fire was extinguished and I knew everyone would be okay, it was time to get some answers. At the top of the list was finding out if my inn was salvageable. My life was tied up with this old place. If it was wrecked beyond repair, then everything about my life was going to change again. I'd need to find somewhere to work and live. Everything had been upended when my mother died, and I moved to Willow Lake. I never wanted to go through another life-altering change like that. It was too soon to do that all again, but what choice would I have?

"It's too dangerous," Gage said.

"I'm not going inside. Not yet. But I need to see. Sure, I'm not a structural engineer, but I can look and see if any of the walls on the back side of the inn are still there or not."

The demon frowned but didn't say anything, although his fingers clenched and unclenched like he wanted to grab me, throw me over his shoulder, and carry me off like he had when the first bomb exploded.

"You can come with me, or I can go alone, but I need to see."

Gage nodded abruptly, but before we'd taken two steps, Jeremy, Adrian, Ash, and Dillon arrived in a rusty pickup truck. They all jumped out. Ash and Dillon went to Van, while Jeremy and Adrian came our way.

"How can we help?" Adrian asked.

"My magic. It's supposed to heal, right? That's what we think, right? Let me…" Jeremy's face was ashen as he eyed the injured people sprawled around us. His face scrunched up like he was concentrating, then he scowled. "It isn't working. Why does this freaking magic never work when I want it to?"

"Jer," Adrian said softly. "It's okay. You can't force it."

Gage rested his hand on Jeremy's shoulder. I didn't like him touching someone else. Jealousy was a foreign feeling. I shoved the feeling down because it was clear the touch wasn't sexual or intimate. I blamed my out-of-control emotions on my shock. It'd been one hell of a day.

"There are ways to help without magic," Gage said softly. "Your powers are still new and there is much we don't know about them. It's possible they can't help in this situation, so, like Adrian said, trying to force it won't help you or anyone else."

When Jeremy frowned but nodded, Gage released his shoulder. He turned his attention to Adrian. "We believe the wolves in the hills are responsible for the bombs—"

"Bombs? Fuck…" Jeremy's eyes bulged.

"Did you find out anything in your interviews today?" Gage continued, ignoring Jeremy's outburst.

"Nothing significant. I would have told you before if we had." Adrian shook his head. As he spoke, his gaze tracked the black cloud marring the otherwise beautiful sky.

"That's fine," Gage said, although the tightness in his

jaw suggested he was disappointed with the lack of answers. "Go and find Isaac and Nelson. They've been helping. They can tell you what still needs to be done."

Adrian seemed surprised by that, and I suspected it would normally be Gage who gave orders and directed people. But he hadn't left my side yet, as if he was my new bodyguard. Although, with people apparently out to get me, I wasn't complaining.

Adrian and Jeremy nodded and left us to find the others. Jeremy was still squishing up his face like he was concentrating or constipated as they walked away. I turned to the inn and moved toward it.

"Where are you going?"

"We talked about this," I huffed. "I need to see what it looks like."

Gage nodded and followed. His eyes darted from shadow to shadow as we walked toward the building, and I was sure if he saw even the littlest thing out of place, I would be carted away through another magical doorway.

As we neared the building, a tight sensation squeezed my chest. Except... It didn't seem like it was my own panic. You couldn't feel someone else's emotions, but as impossible as that sounded, I swore it was like I could feel Gage's anxiety spike as we neared the bomb site.

Footsteps pounded behind us, but I didn't stop.

"What's going on?" Van demanded.

"Jake wants to see the damage," Gage explained.

I glanced at the Chief of Police, ready to argue to be allowed to do this but, surprisingly, he wasn't trying to stop us. That's when I noticed Van hadn't come alone. A whole group of people were following along like my personal posse.

The first responders by the building motioned for us to stop, but Van had a few quick words with them and they let us pass.

"Just stay by the trees," one of the firefighters shouted.

It might have been Carter Jones, hidden behind all his protective gear. I couldn't be sure, but I recalled hearing something about Carter being the fire captain or something like that. He must have joined the other first responders after he'd gone all shimmery and bear-like in the trees. "And stay up wind."

As we neared the inn, I was struck by how normal everything seemed. Well, except for the coating of ash and the smell of something burning. It reminded me of a bonfire, except no one was reaching for marshmallows.

The thick layer of ash muted all the normally bright colors in the landscape. From the foliage to the vehicles in the parking lot, everything was dull and dusty looking.

The pub, which was attached to the right side of the building, appeared unscathed. I hoped it was in as good condition on the inside too. Pretty much all my income came from the pub, so if I still had it, I could still pay my bills.

"Cover your nose and mouth," Gage said.

I tugged the collar of my T-shirt over my nose. Yeah. It wasn't as effective as a proper mask, but it was better than nothing. At least a light breeze was blowing most of the residual smoke and ash away from us now.

So far, so good. The front of the building was mostly fine. Only a few windows were broken. The side of the inn was the same. Then we rounded the corner to the back.

I gaped at the huge crater in the middle of what had been the back patio just a few hours ago. Pieces of deck furniture were scattered all over the yard. One chair was even hanging from the charred branch of an elm tree, at least twenty feet above the ground. All the windows on this side of the building had been shattered. Bits of jagged glass hung in the sills like teeth in yawning mouths. Only blackened wooden posts and a few roof joists were still standing around what had once been the dining room. The siding, the insulation, and the windows were just gone. Inside, the furniture was barely recognizable as tables and chairs; they were just mangled bits of broken wood and upholstery.

We'd been gathering in there, in that exact spot, for the potluck.

It was a miracle any of us had survived.

"The last two blasts must have been worse," Van muttered. "There wasn't this much damage after the first one."

If Gage hadn't gotten us out...

"Hey," he whispered as his arms wrapped around me and pulled me into a tight hug. "I've got you. Everyone is safe. It's okay. It's just stuff. Nothing that can't be replaced."

When had I started shaking?

"It looks like the dining room was an addition," Isaac said. It was odd to see the seemingly easygoing guy look so serious, but the way he assessed the damage made me think he understood what he was seeing.

"Yeah," Hayden agreed. "Built in the sixties, I think."

"That's where most of the damage is. Should be straightforward to fix."

Hayden nodded. "The original building was constructed during the pack wars over a hundred years ago. They built it to withstand a lot of abuse. The addition wouldn't have been built to the same standard."

Hayden knew a lot about the inn. It almost sounded like he'd lived here once. Although, come to think of it, he always knew obscure facts about Willow Lake. What kind of supernatural had Gage said he was again? I shook my head. I couldn't remember, except that he was supernatural.

Like me.

I'd only known I was magical for like five seconds and someone was already trying to kill me. Was this normal for supernatural beings? I hoped not.

"I bet the bombs were in that damn tunnel." Van stepped forward and gestured at the ground. Sure enough, the crater had an oblong sort of shape to it, which extended out a bit on either end.

I'd only found out about the tunnel after the inn was robbed. Ash had been shot in the basement while stopping others from coming in from that tunnel. Van and the others had told me they sealed it, but I suspected they just sealed both ends. Which meant if anyone wanted to use the tunnel to say... plant bombs close to the inn or whatever... all they'd have to do was tap into it in the middle somewhere.

But the tunnel wasn't what I cared about. And it was definitely collapsed now. No one would be using it to get close to the inn again.

Now that I knew everyone was safe, all I cared about was finding out if Hayden and Isaac were right. If the bulk of the repair work involved replacing windows and fixing the siding, that wouldn't be so bad.

Did insurance cover bomb damage? I hoped so.

"I thought you said it was blocked," Gage said. He punctuated his words with a heady and ominous pulse of *something* that vibrated against my back. *Magic*. It was the only explanation.

"I thought it was." Van scowled. Smoke curled from his nostrils. When had he taken up smoking? And where was his cigarette? His eyes flickered strangely, like they were reflecting flames, except nothing was burning now.

"When can we get inside?" I asked.

"Not for a while," Van said. "They'll need to make sure there are no more bombs, gather evidence, check the structural stability of the place..."

"I guess two of my goals are getting put on hold..." I muttered as I slumped against Gage's chest.

"You can stay with me," Gage said, rubbing his hand over my arm.

His team members all raised their eyebrows at that. Jeremy grinned and winked at me. Did Gage not invite people over very often? I hoped that was true, even if I couldn't figure out why he'd want to spend more time with me. After all, since we'd met, I'd molested him in the hall-way, I'd puked on him, and I'd almost gotten him blown up.

Who knew I could be so high maintenance?

"In your motorhome?" Van asked. Now he was doing the eyebrow thing too.

Gage's arms tightened around me. "Yes."

Van held my gaze for a moment. His eyes were still doing that strange fire thing. "You have options, Jake. We won't let this investigation take any longer than necessary, but I agree you'll need a place for a few days. The Tarbeck Motel has some vacancies, or I'm sure Sally or Alice has an extra room."

Gage's arms tightened even more. "Did you find out who gave the information to the wolves?"

Van gritted his teeth. "Daphne Rivers posted a picture of it on social media. She meant well, but she made our task a lot more difficult. Apparently, it got shared by a lot of people."

"So you don't know anything useful and you don't know if someone else will be coming for him."

Van's mouth flattened but he didn't deny Gage's accusations.

"Then he's staying with me, where he'll be safe," Gage said.

The hellhound's lips flattened even more, although I wasn't sure how that was even possible. Fire danced in his eyes.

"It's okay," I said, eager to smooth over the tension. "I want to go with Gage."

What could I say? I felt safe with Gage, demon or not.

And horny.

I felt that too.

But I'd never tell Van that.

I didn't want to be away from Gage. From the moment I'd seen him, I'd been attracted to him. I'd wanted him in my bed, even when I thought he was a hallucination. And, if he was still willing to share his bed with me after everything that had happened, all I could think was *hell, yes!*

Something good had to come from all this, right?

I wished my inn didn't have to blow up for that to happen, but maybe this was all supposed to happen the way it did, because now that I thought about it... I remembered some of those black-and-white paintings I had stashed away in my room. They showed Gage and me doing fun naked things inside what appeared to be an RV.

If I really was an oracle, that was one monumentally big green light for spending the night with him, right? Who was I to turn my back on this whole supernatural business?

Chapter Twenty-Three

JAKE

No more bombs were found.

Hours later, a few firefighters were still poking around at the back of the inn, but most of the emergency crews had finally departed. After so long of nothing new happening, the well-meaning but snoopy residents of Willow Lake had left too, thankfully, because I was ready to drop. All I wanted was to curl up in my bed and go to sleep.

Since the explosions, it felt like every conversation consisted of the same questions: Did you have a vision about this? Are you going to rebuild? What did your insurance company say? And, occasionally, how can I help?

It was exhausting.

When I'd first agreed to spend the night with Gage, I'd had grand plans, but now that the adrenaline and shock had worn off, my eyes refused to stay open. It'd be so easy to just drop down someplace and drift off. I eyed a bit of grass beside the parking lot. That could work.

"Come on," Gage said gently. "Let's get you settled inside."

I nodded and let him guide me toward the motorhome.

"I had big plans for tonight," I mumbled. I sounded tipsy, even to my own ears. Hell, I felt tipsy too.

Gage's mouth twitched, like he was fighting a smile, but didn't say anything. Did he understand what I was saying? Maybe I needed to explain.

"You know the kind…" I leaned toward him as I whispered. "Things that involve a lot of bare skin and a boatload of lube." My cheeks heated as soon as the words were out. Since I was sober, I shouldn't be acting this drunk. Except I was always a little loopy when I was tired. It'd made for some interesting all-nighters at the studio when I was in art school. I liked to believe my classmates had laughed with me, not at me, but I doubted that was the case.

When Gage let out a soft laugh, though, unlike my fellow art students he sounded indulgent, not mocking. "Maybe that should wait."

"Yeah." I sighed dramatically. My sigh quickly turned into a jaw-breaking yawn. "I'm glad your motorhome is here, and that we aren't going somewhere else. Even if I can't go inside the inn, I don't want to leave it."

"Whatever you need," he said. His hand, which had been a light, warm pressure on my lower back, moved in a soft, soothing caress. I even thought he meant what he said.

I hadn't been able to explain my reluctance to go too far away from the inn, but Gage seemed to get it. The inn was both the only thing I owned and the only tangible connection I still had to my family. For so long, my mother had refused to talk about my father or where she'd come from or who her family was. Not knowing those things left me feeling unmoored, although I hadn't recognized that until my grandfather came along and changed everything. I may not have known him long but meeting him had given me a sense of belonging I'd never felt before. I didn't want to lose that. I didn't want to lose the inn. Without it, what was I? Would I have another gaping hole in my world again?

The idea that someone—like those *wolves in the hills* everyone kept talking about—might try to raid the inn while it was empty and vulnerable also made me queasy. Especially since I was beginning to understand more about the supernatural world. If my grandfather had as many magical artifacts as everyone said, those things needed to be protected. I doubted I could fight off a determined werewolf—oh, let's face it, even a determined human would be too much for me to handle—but I couldn't just abandon the place either.

Gage's friends had followed our trek toward the motorhome, and now he turned to address them.

"You don't have to stay. Jeremy, Adrian, go on back to your room. Your cat probably needs to be fed. Isaac and Nelson can go with you and grab a room there too. You'll be safe at the minotaur's place."

Minotaur? That had to be Levi. I should be shocked to find out Levi was a mythical creature, right? But my brain just didn't have the energy.

"I finally cornered Simon today. He's a cat shifter who

works as a security guard over there. Anyway, I'm working on him…"

"The guy is scared of you," Adrian said.

"Meh," Jeremy said with a shrug. "He's scared of everyone, but he'll come around. As I was saying—" he glared at his boyfriend, as if daring him to interrupt again, "—I saw him here after the place went boom, and he's agreed to feed Clawie and Emma if we aren't back when he starts his nightshift," Jeremy said, crossing his arms in front of his chest. "No way are we leaving you guys here by yourself. You might be an all-powerful demon, Mr. Dimples, but you aren't getting rid of us."

"We're all staying," Isaac agreed.

"We're taking shifts." Adrian nodded. "Jeremy and I are taking the first one."

Without waiting for any other discussion, Adrian opened a compartment under the motorhome and pulled out a couple of lawn chairs. Jeremy flopped into one and pulled out his ever-present notebook. The others joined us inside the motorhome.

"Isaac, you take the sofa," Nelson said once we were inside.

"You sure, man? I know the table converts into a bed too, but it's fucking uncomfortable. After the way you sprinted through the forest today, you deserve a better sleep. Take the couch."

"You're built like a fucking giraffe. There is no way your legs will fit on that bed."

So, yeah. Maybe being too tired for sex was a good thing, because I'd never instigate anything while Gage's friends were in the same RV as us. Not for our first time together. Or my first time ever. Because, seriously, what if things went wrong again? What if my dick made a dick move and suddenly decided it wasn't interested? It'd happened before. If it happened again, I wouldn't be able to sleep in the same bed as Gage, and where would I go if Isaac and Nelson were in the main part of the motorhome?

Nelson and Isaac continued to argue about who was sleeping where, but I tuned them out as I trudged down the small, narrow hallway. I'd been in the bathroom already to shower a few hours ago. I think Gage had whipped me away through a portal to his motorhome and insisted I go clean up earlier mostly because I was ready to punch the next person to ask me why I hadn't seen the bombing in a vision.

The break had helped.

It would have been even nicer to come out and find a clean change of clothes even when I'd cleaned up, but I hadn't been in Gage's room, his inner sanctuary. I paused in the doorway and peered inside. The room was small compared to a bedroom in a house or an apartment, and the bed filled most of it. A narrow aisle wrapped around three sides of the expansive mattress. I had to shuffle along one of those aisles, my legs brushing the bed because it was *right there*, so Gage could enter too. He shut the narrow door behind us.

We were alone.

The RV rocked a bit as the other guys moved around in the living and dining room space, but Gage and I didn't move at all. Seeing his bed brought home exactly what we'd both agreed to. Were we ready for this? Even without sex, sleeping together was an enormous step. With sex, I imagined that even though you bared your body, you were still awake so you could hold onto the illusion that if you didn't like something, you could take control of the situation. With sleep, you were vulnerable and helpless. That required a lot of trust.

"So... uh..." I cleared my throat. "Sleep?"

"I think you've already figured this out, but I don't want any misunderstandings between us." Gage reached out, oh so slowly, and brushed his fingers along the side of my face and down my neck. "I'm attracted to you."

Heat blossomed over my cheeks. "I... uh... I like you too."

"But I want to take this slow, okay? We aren't going to do anything tonight. We're just going to sleep. Today scared me. When I heard there were bombs there and I couldn't see you right away..." He shivered. "I just want to hold you tonight, okay?"

I rested my hand on Gage's chest. "I'd like that too."

We leaned closer. Our lips met in a soft kiss that was over too soon according to the blood racing through me, which was valiantly trying to rally some kind of physical response. But another ginormous yawn killed that fleeting idea.

"Let's get into bed," Gage suggested.

"Yes."

I wished I had some pajama pants, a T-shirt, and a partition to hide behind to change into them, but I didn't have any of those things. If I wanted privacy, I'd need to strip in the itsy-bitsy bathroom. But the only way to get from the bathroom back to the bedroom was to walk down the hallway, where Nelson or Isaac could see me. I refused to do that in only my underwear.

And, really, how was walking into the bedroom in my underwear any different from just stripping down to the same underwear in this room?

Except it *did* feel different.

A bit like a striptease.

Should I make it sensual? What would I even do to make it enticing? Suck on my fingers before dragging them over my skin? I think I read a scene like that in a book once.

I couldn't imagine doing it in real life. I'd look like an idiot.

This wasn't how I'd imagined taking my clothes off in front of Gage for the first time. I felt ridiculous but I didn't know why. I wasn't ashamed of my body. So why was this becoming such a huge deal in my head?

"I'll turn around," Gage said.

I thought about saying *don't worry about it* or *it's fine*. But all I felt was relief. I yanked off my clothes, leaving only my bright orange boxers adorned with skiing polar bears. I suddenly regretted choosing these boxers after my shower this afternoon, but I couldn't have anticipated this day would turn out like it had. And it was too late now.

I still hadn't been allowed into the building yet, not even to grab a change of clothing or different underwear. Oh well. We were just sleeping, right? Under blankets and everything. Gage never had to see what I was wearing. I balled up my dirty clothes and shoved them into the corner on my side of the bed, so they were out of the way. Then I climbed into bed and pulled the blanket up until only my head was exposed.

"Done."

Gage turned around. A pulse of power pushed through the room, like the demon was having trouble controlling himself at the sight of me in his bed, even if he was seeing less of my body than a minute ago when I was still dressed.

Then Gage began to strip.

He tugged off his shirt, carefully folded it, and tucked it into a laundry basket in one of his cupboards. Nothing about how he moved was overtly sensual, but my heart pounded, and my cock tried to rally again. I swallowed hard. I stared as more of his beautiful body was revealed.

"Oh… I should… Sorry…" I snapped my eyes shut and pulled the blanket over my face to remove the temptation to open my eyes and watch him undress.

"Jake," Gage said softly.

"Mm hmm?" I squeezed my eyes shut tighter.

"Don't hide from me. I want you to look at me. I want you to see me."

My eyes sprang open, but I was still under the blanket so I couldn't see anything. "Uh… What?"

"Look at me." Gage's deep voice rumbled through the quiet room.

I sucked in a quick breath. The blanket carried Gage's scent. At some point earlier today, when we were talking about the stink the bombs had left behind, Hayden mentioned Gage smelled like brimstone and ash to him, but he didn't smell like that to me. No. To me, Gage smelled of home, of the way the air smelled on a blistering hot summer day, of red-hot charcoals on the barbecue, of my favorite blanket right from the dryer.

"Jake?" Gage said, so softly I almost didn't hear it.

I drew the blanket down my face until just my eyes were exposed.

"Watch me," Gage said. "I want your eyes on me."

The intense way he stared into my eyes made my body come alive. Then I couldn't look away again, even if I tried. He leisurely peeled away the rest of his clothing, as if savoring the way my gaze caressed him.

When he was bare of everything except a tight pair of black boxer briefs, Gage stood at the end of the bed and let me look at him. So I did. My gaze flowed down his sculpted chest, cascaded over the ripples of his defined stomach muscles, slid along the vee of his Adonis belt, then stumbled over the very noticeable and generous bulge at the apex of his legs. And that was it. My eyes wouldn't move on. They were stuck there. Staring at the outline of his cock as it strained against the tight fabric.

I licked my lips.

Gage reached down and adjusted himself. I was pretty sure I whimpered at the sight of his long thick fingers wrapped around the long thick line of his dick. Gage grinned.

"Not tonight," he said.

I swallowed. "I wish I had more energy to argue with you, but I don't want our first time together to be any more disappointing than necessary." Feigning a boldness I didn't really feel, I pulled the bedding aside and patted the mattress. "Come on. Let's get some sleep."

Gage crawled over the mattress until he was beside me.

Then he adjusted the blanket over his body, hiding all his beautiful skin and muscles from view. We faced one another and I was once again struck by the intimacy of being with him like this.

"Before I turn off the light, I need to look you in the eye and address what you just said. I don't know what happened to you in the past, but I will never be disappointed by anything we do together. I can't say it bothers me to hear that your past experiences weren't great. But I can see it bothers you. The way I see it, though, whoever you were with wasn't your person. But you and me? I know it's fast, but I think there could be something more here between us. If you want it. I won't pressure you, but whatever you want to offer, I want that with you."

I nodded. I got the sense he had more he could say, but I didn't press him for details. I was too tired to have a deep conversation. But I couldn't deny the way his words filled me with hope.

Could he be *my* person? My mother had scoffed at the idea of soulmates and had done her best to indoctrinate me to believe the same, but I couldn't ignore the way I felt around Gage. My reaction to him was unlike anything I'd ever experienced.

"I think it'll be different with you too," I whispered, scared to voice my hopes too loudly. "I'm just... In the past, it wasn't... I wasn't..."

"You're all I want. Nothing more, nothing less," he soothed when it was clear I was having trouble finding words, and I melted a little inside. "If we decide to do more, we will learn about each other together. That's all I want. I want to know what you like. What makes you moan. What has you begging for more. I can't think of anything better."

"Yes." I gulped. "I want to know all that about you too."

The red I'd come to associate with his demon form washed over his eyes at my breathless confession. I shivered and inched closer to him. Why did I find evidence of his monstrous side so hot?

"Will you hold me?"

"I was hoping you'd let me." Gage reached up and turned off the light in the room, then he reached under the covers for me. His warm hand collided with my bare chest, causing goosebumps to jump up all over my body. "Are you chilled? Why don't you turn around so I can hold you tight and warm you up?"

"Not cold," I murmured, then I wiggled closer to him. "I want to kiss you."

The room was darkened, but there was still enough light filtering in through the curtains that I could see him. His steady gaze met mine as he gently slid his hand over me until it rested on my waist. When Gage didn't do anything more, I wondered if I'd gotten things mixed up. But I was in his bed. That had to count for something, right?

"Do you not want to kiss me?" I sounded needy.

His fingers flexed on my waist, then he slid his hand around to my lower back. He pulled me closer.

"I want to do so much more than kiss, but I don't think you're ready for that tonight," he whispered.

A little parade of butterflies started doing the conga in my stomach. I grinned and reached for him. My fingers brushed over the dark scruff covering his jaw. When I slid them over his cheeks, his eyelids fluttered for a moment, and he hummed as if enjoying my touch.

"You're beautiful," I whispered.

Then I swept my lips over his and Gage hugged me closer, opening his mouth to mine. Given my terrible experiences with other men, I was a novice kisser. But I should have known, if only from fiction, that there were different kinds of kisses. This was different from the one we'd shared earlier. This one was sweet and innocent and beautiful. It was comfort and pleasure and felt like coming home. It was safety and warmth and belonging.

Our mouths moved together in a sensual exploration. But even as our bodies tangled together—my leg over his hips, his hand cupping the back of my head, the soft scrape of his bristles against my skin—everything remained quite PG. Tonight wasn't for sex. It was for getting to know one another. A deep sense of peace and contentment welled inside me. It felt like mine... but more. Almost like our emotions had tangled as closely as our bodies, and now everything was mixed up together and amplified.

I don't know how long we kissed, but when it ended, neither of us moved apart. We lay entwined under the covers. I'd never felt so safe and happy in my whole life. I'd never imagined feeling this way. It was wonderful and heady, and I wanted more and more and more.

I wasn't sure why, but I was sure Gage would give me that and anything else I might want. With those happy thoughts, I smiled and settled into Gage's warm embrace to sleep.

Chapter Twenty-Four

GAGE

I did not sleep.

The motorhome had been closed up when the explosions had happened, but everything still reeked of ash and chemicals and smoke. The longer I breathed in those reminders of what had happened, the more my rage grew. In the dead of night, with darkness all around me, one thought consumed me: someone had tried to harm my mate.

That was unacceptable.

I rarely used the full extent of my powers, although I'd come close with that massive portal. If I hadn't received those gifts from the locals, I would never have managed to do such a thing and stay in control. Each time I dipped into the well of my magic, I worried a little more of my control would slip away. I'd seen it happen to my father and I'd vowed to myself to do better. But to protect my mate? I would surrender to the full depth of my magic to annihilate the threat.

Consequences be damned.

Jake was precious. Any risk to him needed to be neutralized. Permanently.

My ever-weakening tether to my home and team frayed more with each passing second. The only thing preventing me from going out to the wolf settlement in the woods right now was Jake. He was with me. Sleeping. If I left, he would be vulnerable. I couldn't trust anyone, not even my team, who were sleeping on the other side of the flimsy wall, to protect him. He was mine. And I was the only one capable of guaranteeing his safety.

Tomorrow, when the sun was up and the hellhounds were awake, I would call on them. As a demon, it was my right to demand their service in the quest for justice. From the beginning of time, angels and demons were the judges, and hellhounds our partners in meting out justice. They were the tools for exacting punishments. Although the world had changed a lot over time, the hellhounds' purpose hadn't. It was a calling they couldn't ignore or deny.

So, as I waited for dawn, I held Jake in the safety of my arms and planned my attack.

Some might say there were members of the pack who should be spared, but I didn't feel merciful. They had made their choice when they decided to follow such a weak and conniving alpha. As my temper grew and my plan solidified, my demonic power rose. I tried to tamp it down, but it would not settle. My team was mostly immune to it since they were bound to me, but I was surprised Jake didn't wake.

The benefit of my magic leaking everywhere was that if anyone—human or supernatural being—approached or got too near to where we rested, my magic would warn them to stay away. Anyone stupid enough to disregard that warning would face the consequences. But once I unleashed my powers, I doubted they'd easily be contained again.

What if I never regained control? What if this was what drove me utterly mad? What if doing this meant my team would have to kill me as they had vowed?

Jake whimpered in his sleep, as if aware of the dark turn of my thoughts.

I would never hurt him or my team, at least not physically, but if Jake lost me so soon after finding me, what would happen to him? As an unanchored oracle, he was at risk. I knew that.

And as his mate, I was the logical, perhaps even the only, choice to be his anchor.

But if I didn't destroy those wolves…

I gritted my teeth and more of my power rippled out from me.

I'd known my day of reckoning would come, but I'd never expected it to happen like this.

Jake whimpered again in his sleep, and I stroked his back to soothe him.

"Hush," I murmured. "I am here. You are safe."

He shifted restlessly in my arms until I was forced to loosen my hold. I expected him to turn over or wiggle around until he was comfortable. But as soon as I opened my arms, he jolted upright and threw off the covers.

"Jake?"

He didn't respond. Instead, he moved toward the bedroom door. I grabbed his hand to stop him. Jake spun toward me and chopped his other hand against my wrist. Stunned, I let go. I could have kept hold of him, but this wasn't Jake. I saw that now. His eyes were open, but I knew he wasn't seeing anything of his surroundings. He was in the grip of his oracle magic.

I wished I could stop him long enough to get him dressed. I wished I could make him sit down and wait for me to retrieve his drawing supplies. But Magic was a demanding bitch.

Jake wrenched the door open. The hollow door clattered against the thin wall. Then Jake trudged into the kitchen area. I followed, not bothering with clothes or shoes, needing to keep him in my sight. Based on what I'd seen when he'd had his vision yesterday in the park, I knew he was on the hunt for something to draw with. Did I even have any pens or paper? Everyone on the team—except for me—used their phones to take notes, while I just relied on my own memory.

Nelson and Isaac sat up and grabbed their weapons.

"Jake needs a pen and paper," I said. "Do you have —?" Then I remembered the pencil I kept with my maps. I was about to retrieve it when Jake walked right through the small living room and kitchen area and let himself outside. "Shit." I needed to chase him.

Behind me, Nelson and Isaac scrambled out of their beds to follow.

Jake exited the motorhome and turned to his right. His

bare feet crunched over the gravel, but he didn't wince or hesitate. New offerings of flowers and gift baskets were stacked along the length of the dirty motorhome. The mere sight of them had my magic rejoicing, but Jake didn't seem to notice them at all as he stepped on them. His body pushed out a soft sigh, almost as if he was relieved, then he raised his hand. He drew his fingertip through the mess of mud, ash, and soot I hadn't washed away yet. It made my eye twitch to see my poor motorhome look so dirty, but Jake seemed happy. I guessed he'd found his new canvas.

I scrambled to remove obstacles from Jake's path, flinging trinkets, bottles, and bouquets out of his way so he wouldn't trip over them. Each item landed with a thud, some accompanied by the sound of breaking glass. One was met with a grunt.

"Hey, watch where you're throwing that stuff," Isaac said.

But I didn't stop until the area was clear.

Jake seemed oblivious to everything around him, including me. Was that how he would be when his untethered magic finally overpowered him? Would he be merely an unthinking, unfeeling zombie to his visions until he died? And how long would it take for death to seize him? Would anyone be able to coax him to eat? To sleep? To do anything but sketch out vision after vision?

The thought was sobering.

With his fingernails, Jake cut through the dirt, and with broad sweeping motions, he covered the side of the bus with thin lines. Then, using his fingertips and every other part of his hands, he filled in more and more details. He worked ceaselessly until every inch of space he could reach was covered.

I watched, mesmerized, as an intricate but grisly scene came to life on the side of the Pink Lady. The light in the parking lot wasn't overly bright, but I didn't need it. One of the benefits of being a demon was the ability to see in the dark, but I wondered how Jake was managing to do the same. Then I remembered the vacant look in his eyes when he'd painted his vision earlier, and I knew that as a vessel to deliver the Eternal Magic's message, Jake didn't need his sight.

Nelson and Isaac were right beside me, and it only took a few seconds before Jeremy and Adrian joined us. They had apparently been doing a sweep around the inn when we'd emerged.

"Are those polar bears on his underwear skiing?" Isaac whispered.

"Fuck, Isaac," Nelson reprimanded. "Why are you looking at his ass?"

"What? Like you weren't?"

"Turn around." A pulse of power ripped out of me. "Don't look at him."

I didn't have to look at them to know my team obeyed. A hint of fear tinged the air as they spun around. But I still drew on my demonic form, letting it wash over me, and I spread my wings to shield my mate from view of anyone else who might come upon us.

"Fucking idiot," Adrian mumbled. "You know better than to provoke an ancient fucking demon."

"Whatever. We were all thinking it," Isaac muttered, then he didn't say anything more.

But now that Isaac had brought up my mate's body, my gaze caught the way the muscles in his legs shifted as he stretched up on his tiptoes, the way the muscles in his back rippled as he swung his arm, and the way his graceful fingers danced with such sharp, precise movements as he brought the vision to life in front of me. He was gorgeous and talented, and watching him did something strange to the anger I'd been fanning to life all night.

Those who threatened him needed to be crushed, but doing so did not require any particular skill. Others could kill as easily as I could. But… there was one thing that only I could do: become Jake's tether. That would be protecting him too.

My need for revenge hadn't faded, but my need to care for my mate was stronger.

My mate was everything.

The oppressive weight of my demonic anger slowly lessened. My control had slipped more in this one night than it had in years, but the possible catalyst for my final destruction—my temper—had subsided for the moment.

When Jake's arm finally dropped to his side, he sagged. A shudder rolled over him. He gasped, then wrapped his arms over his stomach.

"No, not again," he cried out with a whimper, then ran toward the back bumper of the motorhome.

He must have felt the jagged edges of the gravel now because he cursed and staggered, but he didn't stop until he rounded the corner. I dashed after him, only to find him hunched over, expelling the contents of his stomach. I stepped closer, but he held up his hand to stop me from getting nearer. When the worst had passed, he wiped his mouth with the back of his hand and groaned.

"Fuck," he said and pushed himself upright. "I hate waking up like that. I swear it's getting worse every day."

"Come on," I said quietly. "Let's get you cleaned up and back to bed."

"What did I draw this time?"

"We'll deal with it in the morning," I said. My priority was making sure he was comfortable. Then, once he was safe and warm in bed again, I'd document the message from the Eternal Magic.

I glanced up at the sky. The stars were sparkling overhead with no clouds in sight. Good. That made it easier. If rain had been close, I would have needed a different plan.

Jake winced as he stepped on the gravel. Without asking permission, I swept him into my arms and carried him into the motorhome. It was a little tricky getting him through the narrow doorway, but I refused to let him down.

"I can walk, you know," he muttered.

I ignored him. Besides, he wasn't struggling to be set down, so I figured he was weaker than he wanted to admit.

I took him to the bathroom first. I found a new toothbrush and a fresh cloth for him. The bathroom was too small for two grown men, even when one was as small as Jake, but I squeezed in there with him anyway. For my next motorhome, I'd have to find one with enough room for both of us. Then again, would I even need another motorhome?

"Do you want a shower?"

He shook his head. "Later... I'm going to crash soon,

and I don't want to do that in the bathroom. Please, go do something else. I can take care of myself."

"You don't have to," I whispered. "You aren't alone anymore, my prince."

Terms of endearment weren't usually my thing, but this one rolled off my tongue before I could catch it.

Jake's mouth twisted in an amused grin. "Your prince?"

"Yes, because you rule over me." I grinned back at him as I brushed my lips over his sweaty forehead. "Let me help you; I am your servant."

"You're oddly sappy all of a sudden." He grinned sleepily as he nudged me gently toward the door. "But I've got this, really."

Since Jake seemed alert enough for the moment, I reluctantly let him have the bathroom to himself. I wasn't going far though. Just in case.

I poked my head outside to find my team with their phones out, taking photos of the image Jake had drawn. The drawing filled the side of the bus from the door to the back bumper, so there was a lot to document.

I was still pissed about Isaac commenting on Jake's underwear, but when it came to their jobs, I trusted my team to do good work. A noise from the bathroom drew me back inside. I was waiting in the hallway when Jake lurched out of the small room. I steered him toward my bed.

"Don't worry," he said with a yawn. His breath smelled fresh and clean. "I think I got most of the dirt off my hands and feet."

"I'm not worried," I reassured him. At least I wasn't worried about that, at any rate.

He crawled into bed, and I pulled the covers up over him again.

"You coming?"

I thought about saying no, but the look on Jake's face told me he needed me right now. The vision he'd portrayed wasn't going anywhere. It could wait, but Jake couldn't. I settled in bed beside him, and he snuggled close.

Within minutes, he was asleep again.

Chapter Twenty-Five

GAGE

I wanted to stay in bed with Jake—I loved having him in my arms—but I couldn't rest until I checked on my team again. So, once I was sure he was sleeping deeply, I pried myself away. When I stepped out of the motorhome, my team paused what they were doing, waiting for my instructions. But, first, I needed to see the drawing again.

Jake had moved so quickly while creating it, I hadn't seen or understood everything at the time. I stepped away from the motorhome until I could take in the whole image. For a sketch done using fingertips through dirt and ash, the drawing was surprisingly detailed.

"Are those the wolf pack lands?" I asked, not recognizing the settlement Jake had drawn.

"Yeah. It's the same place Babette took me," Jeremy said with a shudder.

Adrian wrapped his arms around his mate.

The macabre scene showed the pack lands being

destroyed. Satisfaction welled inside me at the thought of its destruction, and I hoped it would happen soon. Since Jake had only been channeling visions for a year now, it was impossible to know how far into the future his visions projected. The event foretold here could be minutes away or decades.

"We've got a recording of it, boss," Isaac said, lifting his phone as if I wouldn't know what he was talking about. "But we'll grab more pictures in the morning after the sun is up."

I nodded and stared at the drawing. "Anything of interest? Besides the obvious."

"It is the view looking west, as if you were in the air following the road from the highway into the pack lands." Nelson gestured toward a road at the bottom of the drawing. "Like I said, the alpha's house is here, and it appears to be used as the hub of all pack activities, from meetings to food prep. Beside it, over here, is a garage. It's been converted to barracks for his enforcers." Nelson pointed to the drawing as he spoke. "I didn't count the smaller shacks around the estate, but this appears to be consistent with what I observed. They're used for couples or families."

"We should get Dillon here," Adrian said. "He lived there for a bit."

"Do it," I said.

I tallied the smaller buildings. If each contained two or three people, Rob had a sizable pack. And each and every one of those people thought it was a good idea to follow that asshole. Unbelievable. It didn't speak well for the education system here; I'd have to revamp it after I bound myself to the land. I refused to be tied to a place filled with idiots. I would kill the people I was supposed to protect within weeks, if not days. I had no tolerance for stupidity.

As if sensing my thoughts about binding here, the inherent magic of the place fluttered over me in an enthusiastic rush. I let my magic seep out and brush over it, like petting an excited puppy.

Some part of me still worried I was seeing things in Willow Lake that weren't there, but the eager energy in the magic went a long way to easing my worries. The paintings Jake had made of our future also went a long way to easing my worries, but I still shuddered to think what would happen if I was wrong.

I'd never been so indecisive or paranoid, but I couldn't help myself. The risks were too high. I wouldn't forget the way my father had looked at me that last time, after he'd made that same mistake. I refused to give anyone else a similar memory…

My father had ensured I knew how quickly demons could turn dangerous, even before he tried to kill me. He hadn't been a violent man, at least no more so than any other man of that era. Not until the end, at least. Then everything changed.

But he often told the story of how he'd barely been able to escape with me. How his own father had planned to kill him. How my own life would have been forfeit. All because my grandfather, a tethered demon, couldn't tolerate another demon in his territory. Instinct made it impossible for us to coexist.

Over the years, I'd come to suspect there was more to the story than what my father had told me, but by that time it'd been too late. And I couldn't risk asking Teague to summon him so I could have my answers. After such a terrible last day, my father could easily come back as a vengeful or malevolent spirit. I couldn't risk it, not just to answer my personal questions. I just wished I'd asked him earlier, before I had to kill him.

A familiar pang of guilt and regret reverberated through me. I wiped my hands together; like Lady MacBeth, I could still see the blood there.

But, looking at my past now, it was difficult to believe every single being in my species would eventually try to kill their offspring. It made us no better than wild animals who turned on their young. It was primitive and unsettling. And I refused to follow that well-worn path.

I was determined to be better than that, but a demon's nature wasn't always ruled by logic or compassion. So I also didn't take any unnecessary risks. I didn't have any offspring… at least none with my blood in their veins. In many ways, the members of my team were like my children. My found family. Under my care by mutual choice.

But, in the end, would that be enough to save them?

"The attack," Nelson continued, unaware of the dark turn of my thoughts, "appears to start in the south."

"Can we tell who the attackers are?" I glanced to the left side of the drawing, which I believed should be south, based on what Nelson had said. "Is it our team?"

"Nah." Isaac shook his head and gestured to a different part of the drawing. "Look at these… It looks like there might be bears, trolls, or goblins in the mix."

I squinted at the area he'd indicated. It was difficult to interpret what I was looking at, but he was right. It didn't look like anyone from our team. The beings appeared to be bulky and round, and I agreed with Isaac that they were likely bears, trolls, or goblins. I was mildly disappointed I wouldn't be the one to tear the pack apart, but I'd live with it. It was better this way.

My demon blood had been boiling and surging through my veins since the attack on the inn. It wouldn't take much for it to erupt. I'd need to tether soon if I wanted to avoid losing complete control. How ironic would that be? Finally finding my place, only to have my demon go on a rampage.

"The others will be here by daybreak," Isaac said. "Teague and Davie just texted a few minutes ago. They are coming here straight away. The situation at the morgue has been dealt with. Adrian and Jeremy are heading to their room at the motel to rest for a few hours. It's time for Nelson and me to take our shift."

I lifted my eyebrow and stared at the centaur. He didn't look away or stammer like most people would. Isaac was the newest member of the team. It wasn't his role to tell people what to do or when, but I didn't disagree with what he was suggesting. I might need to start giving him more responsibility. He looked like he spent all his time baking in the sun rather than paying attention to anything, but I'd always known he had intelligence and depth. I wouldn't have invited him onto my team otherwise.

"Good. We'll have a team meeting then." I nodded. "Until then, protect the drawing."

It made my eye twitch to have to say that because what I really wanted was to wash away all the dirt and soot and ash. I hated seeing the Pink Lady in such a mess. Seeing the drawing itself was equally disturbing. It was a reminder of just how vulnerable Jake was and how much he needed a tether. But Jake's vision needed to be preserved until we were sure we'd captured all of it.

"Already on it, boss," Isaac said.

I glanced at Nelson, who simply nodded. "We've got it covered. You can go back to Jake. He needs you more than we do right now."

Under normal circumstances, I would have sent everyone on my team to bed and guarded the area myself. But these were not normal circumstances. I had my mate in my bed right now and all I wanted was to return to his warm soft body. It made the back of my neck itch to have him out of my sight.

So I nodded sharply and climbed back into the motorhome. When I got to the bedroom, I slid the door closed as quietly as I could. Then I stared at Jake in my bed, curled around my pillow. He looked so peaceful. If it weren't for the dark circles under his eyes and how his bones appeared too sharp under his thin frame, I would think he was untroubled. But it was obvious his health was suffering under the weight of his oracle magic.

Oracle magic was rare; I'd only encountered it a few times in my long life. So I didn't have a thorough understanding of how it worked. But to be so young and already be suffering struck me as unusual.

The Eternal Magic wasn't usually so cruel.

I doubted we'd ever know for certain, without summoning her spirit, but I suspected his mother had put the curse on Jake when he first showed signs of being an oracle. From everything Jake had said about her, I figured she'd been determined to protect him. And what would scare a mother more than the thought of her child losing his grip on reality and succumbing to his magic? It wouldn't have been much of a leap for her to decide that if Jake couldn't have visions, he'd be protected.

Except magic always won.

And now that the curse was lifted, it was like all the magic he should have experienced as a trickle over the years was flooding through him all at once, like a magic-laden tsunami battering at his sanity and eroding it quicker than it would have otherwise.

Perhaps I was wrong to have ripped the curse from him when he wasn't tethered yet.

I hoped Teague could assess the state of Jake's magic when he arrived. The death mage could see things others couldn't. Then we'd know what we were dealing with.

It was a question for tomorrow.

For now, all I wanted to do was hold Jake.

I crawled into bed beside him for the third time that night. As soon as I settled, he gravitated to me, as if, even in his sleep, he knew I would protect him and welcome him into my arms.

Chapter Twenty-Six

JAKE

When I woke from a deep sleep, I was disoriented.

The mattress under me felt different. The bedding smelled different. The arms around me were definitely different.

Where was I?

I forced my eyes open and all the little details of the room, and the bed, and the man beside me filtered in. Right on the heels of those memories, everything else from the day before rushed back.

And what a long and fucked up day that'd been. It started normal enough and then it was just one bizarre thing after the other.

I stared up at the ceiling in the strange little bedroom in Gage's motorhome. The room was tiny. I was surprised Gage liked it so much: he wasn't a small man. This confined space couldn't be comfortable.

He was also a hot man, figuratively and literally.

Right now, I was thinking mostly about the heat pouring from his body. Everywhere my body touched his was sweaty, but I didn't move away. I loved being close to him and never wanted to leave the shelter of his embrace. I wished I could spend the whole day like this, locked away from the rest of the world.

Then I wouldn't have to think about my wrecked inn or someone trying to kill me.

Yeah. It was better to stay here.

But then Gage's hand started moving over my back. Huh. So he wasn't asleep either. He'd soothed me by stroking my back yesterday too, but now, as his hand dipped lower, sneaking under my underwear to cup my ass, I knew this was something different.

Holy shit. Sex. He was initiating sex.

My brain cells exploded, taking my thoughts in a thousand different directions all at once.

First, I needed to check on my dick. I wiggled. Yep. Dick was engaged. Cock was hard. Good. What next? I'd had a shower at the end of yesterday so I should be okay. And I'd brushed my teeth after my middle of the night painting escapade, so no worries there.

He squeezed my ass.

Every thought scattered.

Fuck. What else?

This was my chance. I couldn't fuck it up. I shivered against him and rolled my hips a little to press my ass into his hand. His palm was so deliciously hot against my skin, and so fucking good. When his finger slipped between my ass cheeks, I jumped like I'd been electrocuted.

He ripped his hand away.

"No, no, no," I moaned. "Put it back."

"Jake?" His voice was rough with sleep. "I didn't mean to push you into something you aren't ready for."

Did we have to talk about this? I hid my face against his chest and pushed my ass out, seeking his touch again.

"I didn't mean to make you uncomfortable," he murmured against my hair.

Why was he still talking about this? Couldn't he tell I wanted him to put his hand back on my ass? Words weren't necessary. He had to feel how hot my cheeks were since my face was smashed against his chest. He probably thought I had a fever.

My lack of experience was biting me in the ass right now.

Or…

Well…

I mean, I wouldn't mind being bitten in the ass, but by Gage, not my embarrassment. But I was an adult. I had been for quite some time. Just because my previous sexual encounters had been abysmal and awkward didn't mean I was incapable of asking for what I wanted.

And, man oh man, I did want it… him… everything.

My dick was so freaking hard I could probably cut glass with it. I frowned. No. I didn't want glass anywhere near my dick.

I even sucked at sexy analogies.

But if I ever wanted to unsuck myself… No. No, no, no.

Although, there was some sucking during sex, right?

Why wouldn't my mind just act normal?

"I wasn't uncomfortable," I managed to say. "You just

surprised me." I lifted my head so I could look at him, valiantly trying to ignore how embarrassed I was. "I liked it. I think we should do more of that."

Gage's lips kicked up in a sexy grin. His dimple flashed, as if saying hello. "More of that, hey?"

"Yes," I nodded. "All the stuff."

"Jake, are you saying you want to have sex with me?"

"You said you could read someone's wishes. Can't you see what I'm wishing for right now?"

"I'd never abuse you like that…"

"I'm giving you permission. Look inside me and you'll see."

Gage's eyes darkened to a beautiful crimson and his skin did too, as if his demon half was surging to the surface. I couldn't imagine what it would be like to be able to change my body into different shapes, but I was wildly curious about what he could do. Seeing this magical side of him was kind of turning me on.

Wait. Did I have a monster kink? Jeremy had mentioned something about an idea he had for a monster kink book when he'd helped bartend the other night. The term seemed self-explanatory, so I hadn't asked for a definition, but maybe I should have.

Then Gage flipped us so suddenly everything around me blurred for a second. My back landed on the mattress with a soft thud and he was over me. His eyes were full red now—not a bit of white to be seen. The air between us grew heavy, laden with his power. I grinned up at him, knowing I'd triggered this response in him. It was a heady feeling.

My previous worries faded. I may not be a sex god…

or demon, as the case may be… but I didn't doubt Gage wanted me. And that was all I needed to know.

"Kiss me," I said. I licked my lips.

"Always demanding kisses," he murmured, then his mouth crashed against mine in a flurry of lips and tongue and heat and wetness. I reached for him, but he grabbed my hands and pinned them to the mattress on either side of my head. A deep, satisfied moan rumbled through him. I smiled against his mouth.

He jolted back.

"Why did you stop?"

"You're smiling…" He sounded confused.

"Shouldn't I be?"

"I didn't scare you?"

"No way," I said, and I meant it. Suddenly, all the words I was too timid to say aloud earlier came flowing out. "I'm not scared of you. I want you, Gage. I want to feel your skin on mine. I want to feel your cock on my tongue. I want to feel you inside me."

"My mate is perfect," he whispered. Then he stopped my words with more kisses.

I doubted he meant mate the same way Jeremy had. Maybe it was like boyfriend or something. But I didn't want to stop to ask him for more information, not when I was so close to having the mind-blowing sex I'd always dreamed about.

Gage let go of my hands long enough to strip away his underwear and then mine. My dick was still wonderfully hard. It bobbed and jerked, and I couldn't have been prouder of it. *Good job, dick. Good job at staying hard and on board with what's going on. You're about to get a nice reward.*

As if hearing my thoughts—and who knew, maybe he *was* seeing what was in my head—Gage lightly licked the tip of my cock. Once. Twice. My whole body shivered at the sensation. His tongue glided softly, teasingly, over my skin until I was trembling. Then he opened his mouth and took me all the way to the root. Fuck. No wonder people always raved about blowjobs. Lust rocketed through me, but it was stronger than I would have expected. It was like I was experiencing both my and Gage's desires all at once. It was overwhelming in the best possible way.

"Yes," I hissed as I bucked into his hot, wet mouth.

This was a gazillion times better than my last failed attempt at sex.

Some part of me knew I should want to stretch this moment out, but it felt so good—*Gage* felt so good. All these years I'd believed I was a failure at sex when all I'd needed was Gage. My demon. I reached blindly for him, needing to feel connected to him in every way possible as his mouth moved up and down over my shaft. I combed my fingers into his hair where they collided with his horns. He moaned encouragingly, and I wondered if his horns were sensitive. I grabbed the hard velvet length of them and held tight.

He slurped and hummed up and down my length, and I couldn't do anything but take it. His tongue teased my tip until tears streamed from my eyes at the helpless wonderfulness of it all. I came suddenly and without warning. My world exploded as I shot down Gage's throat. He held onto my hips, his fingers digging into my skin, and took everything.

When I collapsed, he gave my dick one last lick, then began dropping kisses over my hips and my inner thighs before working up to my stomach and higher. The bristles from his facial hair tickled over my skin, making me shiver. When he reached my mouth, he let his kisses linger and explore lazily, as if knowing my bones still felt like mush and I couldn't do more than move my lips right now. When his mouth traveled away from my lips to my cheek and my jaw and my neck, I finally found words.

"Is being good at blowjobs part of a demon's magic? Because holy fuck…"

Gage laughed at my question. "Nothing demonic. Just trying to please my mate. I see a lot of blowjobs in your future. Consider that the first of many. I plan to shower you with pleasure and give you everything you could ever want or need."

"You don't need to do that, but I definitely wouldn't turn down another blowjob. That was… wow…" I stretched and smiled. I don't think I'd ever felt so contented. My dick was spent and limp and happy. Then I thought about what I'd said. "But not right now," I added. "I don't think I could come again."

Gage grinned at me. "Is that a challenge?"

"It really isn't," I said.

But Gage wasn't listening. He stretched out beside me, bracing himself on one hand while the other coasted up and down my chest. His cock was still hard and leaking against my leg. I started to sit up so I could tend to him, but he pushed me back to the mattress. And when I reached for him, he shifted his hips away from my questing hand. When I looked up, I found him watching me.

"Were you serious about letting me fuck you?" Gage asked quietly.

I blinked. "You want to? Now?"

His hand paused in its exploration of my body. "Do you not wish to do more?"

I swallowed. "I mean. Uh… we could. I just thought I shouldn't push my luck, you know?"

His forehead creased in confusion. "What are you talking about?"

"I'm not good with sex. I've never been able to stay hard with anyone before today. I tried. A few times. And it was miserable. I don't want to push my luck and try to do more."

The darkness in Gage's eyes faded as he considered what I was saying. "You've never reacted to someone before?"

"Never."

Then he nodded. "Your sexual interest was likely blocked by the curse at the same time your oracle magic was. Both of those are in the same parts of your core."

"Someone took away my ability to have sex? Wow. That's harsh."

"We could experiment if you want." His eyes were turning crimson again.

"For science?"

"Of course."

"I wasn't very good at science either," I confessed, "but we could try."

He grinned wickedly at me, and my dick tried rallying again even though it'd only been a few minutes since I'd come harder than I ever had before.

My first successful blowjob. I wanted to commemorate it. Remember it forever. Would it be weird to immortalize this moment in paint?

Then again, I did have a lot of pictures of the two of us already painted by my oracle alter-ego. I could have already painted this moment... I really needed to look at all those paintings again, so I knew what would come next.

Hmm, this oracle gig might have some perks after all.

Chapter Twenty-Seven

GAGE

I'd been alive for a long, long time, but having Jake naked in my arms was unlike anything I'd ever experienced. I wanted to cherish him. I wanted to give him more pleasure than he thought he could endure. I wanted to breathe in his intoxicating scent as it blossomed when he came on my cock.

My dick was achingly hard just from taking him in my mouth and tasting him, but I could wait. Jake wasn't prepped or ready for me yet. I would never risk injuring him, especially not during sex. But before I could grab the lube and get him ready, he pushed me to my back.

"Need to feel you," he murmured. "So I know this is real."

I loved the feel of his hands dancing over my body. His feather-light touches teased and tormented in equal measure. He wasn't experienced—even if he hadn't told me, I would have been able to guess—but his shyness had faded. Since he'd hinted this was the first time being with someone where he wasn't freaking out, I let him explore.

When his hand wrapped around my length, my whole body jolted, and I almost came.

Jake's face lit up as he leaned over me, as if giddy with the power he had over me. His tongue darted out of his mouth and lapped at my ruddy crown. The little tease was mimicking what I'd done to him. He hummed in appreciation as his tongue slid along the slit.

"Jake," I moaned. I was seconds from throwing him down on the mattress and taking him.

He glanced up at me. His glistening reddened lips were millimetres from my dick. His hot breath washed over my heated skin like a caress. It'd be so easy to knot my fingers in his hair and take control. He would look so fucking hot with my dick sliding in and out of those plump lips. More precum dribbled out of my cock.

"If you want me to fuck you," I said, "you're going to have to stop what you're doing."

He bit his bottom lip, showing his indecision.

"What do you want, Jake?"

"I want it all." He pouted. "Why do I have to choose?"

"We can do it all, but not all at once." I cupped the side of his face in my hand, and he leaned into it. "We'll have an eternity together."

He sat up a little. I thought he'd ask me what I meant, since I hadn't had the chance to explain about us being mates yet, or about the bond I sensed was growing between us, but instead he let go of my dick and said, "Want you inside me."

I comforted myself with the knowledge that a bond

couldn't form accidently. He could still reject me. The only one I might hurt by continuing was myself.

"Come here, then," I whispered.

He crawled over me to straddle me. His knees hugged my hips. When our cocks rubbed together, I realized he was getting hard again. I reached up and wrapped my hand around the back of his neck and pulled him down so I could kiss his mouth.

As our mouths met, I slid my hands down his back to cup his ass. The soft round globes filled my hands perfectly. I squeezed and pulled him hard against my erection. It was dangerous to do that. Every brush of his body against mine pushed me closer to coming. But he felt so good on top of me; I couldn't resist grinding our bodies together.

Then I slipped my finger down until I found his entrance.

Shit. I forgot the lube.

I pulled away for a moment and Jake grunted his disapproval.

"Just a minute, sweetling," I whispered gruffly as I grabbed the container from the compartment in the built-in headboard.

I squirted the lube onto my fingers and reached for him again. When my slippery finger brushed over his opening, he gasped. He pushed his ass against my hand, wordlessly asking for more. This time, I didn't stop. I teased his opening until I felt him soften, then I pushed a finger in. Just a little to start.

"Oh," he breathed, just the one word. He wiggled against the intrusion. With his eyes locked on mine, he smiled shyly at me. That soft, tentative smile undid me. If all we did was this and nothing else, I would be happy.

When he finally asked for more, I pushed deeper. His body clenched around my finger, and I closed my eyes at the sensation. It took everything I had to stop myself from replacing my finger with my cock. I bucked my hips, desperate to feel him moving against me and eager to feel that wet tight heat around my cock.

My thoughts died away as he rocked against my hand, fucking himself on it. Now that his inhibitions were gone, he let himself go after what he wanted. Our cocks ground together with each movement, until I was blind with need for him.

"Jake," I groaned. It was a warning and a plea and a hint of something more.

"Gage, I need more," he said on a gasping breath.

I finished prepping him as quickly and thoroughly as I could. No more teasing. No more lingering. When he was ready, I broke our kiss. He braced himself on his arms, lifting his face up only high enough to look into my eyes.

He was beautiful like this with his rosy cheeks, swollen lips, and riot of messy hair. Had he ever painted himself looking this debauched? I hadn't flipped through the numerous paintings he'd done of the two of us, but I hoped one showed him exactly like this. I wanted it. I'd hang it in our bedroom and look at it every day as a reminder of how lucky I was.

"Ready?" I asked.

He nodded. His eyes looked dazed, but happy. I'd originally planned to have him lie on his stomach and take him from behind, but I needed to see his face.

"You're going to ride me," I whispered.

His eyes widened in surprise. "Uh…"

"Supes don't get sexual infections or diseases like humans do."

"So no condoms?"

"No condoms," I agreed. "Unless that's what you want."

He thought about it for a minute then shook his head. I'd never hurt him, but that he believed me… That was something precious. Humbling.

"Sit up," I whispered. Emotion choked my voice, making it rough and deep. "Then lower yourself onto me."

He rose on his knees, showing off his dick, which was hard again. I wanted to grab him by the hips and drag him up my body and suck his dick again, but there would be time to do that next time. Or the time after.

Instead, I put more lube on my fingers, then reached between us to spread it over my cock. Liberally. I wanted Jake's first experience to be beautiful and euphoric. I grabbed my length and held it in place. It brushed against him. His mouth opened slightly in a panting breath as he felt the tip of my cock against him. He shivered, and his gaze once again sought mine.

Fuck, he was beautiful like this. Flushed. Full of desire. Desperate for my cock.

I rubbed my crown against his opening, teasing us both, prolonging the anticipation. When neither of us could take any more, I held myself still.

"Now slowly lower yourself…" My words trailed off as he did as I said. His gaze clung to mine. The crown of my cock pushed against his opening. I trembled as I breached his entrance and slid inside. "Yes, just like that..." I groaned.

As we stared into one another's eyes, joined as closely as two people could be, our magic bloomed between us. I'd never seen Jake's magic manifest before, but I recognized it instantly. The light from his frolicked with the smoky darkness of my own. They twisted and entwined between us, as if we were joining in ways that weren't merely physical.

"Gage." His whisper was full of awe.

"There, that's it," I encouraged. "Keep going."

He inhaled sharply, pausing for a moment. I gripped his hips to steady him. His thighs shook as he took me deeper. Then Jake sank down more, taking my full length inside his hot channel. His eyelashes fluttered and his fingers dug into my chest where he was bracing himself. I loved the pinch of pain; I hoped he left marks on my body. Even if they would heal quickly, I wanted them. I wanted everything Jake gave me.

My hands clenched around his hips as he sat on my cock, not moving, adjusting to having me deep inside. I ached to move, to slide in and out of him, to feel the way his muscles squeezed me. When his face softened into a look of awe and his hips twitched, I gave in to instinct and rolled my hips. He moaned in pleasure. He was stunning like this. I couldn't believe the Eternal Magic had chosen such a beautiful man to be my mate.

Then, driven by instinct and need, we moved together like we'd been made for one another... because we had. Every whispered phrase, every panting breath, every slap of our bodies colliding created our own unique and precious song. One I wanted to hear every day for the rest of my life. I reached between us and wrapped my hand around his cock as he lost himself in pleasure. He threw his head back and gave himself over to the magic between us.

Jake was everything I'd ever dreamed of, and he felt even better.

As I chased my release, my eyes started to close, but suddenly the manifestation of our magics took on a fervent rhythm that matched our bodies. I stared in awe as the white light of Jake's magic came to life between us, painting pictures in the air—ethereal visions of the two of us, foretelling the life we might share. My own magic surged to weave through the images. Where our magics had started separately, they were merging between us, my black-and-red wisps with Jake's white. I'd never seen anything so breathtaking.

I wanted to linger in this moment, but I was too close to the edge. I couldn't stop. With a groan, I came hard, holding Jake tight as I filled him. He followed me a moment later, spilling over my stomach, marking me as his.

When some supes had sex, their magics united and made the experience even better. Or so I'd heard. I'd never experienced it myself, not until this moment. I didn't think any other union could produce what we shared, and I felt pity for those other people who would never experience a moment like this.

The scenes of us floated around us as our bodies cooled. Then the images created by our joined magics drifted closer. I expected the magic to simply fall into our bodies and be absorbed inside us again. But when the images settled over our heated, sweaty skin, they didn't disappear. They merged with our skin, molding to the contours of our bodies. When the energy of our magic dissipated, the tattoo-like images on our bodies remained.

Eyes wide with wonder, Jake reached for the one on my chest. I couldn't make out all the details on my own body, which made me want to find the closest mirror. But the one on Jake showed the two of us in an embrace much like we were in now. I hoped mine was the same. When he traced his finger along the lines on my skin, the image didn't move or fade.

"How…?"

"I don't know," I admitted. "I've heard supes can exchange energy through sex, but I've never had anything like this happen before."

His gaze snapped to mine. "Is this like the tattoos Ash and Dillon have? Or the markings on Jeremy and Adrian?"

I sucked in a breath. Had we bonded already? So easily? I should have asked Adrian for more details when he bonded with his mate, but I'd never expected to need that information. I'd never expected the Eternal Magic to bless me with a mate. Then I remembered what I'd heard about bonds years ago. The mating bond wouldn't finalize until both parties knew what was happening, and each person decided they wanted the bond. Jake and I had too many secrets between us still for that to happen.

"No… I don't think we're bonded. Not yet," I said. "Perhaps it is because as an oracle you need a strong tether, and your magic is seeing if I could be that for you.

Or it could simply be because you could be my mate if you wanted to be."

His gaze snapped to mine. "Mate?"

I nodded.

"Like what Jeremy talked about the other day?"

"Why don't we clean up? Then we can talk."

I reluctantly moved Jake off me and rolled out of bed. No one was in the motorhome, so I didn't bother with clothing as I went to the bathroom to wet a cloth. The sun had already risen, though, so I doubted we'd have privacy for much longer.

After we cleaned up, a process that had Jake blushing again as I wiped the sweat and our spend from his skin, I rested against the headboard and opened my arms. Jake climbed into my lap and once again I was struck by how simple and right this all felt. It was like he was always meant to be beside me.

"So, mates?" he asked.

I brushed a kiss against his hair and took a deep breath. "I hadn't planned to tell you so soon. You only just found out about the Eternal Magic yesterday, so I didn't want to overwhelm you. But I believe we could be mates."

"I know you've already explained that to me, but that was before I knew you thought I could be yours. I have more questions now."

"Like I said before, fated mates are two beings who are destined to be together. Some people say each person has more than one possible mate, but given how few people actually find theirs, I'm not convinced that is true." I swallowed as emotions welled inside me. "Honestly, I never expected to find mine, and yet here you are."

"And I'll become immortal like you. That's what you said, right? My life expectancy would change to match yours."

I nodded. "If the Eternal Magic doesn't do it, I will find a way to do it myself… if you agree. I'd never bind us without your consent." My chest tightened at the thought of Jake choosing to hang on to his mortality and having to watch him grow old and die. I wouldn't survive it.

Jake was silent for quite a long time after I stopped talking. Finally, he asked, "Why do you think we're fated?"

"You don't think it is prophetic that you painted so many pictures of the two of us, long before we met? Your visions don't lie. But more than that, it is the way I feel toward you. You fill my thoughts. You've given me hope."

"I thought I was going crazy, painting the same stranger over and over again," he whispered. "When you walked down my hallway that first time, I thought I was hallucinating."

He pressed his face into my neck, and I hugged him tighter. "I am sorry you went through all that. I don't understand why your family never spoke of magic with you, since one of your parents must have been a supe." It was shockingly cruel to leave him so ill-prepared and vulnerable. "Magic like yours doesn't pop up in random humans."

"What about Jeremy? It sounds like that's what happened to him."

"He is the only human I know who was blessed with magic without having it in his family. In every other situation, magic is hereditary." I brushed a kiss against his hair.

"Like a wolf shifter will have children who are also wolf shifters?"

"Yes, exactly like that," I said.

"So one of my parents was an oracle? My mother never talked about my father, but it must have been him, right? No wonder she was so freaked out by anything magical."

"I suspect your magic is more akin to a mage's," I said slowly, not looking forward to telling him my suspicions about his mother. "A mage's child will be able to work magic but may not have the same type as their parent. In your case, oracles are incredibly rare. I doubt either of your parents was an oracle, but at least one of them must have had magic. And if your grandfather was as powerful as everyone says, it would pass to his child. Was that your mother?"

"Yes," he said. "She was his only child, like I was hers. It was just my mom and I for a long time. I didn't meet my grandfather until she passed almost a year ago. He invited me to Willow Lake, said he wanted to get to know me. And then I'd only been here about a month when he died too."

"I am so sorry." I stroked his back. "Having all of those tragedies happen so close together couldn't have been easy."

He swallowed and shook his head slightly. I rubbed long soothing strokes across his back.

"It was a year ago, you said?" I asked after a few minutes.

"Yeah, just before my birthday. Why?"

His birthday was coming up soon. That was good to

know. I couldn't wait to spoil him. I wanted to ask him about it now, but that would have to wait. Finding out about the curse was more important. I needed to keep the conversation focused on that.

"Did your mother do anything that seems strange when you think about it now?" It was perhaps heartless to ask him this question, with everything else going on, but I needed to know if it really was his mother who'd cursed him. If it was someone else, he could have another unknown enemy out there. One I'd need to deal with.

Jake stilled. He cleared his throat. My senses weren't as strong as Adrian's, but in the quiet of the room, I didn't need to be a wolf shifter to hear his heart racing. "Why?"

"Just a thought…"

"She never wanted me to meet my grandfather," he said. "She even told me he was dead."

"Hmm… It must have been a surprise then to discover he was alive."

"You think you know why she lied to me, don't you?"

I hesitated. "Do you not have any ideas?"

"Would she have been able to sense I had magic?"

"Yes. Even if she didn't have much herself, she would have sensed yours. Your oracle magic is very strong. I doubt she would have missed it."

He huddled closer to me, curling into himself. "You think she tried to stop my magic. You think she's the one who cursed me."

I didn't say anything. I just continued to stroke his back. Because it wasn't so much what I thought; it was what he thought. And chances were, he knew more than he was acknowledging, even to himself. He reached for the duvet we'd kicked off during sex and pulled it around us, wrapping us in a warm cocoon. Then he trembled in my arms for a long while, while I tried to soothe him as best I could.

"On my birthday," he whispered, "she'd make me a weird drink. It tasted like dirt and grass clippings with a coppery taste that reminded me of blood. Disgusting. She wrote down the recipe, but I never read it. I couldn't tell you what the ingredients are; I never tried making it. She said it was a family tradition. She made me promise to keep the tradition alive no matter where I went or if I was with her. But when she died, I didn't want to remember our traditions. It was too difficult. So I didn't make it last year…"

"And that's when your visions started."

"So my own mother cursed me…"

"She was probably trying to protect you. She may not have understood that magic can't be stopped." I pressed another kiss on his hair. "When I saw the remnants of the curse, it was severely deteriorated. Even if you'd continued to poison yourself with your mother's potion, the curse would have unravelled sooner or later. The Eternal Magic hates being contained. In some ways, you were lucky it happened as it did. If the magic had been forced to fight its way free, you might never have recovered."

"But why?"

I hesitated.

Jake looked up at me then. "What else haven't you told me?"

I sighed and reminded myself this conversation was

long overdue. "Like any magic, an oracle's requires balance. Because your visions are of the future, you need something to anchor you to the present. If you don't have a tether, you will get lost in your visions. When that happens…" I didn't want to say it, but I knew he needed to know. "When that happens, you will forget to live in the present. Untethered oracles get caught in an unending cycle of having one vision after another." *Until they die,* I left unsaid.

Jake shuddered and wrapped his arms over his stomach. "Is that what's going on? My visions, as you call them, are happening more frequently. In the beginning, I'd just feel a little dizzy, but now…" His words drifted off.

"When Adrian needs to balance his magic, he eats protein. For Teague, another from my team who you haven't met yet, he needs an apple. For you, it is a little different. From what I understand about oracles, you need a tether."

"Which is what exactly?"

"It's a bond between you and something firmly anchored in the present. It might be a place, or a friend, or…"

"A mate?" he guessed.

"Yes, except…"

He stiffened in my arms. "You think we're mates, but you don't want to be my tether?"

"It isn't that I don't want to be your tether." I hated having to talk about this, but it was necessary. "When I used my magic to heal you after the bombs, I made my decision. You are the only one for me. My magic and I see

289

you as mine, but that doesn't mean you can't still walk away."

"What did you do?" He didn't sound worried, just curious. "Because I've felt things since then. Almost like I could feel you inside me..." His cheeks darkened. "I mean, not like *sex*, but like your feelings or something. I'm not doing a very good job of explaining this."

"I... I didn't know it would do that." I paused. "I'm sorry. I didn't realize..."

"It's fine," he said, dismissing my apology more easily than he should have. "But if you've chosen me like you said, then what's the problem?"

"My demon magic is a little different too. Most of my magic is balanced through negotiations and promises. I make deals with people. They offer me something, and in exchange I use my magic to help them. If I use magic without having a deal in place, it can become unbalanced. A demon who isn't stable becomes dangerous, to themselves or anyone around them."

"Okay..." Jake said, drawing the word out. "I get the sense there is more that you aren't telling me."

"Like oracles, demons eventually need tethers too. I'm nearing the age when finding my own tether is becoming a necessity. But for me, it can only be a place. Once I bind to it, I would become its guardian."

"But if the deals balance your magic, why do you need a tether too?"

I shrugged a little, but I wasn't sure if Jake noticed. "I don't know. I'm not sure if anyone does. I've given it a lot of thought over the years and I've come up with two possible scenarios. There may be a limit to how much magic my demon side can access and as I get closer to using everything I have been allocated by the Eternal Magic, it grows more unstable. My other theory is that a residue gets left behind whenever I use my magic, and over time it accumulates to unmanageable quantities and interferes with my ability to access more."

"Like a magical heart attack brought on by magical cholesterol." Jake's forehead furrowed as he mulled over everything I'd said. "So, if you don't find a place, you become dangerous. When does it happen? How much time do we have?"

I smiled at his use of the word *we*, as if he expected to be at my side from now on, helping any way he could.

"I am already much older than my father was when it happened to him."

"So you think it's getting close?" Jake's fingers tightened where he was holding me.

My father's red eyes flashed in my mind's eye, always so close to my thoughts, never fading with time. I didn't want to discuss him with Jake, but what choice did I have?

Chapter Twenty-Eight

GAGE

Jake cupped my cheek as he held my gaze for a long moment. "Do you want to talk about it?"

I grimaced. I didn't, but it really was the best way for him to understand the reality of becoming involved with me... a demon.

"I was born in a small village along what is now the border between Scotland and England," I started. "My grandfather had tethered to the place when he was a young man. I have a few memories of how the villagers would come to our home. It seemed there were always strangers about, but at that age I hadn't come into my magic yet. My father would assist my grandfather with his work, until one day my father woke me in the dead of night, insisting we needed to flee."

"How old were you?"

"Around ten, I think... Old enough to have clear memories of that night, even after all these years."

"Why did you need to run?"

"My father said my grandfather had become jealous of his magic. Having bonded with the place, he couldn't tolerate another demon in his territory."

"But wouldn't that have always been the case, as soon as your grandfather tethered there? Why would it come to a head so many years later?"

I nodded. "I've asked myself that same question many times."

Jake brushed his fingers through my hair. His soft touch soothed me as he waited for me to continue. I considered leaving my explanation there, but it wouldn't be fair. He deserved to know who he was in bed with. I should have told him before things had gotten this far between us.

"My parents and I traveled the world over the next several decades as my father searched for a place that called to him. I feared and hoped he'd find it in equal measure. And, as time wore on, he became more unpredictable and volatile. The smallest inconvenience or perceived slight would set him off. I hoped if he tethered to a place he would calm. But at the same time…"

"You feared he'd turn on you like his own father had…"

"Yes," I admitted quietly. I hated remembering those selfish worries. "When my mother died of old age, he became worse."

"They weren't mates?"

I shook my head. I often wondered, though, why my father hadn't bound my mother to him the same way I had my team. They weren't true mates, so the Eternal Magic hadn't stepped in to do it, but he could have lengthened her life. She was devoted to him. I was sure, if he'd offered to extend her life so they had more time together, she'd have given him anything he asked of her to balance his magic.

It was just one more thing I'd never know the answer to.

"So what happened?"

"One day my father just... broke. I don't know how else to explain it. It was winter and we'd been caught in a terrible blizzard. When we finally found a room in a little hamlet where we could rest and wait out the storm, I fell asleep. Although I remember my father mumbling about the energy in the place, I didn't sense anything significant. But I wouldn't have if the place wasn't meant to be mine." I paused for a moment, needing to brace myself to finish the rest of the grisly story. Jake just continued to pet my hair. "My father killed the entire village while I slept. When I woke, it was to find him looming over me. Blood coated his hands. His red eyes stared at me like I was a stranger. Then he swiped at me, going for my throat."

Jake sucked in a sharp breath. His hand tightened for a moment in my hair, but I didn't mind. I welcomed the bite of pain, since it reminded me I wasn't in that cold dark room facing off against my father.

"I killed him. Eventually," I admitted with a ragged breath. I hadn't actually told anyone that before. I simply told my team I'd had to kill a demon who lost his mind because he never found his place. I never confessed it was my father I'd killed. "It was him or me... and I couldn't let him kill anyone else."

Jake wrapped his arms around me and squeezed. "I'm so sorry, Gage. I am so very sorry."

I leaned into the comfort he offered, but I couldn't stop yet. There was still more to say. "I chose my family—my team—because I need people around me who can kill me if my demonic side breaks. Given my age, I know I'm on borrowed time. Every time my demonic magic surges, I risk it shattering altogether. And a demon who has no control is dangerous, not just to themselves but to anyone they see." I paused and looked straight into his eyes. "If you tethered to me right now, it could destroy us both if I lost control because of how strong our connection would be."

Jake clung to me.

"I think I could tether to Willow Lake," I admitted quietly.

He sat up abruptly, smiling. "That's good, then, right? You won't have to leave."

"If I could tether here, you're right. I would stay, but…"

Jake tensed.

"If I'm wrong and Willow Lake isn't mine, the results could be catastrophic. I suspect that's what my father tried to do… bind to a place that wasn't meant to be his. And that was what ultimately broke his already fragile hold on his magic."

"Well, fuck," Jake muttered. And I couldn't agree more.

Chapter Twenty-Nine

JAKE

It could destroy us both…

That cheery pronouncement haunted me as we dressed, me in clothes that either Ash or Jeremy must have dropped off for me while we were sleeping. One thing about all the talk of mates, curses, tethers, and murderous family members was that it had distracted me from what had happened to the inn the day before.

Just before we left the bedroom, I pulled Gage to me for a kiss and a hug. I had to stand on my tiptoes to reach his mouth, but it was worth it when our mouths met.

"We're going to figure this out," I said.

It was a presumptuous statement, considering I didn't know anything about magic, but I had painted a lot of scenes of the two of us and we hadn't done everything in those pictures yet. Even the ones that'd danced around us when we made love had said the same thing. We were going to get through this. It was going to work out. Somehow.

I glanced at the sliver of his chest that was visible where his collar was open. The edge of the magical love tattoo was still there, like a reminder it'd all be okay. I might not have believed in visions a few days ago, but I did now. And I refused to believe they were filled with lies, because fuck that shit.

Except...

"Wait," I said as I yanked his shirt open to expose more of his chest.

"What are you doing...?" Gage's question trailed off when he looked down at his exposed skin. The tattoo was fading. Our eyes met. My worry was reflected in his face.

"It doesn't mean anything bad," I said. My eyes were stinging.

"Doesn't mean anything bad at all," he agreed in a gruff voice. Gage's eyes must have been burning too, because he blinked a few times as he pulled me into a hug. "It makes sense the markings would fade, so new ones can form in their place."

"Should we find out?" I liked the idea of going back to bed with my sexy demon, and I wanted to confirm his theory. I needed to know the tattoos' fading wasn't an omen of anything bad. Hiding in the bedroom was also a great way to avoid all the shit we'd be slapped with the moment we went outside. From the damage to the inn to the threat to my life, I didn't want to face any of it.

But this was probably just me avoiding reality again, just like I had for the last year whenever my visions hit.

"I wish we could." Gage shook his head. "But I need to

talk to my team. They've been protecting your drawing all night. And now that the sun is up, we should be able to see it more clearly."

Right. How could I have forgotten about having a vision in the middle of the night?

"Oh no... Did I go out there in my underwear?" I squirmed at the idea of Gage's friends seeing me in my underwear. My orange polar bear underwear. At least I hadn't been wearing my Bob Ross ones. Although... *would* that have been worse?

"Yes, you did." Gage scowled at the memory.

Did that mean they'd discussed my underwear? I hoped no one would comment, and we could all just forget that it ever happened. I crossed my fingers.

If I could ignore the fire in Van's eyes or the way Hayden's eyes flashed when someone annoyed him, I could pretend no one had seen me strutting around in my undies.

Actually, now that I thought about it, Gage's eyes turned colors too. Did that mean all supernatural beings had strange eyes?

"Does anything happen to my eyes when I go all oracle?"

Gage lifted an eyebrow. "Not really. It just looks like you're staring off into space or daydreaming."

"How boring," I muttered as Gage passed me a couple of breakfast bars. I tore one open as Gage opened the door to the outside.

I chewed as I gave myself a silent pep talk. *Everything is fine. No one saw my underwear. Everything is fine. No one saw my underwear.*

I was right behind Gage on the steps, admiring his broad shoulders, when I realized the chatter and noise outside was louder than I'd expected. A lot louder. Seeing all the people who'd gathered, I choked on the bite I'd just taken of the granola bar. My cheeks bulged as I tried to chew, and I was pretty sure I was doing a good imitation of a chipmunk storing nuts for later.

A mob of people turned to look at me.

Why were all these people here?

Had they heard us when we'd… you know… been doing it?

Of course they would have. The walls had about as much soundproofing as a sheet.

Would anyone notice if I ran back inside and hid in Gage's bedroom?

Because this was more embarrassing than knowing I'd been doing my mad zombie painter act while only wearing my skiing polar bear underwear.

Had I made loud noises?

Had the motorhome been a-rocking, so they didn't come a-knocking? I groaned. Why had my brain gone there?

I inhaled sharply and bits of granola made a run for my windpipe. Fuck. I coughed and chunks of granola spewed out in every direction, hitting Gage's back and the few unlucky people who were standing closest to me. People shouted in surprise and stepped back. I tried to apologize but all I could do was cough and wonder if I was dying.

Gage spun around, pulled me off the step, then whacked me on the back to dislodge more granola.

"Water…" I croaked between more sputtering coughs.

He rushed inside and returned at lightning speed. He shoved a water bottle in my face, then thumped me on the back a few more times.

A man I'd never met approached. He was sweet looking, like the boy next door... well, if the boy next door had black smoke curling up from his fingers, but whatever.

"I'm Teague," he said. "Let me help."

"You can trust him," Gage said. "He's a mage."

So I nodded and Teague placed his hand on my upper chest. A strange pulse of something—magic, I supposed—jumped from him into my body. Teague hummed and the magical pulse intensified. Then it faded as quickly as it had started.

It was like the last few minutes never happened. My throat felt normal. And, more importantly, I could breathe again without coughing.

"Wow. Thank you."

Teague's hand dropped to his side while he brought the other up to the side of the motorhome to brace himself. Gage stopped him before he touched the wall, stepping closer to steady Teague.

"Can you grab him an apple?" Gage asked me.

As I ran inside and grabbed the first apple I saw in the crisper of the small fridge, I heard Gage asking Teague if he was having problems adjusting to being in Willow Lake.

"It's a lot," the mage said, "but nothing I can't handle. Davie says there are a lot of ghosts, like you thought there would be. But it's all been manageable so far." Teague smiled at me when I returned and gave him the apple.

As soon as Teague bit into the fruit, Gage turned back to me. "How are you feeling?"

I swallowed, testing out my throat. "I feel fine. What did he do?"

"Magic," Teague said between bites.

The people who'd been standing outside formed a ring around us now.

"Now that the drama is over," a woman said from the far side of the group, "tell me who the hell this is and what the hell has been going on. I knew I shouldn't have left you all alone this long."

With her hands on her hips, she looked tiny but fierce. I didn't doubt she could take down any of the beefy guys standing close to her. If I'd been into women at all, I'm pretty sure she'd be my type. Because apparently I had a thing for confident, take-control types.

She had a Katharine Hepburn thing going on with a short-sleeved blouse, and slacks with flowing pantlegs. Her platinum blonde hair was styled in victory rolls at the front and shoulder-length curls in the back. It reminded me a bit of a mullet, but a classy one.

"Davina," Gage said behind me. "You're here. Good. Come, you haven't met Jake yet."

The woman marched over to us with her eyes narrowed. As soon as she was close to Gage, she ripped the collar of his shirt open.

"What is that?" She stabbed her finger at the fading mark left on Gage's skin from when we'd had sex. I wanted to knock her hand away.

Gage ignored her question. "This is Davina. She is second in command of my team. She's my failsafe. She is also a medium capable of talking with and banishing ghosts and other spirits."

My stomach twisted when he called her his failsafe. I knew instantly what he meant, and it was nothing good. She was the one who'd decide if he needed to be killed. With the look she'd shot in my direction, I didn't doubt she'd be capable of murdering someone.

"Davina, this is Jake. And I believe he is my mate."

"What?" Davina shrieked. "You found your mate? Is it fait accompli? Is that what those marks are?"

"Not yet."

"Still, why didn't you tell me?" She spun around to the others on their team. "Why didn't anyone text me?"

Nelson stepped back into one of the long morning shadows cast by the trees lining the driveway leading to the inn. Then I blinked and he disappeared. Isaac was laughing in that weird horse-like way of his. Meanwhile, Teague just rolled his eyes at Davina, and I was impressed by his calm in the face of her intense scrutiny. Then again, he wouldn't have known either.

"We didn't know," Adrian said, rubbing the back of his neck.

Davina frowned and if looks had powers, Adrian and the others would have been on their knees.

"Oh... I like her." Jeremy whispered, loud enough even I could hear. He adjusted the strap on the backpack he wore as something inside it shifted around. Then a little head popped out. It was the strangest looking thing I'd ever seen. Its bright green eyes bounced around the circle, as if assessing us.

Jeremy didn't seem to notice either the animal or

Davina's scowl. He pulled out a small notebook from his back pocket and started jotting down notes.

"Is that an Emerald Mackobant?" Davina narrowed her eyes at the creature in Jeremy's backpack.

Jeremy glanced up and smiled. He scratched the animal on its chin, and it cooed happily.

"Isn't she adorable? Her name is Emma. We found her at an RV lot and she decided to come home with us. She and Clawie had a little squabble this morning, so we didn't think it would be good to leave them alone without supervision."

"It's a wild animal," Davina said. "You shouldn't try to domesticate it."

Jeremy gasped and tried to cover the creature's ears.

"We've tried to let her free in the woods here, but she refuses to leave us," Adrian said quickly.

Davina just shook her head and continued scowling at everyone.

Van, Hayden, Dillon, and Ash were all here too, but they didn't react to Davina's glower, which made sense since I didn't think they were on Gage's team. He'd talked about his team but, let's face it, I'd had a lot of things on my mind these last few days. Now I wished I'd paid more attention. Just so I understood the group dynamic. I needed to know everything about them so I could figure out how to get them to like me.

If they didn't, would he drop me? Fated mates or not?

No. I refused to let that happen. I couldn't let him go now. When Jeremy had first suggested we might be mates, I'd dismissed it. But now I was ready to fight for my spot at Gage's side. And, with Gage's team being so important to him, I needed them to accept me.

And while I was at it, I would also make sure they understood Gage was not to be murdered until every other possible option had been exhausted. I didn't care if he turned evil. I didn't care what happened when a demon snapped. If they hurt him, I would go after them. He was mine and I'd make sure everyone knew it.

I blinked.

Whoa.

My brain had just leapfrogged into murderous territory. That wasn't normal, was it? I was pretty sure that was a relationship red flag. Then again, maybe it wasn't for supes. I'd thought I'd been going crazy just a few days ago and it ended up just being normal supernatural behaviour, so it stood to reason that crazy possessive murderous thoughts might be too, right? I swallowed. I'd ask Gage later. In private. Far away from where the Chief of Police might hear.

Then Davina turned her attention back to us. Wowser, she was intense.

"And that?" She prodded the fading mark on Gage's skin.

"It happened this morning…" Gage said. He glanced at me.

My cheeks were burning at the memory of what we'd been doing at the time, but I waved at him to continue. I suspected his team didn't have many secrets. It'd be too dangerous. And they probably all knew we'd had sex. Not that our sex life was a secret… It was just private.

"When we made love this morning, our magics merged

and…" He gestured toward his chest. "I suspect it has to do with his magic as an oracle."

Jeremy made a delighted squeal and scribbled madly in his notebook.

"This is the oracle everyone's been talking about?" Davina skewered me with another penetrating look.

If she was always this intense, I bet the ghosts she encountered ran to the afterworld just to escape her.

"Hi," I said. My voice cracked over the single syllable. I waved awkwardly.

Then she grabbed me and yanked me into an aggressive and uncomfortably tight hug. Was she trying to break my ribs?

"Thank Mother Magic he found you," she whispered quietly in my ear. And she sounded almost happy… emotional even… taking me completely by surprise.

Then she patted me hard on the back and released me from the hug. I sagged and Gage caught me. He wrapped his arm around my waist to steady me as I sucked in air to fill my lungs again.

Teague stepped up next to hug me. He didn't squeeze me as tightly, but it was still awkward. My mother had never been much of a hugger. My grandfather had been, but I'd only been with him for a month before he was gone. It wasn't long enough to convert me into being a hugger too.

"Congratulations and welcome to our strange little family," Teague said. He patted me on the back. "I guess this means I'll have to give you a fair price when I try to buy all the magical artifacts I keep hearing about."

I laughed awkwardly. I still hadn't come to terms with

all the problems that'd arisen from the robbery. I wasn't ready to joke about it. And, honestly, I would be happy to give the stuff to Teague. He'd do a better job of protecting it. But, given how little I knew about everything magical, perhaps I should ask someone for advice first. I didn't want to make another magical misstep.

Before I figured out what to say to him, he broke his hug and went to embrace Gage. Then it seemed like everyone from the team and a few local Willow Lake people came over to congratulate us.

"Alright," Gage said a few minutes later, "enough. Anyone who hasn't met yet, make your introductions now. We have work to do."

Chapter Thirty

JAKE

I wished I was anywhere but here as everyone turned to stare at what I'd drawn on the side of the motorhome. They all studied the awful, horrible drawing like it was fascinating, and I couldn't force myself to do more than take a few glances at it before turning toward the sunrise. I pretended to study the colors so I could paint them later, but really, I was just trying to ignore that I'd drawn a massacre—like, WTF, brain?

"It looks like the wolf pack…" someone murmured.

"Does this mean they're all going to die?" someone else whispered.

"Is this connected to the bombing? A kind of retribution?" someone else queried.

Alarmed, I looked at Hayden.

"I didn't do this," I said. "I mean… Yes, I drew it, but I'm not… I don't know… inciting the Eternal Magic to take revenge or whatever."

"I didn't think you did," Hayden assured me, even though his voice wasn't as strong and steady as usual. "I know oracles are vessels for Mother Magic's messages, nothing more."

I had to look away from Hayden. The haggard look on his face was breaking my heart. It couldn't have been easy for him to see what I'd drawn, knowing he had family out there. I wanted to say I was sorry. That I didn't mean it. But he was right, I couldn't control what I painted. Thankfully, everyone here seemed to accept that.

Meanwhile, the rest of the group just continued to murmur and point at things while Van took photos. Jeremy was busy writing a dissertation in his notebook. His strange creature had emerged from the backpack now and was draped over Adrian's shoulders. I blinked at it. The thing had four arms and two legs. That just wasn't right. Where had he found such a thing? I edged away from where they were standing.

I ignored them all until Isaac leaned over to whisper something in Teague's ear. I distinctly heard the words *polar bears*. Teague chuckled, then his gaze darted to me. I scowled at Isaac with my hands on my hips. He didn't need to tell everyone about my underwear. He raised his hands in surrender, but he was laughing now too.

"Come on," he said. "It was funny. I mean... the polar bears were so damn cute on those skis."

Gage's scowling face was much more effective than mine. The smiles dropped right off Isaac and Teague's faces. Shit. Was I being an ass? They probably ribbed one another all the time. Was this Isaac's way of bonding with me? I'd never had brothers or friends who did that, but it was a good thing, right?

I hadn't caffeinated enough yet to make decisions like this or deal with people today.

Then the other chatter quieted too.

"Let's talk about next steps." Van looked each of us in the eye.

Nelson lifted his hand. "I want to go back to the pack today. See what is happening. Try to gather evidence about the bombs."

"My deputies and I have already been to the pack," Van said. "Robbie turned over two pack members, saying they were responsible. He denies having any knowledge of what happened."

"Well, that's bullshit," Nelson muttered. "I heard him talking. There is no way he didn't orchestrate the whole damn thing."

"The wolves we arrested have confessed." Van frowned. "And Robbie was careful not to lie to my face. He knows hellhounds are walking lie-detectors and has learned how to phrase things without implicating himself. But there isn't much more we can do to the pack unless something else turns up."

"So that's why we need to go and look," Nelson said.

"My deputies and I should be the ones to gather evidence."

Nelson rolled his eyes. "You've spent too long working in a human police department. You're thinking like a human. We're trained enforcers for the SC. This is what we do."

Van looked at Gage, who merely nodded. Then he turned to Hayden, who didn't do anything but grind his teeth together.

"Fine," the hellhound said, but he didn't sound happy.

Isaac nodded. "I'll go with him."

A vein in Hayden's jaw pulsed as he clenched his teeth. No one else spoke up.

"We're all concerned about Jake's vision." Gage gestured to the drawing. "But we can't predict when it'll happen. It might be months or years from now. We also don't have enough data to know if what is shown in the visions can be altered."

"True." Van stroked his chin. "We still have boxes of magical artifacts unaccounted for too. The vision from yesterday is a problem, because it looks a lot like the trafficking operation you found in the city. And the bombers..." He stumbled over the word. It was strange to see the unflappable Chief of Police so emotional about what had happened. "The bombers are in custody. At least the scapegoats are. I'm not sure there is much more we can do about that."

Gage nodded. "We need to get one of those wolves to break and turn on Rob or Robbie or whatever you want to call him. I doubt he's shared many details with his pack, but they may have noticed something."

"We'll talk to them. See what we can do." Van nodded. "All right. Let's touch base when we know more."

Then the group broke apart.

Nelson and Isaac went to talk to Van, probably to discuss the wolves he'd taken into custody. I hated that they were going out to the pack again. I hated to think of any of Gage's team being in danger. A short time later, most of the people had departed.

"Hey, I feel like I didn't properly welcome you to the newbie supe club, now that you're in the know, and I have so many things to tell you," Jeremy said, patting me on my shoulder. "As I said yesterday, I just found out about magic too. I've been writing up all my observations, kind of a Magic 101 handbook. I'm thinking of calling it *The Amazing Book of Super Supes*, but everything, including the title, is still a work in progress. I'd be happy to share my notes. Sorry, I should have mentioned this yesterday. Most of the supes around here are aware of it because I've been asking to interview them, so I kind of forgot you wouldn't know about it yet."

"Uh… Thanks?"

"It's overwhelming, right? But so freaking awesome at the same time."

"So you just found out about magic?"

"Yes," Jeremy beamed and bounced on his toes. The creature—Emma—had its four arms wrapped around Jeremy's leg now. Its strange beigy-greenish fur shimmered in the sunlight. "Just found out. I'm not very good at it yet, but Adrian's been practicing with me. Okay. Well. The truth is, I suck at it. The white light in the pub the other night, though, that was me. You saw that, right? I'm just not sure why or how it happened. Everyone says to give it time, but seriously? That is the lamest advice ever. Because if I have magic, I want to use it. All the time. It's like my childhood dream come true."

I wished I had that much enthusiasm for my own supernatural awakening.

"Alrighty, then. I have so many questions for you," Jeremy said, adjusting his notebook and pen so he was ready to write down anything I said. "Or do you have questions for me first? I'm sure there are heaps of things you want to know. And don't be worried about your questions. You can ask me anything. Like, I'm sure you've wondered if you can get pregnant now. And the answer is no. Mpreg isn't a thing."

I blinked. Should I have worried about that? Even considering everything I'd questioned over the last day, pregnancy had not made the list. At all.

"Second, biting is fun... but I'm guessing you know that already." He eyed the fading marks on my neck with a knowing smirk.

"Biting?" I asked, covering my neck with my hand. "People bite each other. Is that a good thing? Really?"

"Hmm." Jeremy's forehead wrinkled. "Well, I'm sure Mr. Dimples will get around to that. Okay... now this is a personal question, but inquiring minds want to know... Can you describe his dick? For research. Is there a knot? Something else?"

"What?" My mouth dropped open. I couldn't have heard him right.

"Jeremy. Don't ask him that!" Adrian looked horrified. His face was bright red.

"Fine," Jeremy muttered. "But—"

"Ease up on how much information you're dumping on him, yeah? You're freaking him out," Adrian said. "Not everyone's mind works like yours did when you found out about supes."

Honestly, I suspected no one's mind worked the way Jeremy's did. Period.

"Oops... right. Got it."

"Come over and meet Davie properly," Adrian said, leading his boyfriend toward Davina.

"Fine, but she better not say anything about Emma." Jeremy scowled.

Then he put his hand up to his ear and mouthed *call me*, as soon as Adrian glanced away. Then he bounded over to the woman, with a huge smile on his face and his notebook ready in his hand. Apparently his concern over her attitude to his bizarre pet didn't undermine his natural curiosity. As soon as the introductions were finished, he started bombarding her with questions, as if trying to figure out how her magic worked.

At least Jeremy hadn't done that to me. I had no idea how my magic worked. And that was just one more thing I'd have to figure out at some point. I exhaled slowly. All I wanted to do was go to my room and hide for a while, but the fire department said it was still too dangerous.

Under normal circumstances, by this time of the day, I would have just finished feeding Paws and—

Shit. Where was Paws? I hadn't seen the cat since... I didn't even know when. I turned toward the inn in horror.

Gage rushed to my side. "What? What's wrong?"

"The cat... Paws... I haven't seen him. Do you think...?"

"Fan out, everyone," Gage said. "We're looking for the cat."

"A cat?" Davina looked confused.

"A supernatural cat," Gage clarified. "His name is Paws and he talks."

Davina's elegantly plucked eyebrows rose. "Okay then."

Then everyone started calling Paws' name and searching around the inn for my grandfather's strange cat.

Chapter Thirty-One

GAGE

"Paws!" Jake sounded frantic as he called the cat's name. We'd scoured the yard around the inn and hadn't found any trace of the creature yet. When we rounded the corner to the back of the building, Jake eyed the skeletal remains of his back dining room. His face twisted, betraying his horror at what might have happened. "Do you think he got trapped inside?"

I sighed. "I'll go in and see if I can find him."

Jake lifted his chin. "I'm going with you."

"No, it's too dangerous."

"It's just as dangerous for you as it is for me."

"Hasn't he told you?" Davina came over to us. "He's pretty much indestructible."

Jake frowned and fisted his hands. "No, he isn't. He's told me about the stupid pact you each made. If you can kill him, so can other things. And for the record, we're going to have a long talk about the deal you all made. Violence isn't the answer."

"That's different." Davina paled. She hated talking about the promise she made to me. They all did.

Jake put his hands on his hips and scowled at her. Since he was distracted, I seized the opportunity to open a small portal. When I stepped into the dining room, I took in the destruction. The damage didn't seem so bad today, maybe because it was no longer a shock.

The soles of my shoes crunched over debris as I followed a sound coming from the kitchen. The gas to the building had been turned off the day before, so I wasn't concerned about getting caught in another explosion. The deeper I went into the building, the heavier the scent of smoke and ash became. It would take a lot of time and money to get this place habitable again.

The door to the kitchen was hanging off its hinges at an odd angle, but it still opened when I pushed on it. Just inside, I found the cat gorging himself on the ruined remnants of the potluck. I counted the empty plates. He clearly didn't seem bothered by the bits of glass and ash and other detritus in the food. And weren't most of these bowls and containers in the other room when the bombs went off? How did he get them in here?

I really needed to have a talk with the creature, because in all my years—nearly two millennia worth—I'd never come across a being like him. I had no idea what he was, but he was clearly very powerful and perhaps as indestructible as I was.

"What are you doing?" I demanded of him.

Paws jolted at the sound of my voice.

"What?" Paws squawked indignantly. "The food was going to waste."

"Jake is worried about you. Didn't you hear us calling your name?"

Paws huffed, casting a glance over his questionable feast. Then he shook out his fur and sat back on his haunches. "I can look after myself."

"He is worried," I reiterated sharply.

"Fine. I'm coming, I'm coming," the cat muttered. Then he licked one of his paws and drew it over his face a couple of times. His idea of getting a move on was different from mine.

"Any time now."

Paws narrowed his eyes at me. "Well, get on with it."

"You want me to open a portal for you." I mean, I had been planning on it, but his imperious attitude was irritating.

Paws shook his body, making his fur fluff up. "It took me hours to get the soot out of my fur. I'm not doing that again when I don't have to."

"So you'll owe me a favor?"

He hissed. "Don't try to make a deal with me, demon. I saw those presents lined up by your motorhome. You don't need more than that."

I smirked but waved my hand through the air to open a portal on the grass behind the inn.

"Paws!" Jake shouted enthusiastically when the chunky cat waddled through the portal. He ran over and scooped the cat up in his arms. "Why didn't you come when we called? Bad kitty."

The creature tolerated Jake's hug and scolding with surprising grace.

"I am so happy you're okay." Jake squeezed the cat.

"Okay, okay," Paws said, squirming for freedom. "Enough."

Jake stroked him another half-dozen times before letting the cat escape. "I can't believe he was actually talking to me the entire time I've lived in Willow Lake. When I'd heard him ask me questions before, I thought I was going crazy."

As we followed Paws around the building to the parking lot again, a sense of calm settled over me as I watched my mate interact with my team. I always felt better having my team close and it was even better with Jake here too. Off to the side, Davina was talking animatedly to what appeared to be nothing but empty space. She must have found a ghost. The way Davina's eyes kept sliding over to me and then Jake, I suspected I knew what —or rather who—they were talking about.

Nelson and Isaac were preparing to leave for the pack lands. Teague and Adrian were giving Nelson a hard time about having to ride behind Isaac on the bike. And Jake and Jeremy were whispering quietly, Jeremy scribbling down more things in his notebook.

Willow Lake's magic bubbled around me, as if sensing my mood and rejoicing in it. Was it trying to tell me something? I sucked in a breath, suddenly sure of what I needed to do.

"Everyone, get over here. There is something else I need to say." I waved everyone closer. When the most important people in my life were standing in a half-circle in front of me, I braced my shoulders. "I feel a connection to Willow Lake."

"But… but you said it could be bad." Jake's shocked whisper had me reaching for him. We'd just been talking about this; it was no surprise that he'd figured out immediately what I was going to tell my team.

"But it might also be exactly what I need." I entwined my fingers with his. "And it might be what you need too."

"No." Jake shook his head. "Don't do this for me. If you aren't sure, you should wait. Make certain first. Please."

"I'm as sure as I can be," I said. And even as I said the words, a sense of rightness washed through me. The latent magic in Willow Lake popped and fizzed in the air around me like bubbles in champagne, while mine rushed to join it. Just with those few words, the edges between my magic and the magic in Willow Lake were beginning to blur. It wasn't too different from how my magic had rushed to greet Jake's. This was the way it was supposed to be. I was sure of it.

"Gage…" Jake whispered and threw himself against my chest. "Please. Don't make a rash decision. I know we've only just met, but…"

"Look at me," I said quietly. Jake squeezed me tighter before loosening his embrace enough to look me in the eye. "My magic is happy about this. I have to trust it. Can you trust me to do this? Believe me, I don't want to leave you. I'm doing this for myself, yes, but I'm also doing this for us. We may have only just met, but I didn't lie when I told my team I believe you are my mate. Fate, the Eternal Magic,

Mother Magic, or whatever you want to call her has brought us together. This is meant to be. I'm sure of it."

"But what if it isn't? It's too great a risk…" His voice cracked over the question. I didn't want him to worry, but just hearing that he cared soothed all the jagged edges of my ancient and battered soul.

"But what if it is?"

Jake tugged my shirt until I bent down, then he slammed his mouth against mine. The kiss was hot and desperate and so damn heart-wrenching at the same time. When it ended, Jake still had his hands fisted in my shirt. He peered at me with glassy eyes. "I can't lose you too."

I cupped his face and wiped away one of the stray tears slipping from his beautiful brown eyes. "You've given me something to live for. Believe me. I wouldn't take this risk if I didn't think it would work."

He whined softly and closed his eyes, sending a few more tears cascading down his cheeks. I gently brushed them away.

"Trust me." I pressed my forehead against his.

"I do…" He swallowed hard. "Just… if something seems like it's about to go wrong… Fuck." He stopped and shook his head. "Just stop it, Jake," he muttered to himself. "My visions aren't lying about us." Then he looked at me again. "But, just in case this isn't right, you fight for the life we're going to have together. We'll get away from here. I'll come with you. We never have to come back. I'll take care of you. Okay?"

I dropped a soft kiss to his lips, unwilling to make a promise I wasn't sure I could keep. "Ready to do this?"

"It's not my decision," Jake said. "The question is, are you ready?"

I nodded.

"Okay." He looked like he wanted to puke on me again, but this time it wasn't because of his magic. "Should I try to channel a vision about this?"

"Do you think you could?"

He grimaced. "No, but…"

I shook my head. "Then let's not. We'll focus on one thing at a time."

He trembled as he leaned against me. I glanced up to see Davina watching us closely. The rest of my team had stepped closer. Everyone's face betrayed shock, fear, and a whisper of hope.

"I knew there was something else you hadn't told us." Davina always knew when I was hiding things. That's why she was my second. "Are you saying what I think you're saying?"

I met each of my team member's gaze. They waited silently, which was unusual, but they probably understood just from my demeanor that something momentous was about to happen. "I believe I can tether to Willow Lake."

"For real?" Davina spoke first.

I swallowed. "Yes. I felt it the first day we were here, but I didn't want to say anything until I had a better idea."

"And you know that now?"

"I believe so." I scrubbed my hand over my face.

"If you get it wrong…" Davina let her words trail off.

"I know," I snapped. "But I want to try it."

My team's faces were now all carefully blank except for Isaac's. His face was expressive enough for everyone else. His mouth had dropped open and his face was paler than I'd ever seen.

"Are you sure you should?" Davina asked carefully.

"Are you questioning me?" I bit out. It was one thing for Jake to be worried; he was my mate and we'd only known one another a short time. But I hadn't expected my team to doubt me too. Jake squeezed my hand. His touch calmed my rising anger.

"It's a big step," Teague said, stepping forward, inserting himself in front of Davina. "But I don't think it's the wrong one. The connection between Gage and this place has grown, even in the few hours I've been here."

"Really?" Davina put her hand to her mouth, betraying the emotion she'd tried to hide. "Is this really the place? After all this time?"

Before I could say anything more, my phone rang. It was Van.

"What?"

"Just got a call," he said over the shrill blast of sirens. I heard them through the phone, but I could hear them in the distance now too. They were drawing nearer. It sounded like their whole squad was rushing somewhere. "Something's happening on the pack lands. Not sure if it's related to your mate's vision or not. Have you had an update from the guys on your team who went back there today?"

"They haven't left yet." I shot a look at Nelson and Isaac, and they ran for their bike. "They're on the way. The rest of us will be right behind them."

Everyone else waited for me to end my call.

"It might be happening now." I didn't explain what *it*

was. They'd know. "The police are heading out there. Let's go."

"What? You're going too? But..." Jake's cheeks looked ashen.

"It's what we do." I tugged him into my arms, and he clung to me. "I'll come back."

"I want to go too," he said.

I shook my head. "You aren't trained for this. We are. If you go out there, I'll be too focused on keeping you safe to do what I need to do."

He squeezed me tighter. "I don't want you to go."

"I'm sorry." I pressed a kiss to his head.

"Should you try bonding to Willow Lake first? It's supposed to make you stronger, isn't it?"

"There isn't enough time, and we can't anticipate what'll happen to my magic after the bond is complete. It is too much of an unknown."

"Fuck," Jake muttered as he broke the hug. As he stepped back, he rubbed the heels of his hands into his eyes. "Okay. You're right. I'm being selfish."

"You aren't selfish. I'd feel the same way if things were reversed. But I've been around for a long time. My team has trained for this."

"And we're really good at it," Davina interjected. "The best there is."

A group of cop cars sped past the inn in a flurry of dust and gravel and blasting sirens.

"Go. Help them." Jake waved me away. "But make sure you come back."

I dropped a quick kiss on his mouth, then ran after my team. Jake stayed behind with Jeremy and Paws. He'd be safe there; believing in that was the only way I could make myself leave him.

I slid into the passenger seat of Davina's black-topped vintage muscle car. I never remembered the make or model, but it was fast and that was all I cared about. Adrian, who'd walked over to the inn this morning with Jeremy, and Teague were already in the back seat.

"Neither Isaac nor Nelson are picking up," Adrian said, not looking up from his phone.

"They might not even be there yet," Teague said.

Davina's tires threw up a cloud of dust and gravel as she spun the car in a one-eighty in the parking lot.

"Tell me where I'm going," she said.

"Turn right," Adrian said.

We careened around the corner, then Davina floored it. None of us said anything. She always drove like this. For as many times as I'd been sure she'd wreck the car, she hadn't done it yet.

"Fuck," Adrian muttered as he grabbed the seat in front of him so he didn't crash into Teague. "We're supes, so I know we're hard to kill, but you don't have to take that as a challenge."

"What was with the surge of demonic magic in the middle of the night last night? The ghosts were telling me about it when I got here," Davina asked, ignoring Adrian's whining as she guided the car around a bend in the road.

Teague leaned forward.

I frowned. I'd hoped she'd talk to me about it alone, but she wasn't wrong to do it this way. The team had a right to know we were going into a potentially volatile situation. "Last night I was thinking about the bomb…"

"And how someone was trying to kill your mate." Davina clenched the steering wheel.

"Yes. That too."

I glanced behind me to gauge the others' reactions. Adrian looked ill, although that might just be from Davina's driving.

"I can't imagine if someone tried to kill my mate," the wolf said. "It was bad enough when Babette was riding Jeremy's back and then his magic knocked him out." He shivered. "I don't think I would have been able to handle it if anything more had happened. The damage those bombs caused…"

Just thinking about the bombs and how close I'd come to losing Jake made my control slip. Just a little.

Teague stared at me. "You gonna be okay with this? We can dump your ass on the side of the road right now. You don't need to come."

"I'll be fine," I lied.

Everyone let my statement stand. They were quiet for several long moments.

"What would it mean for you to tether to Willow Lake?" Adrian asked finally. He'd leaned forward like Teague, their heads almost touching as they peered at me over the seat. "We've always talked about it being the ultimate goal, but what does that look like?"

"If I bind myself here, I don't know what the rest of you would do. We need to talk about it. Would any of you even want to stay here—?"

Their chorus of "yes" and "fuck, yes" interrupted what I was saying.

"Really? You could all imagine living here?"

"Yeah," Davina said. "I've only been here for a few hours, but it doesn't matter. If this is the place you need to be, then we'll be right there with you."

"You can't speak for everyone," I said.

Adrian cleared his throat. "Yeah, actually she can. We decided that as a group a long time ago. We all agreed."

My team—my family—would stay with me. Warmth enveloped me. Was this what love felt like? Had they truly been my family all these years? I'd always thought of them as such, but I didn't realize they felt the same way.

"Thank you," I said quietly. "That... helps. I should have talked to you before I announced I wanted to bond with Willow Lake earlier."

I wasn't much for making speeches, but I knew I should say more, to tell them how thankful I was to have them in my life. But half my team wasn't here, and we'd just caught up to the police cars. It wasn't the right time.

"We're getting close. We all know what to do, but let's go over it. Davina..."

"I'll check in with the local ghosts while we get our gear from the trunk." She glanced into the rearview mirror at the others in the backseat. "And everyone is going to wear their fucking earpieces this time. I don't want to hear any whining about it. They've been spelled to work even when you shift, so there is no excuse. I can't update you on what the ghosts are saying if you can't hear me."

Adrian huffed but didn't say anything. He always complained bitterly about those earpieces—something about them hurting his ears—but Davina was right. Being connected would only help us.

"If this is Jake's vision come to life, there is going to

be a lot of people dying," Teague said. "I'll track the people on the edge of life and death. That should get us closer to where the action is."

"Good." I nodded. "And, Adrian, you'll be with me. Let's see if we can stop this before it turns into the massacre Jake's vision predicted."

As soon as Davina turned onto a rutted dirt road behind the cop cars, magic crackled through the air. Something was happening, and I suspected Jake's vision was coming true sooner than any of us had thought. The intensity and grimness of the magic washed over us like an acid bath.

Davina cursed but kept right on the cop car's bumper while the rest of us stared out the windows looking for a sign of what was happening. Then something emerged from the trees at the side of the narrow road. I caught only a blur of motion before our car rocketed to the side and tumbled over onto its roof.

My teammates shouted in surprise and then in pain. Anger blazed through me. It'd been simmering in my blood since the bombs the day before and now this collision had shattered my tenuous control. My demonic bloodlust surged forward faster than it ever had before, obliterating everything but the need for justice and retribution.

"Oh, fuck," the woman groaned. "Not now. It can't be happening now. Not when he's so close to anchoring..."

She was one of mine. Whatever her worry was, I would deal with it. I would end it.

I ripped free of the car, tearing the bent metal door open and tossing it aside. As soon as I was out, my demonic form erupted, obliterating any lingering human-like aspects of my form and my thoughts. My wings snapped out behind me. Heat burned through my blood. My long black and deadly claws tore free.

I roared.

The beast who'd hit our car cowered and tried to shield himself from my wrath with his arms. As if that would stop me. He could not flee fast enough to escape me.

I ensured he would not harm what was mine again, then I walked away. He was no longer a threat. Yes, he was still alive, but I suspected he wished he wasn't. Behind me, I heard those who wore my magic emerge from the broken vehicle. Someone made a retching sound. I didn't stop to find out who or why. I had prey to stalk.

In the shadowy depths of the forest, wailing and begging and whimpering hit me from every direction. I moved toward the loudest screams. I did not rush. I did not need to. No one would escape me this day, especially not the ones who had tried to harm my mate or those under my protection.

My footsteps fell heavily on the forest floor. Leaves shook on their branches with my every step. The few animals that weren't already hiding froze in my presence. I did not care about them. They were no threat to me. I had much larger prey to hunt.

Chapter Thirty-Two

JAKE

I stared at my phone. Jeremy was doing the same thing across the table from me in Gage's motorhome. Emma, Jeremy's strange supernatural creature, had curled up in a ball on his lap as soon as he'd sat down. Given the sound of its little snuffles, I was pretty sure it—she?—was asleep.

Every part of me was on alert. Between bouts of wishing my phone would ring, I scanned our surroundings like I expected someone was going to attack at any moment. My ears strained for any foreign sound, even though I knew the fight was taking place miles from here. The back of my neck itched, my hands were ice cold, and my chest ached.

In other words, I was a mess.

I hated sitting here, not knowing what was going on. Had they even made it to the pack lands yet?

And that was another thing. I'd only found out about

magic and the wolf pack and supernatural beings yesterday, but I didn't question it now. Perhaps the Eternal Magic, as Gage called it, had given me a helping hand in coming to terms with this strange new world I found myself in.

When I heard a vehicle roar up to us, I jumped out of my seat. I glanced around for something—anything—to use as a weapon, but it wasn't like there were guns or even a baseball bat tucked away in here. Of course not. Gage and his people were weapons all on their own. They didn't need anything more.

"It's just Ash and Dillon," Jeremy announced, peering out the window.

"Dillon wasn't with Van and the others?"

Jeremy shook his head. "He's not officially an officer yet. Van must have called him in when they arrived and knew what they were dealing with out there. It isn't like with the human police. These guys call in other civilian supes when things get dicey. It's a thing."

I leaned over to look out the window with Jeremy in time to see a red-faced, scowling Ash jump out of a car I didn't recognize. He slammed the door and Dillon winced from the driver's seat. To say Ash was unimpressed would be like saying boiling water was a tad warm. It was strange to realize he was as magical as all the rest of the people I'd met in Willow Lake. He just seemed so… normal.

I doubted I'd ever stop being surprised about people's powers.

As Ash stomped over to the motorhome and let himself in, Dillon peeled out of the parking lot and followed a cluster of other vehicles heading west out of town. None of those vehicles had sirens or official decals on their doors. They were just ordinary vehicles, driven by *ordinary* supernatural people. And, apparently, they were all responding to Van's call for help.

"I could have helped," Ash muttered as he flung himself into a chair. "Dillon's an asshole. Just because I'm a mage doesn't mean I need to be coddled. Can you believe he actually tried to stop me from even coming here after he had me borrow our neighbor's car?"

"You're still recovering from being shot," Jeremy reminded him. "Your magic isn't fully healed yet either. And, based on all my research, not every supe is built for fighting the way shifters are."

Ash narrowed his eyes at his friend and Jeremy snapped his mouth shut.

Now we were all sitting around the table in Gage's motorhome, waiting for news about what was happening. So far not a single fucking update had come in. The silence was making me crazy.

"So…" I said.

"So…" Ash said.

"So…" Jeremy said.

This was going great.

"Oh, I know," Jeremy said suddenly. "Tell me about Mr. Dimples." He waggled his eyebrows. "For research reasons, I'm asking everyone about what they've got in their pants. So, you know. What's his dick like? Does it look different? Does it do anything special?"

I gaped at him. Then I remembered he'd asked that before. Did he really expect me to answer?

"Jeremy, don't ask him shit like that," Ash reprimanded. Then he looked at me. "Seriously, just ignore him."

"But I need details for my books. If I don't ask, how will I know?"

Ash scowled at him.

"Fine. But if you ever want to talk…"

"Jeremy!" Ash snapped at him.

Silence fell over us again. I couldn't handle it.

"So…" I started again. "Whatever is happening, it has to do with the same werewolves who stole my grandfather's stuff, right?" I asked, more to break up the quiet than anything else. It was hard to make conversation when all you wanted was your phone to ring, but I was trying. I needed to think about something besides Gage and the others going off to fight. "And they are the same ones who bombed the inn too, right?"

"Yeah," Jeremy said as he checked the volume on his phone again, then dropped his hand down to absently pet Emma's fur. "Dot, the officer who shot Ash here, she was a deer shifter, who'd *allegedly* been intimidated by those wolves into helping them rob your place."

"Dot was a shapeshifter?"

Ash snorted. "We just say shifter."

Jeremy nodded and patted my arm. "Like I said before, I've got you covered. It's been quite the thing, learning about all of this. I know where you're coming from. Like, obviously, the word shifter is derived from shapeshifter, right? From an etymological standpoint. But if you say that, people will just think you're weird."

"Or, maybe their bodies shift, so they are shifters, as simple as that," Ash said. "Don't make it difficult."

Jeremy rolled his eyes, but Ash didn't see. He was looking out the window of the motorhome toward the road, where a few more cars were speeding out of town.

"Shifters are pretty cool, regardless of why they are called that," I said. "Is Gage considered a shifter since he can change his body too? Or is that designation only reserved for people who change to animal forms?" I tapped to refresh my text messages again, then went back to the main screen. Still no new messages.

"I call it battle ready... or sometimes high-test... or undiluted. I'm still working out the terminology for my book," Jeremy said, then he looked at Ash. "But Mr. Dimples wouldn't be considered a shifter, right?"

As the only one of the three of us who'd grown up knowing about supernatural beings, Ash was the expert or so I'd discovered at some point yesterday. As a fire mage, he'd always been surrounded by magic. Jeremy's past was more like mine in that he'd been unaware of magic until he met Adrian.

"Right," Ash agreed as he rubbed his hand over his chest. It was something I'd seen him do numerous times before, especially when he seemed upset or sad.

"I feel like we should be there," I whispered.

Ash's gaze snapped to me. "Like... you're having feelings as an oracle? Some kind of lucid vision or something?"

I shook my head. "No. It's just... I need to do something."

"You and me both," Ash muttered.

"Me three," Jeremy agreed.

"Maybe I can try to bring on a vision." I bit the inside

of my cheek. "I've never tried before, but it could help, right? If I could—"

Jeremy's phone rang, cutting off my words. He fumbled to answer the call.

"You still with Jake?" came the frantic question on the phone. The voice on the other end was shouting loud enough we all heard it in the quiet of the motorhome. Was that Adrian? And was someone screaming in the background?

"Yes," Jeremy said.

"Get him over here. Now."

Then the caller was gone.

"Fuck," Ash said as we all stood from the table.

Jeremy, who was starting to glow with a white light, gently lifted Emma and set her on the floor. She woke up long enough to scowl at him, then went back to sleep. We scrambled out of the motorhome. Then we looked around. There were no other vehicles for us to take. We hurried back inside the motorhome and stared at the driver's seat.

"Have either of you driven one of these before?" I asked.

Ash and Jeremy shook their heads.

"Fuck it," Jeremy said. "I'll do it. I started watching RV videos online after Adrian decided we were going to buy a trailer or a motorhome or whatever. It can't be that hard, right?"

He plopped behind the steering wheel, adjusted the seat and mirrors. He was taller than either Ash or me, but he wasn't as tall as Gage, who normally drove this thing. Then he reached for the key in the ignition... Thank Goya Gage hadn't taken it with him when he left. Jeremy cranked on the key and the motor rumbled to life. Then he checked all the mirrors again.

"Fuck. How did he get this beast in here?"

The motorhome lurched forward, then back. Then forward again. Bit by bit, executing the world's most stressful thirty-nine-point turn, Jeremy reoriented the motorhome toward the driveway. After an excruciatingly painful start, he finally got us out of the parking lot and onto the road heading west.

I hadn't been raised to believe in a religion. I hadn't known magic existed. So I'd created a pantheon of my own. My deities were all the painting greats. And, right now, I wanted to thank every single one of them that we didn't meet anyone going east because Jeremy favored the center line… to the point where I was pretty sure he was straddling it.

My heart was racing as I willed him to drive faster, even though I didn't like the odds of us staying on the road if he did speed up. Sweat trickled down my back. Why would they want me out there? I couldn't see an oracle being much good in a fight. Gage had asked me to stay away, so had something happened to make him change his mind?

Or had something happened to Gage himself?

Dread roiled through me like a storm-churned ocean. Then my fingers convulsed. My eye twitched. I exhaled as I spied the notebook and pencil Jeremy had been flipping through earlier. It held his notes and observations, and, I suspected, it was about to hold some of my dreadful visions too.

Fuck… I had wanted a vision five seconds ago, but not

now. Not when Adrian had just called in a panic, asking for me.

I fought the pull of my magic as hard as I could, and for as long as I could. But no amount of fighting it could hold it at bay. This vision was coming whether I wanted it to or not. All I hoped at this point was for it to end quickly... well, and that when I woke, I wouldn't puke on anyone.

Blackness filled my eyes and then everything was lost.

Chapter Thirty-Three

JAKE

"He's waking up," someone was shouting in my ear.

I groaned and tried to turn away from the noise.

"Come on, Jake. Wake up," they urged.

"Go away." I tried to pull my arm over my head to block out the noise and the light, but my arm wouldn't move.

"Jake!" Another shout, followed by a sharp stinging slap to my left cheek.

"Hey!" I forced my eyes open. As soon as I saw Ash's frantic face, I remembered everything. I glanced at the drawing I'd made.

If my stomach hadn't already been churning, that would have done it. Even in the pale gray lines of a hard pencil, the scene was grotesque. People's limbs were strewn all over the place with an obscene amount of blood dripping and pooling everywhere else. In the center of the page was Gage in his demon form, his black wings stretched out behind him, his horns gleaming in the light, his clawed hands clutching a limp, and obviously dead, body.

I ran for the tiny bathroom, barely making it to the toilet, to cast up the contents of my stomach. A moment later, Ash shoved a bottle of water in my face. I took a swig, swirled it around my mouth, then spit it out.

"Here," Ash said, handing me a wet cloth next.

I flushed the toilet, then forced myself to wipe my face and get back in the game. Unfortunately, lethargy was already pulling at me. I wanted to curl up and sleep, but I couldn't. Not until I knew Gage was safe. I hunted through the small cabinet in the bathroom until I found some toothpaste. Minty breath shouldn't have been my priority just then, but I couldn't think clearly when my mouth tasted like puke.

When I emerged from the bathroom, Ash was leaning over Jeremy and peering out the front windshield. The dirt road we were on was rough and littered with dips and tire ruts. The motorhome chugged over them, swaying ominously from side to side as the grooves got deeper.

"What's over there?" Ash pointed ahead. "Is that their car?"

I rushed to the front so I could see too. Off the road to the left, wedged between the aspen trees at the side of the road, the car was upside down with its wheels spinning. The windows were all shattered and at least one door was missing. Luckily, I didn't see any bodies inside or around the car. A little further up, a cop car was in even worse condition.

"What the hell happened?" I whispered.

Then a deafening roar shook the air, making all the windows rattle. An invisible force, like a concussive sound wave, rolled over us.

"Was that magic?" Jeremy asked. His knuckles were white, both with his magic and how tightly he gripped the steering wheel.

Ash glanced over at me; his fear was easy to see.

"Are we too late?" Jeremy pulled the motorhome to a stop when he couldn't manage to get it around the over-turned vehicles blocking the road.

"No," I said. "I need to get to him. I'll tether him. At least until we can get him back to Willow Lake. Then he'll be able to anchor properly. He's going to be fine. I don't care what my vision said. My vision can go fuck itself."

I stomped toward the door leading out of the motorhome, but before I made it there, my fingers twitched, and darkness bled over my sight again.

Fucking fuck fuck.

Not another one.

Chapter Thirty-Four

GAGE

Blood dripped into my eyes from bodies hanging from the trees above, until the world was layered in red. The scent of death clogged my nostrils. Made my fingers slippery. Coated my tongue.

All the while, intermittent screams tore through the humid forest air.

Still, I couldn't find any more of my enemies.

At the beginning of the battle, I'd moved fluidly through the masses of my enemies. Striking them down where they stood, but not killing them. Some part of me longed to eradicate these beasts from the world, but that was not my job. It had never been my job. I was the judge, but I was not the executioner. Not unless every other avenue had been exhausted.

Instead, I incapacitated my enemies, leaving them for those loyal to me to contain.

But now, everywhere I went in these dark woods, I

arrived too late. My enemies had either run away… or died before I found their broken and mangled bodies. I stalked through yet another small clearing, but it was much the same as the last one.

I roared as retribution was stolen from me once again. I wanted justice for my mate.

I fought against the urge to give in to my darkest desires, the ones where I wanted to taste my enemy's fear, suck the blood from their still beating heart, pop one of their eyes into my mouth and squish it between my teeth while their other eye stared at me in horror.

All around me, bits of wolf and troll and goblin lay in untidy heaps. The wolves smelled like these woods, so they must have been from the pack who'd attacked Jake. But the others, they were not from here. I was convinced those were the ones who'd attacked the wolves. The lingering scents in the air suggested whoever had done this was more foe than friend.

I tore through the piles, needing to see if anyone lay hidden and alive beneath the lifeless bodies. Nothing. Again. I scented the air and followed yet another trail through the dense trees.

Beside me, the wolf who bore the blessing of my magic panted harsh and rapid breaths. They stank of fear. Their heart raced at a dangerous speed. Had they seen an enemy I'd missed?

I scanned the still woods, sensing only myself and the wolf.

He wasn't cowering because of me, was he? He had nothing to fear from me. He was mine. I protected what was mine.

Didn't he see? Didn't he know?

The only ones who needed to fear me were my enemies.

I would show him, make him see how I would protect him and the others and my mate. Especially my mate. He was so fragile. I had to be extra vigilant, more ruthless in my pursuit of those who sought to hurt him. Then they would know to stay away.

My wings snapped out behind me as I stalked forward, hunting for more prey. I lifted my face and breathed in. Wolves. The woods were tainted with the smell of wolves and death. It was impossible to separate one from the other. I should take to the air. They might run from me, but I would find them. They dared to threaten what was mine; for that they deserved to face judgment.

One of mine shouted. I ignored them. Even over their noisy jabbering, I heard more racing heartbeats. Had I finally found where my enemies were hiding?

Another shout from that same familiar voice.

They were making too much noise. I growled at them to be silent.

More muddled and unnecessary words. I stalked forward. If I left my companion behind, I could hunt more easily.

More shouting.

Then a word filtered into my head.

Jake.

I blinked. Hesitated.

"Gage," the voice said. "Jake needs you."

I turned toward the voice. The man, who stank of wolf but also of my magic, swallowed hard under my assessing gaze. His clothes were torn and bloody but whatever injuries he'd sustained were already healing. I lumbered toward him. The scent of his fear spiked. But, again, why? He should know I would never hurt him.

"Gage," he said. "You've got to get hold of yourself. It's Jake. Fuck. It's bad, Gage. He's here, but he's having vision after vision… It's going to break him."

I scowled at the interruption. More of my enemies lingered in the forest, just out of view. This wolf shouldn't be bothering me.

"Gage. You've done enough. Van and his officers have things under control now. You don't have to do any more. You just need to get to Jake now. He's your mate. He needs you. No one else can help him."

I turned back to the wolf.

"Jake?" I forced the word from my mouth. It sounded garbled.

Relief lit his face. He nodded frantically. "Yes. Jake. He needs you, Gage. It's bad."

I inhaled deeply. The ones who hid from me were cowering. Several had pissed themselves. The scent of their terror hung in the air like a tangible entity. I grunted. These cowards were no threat to me or mine.

The scent of trolls and goblins and the other beings who'd been fighting the wolves when we'd arrived was fading. They'd abandoned their comrades and fled almost as soon as we'd arrived. But under all those revolting smells was something familiar… Demon. But not me. Another.

Another who, I suspected, had lost himself.

Someone who needed to be put down.

That was the real threat. But their scent was even fainter than those who'd been fighting the wolves. Were they already gone?

"Fuck, Gage," my wolf companion said. He was one of mine, but why was he talking? I was busy. "We need to get to Jake. Van's got everything else under control. There is no one else out here to hunt."

I clenched my teeth. That wasn't true. We both knew he was lying. And I wanted to find the demon. With it still out there, no one was safe, especially not Jake.

"We're going to lose him, Gage. Why the fuck aren't you listening to me?"

I tilted my head and stared at the wolf again. His words made no sense. Jake was far away. Safe.

I inhaled deeply once more.

And this time, I caught my mate's scent on the air.

"No!" I roared.

Then, with one strong flap of my wings, I shot into the air. I followed the scent to my mate. And he wasn't safe, miles away. He was here. On this blood-soaked hill. I dove for the motorhome I'd called home for too many years. Two faces were pressed against the windows as I landed. They were pale, wide-eyed, and open-mouthed. Suddenly a white shield of magic enveloped them.

But even with that magic wrapped around him, the air reeked of my mate's magic. The ozone scent of it, so much like a mage's, dragged me to him. I landed outside the vehicle holding my mate captive. I cursed. I couldn't get to him inside the motorhome in this form. My body was too large. I peered in at the window. The magical shield that glowed brightly with pure white energy protected three people: the same two fearful faces who I'd seen when I'd first arrived and, behind them, my mate, who was slumped over the table. His hand flew over a piece of paper. All around him were pages torn from the notebook. Even from here, I could see drawing after drawing after drawing.

I had to get to him.

I tried to push my body through the small, narrow door. The others inside backed up. They held their hands up, as if in surrender. The glowing white shield surged brighter. And now one of the people held a glowing ball of magic. He didn't throw it, but his fingers twitched like he wanted to. I huffed. I'd left these men to protect my mate. I wouldn't have done that if I planned to harm them.

I pushed against the doorway again.

I couldn't do it.

My body wouldn't fit.

I knew my demonic form fit inside those walls, but I couldn't get it through the door.

I turned and scanned the surrounding forest.

I couldn't be killed very easily in either form, but my demonic form was stronger, making me better able to protect my mate. People rushed forward, breaking out of the tree line.

They were mine.

"Stand guard," I commanded. My demonic power coated the words, compelling them to obey my desires.

They shuddered as their bodies jumped to heed my command. Their wide eyes were fearful as they stared at me. Once again, I registered fear but didn't understand its origin. Did they mean to attack me? No. Of course not. They would never do such a thing.

Then one by one, they turned to form a protective half-circle in front of the entrance to the motorhome. Yes. That was better. They wouldn't have turned their backs on me if they didn't trust me, unless my command had overridden their basic will. Could it do that?

If I was still able to command them against their wills, they would never be able to kill me if I lost control. Not unless I allowed it. That was a flaw I'd never anticipated. I should have. But luckily it didn't matter now. I'd found my mate and my home.

I scanned the woods again. No new threats were revealed. If I was fast, I could save my mate from his magic and then return to my hunt. But my mate came first. I forced my body to change into my smaller human-like form. As soon as I was small enough to get inside the RV, I charged up the steps.

"How long?" I asked. My voice was hoarse and rough.

"An hour or so?" the one with the fire ball said. His name returned to me. That one was called Ash.

"You okay now?" This question came from Jeremy. Yes. That's right. That was the wolf's mate.

I nodded. "I need my mate. Thank you for protecting him."

The white shield flickered then winked out of sight. I rushed to Jake and took him into my arms. He fought me. He clenched the pencil and notebook in his hand as he tried to draw.

"Get Teague," I shouted.

People scrambled to do as I ordered.

I needed to become Jake's tether, but he needed to be awake and alert to make that happen. A small voice inside my head whispered I might already be too late. I refused to listen to it.

"I'm here," Teague said as he stumbled into the motorhome. His magic was nearly exhausted. He swayed on his feet and his face was a sickly color.

I didn't care.

"Save Jake," I commanded. And this time, I didn't hold back on any of my magic and power. I let the full weight of Teague's bargain with me fill the air. The death mage was mine to protect, but also mine to command.

Teague jerked forward under the weight of my order, his body seeking to obey despite his fatigue. Then his eyes rolled back in his head, and he collapsed to the floor. I tried to grab for him, but I couldn't reach him with Jake in my arms. Jake had ripped out the drawing he'd been making from his notebook and was starting another.

I roared my frustration.

Then I saw what the drawing showed, and my heart lightened.

There was still hope.

I held my mate tightly in my arms and drew upon my magic. Then I reached through all the magics rushing through the air and found Jake's. It was familiar to me. I let my mind tumble back to the moment when our magics had danced with one another this morning as I'd held him in my arms. Our connection was still there. It was as faint as the magical tattoos still clinging tenuously to our skin, but it didn't matter. All that mattered was that I saw it. I felt it.

I pushed my magic out to my mate through the thin thread linking us together.

His magic fought mine, but mine was stronger.

I couldn't sever his link to his own magic, but I could make him sleep. Just for a little while. Long enough to get him back to Willow Lake. My intuition told me everything would be okay if I got him back there.

"Stop," I said firmly to him.

Jake trembled in my arms, then slumped forward. The pencil he'd been clutching fell from his fingers and rolled off the table to the floor. I turned his face to mine, needing to feel his breaths heaving in and out of his body as he fought to stay alive. His eyelashes fluttered, then his eyes opened slightly.

His gaze caught on mine and held for the count of one... two...

His mouth twitched and I swore he was trying to smile.

"Sleep, my mate."

Then his eyes drifted closed again and he relaxed in my arms.

"Gather the team," I said. "We need to return to Willow Lake. Now."

A moment later, my team was crammed into the motorhome, even Isaac and Nelson. We could collect the motorbike and Davina's car later. For now, I just needed my family with me. They were bruised, bloody, and exhausted, but they were all still alive.

"Nelson, get Teague off the floor. Adrian, drive us back. Isaac and Davina, get everyone what they need to recover. I'm going to the back with Jake."

Davina's eyes were wet, but she quickly wiped away her tears.

"Are you injured?" I asked her.

She shook her head. "Just so fucking happy you're still with us."

"Yeah, boss man," Isaac said. "It's good to see you."

"What do you mean?" I frowned.

Everyone was staring at me except Nelson, who was still maneuvering an unconscious Teague onto the sofa. Jeremy and Ash were inching away from me as far as they could within the confines of the motorhome. The Emerald Mackobant was perched on Jeremy's shoulder, hissing and baring its teeth at me. Ash's mate was not there. He must still be out assisting Van and the other members of the local police force with the cleanup.

Then Nelson turned to face me too. His skin was as pale as I'd ever seen it, shockingly white against his black hair. He cleared his throat. "We thought it was time. We thought…"

Davina whined a little in the back of her throat, sounding more like a hurt animal than a medium.

"You thought I'd snapped," I said, finally understanding.

They each nodded.

Had I? I thought back to what had happened since we arrived. Was that what it felt like to lose control? I'd thought I was in control. But maybe I always would, even when I wasn't.

"I am sorry I scared you," I whispered. "If it means anything, I recognized you as mine. I only sought to protect you."

"Yeah," Adrian said, hugging Jeremy close to his chest. The Emerald Mackobant forced its way between them and made little chittering noises as it patted their cheeks, as if confirming for itself that they were safe. "We figured that out."

"So did he lose it or not?" Jeremy whispered to Adrian.

Although he hadn't asked me, I knew everyone was wondering the same thing. "No. I was in control, but... I've never allowed my demonic side to dominate like that. My magic ruled my actions, but I understood what I was doing."

"Is that why Jake was having problems too? Because he's your mate and your magic was amped up as high as it can go?" Jeremy asked, more emboldened now.

A chill rolled over my spine. Fuck. That would make sense, wouldn't it? I had initiated a connection between us when I used my blood to heal his injuries from the explosion the day before. And then our magics had merged briefly when we made love this morning. Fuck. He'd said he could sense me, hadn't he? Right then, I should have known it'd cause problems for him. I'd assumed that because we hadn't completed the bond or made me his tether, that he would be safe. I'd been wrong. So very terribly wrong. The link we shared was powerful enough that when my magic surged, Jake's did too.

This was all my fault.

I had to make this right. I *would* make this right. There was no other option.

I gathered my mate in my arms and carried him to the small bedroom at the back of the motorhome without another word.

Chapter Thirty-Five

GAGE

I cradled Jake in my arms, dropping kisses on his tangled hair and rubbing circles on his sweat-soaked back. In my head, the same words circled around and around.

You're going to be okay. Absolutely fucking fine. You're going to be okay. Absolutely fucking fine.

I was back to reciting mantras, but this time my focus wasn't on me and my control. It was all about Jake. He was the only thing that mattered.

Was I wrong to have severed his magic and stopped him from drawing his visions? I hadn't even thought about that when I'd done it. I just needed him to stop before he was so lost to the future he couldn't get back to the present. I had fixed people's magic in the past, but that was when I could access their greatest desires. But when Jake was under the influence of his magic, he didn't have desires or fears or anything. All he had were visions.

His breathing was steady. I clung to that as a sign he

was okay, even though it worried me he still hadn't moved. If I'd harmed him by commanding him to sleep...

I couldn't bear to think about it.

I hugged him tighter.

Of all the things my magic could do, why couldn't it fix this?

As soon as we crossed into the boundary of Willow Lake, my magic sang. Perhaps I had already started to bond with the magic in this place too. Was that why I'd been so out of control in the pack lands? Because my magic knew I no longer belonged anywhere but here?

Not for the first time, I wished there were more of my kind around to ask, but the last one I'd seen had been an obnoxious self-entitled prick. He smugly gloated about finding his place and refused to answer any of my questions. That'd been about two hundred years ago. I hadn't been to see him since.

But would I be any different?

Sure, I might not gloat—I knew what the endless cycles of hope and disappointment felt like, and I would never mock someone while they were suffering—but I couldn't imagine inviting another of my kind into my territory either.

Just scenting the other demon so close to Willow Lake had aggravated everything today. I wished I understood what happened when one of my kind lost control, but I'd been so young when I'd been forced to defend myself against my father. I thought I knew. The memory was etched into my soul. But had I misremembered that fateful day? Were my assumptions wrong?

I would always remember his piercing red eyes and the

way he'd glowered at me. It plagued me for years... because it almost seemed like he knew me. Over and over again through the centuries, I tried to dismiss the thought as a trick of my memory. But what if he *had* recognized me? What if he'd known exactly what he was doing?

From what my team had said, by all appearances, they'd thought I'd succumbed to my demonic powers. My head and heart ached just thinking about it because I'd still been in control.

Which made me wonder... What if my father had been lucid when he attacked me? What if he intentionally tried to hurt me so I would kill him? What if he'd decided he'd had enough and chose to commit suicide by making me take his life for him?

He'd talked about death and darkness so much after we ran away from my childhood home in the dead of night. He went into so much detail about what happened when a demon lost control. But what if everything he told me about that night had been a lie too?

I didn't know what to believe.

And, if I was in control today, had the other demon in the pack lands been in control too?

Now I was questioning everything I'd believed to be true, all those truths that made me who I was and dictated how I lived my life.

Regardless, although the other demon might not have lost control, he was still a danger to me and mine. I needed to be as strong as possible to protect what was mine. The best way to do that was to tether to Willow Lake.

"Where to?" Adrian shouted from the front of the motorhome.

"Go to the inn," I said. I didn't bother shouting. As a werewolf, Adrian would hear me well enough.

I hadn't investigated much of Willow Lake yet, but I knew the inn sat on a nexus of ley lines. It called to me, the way it must have called to the werewolves who'd first claimed this spot for their pack house.

Jake slept in my arms the entire ride back to the inn. His pale face was marred by deep, dark bruises under his eyes. His cheeks were sunken. His lips were chapped. Channeling so much magic all at once had exhausted him. I prayed to the Eternal Magic that the damage was not permanent.

I would never forgive myself if it was.

As soon as the motorhome was parked, I gathered Jake in my arms again and carried him outside. For the first time, I opened myself fully to the special power of Willow Lake and let my magic flow. My true demon form erupted over me. Several startled gasps greeted the arrival of my shifted form.

"What the fuck?" Jeremy muttered. "I thought we were done with all that."

"It's fine… I think," Adrian answered.

"It is," I agreed. The difference was so obvious now. I knew my team. I knew their names and who they were to me. My thoughts didn't devolve into bloodlust. I was a demon, but I was already beginning to sense what it would mean to be the guardian of this place.

Willow Lake was mine, just as Jake was.

I held my mate in my arms like a bride—I was sure he'd hate to be seen like this, particularly since he was unconscious and defenceless, but I couldn't leave him behind in the motorhome. The need to protect him was overwhelming and I doubted it would ever change.

With each step I took over this land, my magic sang louder. It was everything. It was home. And joy. And love. And welcome.

When I found the spot where my magic rejoiced the loudest and the strongest, I dropped to my knees. I placed Jake gently on the ground beside me. His eyes fluttered open. This time he managed a weak smile.

"It will be okay," I assured him. "Rest now and all will be well."

"I trust you," he whispered. "I love you. I knew you'd come back to me." He reached for my hand and squeezed it softly before letting his own hand drop.

I brushed a kiss to his lips and felt the warmth of his love wash over me and fill me. He loved me. I never expected to feel so blessed.

Once I was sure Jake was comfortable, I set my hands upon the grass. My sharp black claws dug into the dirt. Every spot where my body connected with the earth poured magic out from me. It slipped down like water flowing over pebbles. It seeped through the topsoil and the clay and the underwater spring and the bedrock, down and down. I pushed my magic to its limits, then I gave it more.

I had to.

I realized now why no one had ever been able to explain or describe this or how to do it. I was driven by instinct and guided by the Eternal Magic herself. The distance I reached wasn't something to be measured in millimeters or inches or miles or kilometers. I was dipping into the endless well of the world's magic to find the one thread that made this place what it was.

Once my magic latched onto the beautiful shimmering thread that flourished through the heart of Willow Lake, I coaxed it gently forward, inviting it to see me and judge if it would accept me as its worthy guardian. The magic playfully tickled at my fingers before licking up my arms, and onward until it had wrapped itself around me like a warm, familiar hug. It was strange to think of this type of magic as sentient and knowing, but I didn't doubt it for a moment. I knew it as well as I knew my own magic.

This was pure love. Pure joy.

Willow Lake had deemed me worthy.

The magic enveloping me sparkled and shimmered and glowed before tightening its hold on me. Every nerve and pore in my body tingled at once as the foreign essence invaded me and disappeared inside.

I gasped and clutched at the soil as this new power permeated my blood, my flesh, and my bones, until it found the place where my own magic lived, deep inside my core. I fought to accept the intrusion when every part of me wanted to shove it out. This pain was necessary. It was welcome. I shuddered and gasped as my magic was shredded and remade.

When I finally pulled my claws from the earth and sat back on my heels, I lifted my face to the sun to savor the sensation of all this magic dancing through me. It was mine, but not. Familiar, but not. It would take some adjustment to acclimate to the change, but the joining was complete. Willow Lake was mine and I was hers.

Awestruck whispers from the others floated over me.

"Beautiful," Jake murmured, drawing my gaze to him. My mate. He was sitting up now. His cheeks had a little more color than they had a moment earlier, but he still looked exhausted.

"Will you accept me as your anchor?" I asked. Perhaps I should have waited until we were alone, but I didn't want to postpone. I needed to protect Jake in every way possible.

"Always," Jake whispered. "I accept you as my everything. My mate, my love, my tether."

Tears gathered in his eyes as he gazed at me with such love and tenderness. It humbled me. This amazing, strong, and talented man had chosen me. His visions had suggested it, but, in the end, it was Jake who decided to love me.

"I love you," I whispered as I wrapped him in my arms and bent to kiss him. We were both kneeling now, our bodies pressed together from our knees to our mouths. Around us, our friends and family grew quiet.

When our lips met, I closed my eyes. Once again, I allowed instinct and magic to guide me. My magic had never felt stronger as it raced to do my bidding and wrapped us in a gentle embrace. Jake gasped against my mouth. He leaned back to stare into my eyes.

Did he see the black, white, and red ribbons of magic weaving around us? Those ribbons wove together, illustrating our lives together. Vision after vision swirled around us. Too many to count. Too many to see. But they weren't the wild and uncontrolled chaos that Jake had gone through earlier. Jake's magic wasn't generating these moments alone. No, this was the two of us together. And it was balanced and stable and perfect.

Beautiful.

He was beautiful.

Then, just as it had when I'd joined with Willow Lake, the magic binding us together seeped into our bodies. The visions floated over us like a veil as ancient words, unknown but familiar, fell from our lips. I wasn't worried. I recognized the depth of the magic welling inside us. This was the Eternal Magic. The same magic I'd just felt emanating from the center of the earth. The same magic that connected us all.

But this blessing wasn't just to tether him to me to stabilize his oracle magic. It was so much more than that. This was for mates. The Eternal Magic was connecting our lives, joining us together from this moment forward.

This time when the magic settled, a single shimmering thread stretched between us for a long moment, merging our lives together forever.

"Fuck," Davina muttered with a sniffle. "You made me cry."

"Did they just…?" Isaac whispered.

"Yep," Jeremy agreed. "They're all bonded, complete with matching tattoos. But they didn't get to have magical sex when they bonded. Sucks to be them. Where is my pen? I really need to write this down before I forget. It's different seeing it than doing it."

"You were a little preoccupied with other things when it happened," Adrian reminded his mate gruffly.

"Yes, Wolf Man, we had magical sex. But I just feel

like we're gloating by talking about it now since Gage and Jake didn't get that."

"We should really go have magical sex," my mate whispered in my ear.

Adrian snickered. With his wolf hearing, he would have heard Jake's words.

"Excellent idea." I swept my mate into my arms and carried him toward the motorhome. "My mate and I need some time alone."

"You didn't have to tell everyone," Jake murmured as he pressed his heated face into my neck.

"Adrian," Jeremy said, "we should go back to the hotel and get cleaned up too." No one was fooled by what he said. He just wanted to get his mate alone for sex. And, after the impressive way his magic reached out to protect both Ash and my mate today, he deserved to celebrate however he wanted.

"And where are we supposed to get cleaned up if the motorhome is off limits?" Isaac asked.

"The lake is just over there," I shouted over my shoulder, making my mate laugh and the rest of my teams' jaws drop open in surprise. Nothing had ever felt better in my life.

Chapter Thirty-Six

JAKE

As Gage carried me to the motorhome, we were serenaded by catcalls and hooting. A few people laughed about us being eager newlyweds. And it was true. Becoming tethered to Gage reminded me of a marriage ceremony.

We'd been surrounded by his family. The location had been beautiful—he'd found a spot far enough away from the back of the inn that it hadn't been damaged by the bombs. The breeze had even cooperated and blown the lingering smell of smoke and ash in the other direction.

But if I'd known I was getting hitched, I would have preferred to have changed into something I hadn't been sweating in. Something that didn't smell like puke. I mean, just because I'd tried to be careful when I lost my lunch didn't mean I was successful.

I also would have loved it if no one had been blood-splattered at the time.

Still, the way the magic had moved through us was

incredible. And I swore, through the connection I shared with Gage, I was linked to Willow Lake too. It resonated through me and filled me with a sense of awe. It was calm, so unimaginably calm.

I'd never felt so at peace.

I hadn't been capable of peace when I'd been living under the weight of the curse. I didn't think my mom would have wished me a lifetime of unhappiness, but I couldn't be sure. I'd never know why she did it. I had to hope it was because she loved me. I'd never felt like she didn't, and I hated questioning her love for me now.

But, given everything she'd done to hide the supernatural world from me, I also didn't think she'd have been happy to see me tethered to a demon.

"We're married," I said to Gage once we were ensconced in the motorhome and I was on my feet again, "and I don't even know your last name."

"Stewart," he said. "My name is Gage Stewart. Although I haven't always had that name, I've been using it the longest."

I held out my hand to him and grinned. "I'm Jake Townsend. It's nice to be married to you."

He wrapped his hand around mine and shook it gently before tugging me into his arms. "I can't believe everything that's happened today. The Eternal Magic has truly blessed me."

When he went to kiss me, I turned my head. "Nope. No kisses. Not yet. We need to get cleaned up before we do anything like that."

Gage shook his head. "I don't care if you're clean. I only care that you are mine and that you're safe."

"Nope. That's just your emotions talking. I know you. You like things clean and tidy. It's who you are. We'll be able to enjoy ourselves more if we wash off the grime first." I wiggled out of his arms and turned toward the back of the motorhome. "Besides I refuse to kiss you until I brush my teeth again. And you smell like... I don't know what, but it isn't pleasant."

Gage chuckled but let me go. "All right. I'll go turn on the hot water heater."

"Ugh, and I don't even have any clean clothes to change into," I said as I peeled off my shirt and tossed it into the corner of Gage's little bedroom. When I turned to sit on the bed to take off my socks and shoes, I found he'd returned and was staring at my balled-up shirt where it'd fallen. His nose was wrinkled, and his fingers twitched. I sighed. Since we were married now, I knew I should try to be tidier. "It is just there for a few minutes. Then I'll put it back on again."

"No." Gage's eyes snapped to mine. "I'll get you something different to wear."

"Like you'll magic something up? That's cool."

Gage shook his head. "My magic doesn't work that way, but I'll go grab something from your room."

I nodded. "Yes. Let's do that. Go to the inn. We can shower. My shower isn't big, but it is bigger than yours. We both might fit. I think it's worth checking out."

"The water was turned off. Besides we haven't heard if it's safe to go into the building yet."

"Fine." My shoulders slumped.

"I'll go in and retrieve some clean clothes for you."

I frowned as I threw my socks over by my shirt. "If it isn't safe for me, it isn't safe for you either."

"Go," he said. "Have your shower."

"You aren't going to go in there, are you?"

He just rolled his eyes at me, like he thought it was cute I'd worry about him.

"I can always wear one of your shirts."

His eyes flared with the red of his demon. Oh. He liked that idea. "Go shower before I try to change your mind and push you back on the bed and clean you with my tongue."

"Was that supposed to be sexy?" It was… sort of. But sort of not too. I mean, would I like to have his tongue everywhere? What would that feel like? I couldn't decide if it'd feel good or not, mostly because of the spit aspect. Spit just wasn't sexy to me. But I had liked the way his tongue had felt in my mouth when we kissed, so I might like a tongue bath too. And then I remembered how his tongue was forked when he was in his demonic form, how it curled and moved… I gulped. Yep, I'd dismissed his idea too hastily. "We should explore that later. But only after we're both clean."

"Jake…" he whispered as he stalked toward me.

"Nope, don't look at me like that," I said as I shoved my pants and underwear down and kicked them toward the rest of my clothes. "Not until later."

Gage grunted in obvious appreciation of my naked body, which was silly. My body was just average. His, on the other hand… Yummy. I salivated at the mere thought of his muscular torso. My tongue curled in my mouth. I bet it really would be fun to drag my tongue over all the hills and valleys of his pecs and his abs and his Adonis belt…

"Jake…" Gage said again, this time with a hint of warning, like he was barely resisting the urge to throw me onto the bed and do wonderful things to me. But that wasn't happening until I was sure I no longer smelled of puke and sweat and everything gross.

I scurried into the obscenely tiny bathroom with its obscenely tiny shower stall.

The warm water felt amazing. I could have stayed in there forever, but I didn't want to use up all the hot water. I also knew my sexy demon was waiting for me. So I soaped up and rinsed off as quickly as I could. When I was done, I brushed my teeth.

I opened the bathroom door to find Gage waiting for me. Before he got any ideas, I stepped into the hallway and nudged him into the bathroom. He let out an amused huff but took the hint and started stripping off his clothing.

My gaze waltzed over his broad shoulders, across his tight nipples, and down to his belly button. His neck and upper torso were covered in the new tattoo-like lines that'd shown up when we bonded. I wanted to study them, so I knew what the future had in store for us. I knew the visions marking our bodies would be beautiful and amazing and full of love.

Then he slid his pants down and I swallowed hard. Hard, ha! Everything about him was hard, including his erect cock, which was a thing of beauty standing proud with its glistening slit and veined length.

Holy Kandinsky. He was so fucking sexy.

Would he sit for me? Let me paint him? I loved that idea, but the painting would just be for me. No one else got to see my Gage.

I was sure his heated gaze saw my every reaction—the flush racing over my still damp skin, the hardening of my cock under the towel wrapped around my hips, my tongue darting out to wet my lips.

What would a tongue bath entail exactly?

"If you want me showered before we do anything, you need to go into the bedroom and quit looking at me like that."

Did I want that? I mean, my ultimate fantasy was standing right in front of me. Why was I quibbling over cleanliness?

"I'll be right out," Gage said with a gruff voice, then he tugged the towel from my hips and shut the door in my face.

It took way too long for my brain to engage again and send me shuffling into the bedroom.

Spread across the end of the bed were fresh clothes. He had gone into the inn, the reckless idiot. Still, the idea of clean clothes was so appealing I wasn't going to complain about it. He'd found a pair of jeans, some socks, and my boxer briefs with lollipops on them. Was that his way of saying he hadn't forgotten that he wanted to lick me? I shivered in anticipation. The shirt, though, I didn't recognize. It wasn't mine. I held it up. Two of me could fit in it; it had to be Gage's.

I loved it.

My dirty clothes were missing from the corner, and I wondered if Gage had shoved them into his laundry basket. A pang of *something* shuddered through me at the thought of all our dirty clothes being mixed up together. That was weird, right? To feel like my filthy clothes being shoved in with his was some sign of intimacy. But it was just so… domestic.

Then again, we were essentially married.

My brain skittered back a few steps and said that again. *We were essentially married.*

I'd married a guy I'd known less than a week. If my mother were still alive, this would have killed her.

But I didn't regret anything. How we'd come together and how our lives had merged was magical. Like it was meant to be. Gage had called us fated mates, and deep inside I knew it was true.

Shoot. I'd forgotten to check out the new markings on my neck and chest in the little mirror in the bathroom. I looked down at my body and tried to see them, but it was impossible. If it was anything like the markings on the other bonded mates, I suspected mine would match Gage's.

I grinned. I needed him to get out here, so I could show him just how excited I was about our bond. I took the clothes he'd brought me and tucked them into the narrow shelf beside the bed. Then I stretched out on the bed, fully naked, and waited.

Chapter Thirty-Seven

JAKE

Gage didn't keep me waiting long, but it still felt like an eternity. I was almost ready to duck under the covers, increasingly unsettled by my ongoing nakedness, when he stepped into the small room. His mouth stretched into a wicked grin as his gaze swept over me. He tugged the bedroom door shut behind him, even though I was sure no one would come into the motorhome right now.

He dropped the towel and let it fall to the floor in a very un-Gage like action. Then he was crawling over the bed toward me. He didn't stop until his exquisitely muscular body covered mine, and as our hips aligned, our hard lengths rubbed against one another. I groaned and tilted my hips to get more friction. I loved having him against me.

And thank fucking Matisse this morning hadn't been an anomaly. My dick was still behaving.

"I love you," he whispered into my ear when he was

braced over me. "I don't know if I said that earlier, but I do. I know this has all happened quickly, but that is the way with our kind. The Eternal Magic knows what she's doing when she brings us together."

"I love you too," I said, trying to pour all my feelings into that one short, but powerful sentence.

He pressed his face into my neck and shivered. "Without you, I might not have taken the chance at bonding with Willow Lake. I might not have stopped hunting through the pack lands. My team may have decided I was no longer in control. Without you, I might have been killed today. Normally when I change into my demonic form, I am still fully me. But today, I was lost. Little more than a puppet for my demonic side to use. I barely recognized my team other than that they were mine. I didn't know their names. They knew something was different. It would have been impossible for them not to notice. You are the reason I'm here right now. But more than that, you are everything to me. I would do anything for you."

He was right. Things could have gone horribly wrong today. I didn't want to think about that. I just wanted to focus on everything that had gone right.

"Gage," I whispered, overwhelmed by our combined emotions flowing through me.

Then he kissed my neck as his warm, firm touch explored my chest. His hard length rubbed against mine, and I rocked against him. Skin against skin. I should have been exhausted after the day we'd endured but tethering myself to Gage had invigorated me.

"You're going too slow," I complained.

Then his hand clamped onto my waist, and he dragged me with him as he rolled to his side. Our hands and mouths explored and teased. It was exquisite torture, and someday I might want to see how long we lasted just teasing one another.

Today was not that day.

I didn't want to linger and savor and enjoy. I wanted to conquer and be conquered. I wanted to fuck and be fucked. I wanted to come with him over and over again until we passed out from pure exquisite bliss.

When I didn't think I could take anymore, I pushed against his shoulders, and he obliged me by rolling onto his back. Then I reached for his stash of lube in the compartment in his headboard. It was still pretty full, but I wished we'd picked up more.

Did Willow Lake have a late-night delivery service? Probably not. We'd have to make do with what we had. I covered my palm in lube, then reached for him. His cock felt perfect in my hand, and it'd feel even better when it was inside me. I added more lube. He clenched his teeth and dug his fingers into the bedding.

"Fuck... Jake..."

"That's the idea," I said, throwing in a saucy wink just for the hell of it.

He laughed, and I loved how his whole face lit up when he did. He was gorgeous like this, all relaxed and happy. I wanted to make him laugh again and again.

Then I reached around and prepped myself. I was still new to this, but I understood enough to make sure I was loosened enough to accommodate him. Gage was well-endowed, and I didn't want him to call in Teague to work his healing magic on my ass because I'd been too impatient. And I could see Gage doing exactly that if he thought I was hurt.

Finally, I grunted and took my hand away.

"Ready?"

"You know I am," I said as I lowered myself over his cock. This was the same position we'd been in the first time we made love, and I liked the symmetry of doing it like this again now that we'd bonded. I groaned at the way he filled me as I sank lower. "You can see my greatest wish... I have no secrets from you." I panted, bracing myself on his chest as he took control.

Gage's eyes darkened to the rich red of his demon form, chasing away the white, as his magic rose. Fuck, he was hot. Then he moaned at whatever he'd seen in my head. He tightened his grip on my waist and flipped us over. His skin reddened and his horns gleamed as he grinned down at me.

"Everything I have and all that I am, including my wishes and dreams, I am happy to share with you. Always and forever," I promised.

"Mine," he roared. Then he pounded into me, hitting my prostate with every single thrust. Then I felt my magic surge, soaring to meet his. The black-and-red wisps of his twirled with the white of mine until they blended and became one.

The most beautiful images danced between us. It was our life. Together. Forever and ever. I wanted to memorize every part of it, but the pleasure was too much. I couldn't hold back.

I came with a shout, shooting across my chest just a

heartbeat before Gage did. He threw his head back and roared. And the magic we'd created drifted onto our bodies, just like it had before. It filled the gaps left among those images formed when we'd bonded, etching more details and color on our skin in the beautiful story of our life together.

Chapter Thirty-Eight

JAKE

As darkness fell and my stomach protested its hunger, Gage decided we should check on the others and arrange some food. When we joined everyone outside again, I was surprised to see so many familiar faces. Gage's team was there, of course, but so were many of my regulars.

Vehicles of every description were tucked into the parking lot and along the river road like a jigsaw puzzle. Some rebellious people must have ignored the caution tape and snuck into the pub, because the heavy wooden tables and chairs were now scattered around the area too. And people were everywhere, laughing and eating and drinking. It was like a crowded tailgate party.

Gage guided me toward his friends standing with Hayden, Van, Carter, and Levi. On the way, several people rushed over to congratulate us and offer gifts. Most of the presents were for Gage, but a few were for me. Gage suggested they put them beside the motorhome, so we didn't have to carry them around with us. Daphne and Vanessa hurried away to make it happen.

"Finally coming up for air, hey?" Isaac asked, when we made it to where the team was standing.

"Surprised you can both still walk," Davina added with a wink, "after the noises coming out of the motorhome."

Even if my cheeks had been on fire, they wouldn't have been as hot as they became when everyone else joined in with the ribbing. Gage just rolled his eyes and tucked me up against his side.

"How did it go out there after we left?" Gage asked Van after the teasing subsided. "Were any of your people injured?"

The hellhound grimaced. "No. Nothing major, at any rate. From what we can tell, it looks like most of the destruction happened before we got there."

"Yeah. I thought as much too." Gage nodded. "Sorry we had to leave without talking to you first."

Van waved away his concern. "I heard you had a mate to tend to. That was more important."

Gage's grip tightened on me.

"Is everything good now?" Hayden asked. His gaze traveled over us, as if assessing if we were okay. It lingered on the matching marks on our bodies, the evidence of our new bond. The edges of the images were visible at our collars. These ones weren't fading, at least not in the same way as the ones from this morning had. We'd discovered that our bond markings didn't change, but every time we made love smaller details or images or colors would emerge, only to fade again.

"We're good," I said.

"So your magic is tethered?" Hayden asked.

"I mean, I think so? I haven't had a vision yet, so I can't say for sure."

Hayden nodded. "Let me know, okay? When you know."

"He worries," Van said. "That's why he's the alpha, whether he says he is or not."

Hayden just rolled his eyes, like this was a familiar argument between them.

A sharp pain sliced into my leg.

"Ouch. What the—?"

Paws was there, clawing on my shin to get my attention.

"Lift me up," he demanded.

I still wasn't entirely comfortable with my grandfather's supposedly magical cat, but I did as he asked. I gathered him in my arms and hoisted him up. He was surprisingly heavy for being so small.

"Don't hold me like I'm a baby, for fuck's sake," he grumbled as he wiggled out of my arms to climb onto my shoulders. He sprawled behind my neck, stretching from one shoulder to the other like the world's most uncomfortable scarf. "That's better. Now you two-footed assholes will quit ignoring me."

"How many people were arrested?" Nelson asked.

"Not as many as should have been. A lot of people died out there." Van rubbed the back of his neck. "Both from Robbie's wolf pack, and the goblins and trolls who had attacked them."

A soft whimper escaped from Hayden. It was such a strangely vulnerable sound to come from such a brusque man. "We'll mourn their loss," he said. "Even if we haven't been friendly with most of those wolves for more than a decade, a lot of us had family members up there. They weren't pack, but... they were once."

"But you do have some of the attackers in custody, right?" Nelson apparently wasn't one for letting emotions get in the way of finding out answers.

"Yes. We need to talk to them," Gage said. "The reason we came to Willow Lake in the first place was because of the trafficking of supernatural beings. Despite everything, we still don't have any answers or new leads. It's a problem. Given the painting Jake completed the day of the explosions, we know it is still going on. It must be stopped."

"No," Van shook his head. "We have some wolves. None of the others."

"Why did you arrest the wolves?" I asked. "Aren't they the victims? Yes, a few of them tried to hurt me, but you said you had the bombers in custody already. Why did you arrest more of them?"

Hayden heaved out a deep breath and rubbed his eyes. Van reached over and squeezed his friend's shoulder. The wolf closed his eyes for a moment, as if to collect himself. When he opened them again, they flashed with a decidedly supernatural color.

"We didn't arrest them all," Van said. "But when we searched the pack lands, we found some pretty incriminating things. Speaking of which, there were also a few boxes that smelled like Ulric, so those are probably the last of the stolen items from the inn."

"I'll ask Davina to check for ghosts around here. We

might get lucky and be able to compile an inventory list with their help," Gage said. "Is that all?"

I shuddered at the idea of anyone interviewing ghosts. The existence of ghosts was one of the many things my mother had kept from me. The more I thought about it, the more it freaked me out to think of anyone talking to dead people. And the fact that they were just hanging around the place? Watching me? Nope. I didn't want to go there.

Van hesitated, his gaze darting to Hayden. "We found a few phones and computers with information implicating some of them. Those are the ones we arrested. And... we found a shack with five people trapped inside. They were in cages."

Shock rippled through the group.

"So the wolf pack is connected to our investigation." Gage's skin and eyes took on a crimson color as his anger rose. "We need to talk to those people."

"They say they weren't there long, but..." Van shuddered. "Although they don't appear to have any physical injuries, they're in Doc's care for now. Hopefully they'll remember more after they've rested."

"I can't figure out what in the name of Magic he was thinking to do something so... so..." Hayden rubbed the heels of his hands against his eyes.

"We'll keep searching for answers," Gage said.

Van, Dillon, and Adrian stepped closer to Hayden until they were touching him. Did this have something to do with them calling Hayden alpha? Was this a shifter thing? A sort of two-legged puppy pile? The closeness of the others seemed to relax Hayden a little, so it must have worked.

On the other side of the group, Jeremy was watching the interaction carefully while taking notes in one of his many, many books.

"Okay," Isaac said as he clapped his hands. "That's enough of that. Today wasn't a victory, but we all survived. Our illustrious leader has found his mate and his place. And, while the newlyweds have been canoodling in the motorhome all afternoon, I've been talking with some of the locals, and we have a plan for how to fix up the inn. So I suggest we put today behind us and think about the future."

"Yes," Jeremy agreed as he tucked his notebook and pen into his pocket. "Let's do this! Someone crank up some tunes. It's time to celebrate, because did you see my magic today? That shit was amazing!" Then he started bouncing around while singing Pink's "Get the Party Started" at the top of his lungs.

I wanted to know what had been said about the inn, but there'd be time for that later. I stayed by Gage's side— although I suspected he would follow me anywhere I went —as we watched Dillon and Ash start a bonfire in the middle of my gravel parking lot.

And as the flames grew higher like a beacon of hope at the end of a long emotional day, more people arrived.

Even Emma, Jeremy's strange supernatural pet, was having a good time. She'd found more of her kind in the woods by the inn and they'd all chittered excitedly as they introduced themselves. Now a troop of them were bouncing from one person to the next, sniffing thoroughly before moving on to someone else. Occasionally the creatures stopped long enough to snatch food from someone's hands.

Jeremy, between belting out an endless number of old party songs, kept trying to coax her back, clearly wanting to keep her from being a pest, but she only returned long enough to share a few crumbs of her stolen food with him before scurrying off again to be with her own kind.

In addition to Vanessa and Daphne, my other painting ladies were there too. Alice arrived holding Buddy's hand. Both of them were smiling, so I guessed their date the other night had gone well. Alice gave me a long, tearful hug when she saw me.

I suspected I'd be seeing Buddy around a lot more now, given what my vision had shown about the two of them. I might give the painting to them as a wedding present when the time came—even though it was black-and-white and until recently I would have been embarrassed to have anyone see it. But for now, I wouldn't say anything about what I knew about their future. It wasn't my place to influence their relationship.

The Jensens were sitting on either side of Sally, and they were stroking her with delicate-looking tentacles. Their lumpy round bodies sandwiched Sally's much smaller one, but the succubus was grinning and giggling. Actually, they all appeared achingly happy, and I wondered if they were now a confirmed throuple like my painting ladies had predicted. I tore my gaze away from their group when one of Mrs. Jensen's tentacles snaked down Sally's pants. Nope. I might be happy for her, but I really didn't need to see that.

Some people brought food, but I'd ordered pizzas from the Flying Rowan Café too. When Parker, the owner of the café, stepped out of his van at the end of the driveway to deliver them, his eyes went straight to Levi, who was talking with Carter. Parker's crush on Levi wasn't a secret, at least not to me. Watching them flirt when they were at my pub was one of my favorite pastimes. He'd been trying to pin the big guy down for as long as I'd lived in Willow Lake, but he hadn't been successful yet, even though I suspected Levi wasn't as immune to Parker's flirting as he wished he was. Was Levi putting him off because he was human? It'd suck if that was the reason. Parker seemed like a nice guy.

But, as he carried in a ridiculously high stack of pizza boxes, there was no mistaking the hurt in his eyes at seeing everyone gathered. I understood. In his place, I would have wondered why I hadn't been invited too. But it wasn't exactly easy to explain how everyone was just happy to be with their friends and family after surviving a supernatural battle, when someone didn't know magic was real.

It probably didn't help Parker's feelings to see Levi so engrossed in his conversation with Carter that he didn't appear to notice Parker's arrival. But the sudden tension in Levi's stance made me wonder if that was truly the case. Was that all for show to try to rebuff Parker's interest? It was a cowardly way to do it, if it was. My suspicions were confirmed when Levi relaxed as soon as Parker drove away, and Levi was the first one to come over and grab a slice of pizza. He moaned over the first bite. It was ridiculous. But who was I to interfere?

The pizzas didn't last long. Although they weren't as good as when Ash made them, they were still tasty. Then more food showed up. Soon we'd all eaten and drunk more than we should have.

The conversation was easy. Gage's team mingled with the people of Willow Lake in a way I hadn't expected. They were all so… I don't know… *rough and tough* didn't seem like the right description, but they were warriors, while the citizens of Willow Lake were decidedly not. But Gage had told me that since he'd bonded with Willow Lake, his team had decided to stay here too, so I was glad they seemed to be getting along with everyone.

When Davina settled down beside me, I didn't think anything of it at first. She leaned toward me, fiddling with the label on her beer bottle. She swallowed. I had only just met her, but I knew this apprehension wasn't normal for her.

"Is something wrong?"

"Not wrong…" She shook her head. "I can see and speak to ghosts. Did anyone tell you that already?"

I nodded.

"Right. So. There is someone who would like to talk to you, but only if you want."

"Someone… as in a ghost?" My eyebrows shot up my forehead as a shiver rolled down my back. I glanced around, like an apparition would suddenly jump in front of me and shout *boo*. But of course I didn't see anything at all.

"Yes."

My heart started pounding. "Uh… Who is it? Do you know?"

"Your grandfather."

I wrapped my arms around my stomach. "I… um…"

Davina patted my shoulder. "Hey. There is no rush. It doesn't have to be tonight. Or ever, actually. I just thought I should let you know." She glanced to the left. Was that where the ghost was? I stared at the space but didn't see anything unusual. Then she nodded, more like she was confirming things with the ghost than talking to me. "Yeah. No rush."

I knew most people would love to have a conversation with dead relatives, but not me. Not tonight. I just couldn't. These last few days had been too much. Was I being selfish? Probably. I swallowed to clear my guilt. It didn't work.

It wasn't like I didn't have questions for him. I wanted to know if the purple in his hair meant he'd had a fated mate of his own once upon a time. I wanted to know if he knew why my mother would curse me. I wanted to know why he hadn't told me about magic. But it was more than I could handle tonight after everything else.

"Um… would he mind waiting? I just…"

"Of course, love," she said. "For now, he just wants you to know he's proud of you."

"Thank you." I nodded and forced myself to smile in the direction she'd been looking. The place where the ghost of my grandfather was apparently hanging out waiting to talk with me. "I'm sorry."

"It's okay," Davina said. She patted my hand. "He understands. In the meantime, I'll get him to tell me what else was stolen from his suite. It'll be good to have a list to check against what's been recovered."

Then she, and presumably my grandfather's ghost, got up and wandered into the crowd of other visitors again. Gage stalked toward me and wrapped me in his arms.

"What did she want?" he demanded.

I swallowed hard. "Uh… My grandfather wanted to talk."

"I see." He didn't sound surprised. "And did you?"

"No." I shook my head. "Do you think I was wrong to say no? It isn't that I don't ever want to talk to him, but I just… I don't know. I can't do it now. Not today."

"There is no hurry, love."

Just as he finished speaking, Teague cleared his throat. I hadn't noticed him coming up to us. Gage dropped his chin when he saw who'd joined us.

"I'm so sorry, my friend," my demon said. "I should never have asked you to heal Jake when your magic was so depleted. I hope you can eventually forgive me." I didn't know what had happened, but it was obvious Gage royally messed up because of me.

Teague's cheeks darkened. "I understand why you did it."

"It still isn't right," Gage said.

"No," Teague agreed.

"I'll understand if you want to move on," Gage said.

Teague shook his head, then he met Gage's gaze steadily. "No. I don't want that. You're my family, and families make mistakes. Was I hurt by what happened? Yes, but I've already healed. Physically, at least."

"I won't betray your trust like that again," Gage said. "I promise."

A flutter of magic swirled through the air at Gage's

promise. That wasn't the first time I'd noticed that fluttering sensation when he promised something. Obviously, a demon's promise held more weight than most. I guessed that made sense; a promise was a type of contract.

"Thank you." The death mage nodded his acceptance. "But that isn't why I approached you. I overheard what you were saying... about there not being a hurry, and I thought it'd be a good time to say Gage is right."

"I am often right, but what am I right about this time?" Gage winked at me, showing he was joking.

Teague rolled his eyes, but his mouth curled in a small grin. "I can see the bond between you," he said quietly. "I don't tell many people about my ability, but Gage knows."

Gage nodded. I didn't say anything. I'd ask questions later.

"Well, just in case you were wondering, whatever you did earlier, it entwined your lives."

"Thank Magic," Gage said. "It'd felt like we'd bonded, but it is good to have the confirmation."

"You didn't tell me you were worried," I said. "I thought it was a done deal."

"When we said those ancient words and I saw the tattoos, I thought we'd bonded... but it didn't happen the way Adrian said his bond had." He touched Teague's arm. "So I don't need to negotiate with him and offer immortality?"

Teague shook his head. "It's already done."

"You're stuck with me forever." I grinned at Gage as warmth filled my chest.

From the corner of my eye, I saw the death mage nodding.

A joyful smile broke over my demon's face. Then he picked me up and swung me around in a circle. I squealed and laughed, clinging to him. Around us, people hooted and clapped.

"Immortality?" I asked.

He nodded. "Is that okay? I guess we never talked about that, did we?"

I grinned at him. "Of course I'm okay with it. Forever means forever, doesn't it? But it reminds me of something I asked you before. How old are you?"

"Does it matter?" Gage's cheeks darkened.

"What? Are you old enough to be my grandpa or something?" I teased.

"I suspect I am a little older than your grandfather was," he said. "I was born in my grandfather's village, which is close to Hadrian's Wall. I only mention that because I was born the same year the Romans started building it. My grandfather used to say it was an omen that I was destined to be a powerful guardian."

"Wha—" I blinked at him. "Like Hadrian the Emperor of Rome? That Hadrian?"

He merely nodded, although the tension around his eyes betrayed his apprehension. Did he really think that would make a difference to me?

"You look pretty amazing for a fossil," I teased.

He swatted my ass, in one of the most playful gestures I'd ever seen him do. I loved it. It was like tethering had lifted all the stress and worry from his life and he could finally relax. Perhaps for the first time in his long, long life.

"I can't believe you lived all that time without finding someone special."

"I was waiting for you," he said simply. His sincerity made me light and warm. This is where I was meant to be, with this man. Always.

"I love you. I am so happy you found me," I whispered. "So we've bonded, like Ash and Dillon or Jeremy and Adrian, right?" I just needed to make sure.

Gage looked at Teague, who had been watching us with a bemused smile on his face. At my question, the death mage narrowed his eyes as he stared at the air around us. He shook his head. "It's a little different, but the results are the same. Because Gage is going to be both your mate and your tether, the Eternal Magic appears to have jumped the gun a little and already tied your lives together when the tethering process was initiated."

"But we have both?" Gage asked.

"Yes."

Gage hugged the mage. "Thank you, my friend, for telling us."

I marveled over that news for the rest of the night. I'd already known we were bonded, but hearing someone say the words was reaffirming.

The stars twinkled brightly in the sky by the time Gage and I found our way back to his little bedroom. The others on his team had either set up tents or gone to Levi's motel, so it was just us inside tonight.

Although Robbie had escaped, without a pack, he wasn't considered a threat any longer. I wasn't sure that I agreed, but I still had a lot to learn about supes, so maybe they were right. At any rate. Gage decided that with the threat from the wolf pack neutralized, his team should get some rest rather than stand guard over us again.

My stomach swooped in anticipation when I saw the bed. The covers were still mussed from earlier—something that was probably irritating the hell out of my sexy demon — but me, I couldn't wait to make them even messier.

Epilogue

GAGE

"It's my fault," Hayden said, staring into his beer. He'd been working tirelessly to help the few surviving members of his brother's fractured pack. Considering how they'd treated him and everyone else in Willow Lake, I wondered why he bothered. But I wasn't an alpha. As much as I was the leader of my team and would do anything for them, my connection to them wasn't the same as an alpha's.

"It isn't," Van said flatly. "Give it time. You'll see."

The three of us had commandeered the table in the back corner of Jake's pub, not that many people were there yet. The pub had been deemed safe by the engineers and fire investigators a few days ago, but I expected people would be leery about coming to a bombsite for a while yet. This was the first day Jake had opened his doors to the public again.

My little oracle was worried his business wouldn't recover, but I wasn't. It might have been different if someone had died in the blast, but we'd been lucky. I figured the inn would become a local icon soon enough, a symbol of survival and resilience. Then the townsfolk would tell stories around what had happened, and it'd become a local legend.

How did I know?

Well, Jake might have had a vision about that. I had to say, it was handy being mated to an oracle. And there hadn't even been any puking or passing out after he'd sketched the scene.

The tether was working perfectly.

As soon as we discovered that, we had another celebration. A private one. For just the two of us. In our bedroom in our motorhome.

I just wished he had more control over his visions. Having that ace in the hole would be an incredible asset to Davina, who'd decided to stay on the Supernatural Council's payroll but use Willow Lake as her home base.

The rest of my team were staying close too but had decided to pursue different challenges. None of them had told me any details yet. I was curious to see what each of them would do. Jake's visions hadn't revealed anything specific. The Eternal Magic had a mind of her own when it came to what she allowed Jake to show us.

But none of us were stopping completely, at least not right away. We all agreed the trafficking case was still ours. We would find those people.

Over the last few days, my team—although now that we weren't taking on any new cases for the SC and were stepping away from their rigid definitions, perhaps I should simply call them what they were… my family—

and I had scoured the hills inch by inch for survivors. While we were out there, we'd started to gather the dead too.

A grisly task, that.

We'd found a lot of dead wolves and their mystery attackers. We hadn't been able to identify the dead goblins and trolls yet. We had no idea why they'd been there. And that kept me awake at night. Sometimes I swore I scented the other demon in the air, but when I investigated, no one was there. I wished I could figure out if it was just my paranoia playing tricks, or if it was real.

While we were in the hills, Jake and a few of his regulars had tackled the pub, getting it ready for the public again. It wasn't perfect by any means, but it was functional and would work until we came up with a plan. The most worrisome problem was the smell. This part of the building had been protected from any structural damage, but the smoke had still caused its own problems.

So far, Jake and his friends had repainted the walls, scrubbed the floors, and tossed anything with fabric. It still smelled of smoke occasionally, so it wasn't perfect, but it was getting there.

"We haven't found any survivors in days," Hayden said, staring into his pint.

"How many have asked to come back to Willow Lake now?" I asked.

"Twenty-three at the last count." Hayden grimaced.

"They can't come here. You know that, right?" I asked. I couldn't allow those people in my territory. Yes, they were technically refugees, but finding those five supes caged and ready for transport had tainted them all in my eyes. One of the captured supes was a homeless teenager, for fuck's safe. The kid had been hitchhiking on the wrong stretch of road and ended up in Rob's care. No one could argue Rob did everything on his own. His pack knew, which made them just as guilty in my eyes.

"I know." Hayden rubbed his forehead. Then he dropped his hand and stared me right in the eye. "So, you're the guardian now. Does that make you the alpha?"

"Hell, no." I shook my head. "I will protect Willow Lake and its citizens with everything I have, but I am not its leader. That's you."

He snorted like I'd made a joke. But I was being honest. I protected the place and Van enforced the rules. But neither of us was an alpha. Willow Lake needed Hayden just as much as it needed Van and me. But he was too raw to see that right now. I had faith he'd come around, though.

Jake had already had a vision about it, after all.

I hadn't told Hayden that. Not everyone appreciated knowing their future.

"We never found Robbie or any of his top wolves," Van said, making Hayden flinch.

The wolf had to be struggling between relief his brother was apparently still alive and disgust over the guy using the rest of his pack as fodder for his enemy. I couldn't believe the guy had escaped. I wanted to hunt him down and make him pay for what he'd done, but I was still adjusting to being tethered to Willow Lake, and she was turning out to be a greedy boss.

As long as I stayed within the territory, I was stronger than I'd ever been, but as soon as I stepped over the boundary line, the strength of my magic dropped substantially. I hadn't let that stop me from helping clean up the pack lands, but feeling so weak was frustrating. I didn't regret my decision to bind with the place, but it meant I had to lean on my team more than ever.

"So, I've been meaning to talk to you both," I said, not wanting to think or talk about Rob any more than I had to. I didn't fear losing control or snapping like I would have before tethering to the area, but it still made my blood boil and my power surge, which would just make the few patrons in the pub run away. I didn't need Jake pissed at me for scaring away his few paying customers. "Jake and I have a lot of work to do around here." I waved my hand toward the room, but I knew they'd understand I meant the inn as a whole. "We're going to get the place fixed up. The insurance is dragging their feet, but I've got more than enough in my bank account to take care of it all. After it's done, my team is going to move in here too."

Van and Hayden nodded, like they'd expected as much.

"The thing is… There will still be lots of empty rooms, even with my team." I leaned forward and watched them carefully. "So we're thinking of opening it up to people who need sanctuary. Jake might offer some art classes in the dining hall. And I'd like to create a bit of an art gallery in the foyer to showcase Jake's work too. But it is early days yet. Nothing is settled. Two of the supes we saved from those cages have asked to stay. They're willing to help get things going."

"So it won't be an inn?" Van asked.

"Not in the traditional sense." I shook my head.

"Although I got the sense it hasn't really been an inn for a long time, so this isn't that much of a change."

Hayden lifted his eyebrow, then glanced at Van. "Did you know about this?"

"No. First I've heard of it."

"Well, I'm telling you both now," I said. "Do you have a problem with our plan?" I asked the question, but I didn't really care. I didn't need their blessing, but it would be easier to do if they didn't stand in our way.

"It's a bit hypocritical, don't you think?" Hayden muttered. "Not to offer refuge to the people Robbie controlled when you plan on setting up a sanctuary?"

I huffed. I'd known he'd say that. "I'm telling you, the adults who lived out there weren't innocent. None of them. Do you want to separate the kids from their parents? Because those are the only ones I could tolerate in Willow Lake." I leaned back in my chair. "I hadn't planned on saying anything, but you know I can see people's wishes, right?"

"Like read their minds? Fuck. No, I didn't know that." Hayden scowled.

"I see people's greatest wishes."

He blinked. It was easy to see what he was thinking, and I wanted to say—*yes, Hayden, I've seen your greatest wish*. But I refrained. His face paled, but he rallied quickly. "Why are you telling me this?"

"Because all any of those people are wishing is that they don't get caught and punished for the shit they've done."

Hayden's mouth gaped and his shoulders slumped.

"Fuck," Van muttered. He rubbed his forehead. "I'm

going to pretend I didn't hear that. I'm going to hope they take this second chance they've been given and make a better life for themselves. Somewhere else."

Hayden downed the rest of his beer and pushed his glass away. Then he got up and left the pub without another word.

Paws jumped into the seat Hayden had abandoned. "That werewolf takes too much blame on himself. Rob is an ass and so are all the rest of them." He flicked his tail back and forth.

Van heaved out a breath but didn't disagree.

"Since the bet about Jake getting his magic sorted is finished, we should make a new one," Paws said, louder than was necessary if he was just talking to Van and me. His tail flicked back and forth, and his eyes gleamed. "We can place bets on when Hayden finally accepts he is the alpha."

Van rolled his eyes, but the people at the next table immediately started discussing how much each guess should cost and how they'd make sure Hayden didn't find out. I swore the cat grinned, happy with himself.

"Who ended up getting the money from the bet about Jake?" I asked.

Paws flicked his tail aggressively.

"You didn't tell him yet?" Van asked, obviously amused by the cat's attitude.

"Fine," Paws grumbled. "We decided to give it to Jake to help with the cost of fixing the inn. It was stupid to have kept the bet going after we knew he was an oracle. Oracles see the future. They're always going to win."

I laughed and reached over to scratch the grumpy asshole behind the ear. "Thanks, buddy."

"Fuck off," Paws muttered, but even as he complained, he didn't pull away from my pets.

"So," the hellhound said, ignoring Paws, "tell me about this sanctuary idea you have."

THE END

Want to see what happens when Jake paints Gage's portrait… in the woods… and in the buff? (Spoiler: things get spicy!) Sign up for my newsletter and download the bonus scene: www.loriames.com/newsletter

———

Interested in what happens when timid cat shifter Simon finally finds his inner lion and his fated mate? Check out *Cats Never Fly*, the next Willow Lake Supernaturals book!

A Note from the Author

Hi!

I'm so glad you took a chance on Jake and Gage's book! It really holds a special place in my heart. Jake was the first character to introduce himself to me when I started this series. His opening scene is mostly as it was when I first wrote it all the way back in January 2019. (Wow. That was a long time ago. Until I looked up the date just now, I hadn't realized I've been thinking about this series for so long!)

For a while, Jake's book was the first in the series, but there were too many things going on for it to be the first. But, I think it fits perfectly where it is now.

It is funny the things authors worry about (or maybe it is just me) when they write. This book, for as much as I love the story and these characters, was certainly a challenge and kept me awake worrying more than any other book I've written. I sincerely hope you've found it a fun read, then all those worries will have been worth it.

Again, thank you to Kirk Waite at Rare Bird Beta

Reading, my editor June, and the readers who received an early copy of this book and offered feedback. You have all helped me so much as I worked through the final steps on this book. But, as always, if any errors have survived to the final version, that's on me. If you spot any typos, feel free to email me (lori@loriames.com), rather than reporting the book.

Let's see, what else did I want to mention? Oh, yes… Did you figure out that Simon's book is up next? I expect it to release in late spring / early summer 2024, but I haven't put up the pre-order for it yet. If you join my newsletter, you'll receive all the latest news, including an email when my next book is available at Amazon.

Okay, I think that's all I have for now! Wishing you a never ending supply of books you love! <3

Cheers,
Lori

PS… Reviews help other readers decide if a book might be something they want to read, so please consider writing a review of *Oracles Always Win*. That would be wonderful. Even Paws would be pleased.

About the Lori

Lori Ames writes MM romance with touch of magic! When Lori was in elementary school, she wrote a very compelling story about a girl with a prickly personality who turned into a rose. (Sounds amazing, right? She knew you'd agree.) Then she discovered romances in her teens and, well, she knew she wanted to write romances. It took her a little longer to find MM romances, but once she did, she was addicted. She lives in a small town in Alberta with her husband and an elderly black cat.

You can find out more here:

- Patreon: patreon.com/c/LoriAmes
- Facebook Group:
  facebook.com/groups/LoriAmesReaders
- Facebook Page:
  facebook.com/LoriAmesAuthor
- Website: loriames.com
- Newsletter Sign Up: loriames.com/newsletter
- Bluesky: bsky.app/profile/loriames.bsky.social
- MM Wire: themmwire.circle.so/c/lori-ames/

I also have a store with fun merchandise now! Find a link to it on my website: loriames.com

Also by Lori Ames

WILLOW LAKE SUPERNATURALS

MM Paranormal Romance

Ravens Never Fall - *Prequel* (Oak & Mercer)

The prequel is available to my newsletter subscribers as a free download

Hellhounds Never Lie - *Book 1* (Ash & Dillon)

Wolves Always Bite - *Book 2* (Jeremy & Adrian)

Oracles Always Win - *Book 3* (Jake & Gage)

Cats Never Fly - Book 4 (Simon & Ogden)

Alphas Never Hide - Book 5 (Hayden & Ryley)

WILLOW LAKE PACK

Willow Lake Supernaturals Spin-Off Series

The first book is coming soon!

Moody as a Minotaur - Book 1 (Levi & Parker)